Well, we were all standing there like a statue called "People Meet Yeti," when Freds decided to break the ice; he stepped forward and offered the guy a hand. "Namaste!" he said.

"No, no—" Nathan brushed by him and held out the necklace of fossil shells.

"Is this the same one?" I croaked, momentarily at a loss. Because up until that bathroom door opened, part of me hadn't really believed in it all.

The Yeti reached out and touched the necklace and Nathan's hand. Nathan was quivering. I was impressed myself. Freds said, "He looks kind of like Buddha, don't you think? He doesn't have the belly, but those eyes, man. Buddha to the max."

We got to work. I opened my pack and got out baggy overalls, a yellow "Free Tibet" T-shirt, and a large anorak. Slowly, carefully, gently, with many a soft-spoken sound and slow gesture, we got the Yeti into the clothes. With every move I made I said, "Namaste, blessed sir, namaste."

His hands and feet were a problem. His hands were strange, fingers skinny and almost twice as long as mine, and pretty hairy as well; but wearing mittens in the daytime in Kathmandu was almost worse. I suspended judgment on them and turned to his feet....

Lastly I put my blue Dodgers cap on his head. I topped everything off with a pair of mirrored wraparound sunglasses. "Hey, [ma]de of [f] [Sher]pa necklace, made of f[ ] chunks of rough turqu[ ] [sourc]e of distraction, you k[ ]

"God, he loo[ ]

Books by Kim Stanley Robinson

*The Blind Geometer**
*The Gold Coast**
*Green Mars**
Icehenge•
*The Memory of Whiteness**
*The Planet on the Table**
The Wild Shore

*Published by Tor Books
•Forthcoming from Tor Books

ESCAPE FROM
KATHMANDU

KIM STANLEY ROBINSON

A TOM DOHERTY ASSOCIATES BOOK
NEW YORK

Parts of this book have been previously published in *Isaac Asimov's Science Fiction Magazine*.

ESCAPE FROM KATHMANDU

Copyright © 1989 by Kim Stanley Robinson

A Tor Book
Published by Tom Doherty Associates, Inc.
49 West 24th Street
New York, N.Y. 10010

Cover art by Wayne Barlowe

ISBN: 0-812-50059-8

Library of Congress Catalog Card Number: 89-23310

First edition: November 1989
First mass market printing: June 1990

Printed in the United States of America

0 9 8 7 6 5 4 3 2 1

"As we shall see, there is also considerable historical evidence of enormous networks of underground tunnels in both North, South and Central America, but it is not my intention to discuss the facts here, for that would preclude some of the conclusions I have reached concerning them, to which I shall come in later chapters."

— Alec Maclellan, *The Lost World of Agharti*

PART
1

Escape From Kathmandu

I

USUALLY I'M NOT MUCH interested in other people's mail. I mean when you get right down to it, even my own mail doesn't do that much for me. Most of it's junk mail or bills, and even the real stuff is, like, official news from my sister-in-law, xeroxed for the whole clan, or at best an occasional letter from a climbing buddy that reads like a submission to the *Alpine Journal for the Illiterate*. Taking the trouble to read some stranger's version of this kind of stuff? You must be kidding.

But there was something about the dead mail at the Hotel Star in Kathmandu that drew me. Several times each day I would escape the dust and noise of Alice's Second City, cross the sunny paved courtyard of the Star, enter the lobby and get my key from one of the zoned-out Hindu clerks—nice guys all—and turn up the uneven stairs to go to my room. And there at the bottom of the stairs was a big wooden letter rack nailed to the wall, absolutely *stuffed* with mail. There must have been two hundred letters and postcards stuck up there—thick packets, blue airmail pages, dog-eared postcards from Thailand or Peru, ordinary envelopes covered with complex addresses and purple postal marks—all of them bent over the wooden retainer bars of the rack, all of them gray with dust. Above the rack a cloth print of Ganesh stared down with his sad elephant gaze, as if he represented all the correspondents who had mailed these letters, whose messages were never going to reach their destinations. It was dead mail at its deadest.

And after a while it got to me. I became curious. Ten times a day I passed this sad sight, which never changed—no letters taken away, no new ones added. Such a lot of

3

wasted effort! Once upon a time these names had taken off for Nepal, a long way away no matter where they were from. And back home some relative or friend or lover had taken the time to sit down and write a letter, which to me is like dropping a brick on your foot as far as entertainment is concerned. Heroic, really. "Dear George Fredericks!" they cried. "Where are you, how are you? Your sister-in-law had her baby, and I'm going back to school. When will you be home?" Signed, Faithful Friend, Thinking of You. But George had left for the Himal, or had checked into another hotel and never been to the Star, or was already off to Thailand, Peru, you name it; and the heartfelt effort to reach him was wasted.

One day I came into the hotel a little wasted myself, and noticed this letter to George Fredericks. Just glancing through them all, you know, out of curiosity. My name is George, also—George Fergusson. And this letter to George was the thickest letter-sized envelope there, all dusty and bent permanently across the middle. "George Fredericks—Hotel Star—Thamel Neighborhood—Kathmandu—NEPAL." It had a trio of Nepali stamps on it—the King, Cho Oyo, the King again—and the postmark date was illegible, as always.

Slowly, reluctantly, I shoved the letter back into the rack. I tried to satisfy my curiosity by reading a postcard from Koh Samui: "Hello! Do you remember me? I had to leave in December when I ran out of money. I'll be back next year. Hello to Franz and Badim Badur—Michel."

No, no. I put the card back and hoisted myself upstairs. Postcards are all alike. *Do you remember me?* Exactly. But that letter to George, now. About half-an-inch thick! Maybe six or eight ounces—some sort of epic, for sure. And apparently written in Nepal, which naturally made it more interesting to me. I'd spent most of the previous several years in Nepal, you see, climbing and guiding treks and hanging out; and the rest of the world was beginning to seem pretty

4

unreal. These days I felt the same sort of admiration for the ingenuity of the writers of *The International Herald Tribune* that I used to feel for the writers of *The National Enquirer.* "Jeez," I'd think as I scanned a *Tribbie* in front of a Thamel bookstore, and read of strange wars, unlikely summits, bizarre hijackings. "How do they think these things up?"

But an epic from Nepal, now. That was reality. And addressed to a "George F." Maybe they had misspelled the last name, eh? And anyway, it was clear by the way the letter was doubled over, and the envelope falling apart, that it had been stuck there for years. A dead loss to the world, if someone didn't save it and read it. All that agony of emotions, of brain cells, of finger muscles, all *wasted.* It was a damn shame.

So I took it.

II

MY ROOM, ONE OF the nicest in all Thamel, was on the fourth floor of the Star. The view was eastward, toward the tall bat-filled trees of the King's palace, overlooking the jumble of Thamel shops. A lot of big evergreens dotted the confusion of buildings; in fact, from my height it looked like a city of trees. In the distance I could see the green hills that contained the Kathmandu Valley, and before the clouds formed in the mornings I could even see some white spikes of the Himal to the north.

The room itself was simple: a bed and a chair, under the light of a single bare bulb hanging from the ceiling. But what else do you really need? It's true that the bed was lumpy; but with my foam pad from my climbing gear laid over it to level it out, it was fine. And I had my own bathroom. It's true the seatless toilet leaked pretty badly, but since the shower poured directly onto the floor and leaked also, it didn't matter. It was also true that the shower came in two parts, a waist-high faucet and a showerhead near the ceiling, and the showerhead didn't work, so that to take a shower I had to sit on the floor under the faucet. But that was okay—it was all okay—because that shower was *hot*. The water heater was right there in the room hanging over the toilet, and the water that came from it was so hot that when I took a shower I actually had to turn on the cold water too. That in itself made it one of the finest bathrooms in Thamel.

Anyway, this room and bath had been my castle for about a month, while I waited for my next trekkers' group from Want To Take You Higher Ltd. to arrive. When I entered it with the lifted letter in hand I had to kick my way through clothes, climbing gear, sleeping bag, food, books, maps, *Tribbies*—sweep a pile of such stuff off the chair— and clear a space for the chair by the windowsill. Then I sat down, and tried to open the bent old envelope without actually ripping it.

No way. It wasn't a Nepali envelope, and there was some real glue on the flap. I did what I could, but the CIA wouldn't have been proud of me.

Out it came. Eight sheets of lined paper, folded twice like most letters, and then bent double by the rack. Writing on both sides. The handwriting was miniaturized and neurotically regular, as easy to read as a paperback. The first page was dated June 2, 1985. So much for my guess concerning its age, but I would have sworn the envelope looked four or five years old. That's Kathmandu dust for you. A sentence near the beginning was underlined heavily: *"You must not tell ANYBODY about this!!!"* Whoah, heavy! I glanced out the window, even. A letter with some secrets in it! How great! I tilted the chair back, flattened the pages, and began to read.

6

Dear Freds—

I know, it's a miracle to get even a postcard from me, much less a letter like this one's going to be. But an amazing thing has happened to me and you're the only friend I can trust to keep it to himself. *You must not tell ANYBODY about this!!!* Okay? I know you won't—ever since we were roommates in the dorm you've been the one I can talk to about anything, in confidence. And I'm glad I've got a friend like you, because I've found I really have to tell this to somebody, or go crazy.

As you may or may not remember, I got my Master's in Zoology at U.C. Davis soon after you left, and I put in more years than I care to recall on a Ph.D. there before I got disgusted and quit. I wasn't going to have anything more to do with any of that, but last fall I got a letter from a friend I had shared an office with, a Sarah Hornsby. She was going to be part of a zoological/botanical expedition to the Himalayas, a camp modeled on the Cronin expedition, where a broad range of specialists set up near treeline, in as pure a wilderness as they can conveniently get to. They wanted me along because of my "extensive experience in Nepal," meaning they wanted me to be sirdar, and my degree didn't have a thing to do with it. That was fine by me. I took the job and went hacking away at the bureaucratic underbrush in Kathmandu. You would have done it better, but I did okay. Central Immigration, Ministry of Tourism, Forests and Parks, RNAC, the whole horrible routine, which clearly was designed by someone who had read too much Kafka. But eventually it got done and I took off in the early spring with four animal behaviorists, three botanists, and a ton of supplies, and flew north. We were joined at the airstrip by 22 local porters and a real sirdar, and we started trekking.

I'm not going to tell you exactly where we went. Not because of you; it's just too dangerous to commit it to print. But we were up near the top of one of the watersheds, near the crest of the Himalayas and the border with Tibet. You know how those valleys end: tributaries keep getting higher and higher, and finally there's a last set of box canyon–type valleys fingering up into the highest peaks. We set our base camp where three of these dead-end valleys met, and members of the group could head upstream or down depending on their project. There was a trail to the camp, and a bridge over the river near it, but the three upper valleys were wilderness, and it was tough to get through the forest up into them. It was what these folks wanted, however—untouched wilderness, almost.

When the camp was set the porters left, and there the eight of us were. My old friend Sarah Hornsby was the ornithologist—she's quite good at it, and I spent some time working with her. But she had a boyfriend along, the mammalogist (no, not that, Freds), Phil Adrakian. I didn't like him much, from the start. He was the expedition leader, and absolutely Mr. Animal Behavior—but he sure had a tough time finding any mammals up there. Then Valerie Budge was the entomologist—no problem finding subjects for her, eh? (Yes, she did bug me. Another expert.) And Armaat Ray was the herpetologist, though he ended up helping Phil a lot with the night blinds. The botanists were named Kitty, Dominique, and John; they spent a lot of time to themselves, in a large tent full of plant samplings.

So—camp life with a zoological expedition. I don't suppose you've ever experienced it. Compared to a climbing expedition it isn't that exciting, I'll tell you. On this one I spent the first week or two crossing the bridge and establishing the best routes through the forest into the three high valleys; after that I helped Sarah with her project, mostly. But the whole time I entertained myself watching this crew—being an animal behaviorist for the animal behaviorists, so to speak.

What interests me, having once given it a try and decided it wasn't worth it, is why others carry on. Following animals around, then explaining every little thing you see, and then arguing intensely with everyone else about the explanations—for a *career*? Why on earth would anyone do it?

I talked about it with Sarah, one day when we were up the middle valley looking for beehives. I told her I had formed a classification system.

She laughed. "Taxonomy! You can't escape your training." And she asked me to tell her about it.

First, I said, there were the people who had a genuine and powerful fascination with animals. She was that way herself, I said; when she saw a bird flying, there was a look on her face . . . it was like she was seeing a miracle.

She wasn't so sure she approved of that; you have to be scientifically detached, you know. But she admitted the type certainly existed.

Then, I said, there were the stalkers. These people liked to crawl around in the bush tailing other creatures, like kids playing a game. I went on to explain why I thought this was such a powerful urge; it seemed to me that the life it led to was very similar to the lives led by our primitive ancestors, for a million long years. Living in camps, stalking animals in the woods: to get back to that style of life is a powerfully satisfying feeling.

Sarah agreed, and pointed out that it was also true that nowadays when you got sick of camp life you could go out and sit in a hot bath drinking brandy and listening to Beethoven, as she put it.

"That's right!" I said. "And even in camp there's quite a night life, you've all got your Dostoevski and your arguments over E. O. Wilson . . . it's the best of both worlds. Yeah, I think most of you are stalkers on some level."

"But you always say, 'you people,'" Sarah pointed out to me. "Why are you outside it, Nathan? Why did you quit?"

And here it got serious; for a few years we had been on

the same path, and now we weren't, because I had left it. I thought carefully about how to explain myself. "Maybe it's because of type three, the theorists. Because we must remember that animal behavior is a Very Respectable Academic Field! It has to have its intellectual justification, you can't just go into the academic senate and say, 'Distinguished colleagues, we do it because we like the way birds fly, and it's fun to crawl in the bushes!'"

Sarah laughed at that. "It's true."

And I mentioned ecology and the balance of nature, population biology and the preservation of species, evolution theory and how life became what it is, sociobiology and the underlying animal causes for social behavior . . . But she objected, pointing out that those were real concerns.

"Sociobiology?" I asked. She winced. I admitted, then, that there were indeed some excellent angles for justifying the study of animals, but I claimed that for some people these became the most important part of the field. As I said, "For most of the people in our department, the theories became more important than the animals. What they observed in the field was just more data for their theory! What interested them was on the page or at the conference, and a lot of them only do field work because you have to to prove you can."

"Oh, Nathan," she said. "You sound cynical, but cynics are just idealists who have been disappointed. I remember that about you—you're such an idealist!"

I know, Freds—you will be agreeing with her: Nathan Howe, idealist. And maybe I am. That's what I told her: "Maybe I am. But jeez, the atmosphere in the department made me sick. Theorists backstabbing each other over their pet ideas, and sounding just as scientific as they could, when it isn't really scientific at all! You can't test these theories by designing an experiment and looking for reproducibility, and you can't isolate your factors or vary them, or use controls—it's just observation and untestable hypothesis, over and over! And yet they acted like such

10

solid scientists, math models and all, like chemists or something. It's just scientism."

Sarah just shook her head at me. "You're too idealistic, Nathan. You want things perfect. But it isn't so simple. If you want to study animals, you have to make compromises. As for your classification system, you should write it up for the *Sociobiological Review*! But it's just a theory, remember. If you forget that, you fall into the trap yourself."

She had a point, and besides we caught sight of some bees and had to hurry to follow them upstream. So the conversation ended. But during the following evenings in the tent, when Valerie Budge was explaining to us how human society behaved pretty much like ants—or when Sarah's boyfriend Adrakian, frustrated by his lack of sightings, went off on long analytical jags like he was the hottest theorist since Robert Trivers—she would give me a look and a smile, and I knew I had made my point. Actually, though he talked a big line, I don't think Adrakian was all that good; his publications wouldn't exactly give a porter backstrain, if you know what I mean. I couldn't figure out what Sarah saw in him.

One day soon after that, Sarah and I returned to the middle high valley to hunt again for beehives. It was a cloudless morning, a classic Himalayan forest climb: cross the bridge, hike among the boulders in the streambed, ascending from pool to pool; then up through damp trees and underbrush, over lumpy lawns of moss. Then atop the wall of the lower valley, and onto the floor of the upper valley, much clearer and sunnier up there in a big rhododendron forest. The rhododendron blooms still flared on every branch, and with the flowers' pink intensity, and the long cones of sunlight shafting down through the leaves to illuminate rough black bark, orange fungi, bright green ferns—it was like hiking through a dream. And three thousand feet above us soared a snowy horseshoe ring of peaks. The Himalayas—you know.

So we were in good spirits as we hiked up this high valley, following the streambed. And we were in luck, too. Above one small turn and lift the stream widened into a long narrow pool; on the south face above it was a cliff of striated yellowish granite, streaked with big horizontal cracks. And spilling down from these cracks were beehives. Parts of the cliff seemed to pulsate blackly, clouds of bees drifted in front of it, and above the quiet sound of the stream I could hear the mellow buzz of the bees going about their work. Excited, Sarah and I sat on a rock in the sun, got out our binoculars, and started watching for bird life. Goraks upvalley on the snow, a lammergeier sailing over the peaks, finches beeping around as always—and then I saw it—a flick of yellow, just bigger than the biggest hummingbird. A warbler, bobbing on a twig that hung before the hive cliff. Down it flew, to a fallen piece of hive wax; peck peck peck; wax into bird. A honey warbler. I nudged Sarah and pointed it out, but she had already seen it. We were still for a long time, watching.

Edward Cronin, leader of a previous expedition of this kind to the Himalayas, did one of the first extensive studies of the honey warbler, and I knew that Sarah wanted to check his observations and continue the work. Honey warblers are unusual birds, in that they manage to live off the excess wax of the honeycombs, with the help of some bacteria in their gastro-intestinal systems. It's a digestive feat hardly any other creature on earth has managed, and it's obviously a good move for the bird, as it means they have a very large food source that nothing else is interested in. This makes them very worthy of study, though they hadn't gotten a whole lot of it up to that point—something Sarah hoped to change.

When the warbler, quick and yellow, flew out of sight, Sarah stirred at last—took a deep breath, leaned over and hugged me. Kissed me on the cheek. "Thanks for getting me here, Nathan."

I was uncomfortable. The boyfriend, you know—and Sarah was so much finer a person than he was. . . . And besides, I was remembering, back when we shared that office, she had come in one night all upset because the boyfriend of the time had declared for someone else, and what with one thing and another—well, I don't want to talk about it. But we had been *good friends*. And I still felt a lot of that. So to me it wasn't just a peck on the cheek, if you know what I mean. Anyway, I'm sure I got all awkward and formal in my usual way.

In any case, we were pretty pleased at our discovery, and we returned to the honey cliff every day after that for a week. It was a really nice time. Then Sarah wanted to continue some studies she had started of the goraks, and so I hiked on up to Honey Cliff on my own a few times.

It was on one of those days by myself that it happened. The warbler didn't show up, and I continued upstream to see if I could find the source. Clouds were rolling up from the valley below and it looked like it would rain later, but it was still sunny up where I was. I reached the source of the stream—a spring-fed pool at the bottom of a talus slope—and stood watching it pour down into the world. One of those quiet Himalayan moments, where the world seems like an immense chapel.

Then a movement across the pool caught my eye, there in the shadow of two gnarled oak trees. I froze, but I was right out in the open for anyone to see. There under one of the oaks, in shadow darker for the sunlight, a pair of eyes watched me. They were about my height off the ground. I thought it might be a bear, and was mentally reviewing the trees behind me for climbability, when it moved again—it blinked. And then I saw that the eyes had whites visible around the iris. A villager, out hunting? I didn't think so. My heart began to hammer away inside me, and I couldn't help swallowing. Surely that was some sort of *face* there in the shadows? A bearded face?

Of course I had an idea what I might be trading glances with. The yeti, the mountain man, the elusive creature of the snows. The *Abominable Snowman*, for God's sake! My heart's never pounded faster. What to do? The whites of its eyes . . . baboons have white eyelids that they use to make threats, and if you look at them directly they see the white of your eyes, and believe you are threatening them; on the off-chance that this creature had a similar code, I tilted my head down and looked at him indirectly. I swear it appeared to nod back at me.

Then another blink, only the eyes didn't return. The bearded face and the shape below it were gone. I started breathing again, listened as hard as I could, but never heard anything except for the chuckle of the stream.

After a minute or two I crossed the stream and took a look at the ground under the oak. It was mossy, and there were areas of moss that had been stepped on by something at least as heavy as me; but no clear tracks, of course. And nothing more than that, in any direction.

I hiked back down to camp in a daze; I hardly saw a thing, and jumped at every little sound. You can imagine how I felt—a sighting like that . . . !

And that very night, while I was trying to quietly eat my stew and not reveal that anything had happened, the group's conversation veered onto the topic of the yeti. I almost dropped my fork. It was Adrakian again—he was frustrated at the fact that despite all of the spoor visible in the area, he had only actually seen some squirrels and a distant monkey or two. Of course it would have helped if he'd spent the night in the night blinds more often. Anyway, he wanted to bring up something, to be the center of attention and take the stage as The Expert. "You know these high valleys are exactly the zone the yeti live in," he announced matter-of-factly.

That's when the fork almost left me. "It's almost certain they exist, of course," Adrakian went on, with a funny smile.

"Oh, Philip," Sarah said. She said that a lot to him these days, which didn't bother me at all.

"It's true." Then he went into the whole bit, which of

course all of us knew: the tracks in the snow that Eric Shipton photographed, George Schaller's support for the idea, the prints Cronin's party found, the many other sightings. . . . "There are thousands of square miles of impenetrable mountain wilderness here, as we now know firsthand."

Of course I didn't need any convincing. And the others were perfectly willing to concede the notion. "Wouldn't that be something if we found one!" Valerie said. "Got some good photos—"

"Or found a body," John said. Botanists think in terms of stationary subjects.

Phil nodded slowly. "Or if we captured a live one. . . ."

"We'd be famous," Valerie said.

Theorists. They might even get their names latinized and made part of the new species' name. *Gorilla montani adrakianias-budgeon.*

I couldn't help myself; I had to speak up. "If we found good evidence of a yeti it would be our duty to get rid of it and forget about it," I said, perhaps a bit too loudly.

They all stared at me. "Whatever for?" Valerie said.

"For the sake of the yeti, obviously," I said. "As animal behaviorists you're presumably concerned about the welfare of the animals you study, right? And the ecospheres they live in? But if the existence of the yeti were confirmed, it would be disastrous for both. There would be an invasion of expeditions, tourists, poachers—yetis in zoos, in primate center cages, in laboratories under the knife, stuffed in museums—" I was getting upset. "I mean what's the real value of the yeti for us, anyway?" They only stared at me: value? "Their *value* is the fact that they're unknown, they're beyond science. They're the part of the wilderness we can't touch."

"I can see Nathan's point," Sarah remarked in the ensuing silence, with a look at me that made me lose my train of thought. Her agreement meant an awful lot more than I would have expected. . . .

The others were shaking their heads. "A nice sentiment," Valerie said. "But really, hardly any of them would be affected by study. Think what they'd add to our knowledge of primate evolution!"

"Finding one would be a contribution to science," Phil said, glaring at Sarah. And he really believed that, too, I have to give him that.

Armaat said slyly, "It wouldn't do any harm to our chances for tenure, either."

"There is that," Phil admitted. "But the real point is, you have to abide by what's true. If we found a yeti we'd be obliged to say so, because it was so—no matter how we felt about it. Otherwise you get into suppressing data, altering data, all that kind of thing."

I shook my head. "There are values that are more important than scientific integrity."

And the argument went on from there, mostly repeating points. "You're an idealist," Phil said to me at one point. "You can't *do* zoology without disturbing some subject animals to a certain extent."

"Maybe that's why I got out," I said. And I had to stop myself from going further. How could I say that he was corrupted by the tremendous job pressures in the field to the point where he'd do anything to make a reputation, without the argument getting ugly? Impossible. And Sarah would be upset with me. I only sighed. "What about the subject animal?"

Valerie said indignantly, "They'd trank it, study it, put it back in its environment. Maybe keep one in captivity, where it would live a lot more comfortably than in the wild."

Total corruption. Even the botanists looked uncomfortable with that one.

"I don't think we have to worry," Armaat said with his sly smile. "The beast is supposed to be nocturnal." —Because Phil had shown no enthusiasm for night blinds, you see.

"Exactly why I'm starting a high-valley night blind," Phil

snapped, tired of Armaat's needling. "Nathan, I'll need you to come along and help set it up."

"And find the way," I said. The others continued to argue, Sarah taking my position, or at least something sympathetic to it; I retired, worried about the figure in the shadows I had seen that day. Phil watched me suspiciously as I left.

So, Phil had his way, and we set up a tiny blind in the upper valley to the west of the one I had made the sighting in. We spent several nights up in an oak tree, and saw a lot of Himalayan spotted deer, and some monkeys at dawn. Phil should have been pleased, but he only got sullen. It occurred to me from some of his mutterings that he had hoped all along to find the yeti; he had come craving that big discovery.

And one night it happened. The moon was gibbous, and thin clouds let most of its light through. About two hours before dawn I was in a doze, and Adrakian elbowed me. Wordlessly he pointed at the far side of a small pool in the stream.

Shadows in shadows, shifting. A streak of moonlight on the water—then, silhouetted above it, an upright figure. For a moment I saw its head clearly, a tall, oddly shaped, furry skull. It looked almost human.

I wanted to shout a warning; instead I shifted my weight on the platform. It creaked very slightly, and instantly the figure was gone.

"Idiot!" Phil whispered. In the moonlight he looked murderous. "I'm going after him!" He jumped out of the tree and pulled what I assumed was a tranquilizer pistol from his down jacket.

"You can't find anything out there at night!" I whispered, but he was gone. I climbed down and took off after him— with what purpose I wasn't sure.

Well, you know the forest at night. Not a chance of seeing animals, or of getting around very easily, either. I have to give it to Adrakian—he was fast, and quiet. I lost

1 7

him immediately, and after that only heard an occasional snapped branch in the distance. More than an hour passed, and I was only wandering through the trees. The moon had set and the sky was about halfway to dawn light when I returned to the stream.

I rounded a big boulder that stood on the bank and almost ran straight into a yeti coming the other way, as if we were on a busy sidewalk and had veered the same direction to avoid each other. He was a little shorter than me; dark fur covered his body and head, but left his face clear—a patch of pinkish skin that in the dim light looked quite human. His nose was as much human as primate—broad, but protruding from his face—like an extension of the occipital crest that ridged his skull fore-to-aft. His mouth was broad and his jaw, under its ruff of fur, very broad—but nothing that took him outside the parameters of human possibility. He had thick eyebrow crests bent high over his eyes, so that he had a look of permanent surprise, like a cat I once owned.

At this moment I'm sure he really was surprised. We both were as still as trees, swaying gently in the wind of our confrontation—but no other movement. I wasn't even breathing. What to do? I noticed he was carrying a small smoothed stick, and there in the fur on his neck were some objects on a cord. His face—tools—ornamentation: a part of me, the part outside the shock of it all, was thinking (I suppose I am still a zoologist at heart), *They aren't just primates, they're hominid.*

As if to confirm this idea, he spoke to me. He hummed briefly; squeaked; sniffed the air hard a few times; lifted his lip (quite a canine was revealed) and whistled, very softly. In his eyes there was a question, so calmly, gently, and intelligently put forth that I could hardly believe I couldn't understand and answer it.

I raised my hand, very slowly, and tried to say "Hello." I know, stupid, but what do you say when you meet a yeti? Anyway, nothing came out but a strangled "Huhn."

18

He tilted his head to the side inquisitively, and repeated the sound. "Huhn. Huhn. Huhn."

Suddenly he jacked his head forward and stared past me, upstream. He opened his mouth wide and stood there listening. He stared at me, trying to judge me. (I swear I could tell these things!)

Upstream there was a crash of branches, and he took me by the arm and wham, we were atop the stream bank and in the forest. Hoppety-hop through the trees and we were down on our bellies behind a big fallen log, lying side-by-side in squishy wet moss. My arm hurt.

Phil Adrakian appeared down in the streambed, looking considerably the worse for wear. He'd scraped through some brush and torn the nylon of his down jacket in several places, so that fluffy white down wafted away from him as he walked. And he'd fallen in mud somewhere. The yeti squinted hard as he looked at him, clearly mystified by the escaping down.

"Nathan!" Phil cried. "Naaaa—thannnn!" He was still filled with energy, it seemed. "I saw one! Nathan, where are you, dammit!" He continued downstream, yelling, and the yeti and I lay there and watched him pass by.

I don't know if I've ever experienced a more satisfying moment.

When he had disappeared around a bend in the stream, the yeti sat up and sprawled back against the log like a tired backpacker. The sun rose, and he only squeaked, whistled, breathed slowly, watched me. What was he thinking? At this point I didn't have a clue. It was even frightening me; I couldn't imagine what might happen next.

His hands, longer and skinnier than human hands, plucked at my clothes. He plucked at his own necklace, pulled it up over his head. What looked like fat seashells were strung on a cord of braided hemp. They were fossils, of shells very like scallop shells—evidence of the Himalayas' days underwater. What did the yeti make of them? No way of knowing. But clearly they were valued, they were part of a culture.

For a long time he just looked at this necklace of his. Then, very carefully, he placed this necklace over my head, around my neck. My skin burned in an instant flush, everything blurred through tears, my throat hurt—I felt just like God had stepped from behind a tree and blessed me, and for no reason, you know? I didn't deserve it.

Without further ado he hopped up and walked off bowleggedly, without a glance back. I was left alone in the morning light with nothing except for the necklace, which hung solidly on my chest. And a sore arm. So it *had* happened, I hadn't dreamed it. I had been blessed.

When I had collected my wits I hiked downstream and back to camp. By the time I got there the necklace was deep in one of my down jacket's padded pockets, and I had a story all worked out.

Phil was already there, chattering to the entire group. "There you are!" he shouted. "Where the hell were you? I was beginning to think they had gotten you!"

"I was looking for you," I said, finding it very easy to feign irritation. "Who's this *they*?"

"The yeti, you fool! You saw him too, don't deny it! And I followed him and saw him again, up the river there."

I shrugged and looked at him dubiously. "I didn't see anything."

"You weren't in the right place! You should have been with me." He turned to the others. "We'll shift the camp up there for a few days, very quietly. It's an unprecedented opportunity!"

Valerie was nodding, Armaat was nodding, even Sarah looked convinced. The botanists looked happy to have some excitement.

I objected that moving that many people upvalley would be difficult, and disruptive to whatever life was up there. And I suggested that what Phil had seen was a bear. But

Phil wasn't having it. "What I saw had a big occipital crest, and walked upright. It was a yeti."

So despite my protests, plans were made to move the camp to the high valley and commence an intensive search for the yeti. I didn't know what to do. More protests from me would only make it look suspiciously like I had seen what Phil had seen. I have never been very clever at thinking up subterfuges to balk the plans of others; that's why I left the university in the first place.

I was at my wit's end when the weather came through for me with an early monsoon rainstorm. It gave me an idea. The watershed for our valley was big and steep, and one day's hard rain, which we got, would quickly elevate the level of water in our river. We had to cross the bridge before we could start up the three high valleys, and we had to cross two more to get back out to the airstrip.

So I had my chance. In the middle of the night I snuck out and went down to the bridge. It was the usual village job: piles of big stones on each bank, supporting the three half logs of the span. The river was already washing the bottom of the stone piles, and some levering with a long branch collapsed the one on our shore. It was a strange feeling to ruin a bridge, one of the most valuable human works in the Himalayas, but I went at it with a will. Quickly the logs slumped and fell away from each other, and the end of the downstream one floated away. It was easy enough to get the other two under way as well. Then I snuck back into camp and into bed.

And that was that. Next day I shook my head regretfully at the discovery, and mentioned that the flooding would be worse downstream. I wondered if we had enough food to last through the monsoon, which of course we didn't; and another hour's hard rain was enough to convince Armaat and Valerie and the botanists that the season was up. Phil's shrill protests lost out, and we broke camp and left the following

21

morning, in a light mist that turned to brilliant wet sunshine by noon. But by then we were well downtrail, and committed.

There you have it, Freds. Are you still reading? I lied to, concealed data from, and eventually scared off the expedition of old colleagues that hired me. But you can see I had to do it. There is a creature up there, intelligent and full of peace. Civilization would destroy it. And that yeti who hid with me—somehow he _knew_ I was on their side. Now it's a trust I'd give my life to uphold, really. You can't betray something like that.

On the hike back out, Phil continued to insist he had seen a yeti, and I continued to disparage the idea, until Sarah began to look at me funny. And I regret to report that she and Phil became friendly once again as we neared J—, and the end of our hike out. Maybe she felt sorry for him, maybe she somehow knew that I was acting in bad faith. I wouldn't doubt it; she knew me pretty well. But it was depressing, whatever the reason. And nothing to be done about it. I had to conceal what I knew, and lie, no matter how much it screwed up that friendship, and no matter how much it hurt. So when we arrived at J—, I said goodbye to them all. I was pretty sure that the funding difficulties endemic in zoology would keep them away for a good long time to come, so that was okay. As for Sarah— well—damn it . . . a bit reproachfully I said farewell to her. And I hiked back to Kathmandu rather than fly, to get away from her, and work things off a bit.

The nights on this hike back have been so long that I finally decided to write this, to occupy my mind. I hoped writing it all down would help, too; but the truth is, I've never felt lonelier. It's been a comfort to imagine you going nuts over my story— I can just see you jumping around the room and shouting "YOU'RE KIDDING!" at the top of your lungs, like you used to. I hope to fill you in on any missing details when I see you in person this fall in Kathmandu. Till then—

your friend, Nathan

WELL, BLOW MY MIND. When I finished reading that letter all I could say was "Wow." I went back to the beginning and started to reread the whole thing, but quickly skipped ahead to the good parts. A meeting with the famed Abominable Snowman! What an event! Of course all this Nathan guy had managed to get out was "Huhn." But the circumstances were unusual, and I suppose he did his best.

I've always wanted to meet a yeti myself. Countless mornings in the Himal I've gotten up in the light before dawn and wandered out to take a leak and see what the day was going to be like, and almost every time, especially in the high forests, I've looked around and wondered if that twitch at the corner of my sleep-crusted eye wasn't something abominable, moving.

It never had been, so far as I know. And I found myself a bit envious of this Nathan and his tremendous luck. Why had this yeti, member of the shyest race in Central Asia, been so relaxed with him? It was a mystery to consider as I went about in the next few days, doing my business. And I wished I could do more than that, somehow. I checked the Star's register to look for both Nathan and George Fredericks, and found Nathan's perfect little signature back in mid-June, but no sign of George, or Freds, as Nathan called him. The letter implied they would both be around this fall, but where?

Then I had to ship some Tibetan carpets to the States, and my company wanted me to clear three "videotreks" with the Ministry of Tourism, at the same time that Central Immigration decided I had been in the country long enough; and dealing with these matters, in the city where mailing a letter can take you all day, made me busy indeed. I almost forgot about it.

But when I came into the Star late one sunny blue afternoon and saw that some guy had gone berserk at the mail rack, had taken it down and scattered the poor paper corpses all over the first flight of stairs, I had a feeling I might know what the problem was. I was startled, maybe even a little guilty-feeling, but not at all displeased. I squashed the little pang of guilt and stepped past the two clerks, who were protesting in rapid Nepali. "Can I help you find something?" I said to the distraught person who had wreaked the havoc.

He straightened up and looked me straight in the eye. Straight-shooter, all the way. "I'm looking for a friend of mine who usually stays here." He wasn't panicked yet, but he was close. "The clerks say he hasn't been here in a year, but I sent him a letter this summer, and it's gone."

Contact! Without batting an eye I said, "Maybe he dropped by and picked it up without checking in."

He winced like I'd stuck a knife in him. He looked about like what I had expected from his epic: tall, upright, dark-haired. He had a beard as thick and fine as fur, neatly trimmed away from the neck and below the eyes—just about a perfect beard, in fact. That beard and a jacket with leather elbows would have got him tenure at any university in America.

But now he was seriously distraught, though he was trying not to show it. "I don't know how I'm going to find him, then. . . ."

"Are you sure he's in Kathmandu?"

"He's supposed to be. He's joining a big climb in two weeks. But he always stays here!"

"Sometimes it's full. Maybe he had to go somewhere else."

"Yeah, that's true." Suddenly he came out of his distraction enough to notice he was talking to me, and his clear, gray-green eyes narrowed as he examined me.

"George Fergusson," I said, and stuck out my hand. He tried to crush it, but I resisted just in time.

2 4

"My name's Nathan Howe. Funny about yours," he said without a smile. "I'm looking for a George Fredericks."

"Is that right! What a coincidence." I started picking up all the Star's bent mail. "Well, maybe I can help you. I've had to find friends in Kathmandu before—it's not easy, but it can be done."

"Yeah?" It was like I'd thrown him a lifebuoy; what was his problem?

"Sure. If he's going on a climb he's had to go to Central Immigration to buy the permits for it. And on the permits you have to write down your local address. I've spent too many hours at C.I., and have some friends there. If we slip them a couple hundred rupees baksheesh they'll look it up for us."

"Fantastic!" Now he was Hope Personified, actually quivering with it. "Can we go now?" I saw that his heart-throb, the girlfriend of The Unscrupulous One, had had him pegged; he was an idealist, and his ideas shined through him like the mantle of a Coleman lantern gleaming through the glass. Only a blind woman wouldn't have been able to tell how he felt about her; I wondered how this Sarah had felt about him.

I shook my head. "It's past two—closed for the day." We got the rack back on the wall, and the clerks returned to the front desk. "But there's a couple other things we can try, if you want." Nathan nodded, stuffing mail as he watched me. "Whenever I try to check in here and it's full, I just go next door. We could look there."

"Okay," said Nathan, completely fired up. "Let's go."

So we walked out of the Star and turned right to investigate at the Lodge Pheasant—or Lodge Pleasant—the sign is ambiguous on that point.

Sure enough, George Fredericks had been staying there. Checked out that very morning, in fact. "Oh my God no," Nathan cried, as if the guy had just died. Panic time was really getting close.

"Yes," the clerk said brightly, pleased to have found the name in his thick book. "He is go on trek."

"But he's not due to leave here for two weeks!" Nathan protested.

"He's probably off on his own first," I said. "Or with friends."

That was it for Nathan. Panic, despair; he had to go sit down. I thought about it. "If he was flying out, I heard all of RNAC's flights to the mountains were canceled today. So maybe he came back in and went to dinner. Does he know Kathmandu well?"

Nathan nodded glumly. "As well as anybody."

"Let's try the Old Vienna Inn, then."

IV

IN THE BLUE OF EARLY EVENING Thamel was jumping as usual. Lights snapped on in the storefronts that opened on the street, and people were milling about. Big Land Rovers and little Toyota taxis forged through the crowd abusing their horns; cows in the street chewed their cud and stared at it all with expressions of faint surprise, as if they'd been magically zipped out of a pasture just seconds before.

Nathan and I walked single file against the storefronts, dodging bikes and jumping over the frequent puddles. We passed carpet shops, climbing outfitters, restaurants, used bookstores, trekking agents, hotels, and souvenir stands, and as we made our way we turned down a hundred offers from the young men of the street: "Change money?" "No." "Smoke dope?" "No." "Buy a nice carpet?" "No." "Good hash!" "No." "Change money?" "No." Long ago I had simplified walking in the neighborhood, and just said "No" to everyone I passed. "No, no, no, no, no, no, no." Nathan had a different method that seemed to work just as well or better, because the hustlers didn't think I was negative enough; he would nod politely with that straight-shooter look, and say "No, thank you," and leave them open-mouthed in the street.

We passed K.C.'s, threaded our way through "Times Square," a crooked intersection with a perpetual traffic jam, and started down the street that led out of Thamel into the rest of Kathmandu. Two merchants stood in the doorway of their shop, singing along with a cassette of Pink Floyd's *The Wall.* "We don't nèed no education, we don't need no thought control." I almost got run over by a bike. Where the street widened and the paving began, I pushed a black goat to one side, and we leaped over a giant puddle into a tunnellike hall that penetrated one of the ramshackle street-side buildings. In the hall, turn left up scuzzy concrete stairs. "Have you been here before?" I asked Nathan.

"No, I always go to K.C.'s or Red Square." He looked as though he wasn't sorry, either.

At the top of the stairs we opened the door, and stepped into the Austro-Hungarian Empire. White tablecloths, paneled partitions between deep booths, red wallpaper in a fleur-de-lis pattern, plush upholstery, tasteful kitschy lamps over every table; and, suffusing the air, the steamy pungent smell of sauerkraut and goulash. Strauss waltzes on the box. Except for the faint honking from the street below, it was absolutely the real item.

"My Lord," Nathan said, "how did they get *this* here?"

"It's mostly her doing." The owner and resident culinary genius, a big plump friendly woman, came over and greeted me in stiff Germanic English.

"Hello, Eva. We're looking for a friend—" But then Nathan was already past us, and rushing down toward a small booth at the back.

"I think he finds him," Eva said with a smile.

By the time I got to the table Nathan was pumping the

arm of a short, long-haired blond guy in his late thirties, slapping his back, babbling with relief—overwhelmed with relief, by the look of it. "Freds, thank God I found you!"

"Good to see you too, bud! Pretty lucky, actually—I was gonna split with some Brits for the hills this morning, but old Reliability Negative Airline bombed out again." Freds had a faint southern or country accent, and talked as fast as anyone I'd ever heard, sometimes faster.

"I know," Nathan said. He looked up and saw me. "Actually, my new friend here figured it out. George Fergusson, this is George Fredericks."

We shook hands. "Nice name!" George said. "Call me Freds, everyone does." We slid in around his table while Freds explained that the friends he was going to go climbing with were finding them rooms. "So what are you up to, Nathan? I didn't even know you were in Nepal. I thought you were back in the States working, saving wildlife refuges or something."

"I was," Nathan said, and his grim do-or-die expression returned. "But I had to come back. Listen—you didn't get my letter?"

"No, did you write me?" said Freds.

Nathan stared right at me, and I looked as innocent as I could. "I'm going to have to take you into my confidence," he said to me. "I don't know you very well, but you've been a big help today, and the way things are I can't really be. . . ."

"Fastidious?"

"No no no—I can't be over-cautious, you see. I tend to be over-cautious, as Freds will tell you. But I need help, now." And he was dead serious.

"Just giving you a hard time," I reassured him, trying to look trustworthy, loyal, and all that; difficult, given the big grin on Freds's face.

"Well, here goes," Nathan said, speaking to both of us. "I've got to tell you what happened to me on the expedition

28

I helped in the spring. It still isn't easy to talk about, but. . . ."

And ducking his head, leaning forward, lowering his voice, he told us the tale I had read about in his lost letter. Freds and I leaned forward as well, so that our heads practically knocked over the table. I did all I could to indicate my shocked surprise at the high points of the story, but I didn't have to worry about that too much, because Freds supplied all the amazement necessary. "You're kidding," he'd say. "No. Incredible. I can't believe it. Yetis are usually so skittish! And this one just *stood there*? You're *kidding*! In-fucking-credible, man! I can't *believe* it! How great! What?— oh, no! You didn't!" And when Nathan told about the yeti giving him the necklace, sure enough, just as Nathan had predicted, Freds jumped up out of the booth and leaned back in and shouted, "YOU'RE KIDDING!!"

"Shh!" Nathan hissed, putting his face down on the tablecloth. "No! Get back down here, Freds! Please!"

So he sat down and Nathan went on, to the same sort of response ("You tore the fucking BRIDGE DOWN!?!" "*Shhhh!!*"); and when he was done we all leaned back in the booth, exhausted. Slowly the other customers stopped staring at us. I cleared my throat: "But then today, you um, you indicated that there was still a problem, or some new problem . . . ?"

Nathan nodded, lips pursed. "Adrakian went back and got money from a rich old guy in the States whose hobby used to be *big game hunting*. J. Reeves Fitzgerald. Now he keeps a kind of a photo zoo on a big estate. He came over here with Adrakian, and Valerie, and Sarah too even, and they went right back up to the camp we had in the spring. I found out about it from Armaat and came here quick as I could. Right after I arrived, they checked into a suite at the Sheraton. A bellboy told me they came in a Land Rover with its windows draped, and he saw someone funny hustled upstairs, and now they're locked into that suite like it's a fort. And I'm afraid—I think—I think they've *got one up there.*"

Freds and I looked at each other. "How long ago was this?" I asked.

"Just two days ago! I've been hunting for Freds ever since, I didn't know what else to do!"

Freds said, "What about that Sarah? Is she still with them?"

"Yes," Nathan said, looking at the table. "I can't believe it, but she is." He shook his head. "If they're hiding a yeti up there—if they've got one—then, well, it's all over for the yetis. It'll just be a disaster for them."

I supposed that was true enough. Freds was nodding automatically, agreeing just because Nathan had said it. "It would be a zoo up there, ha ha."

"So you'll help?" Nathan asked.

"Of course, man! Naturally!" Freds looked surprised Nathan would even ask.

"I'd like to," I said. And that was the truth, too. The guy brought it out in you, somehow.

"Thanks," said Nathan. He looked very relieved. "But what about this climb you were going on, Freds?"

"No prob. I was a late add-on anyway, just for fun. They'll be fine. I was beginning to wonder about going with them this time anyway. They got themselves a Trivial Pursuit game for this climb, to keep them from going bonkers in their tents. We tried it out yesterday and you know I'm real good at Trivial Pursuit, except for the history, literature and entertainment categories, but this here game was the *British* version. So we get a buzz on and start to playing and suddenly I'm part of a Monty Python routine, I mean they just don't play it the same! You know how when we play it and you don't know the answer everyone says 'Ha, too bad'—but here I take my turn and go for sports and leisure which is my natural forte, and they pull the card and ask me, 'Who was it bowled three hundred and sixty-five consecutive sticky wickets at the West Indian cricket match of 1956,' or whatever, and they like to *died* they were laughing so hard. They jumped up and danced around me and *howled*. 'Yew don't know, dew yew! Yew don't have the slightest fookin' *idear* who bowled those sticky wickets, dew yew!' It was really hard to concentrate on my answer. So. Going with them this time might have been a mistake anyway. Better to stay here and help you."

Nathan and I could only agree.

Then Eva came by with our food, which we had ordered after Nathan's epic. The amazing thing about the Old Vienna Inn is that the food is even better than the decor. It would be good anywhere, and in Kathmandu, where almost everything tastes a little like cardboard, it's simply unbelievable. "Look at this steak!" Freds said. "Where the hell do they get the meat?"

"Didn't you ever wonder how they keep the street cow population under control?" I asked.

Freds liked that. "I can just imagine them sneaking one of them big honkers into the back here. Wham!"

Nathan began to prod dubiously at his schnitzel. And then, over a perfect meal, we discussed the problem facing us. As usual in situations like this, I had a plan.

V

I HAVE NEVER KNOWN baksheesh to fail in Kathmandu, but that week at the Everest Sheraton International the employees were bottled up tight. They didn't even want to *hear* about anything out of the ordinary, much less be part of it, no matter the gain. Something was up, and I began to suspect that J. Reeves Fitzgerald had a very big bankroll indeed. So Plan A for getting into Adrakian's room was foiled, and I retired to the hotel bar, where Nathan was hidden in a corner booth, suitably disguised in sunglasses and an Australian outback hat. He didn't like my news.

The Everest Sheraton International is not exactly like Sheratons elsewhere, but it is about the quality of your average Holiday Inn, which makes it five-star in Kathmandu, and just about as incongruous as the Old Vienna. The bar looked like an airport bar, and there was a casino in the room next to us, which clearly, to judge by the gales of laughter coming from it, no one could take seriously. Nathan and I sat and nursed our drinks and waited for Freds, who was casing the outside of the hotel.

Suddenly Nathan clutched my forearm. "Don't look!"

"Okay."

"Oh my God, they must have hired a whole bunch of private security cops. Jeez, look at those guys. No, don't look!"

Unobtrusively I glanced at the group entering the bar. Identical boots, identical jackets, with little bulges under the arm; clean-cut looks, upright, almost military carriage. . . . They looked a little bit like Nathan, to tell the truth, but without the beard. "Hmm," I said. Definitely not your ordinary tourists. Fitzgerald's bankroll must have been *very* big.

Then Freds came winging into the bar and slid into our booth. "Problems, man."

"Shh!" Nathan said. "See those guys over there?"

"I know," said Freds. "They're Secret Service agents."

"They're *what*?" Nathan and I said in unison.

"Secret Service agents."

"Now *don't* tell me this Fitzgerald is a close friend of Reagan's," I began, but Freds was shaking his head and grinning.

"No. They're here with Jimmy and Rosalynn Carter. Haven't you heard?"

Nathan shook his head, but I had a sudden sinking feeling as I remembered a rumor of a few weeks back. "He wanted to see Everest . . . ?"

"That's right. I met them all up in Namche a week ago, actually. But now they're back, and staying here."

"Oh my God," Nathan said. "Secret Service men, *here*."

"They're nice guys, actually," Freds said. "We talked to them a lot in Namche. Real straight, of course—real straight—but nice. They could tell us what was happening in the World Series, because they had a satellite dish, and they told us what their jobs were like, and everything. Of course sometimes we asked them questions about the Carters and they just looked around like no one had said anything, which was weird, but mostly they were real normal."

"And *what* are they doing here?" I said, still not quite able to believe it.

"Well, Jimmy wanted to go see Everest. So they all helicoptered into Namche just as if there was no such thing as altitude sickness, and took off for Everest! I was talking just now with one of the agents I met up there, and he told me how it came out. Rosalynn got to fifteen thousand feet and turned back, but Jimmy kept on trudging. Here he's got all these young tough Secret Service guys to protect him, you know, but they started to get sick, and every day they were helicoptering out a number of them because of altitude sickness, pneumonia, whatever, until there were hardly any left! He hiked his whole crew right into the ground! What is he, in his sixties? And here all these young agents were dropping like flies while he motored right on up to Kala Pattar, and Everest Base Camp too. I love it!"

"That's great," I said. "I'm happy for him. But now they're back."

"Yeah, they're doing the Kathmandu culture scene for a bit."

"That's too bad."

"Ah! No luck getting a key to the yeti's room, is that it?"

"*Shhhhh*," Nathan hissed.

"Sorry, I forgot. Well, we'll just have to think of something else, eh? The Carters are going to be here another week."

"The windows?" I asked.

Freds shook his head. "I could climb up to them no problem, but the ones to their room overlook the garden and it wouldn't be all that private."

"God, this is bad," Nathan said, and downed his Scotch. "Phil could decide to reveal the—what he's got, at a press conference while the Carters are here. Perfect way to get enhanced publicity fast—that would be just like him."

We sat and thought about it for a couple of drinks.

"You know, Nathan," I said slowly, "there's an angle we haven't discussed yet, that you'd have to take the lead in."

"What's that?"

"Sarah."

"What? Oh, no. No. I couldn't. I can't talk to her, really. It just—well, I just don't want to."

"But why?"

"She wouldn't care what I said." He looked down at his glass and swirled the contents nervously. His voice turned bitter: "She'd probably just tell Phil we were here, and then we'd *really* be in trouble."

"Oh, I don't know. I don't think she's the kind of person to do that, do you, Freds?"

"I don't know," Freds said, surprised. "I never met her."

"She couldn't be, surely." And I kept after him for the rest of our stay, figuring it was our best chance at that point. But Nathan was stubborn about it, and still hadn't budged when he insisted we leave.

So we paid the bill and took off. But we were crossing the foyer, and near the broad set of front doors, when Nathan suddenly stopped in his tracks. A tall, good-looking woman with large owl-eye glasses had just walked in. Nathan was stuck in place. I guessed who the woman must be, and nudged him. "Remember what's at stake."

A good point to make. He took a deep breath. And as the woman was about to pass us, he whipped off his hat and shades. "Sarah!"

34

The woman jumped back. "Nathan! My God! What—what are you doing here!"

Darkly: "You know why I'm here, Sarah." He drew himself up even straighter than usual, and glared at her. If she'd been convicted of murdering his mother I don't think he could have looked more accusing.

"What—?" Her voice quit on her.

Nathan's lip curled disdainfully. I thought he was kind of overdoing the laying-on-of-guilt trip, and I was even thinking of stepping in and trying a less confrontational approach, but then right in the middle of the next sentence his voice twisted with real pain: "I didn't think you'd be capable of this, Sarah."

With her light brown hair, bangs, and big glasses, she had a schoolgirlish look. Now that schoolgirl was hurting; her lip quivered, she blinked rapidly; "I—I—" And then her face crumpled, and with a little cry she tottered toward Nathan and collapsed against his broad shoulder. He patted her head, looking flabbergasted.

"Oh, Nathan," she said miserably, sniffing. "It's so *awful*. . . ."

"It's all right," he said, stiff as a board. "I know."

The two of them communed for a while. I cleared my throat. "Why don't we go somewhere else and have a drink," I suggested, feeling that things were looking up a trifle.

VI

WE WENT TO THE HOTEL Annapurna coffee shop, and there Sarah confirmed all of Nathan's worst fears. "They've got him in there locked in the *bathroom*." Apparently the yeti was eating less and less, and Valerie Budge was urging Mr.

35

Fitzgerald to take him out to the city's funky little zoo immediately, but Fitzgerald was flying in a group of science and nature writers so he could hold a press conference, the next day or the day after that, and he and Phil wanted to wait. They were hoping for the Carters' presence at the unveiling, as Freds called it, but they couldn't be sure about that yet.

Freds and I asked Sarah questions about the setup at the hotel. Apparently Phil, Valerie Budge and Fitzgerald were taking turns in a continuous watch on the bathroom. How did they feed him? How docile was he? Question, answer, question, answer. After her initial breakdown, Sarah proved to be a tough and sensible character. Nathan, on the other hand, spent the time repeating, "We've got to get him out of there, we've got to do it soon, it'll be the *end* of him." Sarah's hand on his just fueled the flame. "We'll just have to *rescue* him."

"I know, Nathan," I said, trying to think. "We know that already." A plan was beginning to fall into place in my mind. "Sarah, you've got a key to the room?" She nodded. "Okay, let's go."

"What, now?" Nathan cried.

"Sure! We're in a hurry, right? These reporters are going to arrive, and they're going to notice Sarah is gone. . . . And we've got to get some stuff together, first."

VII

When we returned to the Sheraton it was late afternoon. Freds and I were on rented bikes, and Nathan and Sarah followed in a taxi. We made sure our cabbie understood that we wanted him to wait for us out front; then Freds and I went inside, gave the all-clear to Nathan and Sarah, and headed straight for the lobby phones. Nathan and Sarah went to the front desk and checked into a room; we needed them out of sight for a while.

I called all the rooms on the top floor of the hotel (the fourth), and sure enough half of them were occupied by Americans. I explained that I was J. Reeves Fitzgerald, assistant to the Carters, who were fellow guests in the hotel. They all knew about the Carters. I explained that the Carters were hosting a small reception for the Americans at the hotel, and we hoped that they would join us in the casino bar when it was convenient—the Carters would be down in an hour or so. They were all delighted at the invitation (except for one surly Republican that I had to cut off), and they promised to be down shortly.

The last call got Phil Adrakian, in room 355; I identified myself as Lionel Hodding. It went as well as the others; if anything Adrakian was even more enthusiastic. "We'll be right down, thanks—we have a reciprocal invitation to make, actually." I was prejudiced, but he did sound like a pain. Nathan's epithet, *theorist*, didn't really make it for me; I preferred something along the lines of, say, *asshole*.

"Fine. Look forward to seeing all your party, of course."

Freds and I waited in the bar and watched the elevators. Americans in their safari best began to pile out and head for the casino; you wouldn't have thought there was that much polyester in all Kathmandu, but I guess it travels well.

Two men and a plump woman came down the broad stairs beside the elevator. "Them?" Freds asked. I nodded; they fitted Sarah's descriptions exactly. Phil Adrakian was shortish, slim, and good-looking in a California Golden Boy kind of way. Valerie Budge wore glasses and had a lot of curly hair pulled up; somehow she looked intellectual where Sarah only looked studious. The money man, J. Reeves Fitzgerald, was sixtyish and very fit-looking, though he did smoke a cigar. He wore a safari jacket with eight pockets on it. Adrakian was arguing a point with him as they crossed the foyer to the casino bar, and I heard him say, "*better* than a press conference."

I had a final inspiration and returned to the phones. I asked the hotel operator for Jimmy Carter, and got connected; but the phone was answered by a flat Midwestern voice, very businesslike indeed. "Hello?"

"Hello, is this the Carters' suite?"

"May I ask who's speaking?"

"This is J. Reeves Fitzgerald. I'd like you to inform the Carters that the Americans in the Sheraton have organized a reception for them in the hotel's casino bar, for this afternoon."

". . . I'm not sure their scheduling will allow them to attend."

"I understand. But if you'd just let them know."

"Of course."

Back to Freds, where I downed a Star beer in two gulps. "Well," I said, "*something* should happen. Let's get up there."

VIII

I GAVE NATHAN and Sarah a buzz and they joined us at the door of Room 355. Sarah let us in. Inside was a big suite—style, generic Holiday Inn—it could have been in any city on earth. Except that there was a slight smell of wet fur.

Sarah went to the bathroom door, unlocked it. There was a noise inside. Nathan, Freds and I shifted around behind her uncomfortably. She opened the door. There was a movement, and there he was, standing before us. I found myself staring into the eyes of the yeti.

In the Kathmandu tourist scene, there are calendars, postcards, and embroidered T-shirts with a drawing of a yeti on them. It's always the same drawing, which I could never understand; why should everyone agree to use the same guess? It annoyed me: a little furball thing with his back to you, looking over his shoulder with a standard monkey face, and displaying the bottom of one big bare foot.

I'm happy to report that the real yeti didn't look anything like that. Oh he was furry, all right; but he was about Fred's height, and had a distinctly humanoid face, surrounded by a beardlike ruff of matted reddish fur. He looked a little like Lincoln—a short and very ugly Lincoln, sure, with a squashed nose and rather prominent eyebrow ridges—but the resemblance was there. I was relieved to see how human his face looked; my plan depended on it, and I was glad Nathan hadn't exaggerated in his description. The only feature that really looked unusual was his occipital crest, a ridge of bone and muscle that ran fore-and-aft over the top of his head, like his skull itself had a Mohawk haircut.

Well, we were all standing there like a statue called "People Meet Yeti," when Freds decided to break the ice; he stepped forward and offered the guy a hand. "Namaste!" he said.

"No, no—" Nathan brushed by him and held out the necklace of fossil shells that he had been given in the spring.

"Is this the same one?" I croaked, momentarily at a loss. Because up until that bathroom door opened, part of me hadn't really believed in it all.

"I think so."

The yeti reached out and touched the necklace and Nathan's hand. Statue time again. Then the yeti stepped forward and touched Nathan's face with his long, furry hand. He whistled something quiet. Nathan was quivering; there were tears in Sarah's eyes. I was impressed myself. Freds said, "He looks kind of like Buddha, don't you think?

He doesn't have the belly, but those eyes, man. Buddha to the max."

We got to work. I opened my pack and got out baggy overalls, a yellow "Free Tibet" T-shirt, and a large anorak. Nathan was taking his shirt off and putting it back on to show the yeti what we had in mind.

Slowly, carefully, gently, with many a soft-spoken sound and slow gesture, we got the yeti into the clothes. The T-shirt was the hardest part; he squeaked a little when we pulled it over his head. The anorak was zippered, luckily. With every move I made I said, "Namaste, blessed sir, namaste."

The hands and feet were a problem. His hands were strange, fingers skinny and almost twice as long as mine, and pretty hairy as well; but wearing mittens in the daytime in Kathmandu was almost worse. I suspended judgement on them and turned to his feet. This was the only area of the tourist drawing that was close to correct; his feet were huge, furry, and just about square. He had a big toe like a very fat thumb. The boots I had brought, biggest I could find in a hurry, weren't wide enough. Eventually I put him in Tibetan wool socks and Birkenstock sandals, modified by a penknife to let the big toe hang over the side.

Lastly I put my blue Dodgers cap on his head. The cap concealed the occipital crest perfectly, and the bill did a lot to obscure his rather low forehead and prominent eyebrows. I topped everything off with a pair of mirrored wraparound sunglasses. "Hey, neat," Freds remarked. Also a Sherpa necklace, made of five pieces of coral and three giant chunks of rough turquoise, strung on black cord. Principle of distraction, you know.

All this time Sarah and Nathan were ransacking the drawers and luggage, stealing all the camera film and notebooks and whatever else might have contained evidence of the yeti. And throughout it all the yeti stood there, calm and attentive: watching Nathan, sticking his hand down a sleeve like a millionaire with his valet, stepping carefully into the Birkenstocks, adjusting the bill of the baseball cap, everything. I was really impressed, and so was Freds. "He really is like Buddha, isn't he?" I thought the physical resemblance was a bit muted at this point, but his attitude couldn't have been more mellow if he'd been the Gautama himself.

When Nathan and Sarah were done searching they looked up at our handiwork. "*God* he looks weird," Sarah said.

Nathan just sat on the bed and put his head in his hands. "It'll never work," he said. "Never."

"Sure it will!" Freds exclaimed, zipping the anorak up a little farther. "You see people on Freak Street looking like this all the time! Man, when I went to school I played football with a whole team of guys that looked just like him! Fact is, in my state he could run for Senator—"

"Whoah, whoah," I said. "No time to waste, here. Give me the scissors and brush, I still have to do his hair." I tried brushing it over his ears with little success, then gave him a trim in back. One trip, I was thinking, just one short walk down to a taxi. And in pretty dark halls. "Is it even on both sides?"

"For God's sake, George, let's go!" Nathan was getting antsy, and we had been a while. We gathered our belongings, filled the packs, and tugged old Buddha out into the hall.

IX

I HAVE ALWAYS prided myself on my sense of timing. Many's the time I've surprised myself by how perfectly I've managed to be in the right place at the right time; it goes beyond all conscious calculation, into deep mystic communion with the cycles of the cosmos, etc. etc. But apparently in this matter I was teamed up with people whose sense of timing was so cosmically awful that mine was completely swamped. That's the only way I can explain it.

Because there we were, escorting a yeti down the hallway of the Everest Sheraton International and we were walking casually along, the yeti kind of bowlegged—very bowlegged—and long-armed, too—so that I kept worrying he might drop to all fours—but otherwise, passably normal. Just an ordinary group of tourists in Nepal. We decided on the stairs, to avoid any awkward elevator crowds, and stepped through the swinging doors into the stairwell. And there coming down the stairs toward us were Jimmy Carter, Rosalynn Carter, and five Secret Service men.

"Well!" Freds exclaimed. "Damned if it isn't Jimmy Carter! And Rosalynn too!"

I suppose that was the best way to play it, not that Freds was doing anything but being natural. I don't know if the Carters were on their way to something else, or if they were actually coming down to attend my reception; if the latter, then my last-minute inspiration to invite them had been really a bad one. In any case, there they were, and they stopped on the landing. We stopped on the landing. The Secret Service men, observing us closely, stopped on the landing.

What to do? Jimmy gave us his famous smile, and it might as well have been the cover of *Time* magazine, it was such a familiar sight; just the same. Only not quite. Not exactly. His face was older, naturally, but also it had the look of someone who had survived a serious illness, or a great natural disaster. It looked like he had been through the fire, and come back into the world knowing more than most people about what the fire was. It was a good face, it showed what a man could endure. And he was relaxed; this kind of interruption was part of daily life, part of the job he had volunteered for nine years before.

I was anything but relaxed. In fact, as the Secret Service men did their hawk routine on Buddha, their gazes locked, I could feel my heart stop, and I had to give my torso a little twist to get it started up again. Nathan had stopped breathing from the moment he saw Carter, and he was turning white above the sharp line of his beard. It was getting worse by the second when Freds stepped forward and extended a hand. "Hey, Mr. Carter, namaste! We're happy to meet you."

"Hi, how are y'all." More of the famous smile. "Where are y'all from?"

And we answered "Arkansas," "California," "M-Massachusetts," "Oregon," and at each one he smiled and nodded with recognition and pleasure, and Rosalynn smiled and said "Hello, hello," with that faint look I had seen before during the Presidential years, that seemed to say she would have been just as happy somewhere else, and we all shuffled around so that we could all shake hands with Jimmy—until it was Buddha's turn.

"This is our guide, B-Badim Badur," I said. "He doesn't speak any English."

"I understand," Jimmy said. And he took Buddha's hand and pumped it up and down.

Now, I had opted to leave Buddha barehanded, a decision I began to seriously regret. Here we had a man who had shaken at least a million hands in his life, maybe ten million; nobody in the whole world could have been more of an expert at it. And as soon as he grasped Buddha's long skinny hand, he knew that something was different. This wasn't like any of the millions of other hands he had shaken before. A couple of furrows joined the network of fine wrinkles around his eyes, and he looked closer at Buddha's peculiar get-up. I could feel the sweat popping out and beading on my forehead. "Um, Badim's a bit shy," I was saying, when suddenly the yeti squeaked.

"Naa-maas-tayy," it said, in a hoarse, whispery voice.

"Namaste!" Jimmy replied, grinning the famous grin.

And that, folks, was the first recorded conversation between yeti and human.

Of course Buddha had only been trying to help—I'm sure of that, given what happened later—but despite all we did to conceal it, his speech had obviously surprised us pretty severely. As a result the Secret Service guys were about to go cross-eyed checking us out, Buddha in particular.

"Let's let these folks get on with things," I said shakily, and took Buddha by the arm. "Nice to meet you," I said to the Carters. We all hung there for a moment. It didn't seem polite to precede the ex-President of the United States down a flight of stairs, but the Secret Service men damn well didn't want us *following* them down either; so finally I took the lead, with Buddha by the arm, and I held onto him tight as we descended.

We reached the foyer without incident. Sarah conversed brightly with the Secret Service men who were right behind us, and she distracted their attention very successfully, I thought. It appeared we would escape the situation without further difficulties, when the doors to the casino bar swung back, and Phil Adrakian, J. Reeves Fitzgerald, and Valerie Budge walked out. (Timing, anyone?)

Adrakian took in the situation at a glance. "They're kidnapping him!" he yelled. "Hey! *Kidnapping!*"

Well, you might just as well have put jumper cables on those Secret Service agents. After all, it's kind of a question why anyone would want to assassinate an ex-President, but as a hostage for ransom or whatnot, you've got a prime target. They moved like mongooses to get between us and the Carters. Freds and I were trying to back Buddha out the front doors without actually moving our legs; we weren't making much progress, and I don't doubt we could've gotten shot for our efforts, if it weren't for Sarah. She jumped right out in front of the charging Adrakian and blocked him off.

"*You're* the kidnapper, you liar," she cried, and slapped

44

him in the face so hard he staggered. *"Help!"* she demanded of the Secret Service guys, blushing bright red and shoving Valerie Budge back into Fitzgerald. She looked so tousled and embattled and beautiful that the agents were confused; the situation wasn't at all clear. Freds, Buddha and I bumped out the front door and ran for it.

Our taxi was gone. "Shit," I said. No time to think. "The bikes?" Freds asked.

"Yep." No other choice—we ran around the side of the building and unlocked our two bikes. I got on mine and Freds helped Buddha onto the little square rack over the back wheel. People around front were shouting, and I thought I heard Adrakian among them. Freds gave me a push from behind and we were off; I stood to pump up some speed, and we wavered side to side precariously.

I headed up the road to the north. It was just wider than one lane, half-paved and half-dirt. Bike and car traffic on it was heavy, as usual, and between dodging vehicles and potholes, looking back for pursuers, and keeping the bike from tipping under Buddha's shifting weight, I was kept pretty busy.

The bike was a standard Kathmandu rental, Hero Jet by brand name: heavy frame, thick tires, low handlebars, one speed. It braked when you pedaled backwards, and had one handbrake, and it had a big loud bell, which is a crucial piece of equipment. This bike wasn't a bad specimen either, in that the handbrake worked and the handlebars weren't loose and the seat wasn't putting a spring through my ass. But the truth is, the Hero Jet is a solo vehicle. And Buddha was no lightweight. He was built like a cat, dense and compact, and I bet he weighed over two hundred pounds. With him in back, the rear tire was squashed flat—there was about an eighth of an inch clearance between rim and ground, and every time I misnavigated a pothole there was an ugly *thump* as we bottomed out.

So we weren't breaking any speed records, and when we

turned left on Dilli Bazar Freds shouted from behind, "They're after us! See, there's that Adrakian and some others in a taxi!"

Sure enough, back a couple hundred yards was Phil Adrakian, hanging out the side window of a little white Toyota taxi, screaming at us. We pedaled over the Dhobi Khola bridge and shot by the Central Immigration building before I could think of anything to yell that might have brought the crowd there into the street. "Freds!" I said, panting. "Make a diversion! Tie up traffic!"

"Right on." Without a pause he braked to a halt in the middle of the road, jumped off and threw his Hero Jet to the pavement. The three-wheeled motorcab behind him ran over it before the driver could stop. Freds screamed abuse, he pulled the bike out and slung it under a Datsun going the other way, which crunched it and screeched to a halt. More abuse from Freds, who ran around pulling the drivers from their vehicles, shouting at them with all the Nepalese he knew: "Chiso howa!" (Cold wind.) "Tato pani!" (Hot water.) "Rhamrao dihn!" (Nice day.)

I only caught glimpses of this as I biked away, but I saw he had bought a little time and I concentrated on negotiating the traffic. Dilli Bazar is one of the most congested streets in Kathmandu, which is really saying a lot. The two narrow lanes are fronted by three-story buildings containing grocery markets and fabric wholesalers, which open directly onto the street and use it for cash register lines and so on, despite the fact that it's a major truck route. Add to that the usual number of dogs, goats, chickens, taxis, young schoolgirls walking three abreast with their arms linked, pedicabs with five-foot-tall operators pedaling whole families along at three miles an hour, and the occasional wandering sacred cow, and you can see the extent of the problem. Not only that, but the potholes are fierce— some could be mistaken for open manholes.

And the hills! I was doing all right until that point, weaving through the crowd and ringing my bell to the point of thumb cramp. But then Buddha shook my arm and I looked back and saw that Adrakian had somehow gotten past Freds and hired another taxi, and he was trailing us again, stuck behind a colorfully painted bus some distance behind. And then we started up the first of three fairly steep up-and-downs that Dilli Bazar makes before it reaches the city center.

Hero Jets are not made for hills. The city residents get off theirs and walk them up inclines like that one, and only Westerners, still in a hurry even in Nepal, stay on and grind up the slopes. I was certainly a Westerner in a hurry that day, and I stood up and started pumping away. But it was heavy going, especially after I had to brake to a dead stop to avoid an old man blowing his nose with his finger. Adrakian's taxi had rounded the bus, in an explosion of honks, and he was gaining on us fast. I sat back on the seat, huffing and puffing, legs like big blocks of wood, and it was looking like I'd have to find a diplomatic solution to the problem, when suddenly both my feet were kicked forward off the pedals; we surged forward, just missing a pedicab.

Buddha had taken over. He was holding onto the seat with both hands, and pedaling from behind. I had seen tall Westerners ride their rental bikes like that before, to keep from smashing their knees into the handlebars on every up-swing. But you can't get much downthrust from back there, and you didn't ever see them doing that while biking up-hill. For Buddha, this was not a problem. I mean this guy was *strong*. He pumped away so hard that the poor Hero Jet squeaked under the strain, and we surged up the hill and flew down the other side like we had jumped onto a motor-cycle.

A motorcycle without brakes, I should add. Buddha did not seem up on the theory of the footbrake, and I tried the handbrake once or twice and found that it only squealed like a pig and reduced our stability a bit. So as we fired down Dilli Bazar I could only put my feet up on the frame and dodge obstacles, as in one of those race-car video games. I rang the bell for all it was worth, and spent a lot of time in the right lane heading at oncoming traffic (they drive on the left). Out the corner of my eye I saw pedestrians goggling at us as we flew by; then the lanes ahead cleared as we rounded a semi, and I saw we were approaching the "Traffic Engineers' Intersection," usually one of my favorites. Here Dilli Bazar crosses another major street, and the occasion is marked by four traffic lights, all four of them *permanently green twenty-four hours a day*.

This time there was a cow for a traffic cop. "Bistarre!" (Slowly) I yelled, but Buddha's vocabulary apparently remained restricted to "Namaste," and he pedaled right on. I charted a course, clamped down the handbrake, crouched over the handlebars, rang the bell.

We shot the gap between a speeding cab and the traffic cow, with three inches to spare on each side, and were through the intersection before I even had time to blink. No problem. Now *that's* timing.

After that, it was just a matter of navigation. I took us the wrong way up the one-way section of Durbar Marg, to shorten our trip and throw off pursuit for good, and having survived that it was simple to make it the rest of the way to Thamel.

As we approached Thamel, we passed the grounds of the Royal Palace; as I mentioned, the tall trees there are occupied day and night by giant brown bats, hanging head down from the bare upper branches. As we passed the palace, those bats must have caught the scent of the yeti, or something, because all of a sudden the whole flock of them burst off the branches, squeaking like my handbrake and flapping their big skin wings like a hundred little Draculas. Buddha slowed to stare up at the sight, and everyone else on the block, even the cow on the corner, stopped and looked up as well, to watch that cloud of bats fill the sky.

It's moments like that that make me love Kathmandu.

In Thamel, we fit right in. A remarkable number of people on the street looked a lot like Buddha—so much so that the notion hit me that the city was being secretly infiltrated by yeti in disguise. I chalked the notion up to hysteria caused by the Traffic Engineers' Intersection, and directed our Hero Jet into the Hotel Star courtyard. At that point walls surrounded us and Buddha consented to stop pedaling. We got off the bike, and shakily I led him upstairs to my room.

X

So. WE HAD liberated the imprisoned yeti. Although I had to admit, as I locked us both into my room, that he was only partway free. Getting him completely free, back on his home ground, might turn out to be a problem. I still didn't know exactly where his home was, but they don't rent cars in Kathmandu, and the bus rides, no matter the destination, are long and crowded. Would Buddha be able to hold it together for ten hours in a crowded bus? Well, knowing him, he probably would. But would his disguise hold up? That was doubtful.

Meanwhile, there was the matter of Adrakian and the Secret Service being on to us. I had no idea what had happened to Nathan and Sarah and Freds, and I worried about them, especially Nathan and Sarah. I wished they would arrive. Now that we were here and settled, I felt a little uncomfortable with my guest; with him in there, my room felt awfully small.

I went in the bathroom and peed. Buddha came in and watched me, and when I was done he found the right buttons on the overalls, and did the same thing! The guy was

49

amazingly smart. Another point—I don't know whether to mention this—but in the hominid-versus-primate debate, I've heard it said that most primate male genitals are quite small, and that human males are by far the size champs in that category. Hurray for us. But Buddha, I couldn't help noticing, was more on the human side of the scale. Really, the evidence was adding up. The yeti was a hominid, and a highly intelligent hominid at that. Buddha's quick under-standing, his rapid adaptation to changing situations, his recognition of friends and enemies, his *cool*, all indicated smarts of the first order.

Of course, it made sense. How else could they have stayed concealed so well for so long? They must have taught their young all the tricks, generation to generation; keeping close track of all tools or artifacts, hiding their homes in the most hard-to-find caves, avoiding all human settlements, practicing burial of the dead. . . .

Then it occurred to me to wonder: If the yetis were so smart, and so good at concealment, why was Buddha here with me in my room? What had gone wrong? Why had he revealed himself to Nathan, and how had Adrakian man-aged to capture him?

I found myself speculating on the incidence of mental ill-ness among yetis, a train of thought that made me even more anxious for Nathan's arrival. Nathan was not a whole lot of help in some situations, but the man had a rapport with the yeti that I sadly lacked.

Buddha was crouched on the bed, hunched over his knees, staring at me brightly. We had taken his sunglasses off on arrival, but the Dodgers cap was still on. He looked observant, curious, puzzled. What next? he seemed to say. Something in his expression, something about the way he was coping with it all, was both brave and pathetic—it made me feel for him. "Hey, guy. We'll get you back up there. Namaste."

He formed the words with his lips.

Perhaps he was hungry. What do you feed a hungry yeti? Was he vegetarian, carnivorous? I didn't have much there in the room: some packages of curried chicken soup, some candy (would sugar be bad for him?), beef jerky, yeah, a possibility; Nebico malt biscuits, which were little cookielike wafers made in India that figured large in my diet. . . . I opened a package of these and one of jerky, and offered some to him.

He sat back on the bed and crossed his legs in front of him. He tapped the bed as if to indicate my spot. I sat down on the bed across from him. He took a stick of jerky in his long fingers, sniffed it, stuck it between his toes. I ate mine for example. He looked at me as if I'd just used the wrong fork for the salad. He began with a Nebico wafer, chewing it slowly. I found I was hungry, and from the roundness of his eyes I think he felt the same. But he was cool; there was a procedure here, he had me know; he handled all the wafers carefully first, sniffed them, ate them very slowly; took the jerky from between his toes, tried half of it; looked around the room, or at me, chewing very slowly. So calm, so peaceful he was! I decided the candy would be okay, and offered him the bag of jelly beans. He tried one and his eyebrows lifted; he picked one of the same color (green) from the bag, and gave it to me.

Pretty soon we had all the food I owned scattered out there on the bed between us, and we tried first one thing and then another, in silence, as slowly and solemnly as if it were all some sacred ritual. And you know, after a while I felt just like it was.

XI

ABOUT AN HOUR AFTER our meal Nathan, Sarah, and Freds all arrived at once. "You're here!" they cried. "All right, George! Way to go!"

"Thank Buddha," I said. "He got us here."

Nathan and Buddha went through a little hand ritual with the fossil shell necklace. Freds and Sarah told me the story of their adventures. Sarah had fought with Adrakian, who escaped her and ran after us, and then with Valerie Budge, who stayed behind with Fitzgerald, to trade blows and accusations. "It was a joy to pound on her, she's been coming on to Phil for months now—not that I care anymore, of course," Sarah added quickly as Nathan eyed her. Anyway, she had pushed and shoved and denounced Budge and Fitzgerald and Adrakian, and by the time she was done no one at the Sheraton had the slightest idea what was going on. A couple of Secret Service men had gone after Adrakian; the rest contented themselves with shielding the Carters, who were being called on by both sides to judge the merits of the case. Naturally the Carters were reluctant to do this, uncertain as they were of what the case was. Fitzgerald and Budge didn't want to come right out and say they had had a yeti stolen from them, so they were hamstrung; and when Freds returned to see what was up, Nathan and Sarah had already ordered a cab. "I think the Carters ended up on our side," Sarah said with satisfaction.

"All well and good," added Freds, "but there I had old Jimmy right at hand, no yeti to keep me polite, and man I had a bone to pick with that guy! I was in San Diego in 1980 and along about six o'clock on election day me and a bunch of friends were going down to vote and I argued *heavily* with them that we should vote for Carter rather than Anderson, because Anderson would just be a gesture whereas I thought Carter might still have a chance to win, since I don't believe in polls. I really went at it and I convinced every one of them, probably the peak of my political career, and then when we got home and turned on the TV we found out that Carter had already conceded the election a couple of hours before! My friends were so mad at me!

John Drummond threw his beer at me and hit me right here. In fact they soaked me. So I had a bone to pick with old Jimmy, you bet, and I was going to go up to him and ask him why he had done such a thing. But he was looking kind of confused by all the ruckus, so I decided not to."

"The truth is I dragged him away before he could," said Sarah.

Nathan got us back to the problem at hand. "We've still got to get the yeti out of Kathmandu, and Adrakian knows we've got him—he'll be searching for us. How are we going to do it?"

"I've got a plan," I said. Because after my meal with Buddha I had been thinking. "Now where is Buddha's home? I need to know."

Nathan told me.

I consulted my maps. Buddha's valley was pretty near the little airstrip at J—. I nodded. "Okay, here's how we'll do it. . . ."

XII

I SPENT MOST OF the next day through the looking glass, inside the big headquarters of the Royal Nepal Airline Corporation, getting four tickets for the following day's flight to J—. Tough work, even though as far as I could tell the plane wasn't even close to sold out. J— wasn't near any trekking routes, and it wasn't a popular destination. But that doesn't mean anything at RNAC. Their purpose as a company, as far as I can tell, is not so much to fly people places as it is to *make lists*. Waiting lists. I would call it their secret agenda, only it's no secret.

Patience, a very low-keyed pigheadedness, and lots of

53

baksheesh are the keys to getting from the lists to the status of ticket-holder; I managed it, and in one day too. So I was pleased, but I called my friend Bill, who works in one of the city's travel agencies, to establish a little backup plan. He's good at those, having a lot of experience with RNAC. Then I completed the rest of my purchases, at my favorite climbing outfitters in Thamel. The owner, a Tibetan woman, put down her copy of *The Far Pavilions* and stopped doing her arm aerobics, and got me all the clothes I asked for, in all the right colors. The only thing she couldn't find me was another Dodgers cap, but I got a dark blue "ATOM" baseball cap instead.

I pointed at it. "What is this 'ATOM,' anyway?" Because there were caps and jackets all over Nepal with that one word on them. Was it a company, and if so, what kind?

She shrugged. "Nobody knows."

Extensive advertising for an unknown product: yet another Great Mystery of Nepal. I stuffed my new belongings into my backpack and left. I was on my way home when I noticed someone dodging around in the crowd behind me. Just a glance and I spotted him, nipping into a newsstand: Phil Adrakian.

Now I couldn't go home, not straight home. So I went to the Kathmandu Guest House, next door, and told one of the snooty clerks there that Jimmy Carter would be visiting in ten minutes and his secretary would be arriving very shortly. I walked through into the pretty garden that gives the Guest House so many of its pretensions, and hopped over a low spot in the back wall. Down an empty garbage alley, around the corner, over another wall, and past the Lodge Pleasant or Pheasant into the Star's courtyard. I was feeling pretty covert and all when I saw one of the Carters' Secret Service men, standing in front of the Tantric Used Book Store. Since I was already in the courtyard, I went ahead and hurried on up to my room.

XIII

"I THINK THEY MUST have followed you here," I told our little group. "I suppose they might think we really were trying a kidnapping yesterday."

Nathan groaned. "Adrakian probably convinced them we're part of that group that bombed the Hotel Annapurna this summer."

"That should reassure them," I said. "When that happened the opposition group immediately wrote to the King and told him they were suspending all operations against the government until the criminal element among them was captured by the authorities."

"Hindu guerrillas are heavy, aren't they?" said Freds.

"Anyway," I concluded, "all this means is that we have a damn good reason to put our plan into effect. Freds, are you sure you're up for it?"

"Sure I'm sure! It sounds like fun."

"All right. We'd better all stay here tonight, just in case. I'll cook up some chicken soup."

So we had a spartan meal of curried chicken soup, Nebico wafers, Toblerone white chocolate, jelly beans, and iodinated Tang. When Nathan saw the way Buddha went for the jelly beans, he shook his head. "We've got to get him out of here *fast*."

When we settled down, Sarah took the bed, and Buddha immediately joined her, with a completely innocent look in his eye, as if to say: Who, me? This is just where I sleep, right? I could see Nathan was a bit suspicious of this, worried about the old Fay Wray complex maybe, and in fact he curled up on the foot of the bed. I assume there weren't any problems. Freds and I threw down the mildewed foam pads I owned and lay down on the floor.

"Don't you think Buddha is sure to get freaked by the flight tomorrow?" Sarah asked when the lights were off.

"Nothing's seemed to bother him much so far," I said. But I wondered; I don't like flying myself.

"Yeah, but this isn't remotely like anything he's ever done before."

"Standing on a high ridge is kind of like flying. Compared to our bike ride it should be easy."

"I'm not so sure," Nathan said, worried again. "Sarah may be right—flying can be upsetting even for people who know what it is."

"That's usually the heart of the problem," I said, with feeling.

Freds cut through the debate: "I say we should get him stoned before the flight. Get a hash pipe going good and just get him *wasted*."

"You're crazy!" Nathan said. "That'd just freak him out more!"

"Nah."

"He wouldn't know what to make of it," Sarah said.

"Oh yeah?" Freds propped himself up on one arm. "You really think those yetis have lived all this time up there among all those pot plants, and haven't figured them out? No way! In fact that's probably why no one ever sees them! Man, the pot plants up there are as big as *pine trees*. They probably use the buds for food."

Nathan and Sarah doubted that, and they further doubted that we should do any experimenting about it at such a crucial time.

"You got any hash?" I asked Freds with interest.

"Nope. Before this Ama Dablam climb came through I was going to fly to Malaysia to join a jungle mountain expedition that Doug Scott put together, you know? So I got rid of it all. I mean, do you fly drugs into Malaysia is not one of the harder questions on the IQ test, you know? In fact I had too much to smoke in the time I had left, and when I was hiking down from Namche to Lukla I was loading my pipe and dropped this chunk on the ground, a really monster chunk, about ten grams. *And I just left it there!* Just left it lying on the ground! I've always wanted to do that.

"Anyway, I'm out. I could fix that in about fifteen minutes down on the street if you want me to, though—"

"No, no. That's okay." I could already hear the steady breathing of Buddha, fast asleep above me. "He'll be more relaxed than any of us tomorrow." And that was true.

XIV

WE GOT UP BEFORE dawn, and Freds dressed in the clothes that Buddha had worn the day before. We pasted some swatches of Buddha's back fur onto Freds's face to serve as a beard. We even had some of the russet fur taped to the inside of the Dodgers cap, so it hung down behind. With mittens on, and a big pair of snow boots, he was covered; slip the shades onto his nose and he looked at least as weird as Buddha had in the Sheraton. Freds walked around the room a bit, trying it out. Buddha watched him with that surprised look, and it cracked Freds up. "I look like your long-lost brother, hey Buddha?"

Nathan collapsed on the bed despondently. "This just isn't going to work."

"That's what you said last time," I objected.

"Exactly! And look what happened! You call that *working*? Are you telling me that things *worked* yesterday?"

"Well, it depends on what you mean when you say *worked*. I mean here we are, right?" I began packing my gear. "Relax, Nathan." I put a hand on his shoulder, and

Sarah put both her hands on his other shoulder. He bucked up a bit, and I smiled at Sarah. That woman was tough; she had saved our ass at the Sheraton, and she kept her nerve well during the waiting, too. I wouldn't have minded asking her on a long trek into the Himal myself, really, and she saw that and gave me a brief smile of appreciation that also said, no chance. Besides, double-crossing old Nathan would have been like the Dodgers giving away Steve Garvey. People like that you can't double-cross, not if you want to look yourself in the mirror.

Freds finished getting pointers in carriage from Buddha, and he and I walked out of the room. Freds stopped and looked back inside mournfully, and I tugged him along, irritated at the Method acting; we wouldn't be visible to anyone outside the Star until we got downstairs.

But I must say that overall Freds did an amazing job. He hadn't seen all that much of Buddha, and yet when he walked across that courtyard and into the street, he caught the yeti's gait exactly: a bit stiff-hipped and bowlegged, a rolling sailor's walk from which he could drop to all fours instantly, or so it seemed. I could hardly believe it.

The streets were nearly empty: a bread truck, scavenging dogs (they passed Freds without even a glance—would that give us away?), the old beggar and his young daughter, a few coffee freaks outside the German Pumpernickel Bakery, shopkeepers opening up. . . . Near the Star we passed a parked taxi with three men in it, carefully looking the other way. Westerners. I hurried on. "Contact," I muttered to Freds. He just whistled a little.

There was one taxi in Times Square, the driver asleep. We hopped in and woke him, and asked him to take us to the Central Bus Stop. The taxi we had passed followed us. "Hooked," I said to Freds, who was sniffing the ashtrays, tasting the upholstery, leaning out the window to eat the wind like a dog. "Try not to overdo it," I said, worried about my Dodgers cap with all that hair taped in it flying away.

We passed the big clock tower and stopped, got out and paid the cabbie. Our tail stopped farther up the block, I was pleased to see. Freds and I walked down the broad, mashed-mud driveway into the Central Bus Stop.

The bus stop was a big yard of mud, about five or eight feet lower than the level of the street. Scores of buses were parked at all angles in the yard, and their tires had torn the mud up until the yard looked like a vehicular Verdun. All of the buses were owned by private companies—one bus per company, usually, with a single route to run—and all of their agents at the wood-and-cloth booths at the entrance clamored for our attention, as if we might have come in without a particular destination in mind, and would pick the agent that made the loudest offer.

Actually, this time it was almost true. But I spotted the agent for the Jiri bus, which is where I had thought to send Freds, and I bought two tickets, in a crowd of all the other agents, who criticized my choice. Freds hunkered down a little, looking suitably distressed. A big hubbub arose; one of the companies had established its right to leave the yard next, and now its bus was trying to make it up the driveway, which was the one and only exit from the yard.

Each departure was a complete test of the driver, the bus's clutch and tires, and the advisory abilities of the agents standing around. After a lot of clutching and coaching this brightly painted bus squirted up the incline, and the scheduling debate began anew. Only three buses had unblocked access to the driveway, and the argument among their agents was fierce.

I took Freds in hand and we wandered around the track-torn mud, looking for the Jiri bus. Eventually we found it: gaily painted in yellow, blue, green and red, like all the rest, ours also had about forty decals of Ganesh stuck all over the windshield, to help the driver see. As usual, the company's "other bus" was absent, and this one was double-booked. We shoved our way on board and through the tightly packed crowd in the aisle, then found empty seats at the back. The Nepalis like to ride near the front. After more boardings, the crowd engulfed us even in the back. But we had Freds at a window, which is what I wanted.

Through the mud-flecked glass I could just see our tail: Phil Adrakian, and two men who might have been Secret Service agents, though I wasn't sure about that. They were fending off the bus agents and trying to get into the yard at the same time, a tough combination. As they sidestepped the bus agents they got in the driveway and almost got run over by the bus currently sliding up and down the slope; one slipped in the mud scrambling away, and fell on his ass. The bus agents thought this was great. Adrakian and the other two hurried off, and squished from bus to bus trying to look like they weren't looking for anything. They were pursued by the most persistent agents, and got mired in the mud from time to time, and I worried after a while that they wouldn't be able to find us. In fact it took them about twenty minutes. But then one saw Freds at the window, and they ducked behind a bus hulk that had sunk axle-deep, waving off the agents in desperate sign language. "Hooked for good," I said.

"Yeah," Freds replied without moving his lips.

The bus was now completely packed; an old woman had even been insinuated between Freds and me, which suited me fine. But it was going to be another miserable trip. "You're really doing your part for the cause," I said to Freds as I prepared to depart, thinking of the cramped day ahead of him.

"No hroblem!" he said liplessly. "I like these 'us trits!"

Somehow I believed him. I weaseled my way upright in the aisle and said good-bye. Our tails were watching the bus's only door, but that wasn't really much of a problem. I just squirmed between the Nepalis, whose concept of personal "body space" is pretty much exactly confined to the space their bodies are actually occupying—none of this

60

eighteen-inch bullshit for them—and got to a window on the other side of the bus. There was no way our watchers could have seen across the interior of that bus, so I was free to act. I apologized to the Sherpa I was sitting on, worked the window open, and started to climb out. The Sherpa very politely helped me, without the slightest suggestion I was going anything out of the ordinary, and I jumped down into the mud. Hardly anyone on the bus even noticed my departure. I snuck through the no-man's-land of the back buses. Quickly enough I was back on Durbar Marg and in a cab on my way to the Star.

XV

I GOT THE CABBIE to park almost inside the Star's lobby, and Buddha barreled into the backseat like a fullback hitting the line. While we drove he kept his head down, just in case, and the taxi took us out to the airport.

Things were proceeding exactly according to my plan, and you might imagine I was feeling pretty pleased, but the truth is that I was more nervous than I'd been all morning. Because we were walking up to the RNAC desk, you see. . . .

When I got there and inquired, the clerk told us our flight had been canceled for the day.

"What?" I cried. "Canceled! What for?"

Now, our counter agent was the most beautiful woman in the world. This happens all the time in Nepal—in the country you pass a peasant bent over pulling up rice, and she looks up and it's a face from the cover of *Cosmopolitan*, only twice as pretty and without the vampire makeup. This ticket clerk could have made a million modeling in New York, but she didn't speak much English, and when I asked her "What for?" she said, "It's raining," and looked past me for another customer.

I took a deep breath. Remember, I thought: RNAC. What would the Red Queen say? I pointed out the window. "It's not raining. Take a look."

Too much for her. "It's raining," she repeated. She looked around for her supervisor, and he came on over; a thin Hindu man with a red dot on his forehead. He nodded curtly. "It's raining up at J—."

I shook my head. "I'm sorry, I got a report on the short-wave from J—, and besides you can look north and see for yourself. It's not raining."

"The airstrip at J— is too wet to land on," he said.

"I'm sorry," I said, "but you landed there twice yesterday, and it hasn't rained since."

"We're having mechanical trouble with the plane."

"I'm sorry, but you've got a whole fleet of small planes out there, and when one has a problem you just substitute for it. I know, I switched planes three times here once." Nathan and Sarah didn't look too happy to hear that one.

The supervisor's supervisor was drawn by the conversation: another serious, slender Hindu. "The flight is canceled," he said. "It's political."

I shook my head. "RNAC pilots only strike the flights to Lukla and Pokhara—they're the only ones that have enough passengers for the strike to matter." My fears concerning the real reason for the cancellation were being slowly confirmed. "How many passengers on this flight?"

All three of them shrugged. "The flight is canceled," the first supervisor said. "Try tomorrow."

And I knew I was right. They had less than half capacity, and were waiting until tomorrow so the flight would be full. (Maybe more than full, but did they care?) I explained the situation to Nathan and Sarah and Buddha, and Nathan stormed up to the desk demanding that the flight fly as scheduled, and the supervisors had their eyebrows raised like they might actually get some fun out of this after all, but I hauled him away. While I was dialing my friend in the travel agency, I explained to him how maddening irate customers had been made into a sport (or maybe an art form) by Asian bureaucrats. After three tries I got my friend's office. The receptionist answered and said, "Yeti Travels?" which gave me a start; I'd forgotten the company's name. Then Bill got on and I outlined the situation. "Filling planes again, are they?" He laughed. "I'll call in that group of six we 'sold' yesterday, and you should be off."

"Thanks, Bill." I gave it fifteen minutes, during which time Sarah and I calmed Nathan, and Buddha stood at the window staring at the planes taking off and landing. "We've got to get out today!" Nathan kept repeating. "They'll never go for another ruse after today!"

"We know that already, Nathan."

I returned to the desk. "I'd like to get boarding passes for flight 2 to J—, please?"

She made out the boarding passes. The two supervisors stood off behind a console, studiously avoiding my gaze. Normally it wouldn't have gotten to me, but with the pressure to get Buddha out I was a little edgy. When I had the passes in hand I said to the clerk, loud enough for the supervisors to hear, "No more cancellation, eh?"

"Cancellation?"

I gave up on it.

XVI

OF COURSE A BOARDING pass is only a piece of paper, and when only eight passengers got on the little two-engine plane, I got nervous again; but we took off right on schedule. When the plane left the ground I sat back in my chair, and the relief blew through me like wash from the props. I hadn't known how nervous I was until that moment. Nathan and Sarah were squeezing hands and grinning in the seats ahead, and Buddha was in the window seat beside me, staring out at Kathmandu Valley, or the shimmy gray circle of the prop, I couldn't tell. Amazing guy, that Buddha: *so* cool.

We rose out of the green, terraced, faintly Middle-Earth perfection of Kathmandu Valley, and flew over the mountains to the north, up into the land of snows. The other passengers, four Brits, were looking out their windows and exclaiming over the godlike views, and they didn't give a damn if one of their fellow passengers was an odd-looking chap. There was no problem there. After the plane had leveled out at cruising altitude one of the two stewards came down the aisle and offered us all little wrapped pieces of candy, just as on other airlines they offer drinks or meals. It was incredibly cute, almost like kids playing at running an airline, which is the sort of thought that seems cute itself until you remember you are at seventeen thousand feet with these characters, and they are now going to fly you over the biggest mountains on earth in order to land you on the smallest airstrips. At that point the cuteness goes away and you find yourself swallowing deeply and trying not to think of downdrafts, life insurance, metal fatigue, the afterlife. . . .

I shifted forward in my seat, hoping that the other passengers were too preoccupied to notice that Buddha had swallowed his candy without removing the wrapper. I wasn't too sure about the two across from **us**, but they were Brits so even if they did think Buddha was strange, it only meant they would look at him less. No problem.

It wasn't long before the steward said, "No smoking, if it please you," and the plane dipped over and started down toward a particularly spiky group of snowy peaks. Not a sign of a landing strip; in fact the idea of one being down there was absurd on the face of it. I took a deep breath. I hate flying, to tell you the truth.

I suppose some of you are familiar with the Lukla airstrip below the Everest region. It's set on a bench high on the side of the Dudh Khosi gorge, and the grass strip, tilted about fifteen degrees from horizontal and only two hundred yards long, aims straight into the side of the valley wall. When you land there all you can really see is the valley wall, and it looks like you're headed right into it. At the last minute the pilot pulls up and hits the strip, and after the inevitable bounces you roll to a stop quickly because you're going uphill so steeply. It's a heavy experience, some people get religion from it, or at least quit flying.

But the truth is that there are at least a dozen RNAC strips in Nepal that are *much worse* than the one at Lukla, and unfortunately for us, the strip at J— was at about the top of that list. First of all, it hadn't begun life as an airstrip at all—it began as a barley terrace, one terrace among many on a mountainside above a village. They widened it and put a wind sock at one end, and tore out all the barley of course, and that was it. Instant airstrip. Not only that, but the valley it was in was a deep one—say five thousand feet—and very steep-sided, with a nearly vertical headwall just a mile upstream from the airstrip, and a sharp dogleg just a mile or so downstream, and really, nobody in their right *minds* would think to put an airstrip there. I became more and more convinced of this as we made a ten-thousand-foot dive into the dogleg, and pulled up against one wall of the valley, so close to it that I could have made a good estimate of the barley count per hectare if I'd been inclined to. I tried to reassure Buddha, but he was working my candy wrapper out of the ashtray and didn't want to be disturbed. Nice to be a yeti sometimes. I caught sight of our landing strip, and watched it grow bigger—say to the size of a ruler—and then we landed on it. Our pilot was good;

we only bounced twice, and rolled to a stop with yards to spare.

XVII

AND SO WE CAME to the end of our brief association with Buddha the yeti, having successfully liberated him from men who would no doubt become major lecturers on the crank circuit forever after.

I have to say that Buddha was one of the nicest guys I've ever had the pleasure of knowing, and certainly among the coolest. Unflappable, really.

But to finish: we collected our packs, and hiked all that afternoon, up the headwall of that valley and along a forested high valley to the west of it. We camped that night on a broad ledge above a short falls, between two monster boulders. Nathan and Sarah shared one tent, Buddha and I another. Twice I woke and saw Buddha sitting in the tent door, looking out at the immense valley wall facing us.

The next day we hiked long and hard, up continuously, and finally came to the site of the expedition's spring camp. We dropped our packs and crossed the river on a new bridge made of bamboo, and Nathan and Buddha led us up the cross-country route, through the forest to the high box canyon where they had first met. By the time we got up there it was late afternoon, and the sun was behind the mountains to the west.

Buddha seemed to understand the plan, as always. He took off my Dodgers cap and gave it back to me, having shed all the rest of his clothes back at camp. I had always treasured that cap, but now it only seemed right to give it back to Buddha; he nodded when I did, and put it back on his head. Nathan put the fossil necklace around Buddha's neck; but the yeti took it off and bit the cord apart, and gave a fossil seashell to each of us. It was quite a moment. Who knows but what yetis didn't eat these shellfish, in a previous age? I know, I know, I've got the timescales wrong, or so they say, but believe me, there was a look in that guy's eye when he gave us those shells that was ancient. I mean *old*. Sarah hugged him, Nathan hugged him, I'm not into that stuff, I shook his skinny strong right hand. "Goodbye for Freds, too," I told him.

"Na-mas-te," he whispered.

"Oh, Buddha," Sarah said, sniffling, and Nathan had his jaw clamped like a vise. Quite the sentimental moment. I turned to go, and sort of pulled the other two along with me; there wasn't that much light left, after all. Buddha took off upstream, and last I saw him he was on top of a riverside boulder, looking back down at us curiously, his wild russet fur suddenly groomed and perfect-looking in its proper context; my Dodgers cap looked odd indeed. That yeti was a hard man to read, sometimes, but it seemed to me then that his eyes were sad. His big adventure was over.

On the way back down it occurred to me to wonder if he wasn't in fact a little crazy, as I had thought once before. I wondered if he might not walk right into the next camp he found, and sit down and croak "Namaste," blowing all the good work we'd done to save him from civilization. Maybe civilization had corrupted him already, and the natural man was gone for good. I hoped not. If so, you've probably already heard about it.

Well, things were pretty subdued in the old expedition camp that night. We got up the tents by lantern light, and had some soup and sat there looking at the blue flames of the stove. I almost made a real fire to cheer myself up, but I didn't feel like it.

Then Sarah said, with feeling, "I'm proud of you, Nathan," and he began to do his Coleman lantern glow, he was so happy. I would be, too. In fact, when she said, "I'm proud of you too, George," and gave me a peck on the cheek, it made me grin, and I felt a pang of . . . well, a lot of things. Pretty soon they were off to their tent. Fine for them, and I was happy for them, really, but I was also feeling a little like old Snideley Whiplash at the end of the Dudley Do-Right episode: left out in the cold, with Dudley getting the girl. Of course I had my fossil seashell, but it wasn't quite the same.

I pulled the Coleman over, and looked at that stone shell for a while. Strange object. What had the yeti who drilled the little hole through it been thinking? What was it *for*?

I remembered the meal on my bed, Buddha and me solemnly chomping on wafers and picking over the supply of jelly beans. And then I was all right; that was enough for me, and more than enough.

XVIII

BACK IN KATHMANDU WE met Freds and found out what had happened to him, over schnitzel Parisienne and apple strudel at the Old Vienna. "By noon I figured you all were long gone, so when the bus stopped for a break at Lamosangu I hopped off and walked right up to these guys' taxi. I did my Buddha thing and they almost died when they saw me coming. It was Adrakian and two of those Secret Service guys who chased us out of the Sheraton. When I took off the cap and shades they were fried, naturally. I said, 'Man, I made a mistake! I wanted to go to Pokhara! This isn't Pokhara!' They were so mad they started yelling at each other. 'What's that?' says I. 'You all made some sort of mistake too? What a shame!' And while they were screaming at each other and all I made a deal with the taxi driver to take me back to Kathmandu too. The others weren't too happy about that, and they didn't want to let me in, but the cabbie was already pissed at them for hiring him to take his car over that terrible road, no matter what the fare. So when I offered him a lot of rupes he was pleased to stick those guys somehow, and he put me in the front seat with him, and we turned around and drove back to Kathmandu."

I said, "You drove back to Kathmandu with the *Secret Service*? How did you explain the fur taped to the baseball cap?"

"I didn't! So anyway, on the way back it was silent city behind me, and it got pretty dull, so I asked them if they'd seen the latest musical disaster movie from Bombay."

"What?" Nathan said. "What's that?"

"Don't you go see them? They're showing all over town. We do it all the time, it's great. You just smoke a few bowls of hash and go see one of these musicals they make, they last about three hours, no subtitles or anything, and they're killers! Incredible! I told these guys that's what they should do—"

"You told the Secret Service guys they should smoke bowls of *hash*?"

"Sure! They're Americans, aren't they? Anyway, they didn't seem too convinced, and we still had a hell of a long way to go to Kathmandu, so I told them the story of the last one I saw. It's still in town, you sure you're not going to see it? I don't want to spoil it for you."

We convinced him he wouldn't.

"Well, it's about this guy who falls in love with a gal he works with. But she's engaged to their boss, a real crook who is contracted to build the town's dam. The crook is building the dam with some kinda birdshit, it looked like, instead of cement, but while he was scamming that he fell into a mixer and was made part of the dam. So the guy and the gal get engaged, but she burns her face lighting a stove.

She heals pretty good, but after that when he looks at her he sees through her to her skull and he can't handle it, so he breaks the engagement and she sings a lot, and she disguises herself by pulling her hair over that side of her face and pretending to be someone else. He meets her and doesn't recognize her and falls in love with her, and she reveals who she is and sings that he should fuck off. Heavy singing on all sides at that point, and he tries to win her back and she says no way, and all the time it's raining cats and dogs, and finally she forgives him and they're all happy again, but the dam breaks right where the crook was weakening it and the whole town is swept away singing like crazy. But these two both manage to grab hold of a stupa sticking up out of the water, and then the floods recede and there they are hanging there together, and they live happily ever after. Great, man. A classic."

"How'd the Secret Service like it?" I asked.

"They didn't say. I guess they didn't like the ending."

But I could tell, watching Nathan and Sarah grinning hand-in-hand across the table, that they liked the ending just fine.

XIX

OH, ONE MORE THING: *you must not tell ANYONE about this!!!* Okay?

PART
2

Mother Goddess
of the World

I

My life started to get weird again the night I ran into Freds Fredericks, near Chimoa, in the gorge of the Dudh Kosi. I was guiding a trek at the time, and was very happy to see Freds. He was traveling with another climber, a Tibetan by the name of Kunga Norbu, who appeared to speak little English except for "Hello" and "Good morning," both of which he said to me as Freds introduced us, even though it was just after sunset. My trekking group was settled into their tents for the night, so Freds and Kunga and I headed for the cluster of teahouses tucked into the forest by the trail. We looked in them; two had been cleaned up for trekkers, and the third was a teahouse in the old style, frequented only by porters. We ducked into that one.

It was a single low room; we had to stoop not only under the beams that held up the slate roof, but also under the smoke layer. Old-style country buildings in Nepal do not have chimneys, and the smoke from their wood stoves just goes up to the roof and collects there in a very thick layer, which lowers until it begins to seep out under the eaves. Why the Nepalis don't use chimneys, which I would have thought a fairly basic invention, is a question no one can answer; it is yet another Great Mystery of Nepal.

Five wooden tables were occupied by Rawang and Sherpa porters, sprawled on the benches. At one end of the room the stove was crackling away. Flames from the stove and a hissing Coleman lantern provided the light. We said Namaste to all the staring Nepalis, and ducked under the smoke to sit at the table nearest the stove, which was empty.

We let Kunga Norbu take care of the ordering, as he had

more Nepalese than Freds or me. When he was done the Rawang stove keepers giggled and went to the stove, and came back with three huge cups of Tibetan tea.

I complained to Freds about this in no uncertain terms. "Damn it, I thought he was ordering chang!"

Tibetan tea, you see, is not your ordinary Lipton's. To make it they start with a black liquid that is not made from tea leaves at all but from some kind of root, and it is so bitter you could use it for suturing. They pour a lot of salt into this brew, and stir it up, and then they dose it liberally with rancid yak butter, which melts and floats to the top.

It tastes worse than it sounds. I have developed a strategy for dealing with the stuff whenever I am offered a cup; I look out the nearest window, and water the plants with it. As long as I don't do it too fast and get poured a second cup, I'm fine. But here I couldn't do that, because twenty-odd pairs of laughing eyes were staring at us.

Kunga Norbu was hunched over the table, slurping from his cup and going "ooh," and "ahh," and saying complimentary things to the stove keepers. They nodded and looked closely at Freds and me, big grins on their faces.

Freds grabbed his cup and took a big gulp of the tea. He smacked his lips like a wine taster. "Right on," he said, and drained the cup down. He held it up to our host. "More?" he said, pointing into the cup.

The porters howled. Our host refilled Freds's cup and he slurped it down again, smacking his lips after every swallow. I slipped some iodine solution into mine from a dropper I keep on me, and stirred it around and held my nose to get down a sip, and they thought that was funny too.

So we were in tight with the teahouse crowd, and when I asked for chang they brought over a whole bucket of it. We poured it into the little chipped teahouse glasses and went to work on it.

"So what are you and Kunga Norbu up to?" I asked him.

"Well," he said, and a funny expression crossed his face. "That's kind of a long story, actually."

"So tell it to me."

He looked uncertain. "It's too long to tell tonight."

"What's this? A story too long for Freds Fredericks to tell? Impossible, man, why I once heard you summarize the Bible to Laure, and it only took you a minute."

Freds shook his head. "It's longer than that."

"I see." I let it go, and the three of us kept on drinking the chang, which is a white beer made from rice or barley. We drank a lot of it, which is a dangerous proposition on several counts, but we didn't care. As we drank we kept slumping lower over the table to try to get under the smoke layer, and besides we just naturally felt like slumping at that point. Eventually we were laid out like mud in a puddle.

Freds kept conferring with Kunga Norbu in Tibetan, and I got curious. "Freds, you hardly speak a word of Nepali, how is it you know so much Tibetan?"

"I spent a couple years in Tibet. I was studying in the Buddhist lamaseries there."

"*You* studied in Buddhist lamaseries in Tibet?"

"Yeah sure! Can't you tell?"

"Well . . ." I waved a hand. "I guess that might explain it."

"That was where I met Kunga Norbu, in fact. He was my teacher."

"I thought he was a climbing buddy."

"Oh he is! He's a climbing lama. Actually there's quite a number of them. See when the Chinese invaded Tibet they closed down all the lamaseries, destroyed most of them in fact. The monks had to go to work, and the lamas either slipped over to Nepal, or moved up into mountain caves. Then later the Chinese wanted to start climbing mountains as propaganda efforts, to show the rightness of the thoughts of Chairman Mao. The altitude in the Himalayas was a little bit much for them, though, so they mostly used Tibetans, and called them Chinese. And the Tibetans with the most actual mountain experience turned out to be Bud-

75

dhist monks, who had spent a lot of time in really high, isolated retreats. Eight of the nine so-called Chinese to reach the top of Everest in 1975 were actually Tibetans."

"Was Kunga Norbu one of them?"

"No. Although he wishes he was, let me tell you. But he did go pretty high on the North Ridge in the Chinese expedition of 1980. He's a really strong climber. And a great guru too, a really holy guy."

Kunga Norbu looked across the table at me, aware that we were talking about him. He was short and skinny, very tough looking, with long black hair. Like a lot of Tibetans, he looked almost exactly like a Navaho or Apache Indian. When he looked at me I got a funny feeling; it was as if he were staring right through me to infinity. Or somewhere equally distant. No doubt lamas cultivate that look.

"So what are you two doing up here?" I asked, a bit uncomfortable.

"We're going to join my Brit buddies, and climb Lingtren. Should be great. And then Kunga and I might try a little something on our own."

We found we had finished off the bucket of chang, and we ordered another. More of that and we became even lower than mud in a puddle.

Suddenly Kunga Norbu spoke to Freds, gesturing at me. "Really?" Freds said, and they talked some more. Finally Freds turned to me. "Well, this is a pretty big honor, George. Kunga wants me to tell you who he really is."

"Very nice of him," I said. I found that with my chin on the table I had to move my whole head to speak.

Freds lowered his voice, which seemed to me unnecessary as we were the only two people in the room who spoke English. "Do you know what a tulku is, George?"

"I think so," I said. "Some of the Buddhist lamas up here are supposed to be reincarnated from earlier lamas, and they're called tulkus, right? The abbot at Tengboche is supposed to be one."

Freds nodded. "That's right." He patted Kunga Norbu on the shoulder. "Well, Kunga here is also a tulku."

"I see." I considered the etiquette of such a situation, but couldn't really figure it, so finally I just scraped my chin off the table and stuck my hand across the table. Kunga Norbu took it and shook, with a modest smile.

"I'm serious," Freds said.

"Hey!" I said. "Did I say you weren't serious?"

"No. But you don't believe it, do you."

"I believe that you believe it, Freds."

"He really is a tulku! I mean I've seen proof of it, I really have. His ku kongma, which means his first incarnation, was as Tsong Khapa, a very important Tibetan lama born in 1555. The monastery at Kum-Bum is located on the site of his birth."

I nodded, at a loss for words. Finally I filled up our little cups, and we toasted Kunga Norbu's age. He could definitely put down the chang like he had had lifetimes of practice. "So," I said, calculating. "He's about four hundred and thirty-one."

"That's right. And he's had a hard time of it, I'll tell you. The Chinese tore down Kum-Bum as soon as they took over, and unless the monastery there is functioning again, Tsong Khapa can never escape being a disciple. See, even though he is a major tulku—"

"A major tulku," I repeated, liking the sound of it.

"Yeah, even though he's a major tulku, he's still always been the disciple of an even bigger one, named Dorjee. Dorjee Lama is about as important as they come—only the Dalai Lama tops him—and Dorjee is one hard, hard guru."

I noticed that the mention of Dorjee's name made Kunga Norbu scowl, and refill his glass.

"Dorjee is so tough that the only disciple who has ever stuck with him has been Kunga here. Dorjee—when you want to become his student and you go ask him, he beats you with a stick. He'll do that for a couple of years to make sure you really want him as a teacher. And then he really puts you through the wringer. Apparently he uses the methods of the Ts'an sect in China, which are tough. To teach you the Short Path he pounds you in the head with his shoe."

"Now that you mention it, he does look a little like a guy who has been pounded in the head with a shoe."

"How can he help it? He's been a disciple of Dorjee's for four hundred years, and it's always the same thing. So he asked Dorjee when he would be a guru in his own right, and Dorjee said it couldn't happen until the monastery built on Kunga's birth site was rebuilt. And he said that *that* would never happen until Kunga managed to accomplish— well, a certain task. I can't tell you exactly what the task is yet, but believe me it's tough. And Kunga used to be *my* guru, see, so he's come to ask me for some help. So that's what I'm here to do."

"I thought you said you were going to climb Lingtren with your British friends?"

"That too."

I wasn't sure if it was the chang or the smoke, but I was getting a little confused. "Well, whatever. It sounds like a real adventure."

"You're not kidding."

Freds spoke in Tibetan to Kunga Norbu, explaining what he had said to me, I assumed. Finally Kunga replied, at length.

Freds said to me, "Kunga says you can help him too."

"I think I'll pass," I said. "I've got my trekking group and all, you know."

"Oh I know, I know. Besides, it's going to be tough. But Kunga likes you—he says you have the spirit of Naropa."

Kunga nodded vigorously when he heard the name Naropa, staring through me with that spacy look of his.

"I'm glad to hear it," I said. "But I still think I'll pass."

"We'll see what happens," Freds said, looking thoughtful.

II

MANY GLASSES OF CHANG later we staggered out into the night. Freds and Kunga Norbu slipped on their down jackets, and with a "Good night" and a "Good morning" they wandered off to their tent. I made my way back to my group. It felt really late, and was maybe eight-thirty.

As I stood looking at our tent village, I saw a light bouncing down the trail from Lukla. The man carrying the flashlight approached—it was Laure, the sirdar for my group. He was just getting back from escorting clients back to Lukla. "Laure!" I called softly.

"Hello George," he said. "Why late now?"

"I've been drinking."

"Ah." With his flashlight pointed at the ground I could easily make out his big smile. "Good idea."

"Yeah, you should go have some chang yourself. You've had a long day."

"Not long."

"Sure." He had been escorting disgruntled clients back to Lukla all day, so he must have hiked five times as far as the rest of us. And here he was coming in by flashlight. Still, I suppose for Laure Tenzing Sherpa that did not represent a particularly tough day. As guide and yakboy he had been walking in these mountains all his life, and his calves were as big around as my thighs. Once, for a lark, he and three friends had set a record by hiking from Everest Base Camp to Kathmandu in four days; that's about two hundred miles, across the grain of some seriously uneven countryside. Compared to that today's work had been like a walk to the mailbox, I guess.

The worst part had no doubt been the clients. I asked him

about that and he frowned. "People go co-op hotel, not happy. Very, very not happy. They fly back Kathmandu."

"Good riddance," I said. "Why don't you go get some chang."

He smiled and disappeared into the dark.

I looked over the tents holding my sleeping clients and sighed.

So far it had been a typical videotrek. We had flown in to Lukla from Kathmandu. My clients, enticed to Nepal by glossy ads that promised them video Ansel Adamshood, had gone wild in the plane, rushing about banging zoom lenses together and so on. They were irrepressible until they saw the Lukla strip, which from the air looks like a toy model of a ski jump. Pretty quickly they were strapped in and looking like they were reconsidering their wills—all except for one tubby little guy named Arnold, who continued to roll up and down the aisle like a bowling ball, finally inserting himself into the cockpit so he could shoot over the pilots' shoulders. "We are landing at Lukla," he announced to his camera's mike in a deep fakey voice, like the narrator of a bad travelogue. "Looks impossible, but our pilots are calm."

Despite him we landed safely. Unfortunately one of our group then tried to film his own descent from the plane, and fell heavily down the steps. As I ascertained the damage—a sprained ankle—there was Arnold again, leaning over to immortalize the victim's every writhe and howl.

A second plane brought in the rest of our group, led by Laure and my assistant Heather. We started down the trail. For a couple of hours everything went well—the trail serves as the Interstate Five of the region, and is as easy as they come. And the view is awesome—the Dudh Kosi valley is like a forested Grand Canyon, only bigger. Our group was impressed, and several of them filmed a real-time record of the day.

Then the trail descended to the banks of the Dudh Kosi

river, and we got a surprise. Apparently in the last monsoon a glacial lake upstream had burst its ice dam, and rushed down in a devastating flood, tearing out the bridges, trail, trees, everything. Thus our fine interstate ended abruptly in a cliff overhanging the torn-to-shreds riverbed, and what came next was the seat-of-the-pants invention of the local porters, for whom the trail was a daily necessity. They had been clever indeed, but there really was no good alternative to the old route; so the new trail wound over strewn white boulders in the riverbed, traversed unstable new sand cliffs, and veered wildly up and down muddy slides that had been hacked out of dense forested walls. It was radical stuff, and even experienced trekkers were having trouble.

Our group was appalled. The ads had not mentioned this.

The porters ran ahead barefoot to reach the next tea break, and the clients began to bog down. People slipped and fell. People sat down and cried. Altitude sickness was mentioned more than once, though as a matter of fact we were not much higher than Denver. Heather and I ran around encouraging the weary. I found myself carrying three videocameras. Laure was carrying nine.

It was looking like the retreat from Moscow when we came to the first of the new bridges. These are pretty neat pieces of backwoods engineering; there aren't any logs in the area long enough to span the river, so they take four logs and stick them out over the river, and weigh them down with a huge pile of round stones. Then four more logs are pushed out from the other side, until their ends rest on the ends of the first four. Instant bridge. They work, but they are not confidence builders.

Our group stared at the first one apprehensively. Arnold appeared behind us and chomped an unlit cigar as he filmed the scene. "The *Death Bridge*," he announced into his camera's mike.

"Arnold, please," I said. "Mellow out."

He walked down to the glacial gray rush of the river. "Hey, George, do you think I could take a step in to get a better shot of the crossing?"

"NO!" I stood up fast. "One step in and you'd drown, I mean look at it!"

"Well, okay."

Now the rest of the group were staring at me in horror, as if it weren't clear at first glance that to fall into the Dudh Kosi would be a very fatal error indeed. A good number of them ended up crawling across the bridge on hands and knees. Arnold got them all for posterity, and filmed his own crossing by walking in circles that made me cringe. Silently I cursed him; I was pretty sure he had known perfectly well how dangerous the river was, and only wanted to make sure everyone else did too. And very soon after that—at the next bridge, in fact—people began to demand to be taken back to Lukla. To Kathmandu. To San Francisco.

I sighed, remembering it. And remembering that this was only the beginning. Just your typical Want To Take You Higher Ltd. videotrek. Plus Arnold.

III

I GOT ANOTHER BIT of Arnold in action early the next morning, when I was in the rough outhouse behind the trekkers' teahouses, very hung over, crouched over the unhealthy damp hole in the floor. I had just completed my business in there when I looked up to see the big glass eye of a zoom lens, staring over the top of the wooden door at me.

"No, Arnold!" I cried, struggling to put my hand over the lens while I pulled up my pants.

"Hey, just getting some local color," Arnold said, backing

away. "You know, people like to see what it's really like, the details and all, and these outhouses are really something else. Exotic."

I growled at him. "You should have trekked in from Jiri, then. The lowland villages don't have outhouses at all."

His eyes got round, and he shifted an unlit cigar to the other side of his mouth. "What do you do, then?"

"Well, you just go outside and have a look around. Pick a spot. They usually have a shitting field down by the river. Real exotic."

He laughed. "You mean, turds everywhere?"

"Well, something like that."

"That sounds great! Maybe I'd better walk back out instead of flying."

I stared at him, wrinkling my nose. "Serious filmmaker, eh Arnold?"

"Oh, yeah. Haven't you heard of me? Arnold McConnell? I make adventure films for PBS. And sometimes for the ski resort circuit, video rentals, that kind of thing. Skiing, hang gliding, kayaking, parachuting, climbing, skateboarding—I've done them all. Didn't you ever see *The Man Who Swam Down the Zambesi*? No? Ah, that's a bit of a classic, now. One of my best."

So he had known how dangerous the Dudh Kosi was. I stared at him reproachfully. It was hard to believe he made adventure films; he looked more like the kind of Hollywood producer you'd tell couch jokes about. "So you're making a real film of this trip?" I asked.

"Yeah, sure. Always working, never stop working. Workaholic."

"Don't you need a bigger crew?"

"Well sure, usually, but this is a different kind of thing, one of my 'personal diary' films I call them. I've sold a couple to PBS. Do all the work myself. It's kind of like my version of solo climbing."

"Fine. But cut the part about me taking a crap, okay?"

"Sure, sure, don't worry about it. Just got to get everything I can, you know, so I've got good tape to choose from later on. All grist for the mill. That's why I got this lens. All the latest in equipment for me. I got stuff you wouldn't believe."

"I believe."

He chomped his cigar. "Just call me Mr. Adventure."

"I will."

IV

I DIDN'T SEE FREDS and Kunga Norbu in Namche Bazaar, and I figured they had left already with Freds's British friends; I probably wouldn't see them again until we got up near their base camp, because I planned to keep my group in Namche a couple days to acclimatize, and enjoy the town. Namche functions as the Sherpas' capital, and a more dramatically placed town you could hardly imagine; it is perched on a promontory above the confluence of the Dudh Kosi and the Bhote Kosi, and the rivers lie about a mile below in steep green gorges, while white peaks tower a mile above all around it. The town itself is a horseshoe-shaped ring of stone buildings and stone streets, packed with Sherpas, trekkers, climbers, and traders dropping in for the weekly bazaar.

It's a fun town, and kept me busy; I forgot about Freds and the Brits, and so was quite surprised to run into them in Pheriche, one of the Sherpas' high mountain villages.

Most of these high villages are occupied only in the summer, to grow potatoes and pasture yaks. Pheriche, however, lies on the trekking route to Everest, so it's occupied almost year-round, and a couple lodges have been built, along with the Himalayan Rescue Association's only aid station. It still looks like a summer pasturage: low rock walls separate potato fields, and a few slate-roofed stone huts, plus the lodges and the tin-roofed aid station. All of it is clustered at the end of a flat-bottomed glacial valley, against the side of a lateral moraine five hundred feet high. A stream meanders by, and the ground is carpeted with grasses and the bright autumn red of berberi bushes. On all sides tower the fantastic white spikes of some of the world's most dramatic peaks—Ama Dablam, Taboche, Tramserku, Kang Taiga—and all in all, it's quite a place. My clients were making themselves dizzy trying to film it.

We set up our tent village in an unused potato field, and after dinner Laure and I slipped off to the Himalaya Hotel to have some chang. I entered the lodge's little kitchen and heard Freds cry, "Hey George!" He was sitting with Kunga Norbu and four Westerners; we joined them, crowding in around a little table. "These are the friends we're climbing with."

He introduced them, and we all shook hands. Trevor was a tall slender guy, with round glasses and a somewhat crazed grin. "Mad Tom," as Freds called him, was short and curly-headed, and didn't look mad at all, although something in his mild manner made me believe that he could be. John was short and compact, with a salt-and-pepper beard, and a crusher handshake. And Marion was a tall and rather attractive woman—though I suspected she might have blushed or punched you if you said so—she was attractive in a tough, wild way, with a stark strong face, and thick brown hair pulled back and braided. They were British, with the accents to prove it: Marion and Trevor quite posh and public school, and John and Mad Tom very thick and North Country.

We started drinking chang, and they told me about their climb. Lingtren, a sharp peak between Pumori and Everest's West Shoulder, is serious work from any approach, and they were clearly excited about it, in their own way: "Bit of a slog, to tell the truth," Trevor said cheerfully.

When British climbers talk about climbing, you have to learn to translate it into English. "Bit of a slog" means don't go there.

"I think we ought to get lost and climb Pumori instead," said Marion. "Lingtren is a perfect *hill*."

"Marion, really."

"Can't beat Lingtren's price, anyway," said John.

He was referring to the fee that the Nepali government makes climbers pay for the right to climb its peaks. These fees are determined by the height of the peak to be climbed—the really big peaks are super expensive. They charge you over five thousand dollars to climb Everest, for instance, and still competition to get on its long waiting list is fierce. But some of the toughest climbs in Nepal aren't very high, relative to the biggies, and they come pretty cheap. Apparently Lingtren was one of these.

We watched the Sherpani who runs the lodge cook dinner for fifty, under the fixed gazes of the diners, who sat staring hungrily at her every move. To accomplish this she had at her command a small wood-burning stove (with chimney, thank God), a pile of potatoes, noodles, rice, some eggs and cabbage, and several chang-happy porter assistants, who alternated washing dishes with breaking up chunks of yak dung for the fire. A difficult situation on the face of it, but the Sherpani was cool: she cooked the whole list of orders by memory, slicing and tossing potatoes into one pan, stuffing wood in the fire, flipping twenty pounds of noodles in midair like they were a single hotcake—all with the sureness and panache of an expert juggler. It was a kind of genius.

Two hours later those who had ordered the meals that came last in her strict sequence got their cabbage omelets on French fries, and the kitchen emptied out as many people went to bed. The rest of us settled down to more chang and chatter.

Then a trekker came back into the kitchen, so he could listen to his shortwave radio without bothering sleepers in the lodge's single dorm room. He said he wanted to catch the news. We all stared at him in disbelief. "I need to find out how the dollar's doing," he explained. "Did you know it dropped *eight percent* last week?"

You meet all kinds in Nepal.

Actually it's interesting to hear what you get on shortwave in the Himal, because depending on how the ionosphere is acting, almost anything will bounce in. That night we listened to the People's Voice of Syria, for instance, and some female pop singer from Bombay, which perked up the porters. Then the operator ran across the BBC world news, which was not unusual—it could have been coming from Hong Kong, Singapore, Cairo, even London itself.

Through the hissing of the static the public-school voice of the reporter could barely be made out. ". . . British Everest Expedition of 1986 is now on the Rongbuk Glacier in Tibet, and over the next two months they expect to repeat the historic route of the attempts made in the twenties and thirties. Our correspondent to the expedition reports—" and then the voice changed to one even more staccato and drowned in static: "—the expedition's principal goal of recovering the bodies of Mallory and Irvine, who were last seen near the summit in 1924, *crackle, buzz* . . . chances considerably improved by conversations with a partner of the Chinese climber who reported seeing a body on the North Face in 1980 *bzzzzkrkrk!* . . . description of the site of the finding *sssssssss* . . . snow levels very low this year, and all concerned feel chances for success are *sssskrkssss*." The voice faded away in a roar of static.

Trevor looked around at us, eyebrows lifted. "Did I understand them to say that they are going to search for Mallory and Irvine's *bodies*?"

A look of deep horror creased Mad Tom's face. Marion

wrinkled her nose as if her chang had turned to Tibetan tea. "I can't believe it."

I didn't know it at the time, but this was an unexpected opportunity for Freds to put his plan into action ahead of schedule. He said, "Haven't you heard about that? Why Kunga Norbu here is precisely the climber they're talking about, the one who spotted a body on the North Face in 1980."

"He *is*?" we all said.

"Yeah, you bet. Kunga was part of the Chinese expedition to the North Ridge in 1980, and he was up there doing reconnaissance for a direct route on the North Face when he saw a body." Freds spoke to Kunga Norbu in Tibetan, and Kunga nodded and replied at some length. Freds translated for him: "He says it was a Westerner, wearing museum clothing, and he had clearly been there a long time. Here, he says he can mark it on a photo—" Freds got out his wallet and pulled a wad of paper from it. Unfolded, it revealed itself as a battered black-and-white photo of Everest as seen from the Tibetan side. Kunga Norbu studied it for a long time, talked it over with Freds, and then took a pencil from Freds and carefully made a circle on the photo.

"Why he's circled half the North Face," John pointed out. "It's fooking useless."

"Nah," Freds said. "Look, it's a little circle."

"It's a little photo, innit."

"Well, he can describe the spot exactly—it's up there on top of the Black Band. Anyway, someone has managed to get together an expedition to go looking for the bodies, or the body, whatever. Now Kunga slipped over to Nepal last year, so this expedition is going on secondhand information from his climbing buds. But that might be enough."

"And if they find the bodies?"

"Well, I think they're planning to take them down and ship them to London and bury them in Winchester Cathedral."

The Brits stared at him. "You mean Westminster Abbey?" Trevor ventured.

"Oh that's right, I always get those two mixed up. Anyway that's what they're going to do, and they're going to make a movie out of it."

I groaned at the thought. More video.

The four Brits groaned louder than I did. "That is rilly dis-gusting," Marion said.

"Sickening," John and Mad Tom agreed.

"It is a travesty, isn't it?" Trevor said. "I mean those chaps belong up there if anybody does. It's nothing less than grave robbing!"

And his three companions nodded. On one level they were joking, making a pretense of their outrage; but underneath that, they were dead serious. They meant it.

V

To UNDERSTAND WHY THEY would care so much, you have to understand what the story of Mallory and Irvine means to the British soul. Climbing has always been more important there than in America—you could say that the British invented the sport in Victorian times, and they've continued to excel in it since then, even after World War Two when much else there fell apart. You could say that climbing is the Rolls Royce of British sport. Whymper, Hillary, the brilliant crowd that climbed with Bonington in the seventies: they're all national heroes.

But none more so than Mallory and Irvine. Back in the twenties and thirties, you see, the British had a lock on Everest, because Nepal was closed to foreigners, and Tibet was closed to all but the British, who had barged in on them with Younghusband's campaign back in 1904. So the mountain was their private playground, and during those years they made four or five attempts, all of them failures, which is understandable: they were equipped like Boy Scouts, they had to learn high-altitude technique on the spot, and they had terrible luck with weather.

The try that came closest was in 1924. Mallory was its lead climber, already famous from two previous attempts. As you may already know, he was the guy who replied "Because it's there" when asked why anyone would want to climb the thing. This is either a very deep or a very stupid answer, depending on what you think of Mallory. You can take your pick of interpretations; the guy has been psychoanalyzed into the ground. Anyway, he and his partner Irvine were last glimpsed, by another expedition member, just eight hundred feet and less than a quarter of a mile from the summit—and at one P.M., on a day that had good weather except for a brief storm, and mist that obscured the peak from the observers below. So they either made it or they didn't; but something went wrong somewhere along the line, and they were never seen again.

A glorious defeat, a deep mystery: this is the kind of story that the English just love, as don't we all. All the public-school virtues wrapped into one heroic Tale—you couldn't write it better. To this day the story commands tremendous interest in England, and this is doubly true among people in the climbing community, who grew up on the story, and who still indulge in a lot of speculation about the two men's fate, in journal articles and pub debates and the like. They love that story.

Thus to go up there, and find the bodies, and end the mystery, and cart the bodies off to England. . . . You can see why it struck my drinking buddies that night as a kind of sacrilege. It was yet another modern PR stunt—a money-grubbing plan made by some publicity hound—a Profaning of the Mystery. It was, in fact, a bit like videotrekking. Only worse. So I could sympathize, in a way.

I TRIED TO THINK of a change of subject, to distract the Brits. But Freds seemed determined to fire up their distress. He poked his finger onto the folded wreck of a photo. "You know what y'all oughta do," he told them in a low voice. "You mentioned getting lost and climbing Pumori? Well shit, what you oughta do instead is get lost in the other direction, and beat that expedition to the spot, and hide old Mallory. I mean here you've got the actual eyewitness right here to lead you to him! Incredible! You could bury Mallory in rocks and snow and then sneak back down. If you did that, they'd never find him!"

All the Brits stared at Freds, eyes wide. Then they looked at each other, and their heads kind of lowered together over the table. Their voices got soft. "He's a genius," Trevor breathed.

"Uh, no," I warned them. "He's not a genius." Laure was shaking his head. Even Kunga Norbu was looking doubtful.

Freds looked over the Brits at me and waggled his eyebrows vigorously, as if to say: this is a great idea! Don't foul it up!

"What about the Lho La?" John asked. "Won't we have to climb that?"

"Piece of cake," Freds said promptly.

"No," Laure protested. "Not piece cake! Pass! Very steep pass!"

"Piece of cake," Freds insisted. "I climbed it with those West Ridge direct guys a couple years ago. And once you top it you just slog onto the West Shoulder and there you are with the whole North Face, sitting right off to your left."

"Freds," I said, trying to indicate that he shouldn't incite his companions to such a dangerous, not to mention illegal, climb. "You'd need a lot more support for high camps than you've got. That circle there is pretty damn high on the mountain."

"True," Freds said immediately. "It's pretty high. Pretty damn high. You can't get much higher."

Of course to people like the Brits this was only another incitement, as I should have known.

"You'd have to do it like Woody Sayres did back in '62," Freds went on. "They got Sherpas to help them up the Nup La over by Cho Oyo, then bolted to Everest when they were supposed to be climbing Gyachung Kang. They moved a single camp with them all the way to Everest, and got back the same way. Just four of them, and they almost climbed it. And the Nup La is twenty miles farther away from Everest than the Lho La. The Lho La's right there under it."

Mad Tom knocked his glasses up his nose, pulled out a pencil and began to do calculations on the table. Marion was nodding. Trevor was refilling all our glasses with chang. John was looking over Mad Tom's shoulder and muttering to him; apparently they were in charge of supplies.

Trevor raised his glass. "Right then," he said. "Are we for it?"

They all raised their glasses. "We're for it."

They were toasting the plan, and I was staring at them in dismay, when I heard the door creak and saw who was leaving the kitchen. "Hey!"

I reached out and dragged Arnold McConnell back into the room. "What're you doing here?"

Arnold shifted something behind his back. "Nothing, really. Just my nightly glass of milktea, you know. . . ."

"It's him!" Marion exclaimed. She reached behind Arnold and snatched his camera from behind his back; he tried to hold on to it, but Marion was too strong for him. "Spying on me again, were you? Filming us from some dark corner?"

"No no," Arnold said. "Can't film in the dark, you know."

"Film in tent," Laure said promptly. "Night."

Arnold glared at him.

"Listen, Arnold," I said. "We were just shooting the bull here you know, a little private conversation over the chang. Nothing serious."

"Oh, I know," Arnold assured me. "I know."

Marion stood and stared down at Arnold. They made a funny pair—her so long and rangy, him so short and tubby. Marion pushed buttons on the camera until the videocassette popped out, never taking her eye from him. She could really glare. "I suppose this is the same film you used this morning, when you filmed me taking my shower, is that right?" She looked at us. "I was in the little shower box they've got across the way, and the tin with the hot water in it got plugged at the bottom somehow. I had the door open a bit so I could stretch up and fiddle with it, when suddenly I noticed this pervert filming me!" She laughed angrily. "I bet you were quite pleased with that footage, weren't you, you peeping Tom!"

"I was just leaving to shoot yaks," Arnold explained rapidly, staring up at Marion with an admiring gaze. "Then there you were, and what was I supposed to do? I'm a filmmaker, I film beautiful things. I could make you a star in the States," he told her earnestly. "You're probably the most beautiful climber in the world."

"And all that competition," Mad Tom put in.

I was right about Marion's reaction to a compliment of that sort—she blushed to the roots, and considered punching him too—she might have, if they'd been alone.

"—adventure films back in the States, for PBS and the ski resort circuit," Arnold was going on, chewing his cigar and rolling his eyes as Marion took the cartridge over toward the stove.

The Sherpani waved her off. "Smell," she said.

Marion nodded and took the videocassette in her hands. Her forearms tensed, and suddenly you could see every muscle. And there were a lot of them, too, looking like thin bunched wires under the skin. We all stared, and instinctively Arnold raised his camera to his shoulder before remembering it was empty. That fact made him whimper, and he was fumbling at his jacket pocket for a spare when the cassette snapped diagonally and the videotape spilled out. Marion handed it all to the Sherpani, who dumped it in a box of potato peels, grinning.

We all looked at Arnold. He chomped his cigar, shrugged. "Can't make you a star that way," he said, and gave Marion a soulful leer. "Really, you oughta give me a chance, you'd be great. Such *presence.*"

"I would appreciate it if you would now leave," Marion told him, and pointed at the door.

Arnold left.

"That guy could be trouble," Freds said.

VII

FREDS WAS RIGHT about that.

But Arnold was not the only source of trouble. Freds himself was acting a bit peculiar, I judged. Still, when I thought of the various oddities in his recent behavior—his announcement that his friend Kunga Norbu was a tulku, and now this sudden advocacy of a Save Mallory's Body campaign—I couldn't put it all together. It didn't make sense.

94

So when Freds's party and my trekking group took off upvalley from Pheriche on the same morning, I walked with Freds for a while. I wanted to ask him some questions. But there were a lot of people on the trail, and it was hard to get a moment to ourselves.

As an opener I said, "So, you've got a woman on your team."

"Yeah, Marion's great. She's probably the best climber of us all. And incredibly strong. You know those indoor walls they have in England, for practicing?"

"No."

"Well, the weather is so bad there, and the climbers are such fanatics, that they've built these thirty- and forty-foot walls inside gyms, and covered them with concrete and made little handholds." He laughed. "It looks dismal— scuzzy old gym with bad light and no heating, and all these guys stretched out on a concrete wall like a new kind of torture. . . . Anyway I visited one of these, and they set me up in a race with Marion, up the two hardest pitches. Maybe 5.13 in places, impossible stuff. Everyone started betting on us, and the rule was someone had to top out for anyone to collect on the bets. But there was a leak getting the wall damp, and I came off about halfway up. So she won, but to collect the bets she had to top out. With the leak it really was impossible, but everyone who had bet on her was yelling at her to do it, so she just grit her teeth and started making these *moves*, man"—Freds illustrated in the air between us as we hiked—"and she was doing them in slow motion so she wouldn't come off. Just hanging there by her fingertips and toes, and I swear to God she hung on that wall for must've been *three hours*. Everyone else stopped climbing to watch. Guys were going home—guys were begging her to come off—guys had tears in their eyes. Finally she topped out and crawled over to the ladder and came down, and they mobbed her. They were ready to make her queen. In fact she pretty much is queen, as far as the English climbers are concerned—you could bring the real one in and if Marion were there they wouldn't even notice."

Then Arnold slipped between us, looking conspiratorial. "I think this Mallory scheme is a great idea," he whispered through clenched teeth. "I'm totally behind you, and it'll make a *great movie*."

"You miss the point," I said to him.

"We ain't doing nothing but climb Lingtren," Freds said to him.

Arnold frowned, tucked his chin onto his chest, chewed his cigar. Frowning, Freds left to catch up with his group, and they soon disappeared ahead. So I lost my chance to talk to him.

We came to the upper end of Pheriche's valley, turned right and climbed to get into an even higher one. This was the valley of the Khumbu Glacier, a massive road of ice covered with a chaos of gray rubble and milky blue melt ponds. We skirted the glacier and followed a trail up its lateral moraine to Lobuche, which consists of three teahouses and a tenting ground. The next day we hiked on upvalley to Gorak Shep.

Now Gorak Shep ("Dead Crow") is not the kind of place you see on posters in travel agencies. It's just above seventeen thousand feet, and up there the plant life has about given up. It's just two ragged little teahouses under a monstrous rubble hill, next to a gray glacial pond, and all in all it looks like the tailings of an extraordinarily large gravel mine.

But what Gorak Shep does have is mountains. Big snowy mountains, on all sides. How big? Well, the wall of Nuptse, for instance, stands a full seven thousand feet over Gorak Shep. An avalanche we saw, sliding down a fraction of this wall and sounding like thunder, covered about two World Trade Centers' worth of height, and still looked tiny. And Nuptse is not as big as some of the peaks around it. So you get the idea.

Cameras can never capture this kind of scale, but you can't help trying, and my crowd tried for all they were worth in the days we were camped there. The ones handling the altitude well slogged up to the top of Kala Pattar ("Black Hill"), a local walker's peak which has a fine view of the Southwest Face of Everest. The day after that, Heather and Laure led most of the same people up the glacier to Everest Base Camp, while the rest of us relaxed. Everest Base Camp, set by the Indian Army this season, was basically a tent village like ours, but there are some fine seracs and ice towers to be seen along the way, and when they returned the clients seemed satisfied.

So I was satisfied too. No one had gotten any bad altitude sickness, and we would be starting back the next morning. I was feeling fine, sitting up on the hill above our tents in the late afternoon, doing nothing.

But then Laure came zipping down the trail from Base Camp, and when he saw me he came right over. "George George," he called out as he approached.

I stood as he reached me. "What's up?"

"I stay talk friends porter Indian Army base camp, Freds find me Freds say his base camp come please you. Climb Lho La find man camera come hire Sherpas finish with Freds, very bad follow Freds."

Now Laure's English is not very good, as you may have noticed. But after all we were in his country speaking my language—and for him English came after Sherpa, Nepali, and some Japanese and German, and how many languages do you speak?

Besides, I find I always get the gist of what Laure says, which is not something you can always say of all our fellow native speakers. So I cried out, "No! Arnold is *following* them?"

"Yes," Laure said. "Very bad. Freds say come please get."

"Arnold hired their Sherpas?"

Laure nodded. "Sherpas finish porter, Arnold hire."

"Damn him! We'll have to climb up there and get him!"

"Yes. Very bad."

"Will you come with me?"

"Whatever you like."

I hustled to our tents to get together my climbing gear, and tell Heather what had happened. "How did he get up there?" she asked. "I thought he was with you all day."

"He told me he was going with you! He probably followed you guys all the way up, and kept on going. Don't worry about it, it's not your fault. Take the group back to Namche starting tomorrow, and we'll catch up with you." She nodded, looking worried.

Laure and I took off. Even going at Laure's pace we didn't reach Freds's base camp until the moon had risen. Their camp was now only a single tent in a bunch of trampled snow, just under the steep headwall of the Khumbu Valley—the ridge that divided Nepal from Tibet. We zipped open the tent and woke Freds and Kunga Norbu.

"All right!" Freds said. "I'm glad you're here! Real glad!"

"Give me the story," I said.

"Well, that Arnold snuck up here, apparently."

"That's right."

"And our Sherpas were done and we had paid them, and I guess he hired them on the spot. They have a bunch of climbing gear, and we left fixed ropes up to the Lho La, so up they came. I tell you I was pretty blown away when they showed up in the pass! The Brits got furious and told Arnold to go back down, but he refused and, well, how do you make someone do something they don't want to up there? If you punch him out he's likely to have trouble getting down! So Kunga and I came back to get you and found Laure at Base Camp, and he said he'd get you while we held the fort."

"Arnold climbed the Lho La?" I said, amazed.

"Well, he's a pretty tough guy, I reckon. Didn't you ever see that movie he made of the kayak run down the Baltoro? Radical film, man, really it's up there with *The Man Who Skied Down Everest* for radicalness. And he's done some other crazy things too, like flying a hang glider off the Grand Teton, filming all the way. He's tougher than he looks. I think he just does the Hollywood sleaze routine so he can get away with things. Anyway those are some excellent climbing Sherpas he's got, and with them and the fixed ropes he just had to gut it out. And I guess he acclimatizes well, because he was walking around up there like he was at the beach."

I sighed. "That is one determined filmmaker."

Freds shook his head. "The guy is a leech. He's gonna drive the Brits bats if we don't haul his ass back down here."

VIII

So THE NEXT DAY the four of us started the ascent of the Lho La, and were quickly engaged in some of the most dangerous climbing I've ever done. Not the most technically difficult—the Brits had left fixed rope in the toughest sections, so our progress was considerably aided. But it was still dangerous, because we were climbing an icefall, which is to say a glacier on a serious tilt.

Now a glacier as you know is a river of ice, and like its liquid counterparts it is always flowing downstream. Its rate of flow is much slower, but it isn't negligible, especially when you're standing on it. Then you often hear creaks, groans, sudden cracks and booms, and you feel like you're on the back of a living creature.

Put that glacier on a hillside and everything is accelerated; the living creature becomes a dragon. The ice of the glacier breaks up into immense blocks and shards, and these shift regularly, then balance on a point or edge, then fall and smash to fragments, or crack open to reveal deep fissures. As we threaded our way up through the maze of the Lho La's icefall, we were constantly moving underneath blocks of ice that looked eternal but were actually precarious—they were certain to fall sometime in the next month or two. I'm not expert at probability theory, but I still didn't like it.

"Freds," I complained. "You said this was a piece of cake."

"It is," he said. "Check out how fast we're going."

"That's because we're scared to death."

"Are we? Hey, it must be only forty-five degrees or so."

This is as steep as an icefall can get before the ice all falls downhill at once. Even the famous Khumbu Icefall, which we now had a fantastic view of over to our right, fell at only about thirty degrees. The Khumbu Icefall is an unavoidable part of the standard route on Everest, and it is by far the most feared section; more people have died there than anywhere else on the mountain. And the Lho La is worse than the Khumbu!

So I had some choice words for our situation as we climbed very quickly indeed, and most of them left Laure mystified. "Great, Freds," I shouted at him. "Real piece of cake all right!"

"Lot of icing, anyway," he said, and giggled. This under a wall that would flatten him like Wile E. Coyote if it fell. I shook my head.

"What do you think?" I said to Laure.

"Very bad," Laure said. "Very bad, very dangerous."

"What do you think we should do?"

"Whatever you like."

We hurried.

Now I like climbing as much as anybody, almost, but I am not going to try to claim to you that it is an exceptionally sane activity. That day in particular I would not have been inclined to argue the point. The thing is, there is danger and there is danger. In fact climbers make a distinction, between objective danger and subjective danger. Objective dangers are things like avalanches and rockfall and storms, that you can't do anything about. Subjective dangers are those incurred by human error—putting in a bad hold, forgetting to fasten a harness, that sort of thing. See, if you are perfectly careful, then you can eliminate all the subjective dangers. And when you've eliminated the subjective dangers, you have only the objective dangers to face. So you can see it's very rational.

On this day, however, we were in the midst of a whole wall of objective dangers, and it made me nervous. We pursued the usual course in such a case, which is to go like hell. The four of us were practically running up the Lho La. Freds, Kunga and Laure were extremely fast and strong, and I am in reasonable shape myself; plus I get the benefits of more adrenaline than less imaginative types. So we were hauling buns.

Then it happened. Freds was next to me, on a rope with Kunga Norbu, and Kunga was the full rope length away—about twenty yards—leading the way around a traverse that went under a giant serac, which is what they call the fangs of blue ice that protrude out of an icefall, often in clusters. Kunga was right underneath this serac when without the slightest warning it sheared off and collapsed, shattering into a thousand pieces.

I had reflexively sucked in a gasp and was about to scream when Kunga Norbu jostled my elbow, nearly knocking me down. He was wedged in between Freds and me, and the rope tying them together was flapping between our legs.

Trying to revise my scream I choked, gasped for breath, choked again. Freds slapped me on the back to help. Kunga was definitely there, standing before us, solid and corporeal. And yet he had been under the serac! The broken pieces of the ice block were scattered before us, fresh and gleaming in the afternoon sun. The block had sheared off and collapsed without the slightest quiver or warning—there simply hadn't been time to get out from under it!

Freds saw the look on my face, and he grinned feebly. "Old Kunga Norbu is pretty fast when he has to be."

But that wasn't going to do. "Ga gor nee," I said—and

then Freds and Kunga were holding me up. Laure hurried up to join us, round-eyed with apprehension.

"Very bad," he said.

"Gar," I attempted, and couldn't go on.

"All right, all right," Freds said, soothing me with his gloved hands. "Hey, George. Relax."

"He," I got out, and pointed at the remains of the serac, then at Kunga.

"I know," Freds said, frowning. He exchanged a glance with Kunga, who was watching me impassively. They spoke to each other in Tibetan. "Listen," Freds said to me. "Let's top the pass and then I'll explain it to you. It'll take a while, and we don't have that much day left. Plus we've got to find a way around these ice cubes so we can stick to the fixed ropes. Come on, buddy." He slapped my arm. "Concentrate. Let's do it."

So we started up again, Kunga leading as fast as before. I was still in shock, however, and I kept seeing the collapse of the serac, with Kunga under it. He just couldn't have escaped it! And yet there he was up above us, jumaring up the fixed ropes like a monkey scurrying up a palm.

It was a miracle. And I had seen it. I had a hell of a time concentrating on the rest of that day's climb.

IX

JUST BEFORE SUNSET we topped the Lho La, and set our tent on the pass's flat expanse of deep hard snow. It was one of the spacier campsites I had ever occupied: on the crest of the Himalaya, in a broad saddle between the tallest mountain on earth, and the very spiky and beautiful Lingtren. Below us to one side was the Khumbu Glacier; on the other was the Rongbuk Glacier in Tibet. We were at about twenty thousand feet, and so Freds and his friends had a long way to go before reaching old Mallory. But nothing above would be quite as arbitrarily dangerous as the icefall. As long as the weather held, that is. So far they had been lucky; it was turning out to be the driest October in years.

There was no sign of either the British team or Arnold's crew, except for tracks in the snow leading around the side of the West Shoulder and disappearing. So they were on their way up. "Damn!" I said. "Why didn't they wait?" Now we had more climbing to do, to catch Arnold.

I sat on my groundpad on the snow outside the tent. I was tired. I was also very troubled. Laure was getting the stove to start. Kunga Norbu was off by himself, sitting in the snow, apparently meditating on the sight of Tibet. Freds was walking around singing "Wooden Ships," clearly in heaven. "'Talkin' about ver-y free—and eeea-sy'—I mean is this a great campsite or *what*," he cried to me. "Look at that sunset! It's too much, too much. I wish we'd brought some chang with us. I do have some hash, though. George, time to break out the pipe, hey?"

I said, "Not yet, Freds. You get over here and tell me what the hell happened down there with your buddy Kunga. You promised you would."

Freds stood looking at me. We were in shadow—it was cold, but windless—the sky above was clear, and a very deep dark blue. The airy roar of the stove starting was the only sound.

Freds sighed, and his expression got as serious as it ever got: one eye squinted shut entirely, forehead furrowed, and lips squeezed tightly together. He looked over at Kunga, and saw he was watching us. "Well," he said after a while. "You remember a couple of weeks ago when we were down at Chimoa getting drunk?"

"Yeah?"

"And I told you Kunga Norbu was a tulku."

I gulped. "Freds, don't give me that again."

"Well," he said. "It's either that or tell you some kind of a lie. And I ain't so good at lying, my face gives me away or something."

"Freds, get serious!" But looking over at Kunga Norbu, sitting in the snow with that blank expression, those weird black eyes, I couldn't help but wonder.

Freds said, "I'm sorry, man, I really am. I don't mean to blow your mind like this. But I did try to tell you before, you have to admit. And it's the simple truth. He's an honest-to-God tulku. First incarnation the famous Tsong Khapa, born in 1555. And he's been around ever since."

"So he met George Washington and like that?"

"Well, Washington didn't go to Tibet, so far as I know."

I stared at him. He shuffled about uncomfortably. "I know it's hard to take, George. Believe me. I had trouble with it myself, at first. But when you study under Kunga Norbu for a while, you see him do so many miraculous things, you can't help but believe."

I stared at him some more, speechless.

"I know," Freds said. "The first time he pulls one of his moves on you, it's a real shock. I remember my first time real well. I was hiking with him from the hidden Rongbuk to Namche, we went right over Lho La like we did today, and right around Base Camp we came across this Indian trekker who was turning blue. He was clearly set to die of altitude sickness, so Kunga and I carried him down between us to Pheriche, which was already a long day's work as you know. We took him to the Rescue Station and I figured they'd put him in the pressure tank they've got there, have you seen it? They've got a tank like a miniature submarine in their back room, and the idea is you stick a guy with altitude sickness in it and pressurize it down to sea level pressure, and he gets better. It's a neat idea, but it turns out that this tank was donated to the station by a hospital in Tokyo, and all the instructions for it are in Japanese, and no one at the station reads Japanese. Besides as

104

far as anyone there knows it's an experimental technique only, no one is quite sure if it will work or not, and nobody there is inclined to do any experimenting on sick trekkers. So we're back to square one and this guy was sicker than ever, so Kunga and I started down towards Namche, but I was getting tired and it was really slow going, and all of a sudden Kunga Norbu picked him up and slung him across his shoulders, which was already quite a feat of strength as this Indian was one of those pear-shaped Hindus, a heavy guy—and then Kunga just took off running down the trail with him! I hollered at him and ran after him trying to keep up, and I tell you I was *zooming* down that trail, and still Kunga ran right out of sight! Big long steps like he was about to fly! I couldn't believe it!"

Freds shook his head. "That was the first time I had seen Kunga Norbu going into *lung-gom* mode. Means mystic long-distance running, and it was real popular in Tibet at one time. An adept like Kunga is called a *lung-gom-pa*, and when you get it down you can run really far really fast. Even levitate a little. You saw him today—that was a *lung-gom* move he laid on that ice block."

"I see," I said, in a kind of daze. I called out to Laure, still at the stove: "Hey Laure! Freds says Kunga Norbu is a tulku!"

Laure smiled, nodded. "Yes, Kunga Norbu Lama very fine tulku!"

I took a deep breath. Over in the snow Kunga Norbu sat cross-legged, looking out at his country. Or somewhere. "I think I'm ready for that hash pipe," I told Freds.

X

IT TOOK US TWO DAYS to catch up to Arnold and the Brits, two days of miserable slogging up the West Shoulder of Everest. Nothing complicated here: the slope was a regular expanse of hard snow, and we just put on the crampons and ground on up it. It was murderous work. Not that I could tell with Freds and Laure and Kunga Norbu. There may be advantages to climbing on Everest with a tulku, a Sherpa long-distance champion, and an American space cadet, but longer rest stops are not among them. Those three marched uphill as if paced by Sousa marches, and I trailed behind huffing and puffing, damning Arnold with every step.

Late on the second day I struggled onto the top of the West Shoulder, a long snowy divide under the West Ridge proper. By the time I got there Freds and Laure already had the tent up, and they were securing it to the snow with a network of climbing rope, while Kunga Norbu sat to one side doing his meditation.

Farther down the Shoulder were the two camps of other teams, placed fairly close together as there wasn't a whole lot of extra flat ground up there to choose from. After I had rested and drunk several cups of hot lemon drink, I said, "Let's go find out how things stand." Freds walked over with me.

As it turned out, things were not standing so well. The Brits were in their tent, waist deep in their sleeping bags and drinking tea. And they were not amused. "The man is utterly daft," Marion said. She had a mild case of high-altitude throat, and any syllable she tried to emphasize disappeared entirely. "We've *oyd* outrunning him, but the Sherpas are good, and he *oyy* be strong."

"A fooking leech he is," John said.

Trevor grinned ferociously. His lower face was pretty sunburned, and his lips were beginning to break up. "We're counting on you to get him back down, George."

"I'll see what I can do."

Marion shook her head. "God knows we've tried, but it does no good whatever, he won't listen, he just rattles on about making me a *stee*, I don't know how to *dee* with that."

She turned red. "And none of these brave chaps will agree that we should just go over there and seize his bloody camera and throw it into Ti*beee*!"

The guys shook their heads. "We'd have to deal with the Sherpas," Mad Tom said to Marion patiently. "What are we going to do, fight with them? I can't even imagine it."

"And if Mad Tom can't imagine it," Trevor said.

Marion just growled.

"I'll go talk to him," I said.

But I didn't have to go anywhere, because Arnold had come over to greet us. "Hello!" he called out cheerily. "George, what a surprise! What brings you up here?"

I got out of the tent. Arnold stood before me, looking sunburned but otherwise all right. "You know what brings me up here, Arnold. Here, let's move away a bit, I'm sure these folks don't want to talk to you."

"Oh, no, I've been talking to them every day! We've been having lots of good talks. And today I've got some real news." He spoke into the tent. "I was looking through my zoom over at the North Col, and I see they've set up a camp over there! Do you suppose it's that expedition looking for Mallory's body?"

Curses came from the tent.

"I know," Arnold exclaimed. "Kind of puts the pressure on to get going, don't you think? Not much time to spare."

"Bugger off!"

Arnold shrugged. "Well, I've got it on tape if you want to see. Looked like they were wearing Helly-Hansen jackets, if that tells you anything."

"Don't tell me you can read labels from this distance," I said.

Arnold grinned. "It's a hell of a zoom lens. I could read their lips if I wanted to."

I studied him curiously. He really seemed to be doing fine, even after four days of intense climbing. He looked a touch thinner, and his voice had an altitude rasp to it, and he was pretty badly sunburned under the stubble of his beard—but he was still chewing a whitened cigar between zinc-oxided lips, and he still had the same wide-eyed look of wonder that his filming should bother anybody. I was impressed; he was definitely a lot tougher than I had expected. He reminded me of Dick Bass, the American millionaire who took a notion to climb the highest mountains on each continent. Like Bass, Arnold was a middle-aged guy paying pros to take him up; and like Bass, he acclimatized well, and had a hell of a nerve.

So, there he was, and he wasn't falling apart. I had to try something else. "Arnold, come over here a little with me, let's leave these people in peace."

"Good *reee*!" Marion shouted from inside the tent.

"That Marion," Arnold said admiringly when we were out of earshot. "She's really beautiful, I mean I really, really, really like her." He struck his chest to show how smitten he was.

I glared at him. "Arnold, it doesn't matter if you're falling for her or *what*, because they *definitely* do not want you along for this climb. Filming them destroys the whole point of what they're trying to do up there."

Arnold seized my arm. "No it doesn't! I keep trying to explain that to them. I can edit the film so that no one will know where Mallory's body is. They'll just know it's up here safe, because four young English climbers took incredible risks to keep it free from the publicity hounds threatening to tear it away to London. It's great, George. I'm a filmmaker, and I know when something will make a great movie, and this will make a great movie."

I frowned. "Maybe it would, but the problem is this climb is illegal, and if you make the film, then the illegal part becomes known and these folks will be banned by the Nepali authorities. They'll never be let into Nepal again."

"So? Aren't they willing to make that sacrifice for Mallory?"

I frowned. "For your movie, you mean. Without that they could do it and no one would be the wiser."

"Well, okay, but I can leave their names off it or something. Give them stage names. Marion Davies, how about that?"

"That's her real name." I thought. "Listen, Arnold, you'd be in the same kind of trouble, you know. They might not ever let you back, either."

He waved a hand. "I can get around that kind of thing. Get a lawyer. Or baksheesh, a lot of baksheesh."

"These guys don't have that kind of money, though. Really, you'd better watch it. If you press them too hard they might do something drastic. At the least they'll stop you, higher up. When they find the body a couple of them will come back and stop you, and the other two bury the body, and you won't get any footage at all."

He shook his head. "I got lenses, haven't I been telling you? Why I've been shooting what these four eat for breakfast every morning. I've got hours of Marion on film for instance," he sighed, "and my God could I make her a star. Anyway I could film the burial from here if I had to, so I'll take my chances. Don't you worry about me."

"I am *not* worrying about you," I said. "Take my word for it. But I do wish you'd come back down with me. They don't want you up here, and I don't want you up here. It's dangerous, especially if we lose this weather. Besides, you're breaking your contract with our agency, which said you'd follow my instructions on the trek."

"Sue me."

I took a deep breath.

Arnold put a friendly hand to my arm. "Don't worry so much, George. They'll love me when they're stars." He saw the look on my face and stepped away. "And don't you try anything funny with me, or I'll slap some kind of kidnapping charge on you, and you'll never guide a trek again."

109

"Don't tempt me like that," I told him, and stalked back to the Brits' camp.

I dropped into their tent. Laure and Kunga Norbu had joined them, and we were jammed in there. "No luck," I said. They weren't surprised.

"Superleech," Freds commented cheerfully.

We sat around and stared at the blue flames of the stove. Then, as usually happens in these predicaments, I said, "I've got a plan."

It was relatively simple, as we didn't have many options. We would all descend back to the Lho La, and maybe even down to Base Camp, giving Arnold the idea we had given up. Once down there the Brits and Freds and Kunga Norbu could restock at the Gorak Shep teahouses, and Laure and I would undertake to stop Arnold, by stealing his boots for instance. Then they could go back up the fixed ropes and try again.

Trevor looked dubious. "It's difficult getting up here, and we don't have much time, if that other expedition is already on the North Col."

"I've got a better plan," Freds announced. "Looky here, Arnold's following you Brits, but not us. If we four pretended to go down, while you four took the West Ridge direct, then Arnold would follow you. Then we four could sneak off into the Diagonal Ditch, and pass you by going up the Hornbein Couloir, which is actually faster. You wouldn't see us and we'd be up there where the body is, lickety-split."

Well, no one was overjoyed at this plan. The Brits would have liked to find Mallory themselves, I could see. And I didn't have any inclination to go any higher than we already had. In fact I was dead set against it.

But by now the Brits were absolutely locked onto the idea of saving Mallory from TV and Westminster Abbey. "It would do the job," Marion conceded.

"And we might lose the leech on the ridge," Mad Tom added. "It's a right piece of work or so I'm told."

"That's right!" Freds said happily. "Laure, are you up for it?"

"Whatever you like," Laure said, and grinned. He thought it was a fine idea. Freds then asked Kunga Norbu, in Tibetan, and reported to us that Kunga gave the plan his blessing.

"George?"

"Oh, man, no. I'd rather just get him down some way."

"Ah come on!" Freds cried. "We don't have another way, and you don't want to let down the side, do you? Sticky wicket and all that?"

"He's your fooking client," John pointed out.

"Geez. Oh, man. . . . Well. . . . All right."

I walked back to our tent feeling that things were really getting out of control. In fact I was running around in the grip of other people's plans, plans I by no means approved of, made by people whose mental balance I doubted. And all this on the side of a mountain that had killed over fifty people. It was a bummer.

XI

But I went along with the plan. Next morning we broke camp and made as if to go back down. The Brits started up the West Ridge, snarling dire threats at Arnold as they passed him. Arnold and his Sherpas were already packed, and after giving the Brits a short lead they took off after them. Arnold was roped up to their leader Ang Rita, raring to go, his camera in a chest pack. I had to hand it to him—he was one tenacious peeping Tom.

We waved good-bye and stayed on the shoulder until they were above us, and momentarily out of sight. Then we hustled after them, and took a left into the so-called Diagonal Ditch, which led out onto the North Face.

We were now following the route first taken by Tom Hornbein and Willi Unsoeld, in 1963. A real mountaineering classic, actually, which goes up what is now called the Hornbein Couloir. Get out any good photo of the North Face of Everest and you'll see it—a big vertical crack on the right side. It's a steep gully, but quite a bit faster than the West Ridge.

So we climbed. It was hard climbing, but not as scary as the Lho La. My main problem on this day was paranoia about the weather. Weather is no common concern on the side of Everest. You don't say, "Why snow would really ruin the day." Quite a number of people have been caught by storms on Everest and killed by them, including the guys we were going to look for. So whenever I saw wisps of cloud streaming out from the peak, I tended to freak. And the wind whips a banner of cloud from the peak of Everest almost continuously. I kept looking up and seeing that banner, and groaning. Freds heard me.

"Gee, George, you sound like you're really hurting on this pitch."

"Hurry up, will you?"

"You want to go faster? Well, okay, but I gotta tell you I'm going about as fast as I can."

I believed that. Kunga Norbu was using ice axe and crampons to fire up the packed snow in the middle of the couloir, and Freds was right behind him; they looked like a roofer on a ladder. I did my best to follow, and Laure brought up the rear. Both Freds and Kunga had grins so wide and fixed that you'd have thought they were on acid. Their teeth were going to get sunburned they were loving it so much. Meanwhile I was gasping for air, and worrying about that summit banner.

It was one of the greatest climbing days of my life.

How's that, you ask? Well . . . it's hard to explain. But it's something like this: when you get on a mountain wall with a few thousand feet of empty air below you, it catches your attention. Of course part of you says oh my God, it's all over. Whyever did I do this! But another part sees that in order not to die you must pretend you are quite calm, and engaged in a semi-theoretical gymnastics exercise intended to get you higher. You *pay attention* to the exercise like no one has ever paid attention before. Eventually you find yourself on a flat spot of some sort—three feet by five feet will do. You look around and realize that you did not die, that you are still alive. And at that point this fact becomes really exhilarating. You really *appreciate* being alive. It's a sort of power, or a privilege granted you, in any case it feels quite special, like a flash of higher consciousness. Just to be alive! And in retrospect, that *paying attention* when you were climbing—you remember that as a higher consciousness too.

You can get hooked on feelings like those; they are the ultimate altered state. Drugs can't touch them. I'm not saying this is real healthy behavior, you understand. I'm just saying it happens.

For instance, at the end of this particular intense day in the Hornbein Couloir, the four of us emerged at its top, having completed an Alpine-style blitz of it due in large part to Kunga Norbu's inspired leads. We made camp on a small flat knob top just big enough for our tent. And looking around—what a feeling! It really was something. There were only four or five mountains in the world taller than we were in that campsite, and you could tell. We could see all the way across Tibet, it seemed. Now Tibet tends mostly to look like a freeze-dried Nevada, but from our height it was range after range of snowy peaks, white on black forever, all tinted sepia by the afternoon sun. It seemed the world was nothing but mountains.

Freds plopped down beside me, idiot grin still fixed on his face. He had a steaming cup of lemon drink in one hand, his hash pipe in the other, and he was singing

"'What a looong, strange trip it's been.'" He took a hit from the pipe and handed it to me.

"Are you sure we should be smoking up here?"

"Sure, it helps you breathe."

"Come on."

"No, really. The nerve center that controls your involuntary breathing shuts down in the absence of carbon dioxide, and there's hardly any of that up here, so the smoke provides it."

I decided that on medical grounds I'd better join him. We passed the pipe back and forth. Behind us Laure was in the tent, humming to himself and getting his sleeping bag out. Kunga Norbu sat in the lotus position on the other side of the tent, intent on realms of his own. The world, all mountains, turned under the sun.

Freds exhaled happily. "This must be the greatest place on earth, don't you think?"

That's the feeling I'm talking about.

XII

WE HAD A LONG and restless night of it, because it's harder than hell to sleep at that altitude. Sleepiness seems to go right out of the mental repertoire, and when it does arrive, you fall into what is called Cheyne-Stokes breathing. Your body keeps getting fooled concerning how much oxygen it's getting, so you hyperventilate for a while and then stop breathing entirely, for up to a minute at a time. This is not a comforting pattern if it is going on in a sleeping person lying next to you; Freds for instance really got into it, and I kept waking up completely during some really long silences, worrying that he had died. He apparently felt the same way about me, but didn't have my patience, so that if

I ever did fall asleep I was usually jerked back to consciousness by Freds tugging on my arm, saying "George, damn it, breathe! Breathe!"

But the next day dawned clear and windless once again, and after breakfasting and marveling at the view we headed along the top of the Black Band.

Our route was unusual, perhaps unique. The Black Band, harder than the layers of rock above and below it, sticks out from the generally smooth slope of the face, in a crumbly rampart. So in effect we had a sort of road to walk on. Although it was uneven and busted up, it was still twenty feet wide in places, and an easier place for a traverse couldn't be imagined. There were potential campsites all over it.

Of course usually when people are at twenty-eight thousand feet on Everest, they're interested in getting either higher or lower pretty quick. Since this rampway was level and didn't facilitate any route whatsoever, it wasn't much traveled. We might have been the first on it, since Freds said that Kunga Norbu had only looked down on it from above.

So we walked this high road, and made our search. Freds knocked a rock off the edge, and we watched it bounce down toward the Rongbuk Glacier until it became invisible, though we could still hear it. After that we trod a little more carefully. Still, it wasn't long before we had traversed the face and were looking down the huge clean chute of the Great Couloir. Here the rampart ended, and to continue the traverse to the fabled North Ridge, where Mallory and Irvine were last seen, would have been ugly work. Besides, that wasn't where Kunga Norbu had seen the body.

"We must have missed it," Freds said. "Let's spread out side to side, and check every little nook and cranny on the way back." So we did, taking it very slowly, and ranging out to the edge of the rampart as far as we dared.

We were about halfway back to the Hornbein Couloir when Laure found it. He called out, and we approached.

115

"Well dog my cats," Freds said, looking astonished.

The body was wedged in a crack, chest deep in a hard pack of snow. He was on his side, and curled over so that he was level with the rock on each side of the crack. His clothing was frayed, and rotting away on him; it looked like knit wool. The kind of thing you'd wear golfing in Scotland. His eyes were closed, and under a fraying hood his skin looked papery. Sixty years out in sun and storm, but always in below-freezing air, had preserved him strangely. I had the odd feeling that he was only sleeping, and might wake and stand.

Freds knelt beside him and dug in the snow a bit. "Look here—he's roped up, but the rope broke."

He held up an inch or two of unraveled rope—natural fibers, horribly thin—it made me shudder to see it. "Such primitive gear!" I cried.

Freds nodded briefly. "They were nuts. I don't think he's got an oxygen pack on either. They had it available, but he didn't like to use it." He shook his head. "They probably fell together. Stepped through a cornice maybe. Then fell down to here, and this one jammed in the crack while the other one went over the edge, and the rope broke."

"So the other one is down in the glacier," I said.

Freds nodded slowly. "And look—" He pointed above. "We're almost directly under the summit. So they must have made the top. Or fallen when damned close to it." He shook his head. "And wearing nothing but a jacket like that! Amazing."

"So they made it," I breathed.

"Well, maybe. Looks like it, anyway. So . . . which one is this?"

I shook my head. "I can't tell. Early twenties, or mid-thirties?"

Uneasily we looked at the mummified features.

"Thirties," Laure said. "Not young."

Freds nodded. "I agree."

116

"So it's Mallory," I said.

"Hmph." Freds stood and stepped back. "Well, that's that. The mystery solved." He looked at us, spoke briefly with Kunga Norbu. "He must be under snow most years. But let's hide him under rock, for the Brits."

This was easier said than done. All we needed were stones to lay over him, as he was tucked down in the crack. But we quickly found that loose stones of any size were not plentiful; they had been blown off. So we had to work in pairs, and pick up big flat plates that were heavy enough to hold against the winds.

We were still collecting these when Freds suddenly jerked back and sat behind an outcropping of the rampart. "Hey, the Brits are over there on the West Ridge! They're almost level with us!"

"Arnold can't be far behind," I said.

"We've still got an hour's work here," Freds exclaimed. "Here—Laure, listen—go back to our campsite and pack our stuff, will you? Then go meet the Brits and tell them to slow down. Got that?"

"Slow down," Laure repeated.

"Exactly. Explain we found Mallory and they should avoid this area. Give us time. You stay with them, go back down with them. George and Kunga and I will follow you guys down, and we'll meet you at Gorak Shep."

Gorak Shep? That seemed farther down than necessary.

Laure nodded. "Slow down, go back, we meet you Gorak Shep."

"You got it, buddy. See you down there."

Laure nodded and was off.

"Okay," Freds said. "Let's get this guy covered."

We built a low wall around him, and then used the biggest plate of all as a keystone to cover his face. It took all three of us to pick it up, and we staggered around to get it into position without disturbing him; it really knocked the wind out of us.

117

When we were done the body was covered, and most of the time snow would cover our burial cairn, and it would be just one lump among thousands. So he was hidden. "Shouldn't we say something?" Freds asked. "You know, an epitaph or whatever?"

"Hey, Kunga's the tulku," I said. "Tell him to do it."

Freds spoke to Kunga. In his snow goggles I could see little images of Kunga, looking like a Martian. Quite a change in gear since old Mallory!

Kunga Norbu stood at the end of our cairn and stuck out his mittened hands; he spoke in Tibetan for a while.

Afterward Freds translated for me. "Spirit of Chomolungma, Mother Goddess of the World, we're here to bury the body of George Leigh Mallory, the first person to climb your sacred slopes. He was a climber with a lot of heart and he always went for it, and we love him for that—he showed very purely something that we all treasure in ourselves. I'd like to add that it's also clear from his clothing and gear that he was a total loon to be up here at all, and I in particular want to salute that quality as well. So here we are, four disciples of your holy spirit, and we take this moment to honor that spirit here and in us, and everywhere in the world." Kunga bowed his head, and Freds and I followed suit, and we were silent; and all we heard was the wind, whistling over the Mother Goddess into Tibet.

XIII

FINE. OUR MISSION was accomplished, Mallory was safely on Everest for all time, we had given him a surprisingly moving burial ceremony, and I for one was pretty pleased. But back at our campsite, Freds and Kunga started acting oddly. Laure had packed up the tent and our packs and left them for us, and now Freds and Kunga were hurrying around repacking them.

I said something to the effect that you couldn't beat the view from Mallory's final resting place, and Freds looked up at me, and said,

"Well, you could beat the view by a *little*." And he continued repacking feverishly. "In fact I've been meaning to talk to you about that," he said as he worked. "I mean, here we are, right? I mean here we are."

"Yes," I said. "We are here."

"I mean to say, here we are at almost twenty-eight thou, on Everest. And it's only noon, and it's a perfect day. I mean a *perfect* day. Couldn't ask for a nicer day."

I began to see what he was driving at. "No way, Freds."

"Ah come on! Don't be hasty about this, George! We're above all the hard parts, it's just a walk from here to the top!"

"No," I said firmly. "We don't have time. And we don't have much food. And we can't trust the weather. It's too dangerous."

"Too dangerous! All climbing is too dangerous, George, but I don't notice that that ever stopped you before. Think about it, man! This ain't just some ordinary mountain, this ain't no Rainier or Denali, this is *Everest.* Sagarmatha! Chomo*lung*ma! The BIG E! Hasn't it always been your secret fantasy to climb Everest?"

"Well, no. It hasn't."

"I don't believe you! It sure is mine, I'll tell you that. It's gotta be yours too."

All the time we argued Kunga Norbu was ignoring us, while he rooted through his pack tossing out various inessential items.

Freds sat down beside me and began to show me the contents of his pack. "I got our butt pads, the stove, a pot, some soup and lemon mix, a good supply of food, and

119

here's my snow shovel so we can bivvy somewhere. Everything we need."

"No."

"Looky here, George." Freds pulled off his goggles and stared me in the eye. "It was nice to bury Mallory and all, but I have to tell you that Kunga Lama and I have had what you'd call an *ulterior motive* all along here. We joined the Brits on the Lingtren climb because I had heard about this Mallory expedition from the north, and I was planning all along to tell them about it, and show them our photo, and tell them that Kunga was the guy who saw Mallory's body back in 1980, and suggest that they go hide him."

"You mean Kunga wasn't the one who saw Mallory's body?" I demanded.

"No, he wasn't. I made that up. The Chinese climber who saw a body up here was killed a couple years later. So I just had Kunga circle the general area where I had heard the Chinese saw him. That's why I was so surprised when we actually ran across the guy! Although it stands to reason when you look at the North Face—there isn't anywhere else but the Black Band that would have stopped him.

"Anyway I lied about that, and I also suggested we slip up the Hornbein Couloir and find the body when Arnold started tailing the Brits, and all of that was because I was just hoping we'd get into this situation, where we got the time and the weather to shoot for the top, we were both just *hoping* for it man and here we are. We got everything planned, Kunga and I have worked it all out—we've got all the stuff we need, and if we have to bivvy on the South Summit after we bag the peak, then we can descend by way of the Southeast Ridge and meet the Indian Army team in the South Col, and get escorted back to Base Camp, that's the yak route and won't be any problem."

He took a few deep breaths. "Plus, well, listen. Kunga Lama has got *mystic reasons* for wanting to go up there, having to do with his longtime guru Dorjee Lama. Remember I told you back in Chimoa how Dorjee Lama had set a task for Kunga Norbu, that Kunga had to accomplish before the monastery at Kum-Bum would be rebuilt, and Kunga set free to be his own lama at last? Well—the task was to *climb Chomolungma*! That old son of a gun said to Kunga, you just climb Chomolungma and everything'll be fine! Figuring that would mean that he would have a disciple for just as many reincarnations as he would ever go through this side of nirvana. But he didn't count on Kunga Norbu teaming up with his old student Freds Fredericks, and his buddy George Fergusson!"

"Wait a minute," I said. "I can see you feel very deeply about this Freds, and I respect that, but I'm not going."

"We need you along, George! Besides, we're going to do it, and we can't really leave you to go back down the West Ridge by yourself—that'd be more dangerous than coming along with us! And we're going to the peak, so you have to come along, it's that simple!"

Freds had been talking so fast and hard that he was completely out of breath; he waved a hand at Kunga Norbu. "You talk to him," he said to Kunga, then switched to Tibetan, no doubt to repeat the message.

Kunga Norbu pulled up his snow goggles, and very serenely he looked at me. He looked just a little sad; it was the sort of expression you might get if you refused to give to the United Way. His black eyes looked right through me just as they always did, and in that high-altitude glare his pupils kind of pulsed in and out, in and out, in and out. And damned if that old bastard didn't hypnotize me. I think.

But I struggled against it. I found myself putting on my pack, and checking my crampons to make sure they were really, really, really tight, and at the same time I was shouting at Freds. "Freds, be reasonable! No one climbs Everest unsupported like this! It's too dangerous!"

"Hey, Messner did it. Messner climbed it in two days from North Col by himself, all he had was his girlfriend waiting down at base camp."

"You can't use Reinhold Messner as an example," I cried. "Messner is insane."

"Nah. He's just tough and fast. And so are we. It won't be a problem."

"Freds, climbing Everest is generally considered a problem." But Kunga Norbu had put on his pack and was starting up the slope above our campsite, and Freds was following him, and I was following Freds. "For one big problem," I yelled, "we don't have any oxygen!"

"People climb it without oxygen all the time now."

"Yeah, but you pay the price for it. You don't get enough oxygen up there, and it kills brain cells like you can't believe! If we go up there we're certain to lose *millions* of brain cells."

"So?" He couldn't see the basis of the objection.

I groaned. We continued up the slope.

XIV

AND THAT IS HOW I found myself climbing Mount Everest with a Tibetan tulku and the wild man of Arkansas. It was not a position that a reasonable person could defend to himself, and indeed as I trudged after Freds and Kunga I could scarcely believe it was happening. But every labored breath told me it was. And since it was, I decided I had better psych myself into the proper frame of mind for it, or else it would only be that much more dangerous. "Always wanted to do this," I said, banishing the powerful impression that I had been hypnotized into the whole deal. "We're climbing Everest, and I really want to."

"That's the attitude," Freds said.

I ignored him and kept thinking the phrase "I want to do this," once for every two steps. After a few hundred steps,

I have to admit that I had myself somewhat convinced. I mean, Everest! Think about it! I suppose that like anyone else, I had the fantasy in there somewhere.

I won't bother you with the details of our route; if you want them you can consult my anonymous article in the *American Alpine Journal*, 1987 issue. Actually it was fairly straightforward; we contoured up from the Hornbein Couloir to the upper West Ridge, and continued from there.

I did this in bursts of ten steps at a time; the altitude was finally beginning to hammer me. I acclimatize as well as anyone I know, but nobody acclimatizes over twenty-six thousand feet. It's just a matter of how fast you wind down.

"Try to go as slow as you need to, and avoid rests," Freds advised.

"I'm going as slow as I can already."

"No you're not. Try to just flow uphill. Really put it into first gear. You fall into a certain rhythm."

"All right. I'll try."

We were seated at this point to take off our crampons, which were unnecessary. Freds had been right about the ease of the climb up here. The ridge was wide, it wasn't very steep, and it was all broken up, so that irregular rock staircases were everywhere on it. If it were at sea level you could run up it, literally. It was so easy that I could try Freds's suggestion, and I followed him and Kunga up the ridge in slow-slow motion. At that rate I could go about five or ten minutes between rests—it's hard to be sure how long, as each interval seemed like an afternoon on its own.

But with each stop we were a little higher. There was no denying the West Ridge had a first-class view: to our right all the mountains of Nepal, to our left all the mountains of Tibet, and you could throw in Sikkim and Bhutan for change. Mountains everywhere: and all of them below us.

The only thing still above us was the pyramid of Everest's final summit, standing brilliant white against a black-blue sky.

At each rest stop I found Kunga Norbu was humming a strange Buddhist chant; he was looking happier and happier in a subtle sort of way, while Freds's grin got wider and wider. "Can you believe how perfect the day is? Beautiful, huh?"

"Uh huh." It was nice, all right. But I was too tired to enjoy it. Some of their energy poured into me at each stop, and that was a good thing, because they were really going strong, and I needed the help.

Finally the ridge became snow-covered again, and we had to sit down and put our crampons back on. I found this usually simple process almost more than I could handle. My hands left pink afterimages in the air, and I hissed and grunted at each pull on the straps. When I finished and stood, I almost keeled over. The rocks swam, and even with my goggles on the snow was painfully white.

"Last bit," Freds said as we looked up the slope. We crunched into it, and our crampons spiked down into firm snow. Kunga took off at an unbelievable pace. Freds and I marched up side by side, sharing a pace to take some of the mental effort out of it.

Freds wanted to talk, even though he had no breath to spare. "Old Dorjee Lama. Going to be. Mighty surprised. When they start rebuilding. Kum-Bum. Ha!"

I nodded as if I believed in the whole story. This was an exaggeration, but it didn't matter. Nothing mattered but to put one foot in front of the other, in blazing white snow.

I have read that Everest stands just at the edge of the possible, as far as climbing it without oxygen goes. The scientific team that concluded this, after a climb in which air and breath samples were taken, actually decided that theoretically it wasn't possible at all. Sort of a bumblebee's flight situation. One scientist speculated that if Everest were just a couple hundred feet taller, then it *really* couldn't be done.

I believe that. Certainly the last few steps up that snow pyramid were the toughest I ever took. My breath heaved in and out of me in useless gasps, and I could hear the brain cells popping off by the thousands, *snap crackle pop.* We were nearing the peak, a triangular dome of pure snow; but I had to slow down.

Kunga forged on ahead of us, picking up speed in the last approach. Looking down at the snow, I lost sight of him. Then his boots came into my field of vision, and I realized we were there, just a couple steps below the top.

The actual summit was a ridged mound of snow about eight feet long and four feet wide. It wasn't a pinnacle, but it wasn't a broad hilltop either; you wouldn't have wanted to hold a dance on it.

"Well," I said. "Here we are." I couldn't get excited about it. "Too bad I didn't bring a camera." The truth was, I didn't feel a thing.

Beside me Freds stirred. He tapped my arm, gestured up at Kunga Norbu. We were still below him, with our heads at about the level of his boots. He was humming, and had his arms extended up and out, as if conducting a symphony out to the east. I looked out in that direction. By this time it was late afternoon, and Everest's shadow extended to the horizon, even above. There must have been ice particles in the air to the east, because all of a sudden above the darkness of Everest's shadow I saw a big icebow. It was almost a complete circle of color, much more diaphanous than a rainbow, cut off at the bottom by the mountain's triangular shadow.

Inside this round bow of faint color, on the top of the dark air of the shadow peak, there was a cross of light-haloed shadow. It was a Spectre of the Brocken phenomenon, caused when low sunlight throws the shadows of peaks and climbers onto moisture-filled air, creating a glory of light around the shadows. I had seen one before.

Then Kunga Norbu flicked his hands to the sides, and the whole vision disappeared, instantly.

"Whoah," I said.

"Right on," Freds murmured, and led me the last painful steps onto the peak itself, so that we stood beside Kunga Norbu. His head was thrown back, and on his face was a smile of pure, childlike bliss.

Now, I don't know what really happened up there. Maybe I went faint and saw colors for a second, thought it was an icebow, and then blinked things clear. But I know that at that moment, looking at Kunga Norbu's transfigured face, I was quite sure that I had seen him gain his freedom, and paint it out there in the sky. The task was fulfilled, the arms thrown wide with joy. . . . I believed all of it. I swallowed, a sudden lump in my throat.

Now I felt it too; I felt where we were. We had climbed Chomolungma. We were standing on the peak of the world.

Freds heaved his breath in and out a few times. "Well!" he said, and shook mittened hands with Kunga and me. "We did it!" And then we pounded each other on the back until we almost knocked ourselves off the mountain.

XV

WE HADN'T BEEN UP there long when I began to consider the problem of getting down. There wasn't much left of the day, and we were a long way from anywhere homey. "What now?"

"I think we'd better go down to the South Summit and

dig a snow cave for the night. That's the closest place we can do it, and that's what Haston and Scott did in '75. It worked for them, and a couple other groups too."

"Fine," I said. "Let's do it."

Freds said something to Kunga, and we started down. Immediately I found that the Southeast Ridge was not as broad or as gradual as the West Ridge. In fact we were descending a kind of snow-covered knife edge, with ugly gray rocks sticking out of it. So this was the yak route! It was a tough hour's work to get down to the South Summit, and the only thing that made it possible was the fact that we were going downhill all the way.

The South Summit is a big jog in the Southeast Ridge, which makes for a lump of a subsidiary peak, and a flat area. Here we had a broad sloping expanse of very deep, packed snow—perfect conditions for a snow cave.

Freds got his little aluminum shovel out of his pack and went to it, digging like a dog after a bone. I was content to sit and consult. Kunga Norbu stood staring around at the infinite expanse of peaks, looking a little dazed. Once or twice I summoned up the energy to spell Freds. After a body-sized entryway, we only wanted a cave big enough for the three of us to fit in. It looked a bit like a coffin for triplets.

The sun set, stars came out, the twilight turned midnight blue; then it was night. And seriously, seriously cold. Freds declared the cave ready and I crawled in after him and Kunga, feeling granules of snow crunch under me. We banged heads and got arranged on our butt pads so that we were sitting in a little circle, on a rough shelf above our entrance tunnel, in a roughly spherical chamber. By slouching I got an inch's clearance above. "All right," Freds said wearily. "Let's party." He took the stove from his pack, held it in his mittens for a while to warm the gas inside, then set it on the snow in the middle of the three of us, and lit it with his lighter. The blue glare was blinding, the roar deafening. We took off our mitts and cupped our hands so there was no gap between flame and flesh. Our cave began to warm up a little.

You may think it odd that a snow cave can warm up at all, but remember we are speaking relatively here. Outside it was dropping to about ten below zero, Fahrenheit. Add any kind of wind and at that altitude, where oxygen is so scarce, you'll die. Inside the cave, however, there was no wind. Snow itself is not that cold, and it's a great insulator: it will warm up, even begin to get slick on its surface, and that water also holds heat very well. Add a stove raging away, and three bodies struggling to pump out their 98.6, and even with a hole connecting you to the outside air, you can get the temperature well up into the thirties. That's colder than a refrigerator, but compared to ten below it's beach weather.

So we were happy in our little cave, at first. Freds scraped some of the wall into his pot and cooked some hot lemon drink. He offered me some almonds, but I had no appetite whatsoever; eating an almond was the same as eating a coffee table to me. We were all dying for drink, though, and we drank the lemon mix when it was boiling, which at this elevation was just about bath temperature. It tasted like heaven.

We kept melting snow and drinking it until the stove sputtered and ran out of fuel. Only a couple of hours had passed, at most. I sat there in the pitch-dark, feeling the temperature drop. My spirits dropped with it.

But Freds was by no means done with the party. His lighter scraped and by its light I saw him punch a hole in the wall and set a candle in it. He lit the candle, and its light reflected off the slick white sides of our home. He had a brief discussion with Kunga Norbu.

"Okay," he said to me at the end of it, breath cascading whitely into the air. "Kunga is going to do some *tumo* now."

"Tumo?"

"Means, the art of warming oneself without fire up in the snows."

That caught my interest. "Another lama talent?"

"You bet. It comes in handy for naked hermits in the winter."

"I can see that. Tell him to lay it on us."

With some crashing about Kunga got in the lotus position, an impressive feat with his big snow boots still on.

He took his mitts off, and we did the same. Then he began breathing in a regular, deep rhythm, staring at nothing. This went on for almost half an hour, and I was beginning to think we would all freeze before he warmed up, when he held his hands out toward Freds and me. We took them in our own.

They were as hot as if he had a terrible fever. Fearfully I reached up to touch his face—it was warm, but nothing like his hands. "My Lord," I said.

"We can help him now," Freds said softly. "You have to concentrate, harness the energy that's always inside you. Every breath out you push away pride, anger, hatred, envy, sloth, stupidity. Every breath in, you take in Buddha's spirit, the five wisdoms, everything good. When you've gotten clear and calm, imagine a golden lotus in your belly button. . . . Okay? In that lotus you imagine the syllable *ram*, which means fire. Then you have to see a little seed of flame, the size of a goat dropping, appearing in the *ram*. Every breath after that is like a bellows, fanning that flame, which travels through the *tsa*s in the body, the mystic nerves. Imagine this process in five stages. First, the *uma tsa* is seen as a hair of fire, up your spine more or less. . . . Two, the nerve is as big around as your little finger. . . . Three, it's the size of an arm. . . . Four, the body becomes the *tsa* itself and is perceived as a tube of fire. . . . Five, the *tsa* engulfs the world, and you're just one flame in a sea of fire."

"My Lord."

We sat there holding Kunga Norbu's fiery hands, and I imagined myself a tube of fire: and the warmth poured into me—up my arms, through my torso—it even thawed my frozen butt, and my feet. I stared at Kunga Norbu, and he stared right through the wall of our cave to eternity, or wherever, his eyes glowing faintly in the candlelight. It was weird.

I don't know how long this went on—it seemed endless, although I suppose it was no more than an hour or so. But then it broke off—Kunga's hand cooled, and so did the rest of us. He blinked several times and shook his head. He spoke to Freds.

"Well," Freds said. "That's about as long as he can hold it, these days."

"What?"

"Well . . ." He clucked his tongue regretfully. "It's like this. Tulkus tend to lose their powers, over the course of several incarnations. It's like they lose something in the process, every time, like when you keep making a tape from copies or whatever. There's a name for it."

"Transmission error," I said.

"Right. Well, it gets them too. In fact you run into a lot of tulkus in Tibet who are complete morons. Kunga is better than that, but he is a bit like Paul Revere. A little light in the belfry, you know. A great lama, and a super guy, but not tremendously powerful at any of the mystic disciplines, anymore."

"Too bad."

"I know."

I recalled Kunga's fiery hands, their heat pronging into me. "So . . . he really is a tulku, isn't he."

"Oh yeah! Of course! And now he's free of old Dorjee Lama, too—a lama in his own right, and nobody's disciple. It must be a great feeling."

"I bet. So how does it work, again, exactly?"

"Becoming a tulku?"

"Yeah."

"Well, it's a matter of concentrating your mental powers. Tibetans believe that none of this is supernatural, but just a focusing of natural powers that we all have. Tulkus have gotten their psychic energies incredibly focused, and when you're at that stage, you can leave your body whenever you want. Why if Kunga wanted to, he could die in about ten seconds."

"Useful."

"Yeah. So when they decide to go, they hop off into the Bardo. The Bardo is the other world, the world of spirit, and it's a confusing place—talk about hallucinations! First a light like God's camera flash goes off in your face. Then it's just a bunch of colored paths, apparitions, everything. When Kunga describes it it's really scary. Now if you're just an ordinary spirit, then you can get disoriented, and be re-born as a slug or a game show host or *anything*. But if you stay focused, you're reborn in the body you choose, and you go on from there."

I nodded dully. I was tired, and cold, and the lack of oxygen was making me stupid and spacy; I couldn't make any sense of Freds's explanations, although it may be that that would have happened anywhere.

We sat there. Kunga hummed to himself. It got colder. The candle guttered, then went out.

It was dark. It continued to get colder.

After a while there was nothing but the darkness, our breathing, and the cold. I couldn't feel my butt or my legs below the knee. I knew I was waiting for something, but I had forgotten what it was. Freds stirred, started speaking Tibetan with Kunga. They seemed a long way away. They spoke to people I couldn't see. For a while Freds jostled about, punching the sides of the cave. Kunga shouted out hoarsely, things like "Hak!" and "Phut!"

"What are you doing?" I roused myself to say.

131

"We're fighting off demons," Freds explained.

I was ready to conclude, by watching my companions, that lack of oxygen drove one nuts; but given who they were, I had to suspend judgement. It might not have been the oxygen.

Some indeterminate time later Freds started shoveling snow out the tunnel. "Casting out demons?" I inquired.

"No, trying to get warm. Want to try it?"

I didn't have the energy to move.

Then he shook me from side to side, switched to English, told me stories. Story after story, in a dry, hoarse, frog's voice. I didn't understand any of them. I had to concentrate on fighting the cold. On breathing. Freds became agitated, he told me a story of Kunga's, something about running across Tibet with a friend, a *lung-gom-pa* test of some kind, and the friend was wearing chains to keep from floating away entirely. Then something about running into a young husband at night, dropping the chains in a campfire . . . "The porters knew about *lung-gom*, and the next morning they must have tried to explain it to the British. Can you imagine it? Porters trying to explain these chains come out of nowhere . . . explaining they were used by people running across Tibet, to keep from going orbital? Man, those Brits must've thought they were invading Oz. Don't you think so? Hey, George? George? . . . George?"

XVI

BUT FINALLY THE NIGHT passed, and I was still there.

We crawled out of our cave in the predawn light, and stamped our feet until some sensation came back into them, feeling pretty pleased with ourselves. "Good morning!" Kunga Norbu said to me politely. He was right about that.

There were high cirrus clouds going pink above us, and an ocean of blue cloud far below in Nepal, with all the higher white peaks poking out of it like islands, and slowly turning pink themselves. I've never seen a more otherworldly sight; it was as if we had climbed out of our cave onto the side of another planet.

"Maybe we should just shoot down to the South Col and join those Indian Army guys," Freds croaked. "I don't much feel like going back up to the peak to get to the West Ridge."

"You aren't kidding," I said.

So down the Southeast Ridge we went.

Now Peter Habeler, Messner's partner on the first oxygenless ascent of Everest in 1979, plunged down this ridge from the summit to the South Col in *one hour*. He was worried about brain damage; my feeling is that the speed of his descent is evidence it had already occurred. We went as fast as we could, which was pretty alarmingly fast, and it still took us almost three hours. One step after another, down a steep snowy ridge. I refused to look at the severe drops to right and left. The clouds below were swelling up like the tide in the Bay of Fundy; our good weather was about to end.

I felt completely disconnected from my body, I just watched it do its thing. Below Freds kept singing, "'I get up, I get dow-wow-wown,'" from the song "Close to the Edge." We came to a big snow-filled gully and glissaded down it carelessly, sliding twenty or thirty feet with each dreamy step. All three of us were staggering by this point. Cloud poured up the Western Cwm, and mist magically appeared all around us, but we were just above the South Col by this time, and it didn't matter. I saw there was a camp in the col, and breathed a sigh of relief. We would have been goners without it.

The Indians were still securing their tents as we walked up. A week's perfect weather, and they had just gotten into the South Col. Very slow, I thought as we approached. Siege-style assault, logistical pyramid, play it safe—slow as building the other kind of pyramid.

As we crossed the col and closed on the tents, navigating between piles of junk from previous expeditions, I began to worry. You see, the Indian Army has had incredible bad luck on Everest. They have tried to climb it several times, and so far as I know, they've never succeeded. Mostly this is because of storms, but people tend to ignore that, and the Indians have come in for a bit of criticism from the climbing community in Nepal. In fact they've been called terrible climbers. So they are a little touchy about this, and it was occurring to me, very slowly, that they might not be too amused to be greeted in the South Col by three individuals who had just bagged the peak on an overnighter from the north side.

Then one of them saw us. He dropped the mallet in his hand.

"Hi there!" Freds croaked.

A group of them quickly gathered around us. The wind was beginning to blow hard, and we all stood at an angle into it. The oldest Indian there, probably a major, shouted gruffly, "Who are you!"

"We're lost," Freds said. "We need help."

Ah, good, I thought. Freds has also thought of this problem. He won't tell them where we've been. Freds is still thinking. He will take care of this situation for us.

"Where did you come from?" the major boomed.

Freds gestured down the Western Cwm. Good, I thought. "Our Sherpas told us to keep turning right. So ever since Jomosom we have been."

"Where did you say!"

"Jomosom!"

The major drew himself up. "Jomosom," he said sharply, "is in *western* Nepal."

"Oh," Freds said.

And we all stood there. Apparently that was it for Freds's explanation.

I elbowed him aside. "The truth is, we thought it would be fun to help you. We didn't know what we were getting into."

"Yeah!" Freds said, accepting this new tack thankfully. "Can we carry a load down for you, maybe?"

"We are still climbing the mountain!" the major barked. "We don't need loads carried down!" He gestured at the ridge behind us, which was disappearing in mist. "This is Everest!"

Freds squinted at him. "You're kidding."

I elbowed him. "We need help," I said.

The major looked at us closely. "Get in the tent," he said at last.

XVII

WELL, EVENTUALLY I CONCOCTED a semiconsistent story about us idealistically wanting to porter loads for an Everest expedition, although who would be so stupid as to want to do that I don't know. Freds was no help at all—he kept forgetting and going back to his first story, saying things like "We must have gotten on the wrong plane." And neither of us could fit Kunga Norbu into our story very well; I claimed he was our guide, but we didn't understand his language. He very wisely stayed mute.

Despite all that, the Indian team fed us and gave us water to slake our raging thirst, and they escorted us back down their fixed ropes to the camps below, to make sure they got us out of there. Over the next couple of days they led us all the way down the Western Cwm and the Khumbu Icefall to Base Camp. I wish I could give you a blow-by-blow account of the fabled Khumbu Icefall, but the truth is I barely remember it. It was big and white and scary; I was tired. That's all I know. And then we were in their Base Camp, and I knew it was over. First illegal ascent of Everest.

XVIII

WELL, AFTER WHAT WE HAD been through, Gorak Shep looked like Ireland, and Pheriche looked like Hawaii. And the air was oxygen soup.

We kept asking after the Brits and Arnold and Laure, and kept hearing that they were a day or so below us. From the sound of it the Brits were chasing Arnold, who was managing by extreme efforts to stay ahead of them. So we hurried after them.

On our way down, however, we stopped at the Pengboche Monastery, a dark, brooding old place in a little nest of black pine trees, supposed to be the chin whiskers of the first abbot. There we left Kunga Norbu, who was looking pretty beat. The monks at the monastery made a big to-do over him. He and Freds had an emotional parting, and he gave me a big grin as he bored me through one last time with that spacy black gaze. "Good morning!" he said, and we were off.

So Freds and I tromped down to Namche, which reminded me strongly of Manhattan, and found our friends had just left for Lukla, still chasing Arnold. Below Namche we really hustled to catch up with them, but we didn't succeed until we reached Lukla itself. And then we only caught the Brits—because they were standing there by the Lukla airstrip, watching the last plane of the day hum down the tilted grass and ski jump out over the deep gorge of the Dudh Kosi—while Arnold McConnell, we quickly found out, was on that plane, having paid a legitimate passenger a fat stack of rupees to replace him. Arnold's Sherpa companions were lining the strip and waving good-bye to him; they had all earned about a year's wages in this one climb, it turned out, and they were pretty fond of old Arnold.

The Brits were not. In fact they were fuming.

"Where have you been?" Trevor demanded.

"Well. . . ." we said.

"We went to the top," Freds said apologetically. "Kunga had to for religious reasons."

"Well," Trevor said huffily. "We considered it ourselves, but *we* had to chase *your* client back down the mountain to try and get his film. The film that will get us all kicked out of Nepal for good if it's ever shown."

"Better get used to it," Mad Tom said gloomily. "He's off to Kathmandu, and we're not. We'll never catch him now."

Now the view from Lukla is nothing extraordinary, compared to what you can see higher up; but there are the giant green walls of the gorge, and to the north you can see a single scrap of the tall white peaks beyond; and to look at all that, and think you might never be allowed to see it again. . . .

I pointed to the south. "Maybe we just got lucky."

"What?"

Freds laughed. "Choppers! Incoming! Some trekking outfit has hired helicopters to bring its group in."

It was true. This is fairly common practice, I've done it myself many times. RNAC's daily flights to Lukla can't fulfill the need during the peak trekking season, so the Nepali Air Force kindly rents out its helicopters, at exorbitant fees. Naturally they prefer not to go back empty, and they'll take whoever will pay. Often, as on this day, there is a whole crowd clamoring to pay to go back, and the competition is fierce, although I for one am unable to understand what people are so anxious to get back to.

Anyway, this day was like most of them, and there was a

whole crowd of trekkers sitting around on the unloading field by the airstrip, negotiating with the various Sherpa and Sherpani power brokers who run the airport and get people onto flights. The hierarchy among these half-dozen power brokers is completely obscure, even to them, and on this day as always each of them had a list of people who had paid up to a hundred dollars for a lift out; and until the brokers discussed it with the helicopter crew, no one knew who was going to be the privileged broker given the go-ahead to march his clients on board. The crowd found this protocol ambiguous at best, and they were milling about and shouting ugly things at their brokers as the helicopters were sighted.

So this was not a good situation for us, because although we were desperate, everyone else wanting a lift claimed to be desperate also, and no one was going to volunteer to give up their places. Just before the two Puma choppers made their loud and windy landing, however, I saw Heather on the unloading field, and I ran over and discovered that she had gotten our expedition booked in with Pemba Sherpa, one of the most powerful brokers there. "Good work, Heather!" I cried. Quickly I explained to her some aspects of the situation, and looking wide-eyed at us—we were considerably filthier and more sunburnt than when we last saw her—she nodded her understanding.

And sure enough, in the chaos of trekkers milling about the choppers, in all that moaning and groaning and screaming and shouting to be let on board, it was Pemba who prevailed over the other brokers. And Want To Take You Higher Ltd.'s "Video Expedition To Everest Base Camp"—with the addition of four British climbers and an American—climbed on board the two vehicles, cheering all the way. With a *thukka thukka thukka* we were off.

"Now how will we find him in Kathmandu?" Marion said over the noise.

"He won't be expecting you," I said. "He thinks he's on

138

the last flight of the day. So I'd start at the Kathmandu Guest House, where we were staying, and see if you can find him there."

The Brits nodded, looking grim as commandos. Arnold was in trouble.

XIX

WE LANDED AT THE KATHMANDU airport an hour later, and the Brits zipped out and hired a taxi immediately. Freds and I hired another one and tried to keep up, but the Brits must have been paying their driver triple, because that little Toyota took off over the dirt roads between the airport and the city like it was in a motocross race. So we fell behind, and by the time we were let off in the courtyard of the Kathmandu Guest House, their taxi was already gone. We paid our driver and walked in and asked one of the snooty clerks for Arnold's room number, and when he gave it to us we hustled on up to the room, on the third floor overlooking the back garden.

We got there in the middle of the action. John and Mad Tom and Trevor had Arnold trapped on a bed in the corner, and they were standing over him not letting him go anywhere. Marion was on the other side of the room doing the actual demolition, taking up videocassettes one at a time and stomping them under her boot. There was a lot of yelling going on, mostly from Marion and Arnold. "*That's* the one of me taking my bath," Marion said. "And *that's* the one of me changing my shirt in my tent. And *that's* the one of me taking a pee at eight thousand meters!" and so on, while Arnold was shouting "No, no!" and "Not that one, my God!" and "I'll sue you in every court in Nepal!"

"Foreign nationals can't sue each other in Nepal," Mad Tom told him.

But Arnold continued to shout and threaten and moan, his sun-torched face going incandescent, his much-reduced body bouncing up and down on the bed, his big round eyes popping out till I was afraid they would burst, or fall down on springs. He picked up the fresh cigar that had fallen from his mouth and threw it between Trevor and John, hitting Marion in the chest.

"Molester," she said, dusting her hands with satisfaction. "That's all of them, then." She began to stuff the wreckage of plastic and videotape into a daypack. "And we'll take this along, too, thank you very much."

"Thief," Arnold croaked.

The three guys moved away from him. Arnold sat there on the bed, frozen, staring at Marion with a stricken, bug-eyed expression. He looked like a balloon with a pinprick in it.

"Sorry, Arnold," Trevor said. "But you brought this on yourself, as you must admit. We told you all along we didn't want to be filmed."

Arnold stared at them speechlessly.

"Well, then," Trevor said. "That's that." And they left.

Freds and I watched Arnold sit there. Slowly his eyes receded back to their usual pop-eyed position, but he still looked disconsolate.

"Them Brits are tough," Freds offered. "They're not real sentimental people."

"Come on, Arnold," I said. Now that he was no longer my responsibility, now that we were back, and I'd never have to see him again—now that it was certain his videotape, which could have had Freds and me in as much hot water as the Brits, was destroyed—I felt a little bit sorry for him. Just a little bit. It was clear from his appearance that he had really gone through a lot to get that tape. Besides, I was starving. "Come on, let's all get showered and shaved and cleaned up, and then I'll take you out to dinner."

"Me too," said Freds.
Arnold nodded mutely.

XX

KATHMANDU IS A FUNNY CITY. When you first arrive there
from the West, it seems like the most ramshackle and un-
sanitary place imaginable: the buildings are poorly constructed of old brick, and there are weed patches growing
out of the roofs; the hotel rooms are bare pits; all the food
you can find tastes like cardboard, and often makes you
sick; and there are sewage heaps here and there in the mud
streets, where dogs and cows are scavenging. It really
seems primitive.

Then you go out for a month or two in the mountains, on
a trek or a climb. And when you return to Kathmandu, the
place is utterly transformed. The only likely explanation is
that while you were gone they took the city away and re-
placed it with one that looks the same on the outside, but is
completely different in substance. The accommodations are
luxurious beyond belief; the food is superb; the people look
prosperous, and their city seems a marvel of architectural
sophistication. Kathmandu! What a metropolis!

So it seemed to Freds and me, as we checked into my
home away from home, the Hotel Star. As I sat on the floor
under the waist-high tap of steaming hot water that
emerged from my shower, I found myself giggling in mindless rapture, and from the next room I could hear Freds
bellowing "Going to Kathmandu": "K-k-k-k-k-Kat-Man-
Du!"

An hour later, hair wet, faces chopped up, skin all prune-
shriveled, we met Arnold out in the street and walked
through the Thamel evening. "We look like coat racks!"
Freds observed. Our city clothes were hanging on us. Freds

and I had each lost about twenty pounds, Arnold about thirty. And it wasn't just fat, either. Everything wastes away at altitude. "We'd better get to the Old Vienna and put some of it back on."

I started salivating at the very thought of it.

So we went to the Old Vienna Inn, and relaxed in the warm steamy atmosphere of the Austro-Hungarian Empire. After big servings of goulash, schnitzel Parisienne, and apple strudel with whipped cream, we sat back sated. Sensory overload. Even Arnold was looking up a little. He had been quiet through the meal, but then again we all had, being busy.

We ordered a bottle of rakshi, which is a potent local beverage of indeterminate origin. When it came we began drinking.

Freds said, "Hey, Arnold, you're looking better."

"Yeah, I don't feel so bad." He wiped his mouth with a napkin streaked all red; we had all split our sun-destroyed lips more than once, trying to shovel the food in too fast. He got set to start the slow process of eating another cigar, unwrapping one very slowly. "Not so bad at all." And then he grinned; he couldn't help himself; he grinned so wide that he had to grab the napkin and stanch the flow from his lips again.

"Well, it's a shame those guys stomped your movie," Freds said.

"Yeah, well." Arnold waved an arm expansively. "That's life."

I was amazed. "Arnold, I can't believe this is you talking. Here those guys took your videotapes of all that *suffering* you just put us through, and they *stomp* it, and you say, 'That's life'?"

He took a long hit of the rakshi. "Well," he said, waggling his eyebrows up and down fiendishly. He leaned over the table toward us. "They got one copy of it, anyway."

Freds and I looked at each other.

"Couple hundred dollars of tape there that they crunched, I suppose I ought to bill them for it. But I'm a generous guy; I let it pass."

"One copy?" I said.

"Yeah." He tipped his head. "Did you see that box, kind of like a suitcase, there in the corner of my room at the Guest House?"

We shook our heads.

"Neither did the Brits. Not that they would have recognized it. It's a video splicer, mainly. But a copier too. You stick a cassette in there and push a button and it copies the cassette for storage, and then you can do all your splicing off the master. You make your final tape that way. Great machine. Most freelance video people have them now, and these portable babies are really the latest. Saved my ass, in this case."

"Arnold," I said. "You're going to get those guys in trouble! And us too!"

"Hey," he warned, "I've got the splicer under lock and key, so don't get any ideas."

"Well you're going to get us banned from Nepal for good!"

"Nah. I'll give you all stage names. You got any preferences along those lines?"

"Arnold!" I protested.

"Hey, listen," he said, and drank more rakshi. "Most of that climb was in Tibet, right? Chinese aren't going to be worrying about it. Besides, you know the Nepal Ministry of Tourism—can you really tell me they'll ever get it together to even see my film, much less take names from it and track those folks down when they next apply for a visa? Get serious!"

"Hmm," I said, consulting with my rakshi.

"So what'd you get?" Freds asked.

"*Everything*. I got some good long-distance work of you guys finding the body up there—ha!—you thought I didn't

143

get that, right? I tell you I was filming your *thoughts* up there! I got that, and then the Brits climbing on the ridge—everything. I'm gonna make stars of you all."

Freds and I exchanged a relieved glance. "Remember about the stage names," I said.

"Sure. And after I edit it you won't be able to tell where on the mountain the body was, and with the names and all, I really think Marion and the rest will love it. Don't you? They were just being shy. Old-fashioned! I'm going to send them all prints of the final product, and they're gonna love it. Marion in particular. She's gonna look beautiful." He waved the cigar and a look of cowlike yearning disfigured his face. "In fact, tell you a little secret, I'm gonna accompany that particular print in person, and make it part of my proposal to her. I think she's kind of fond of me, and I bet you anything she'll agree to marry me when she sees it, don't you think?"

"Sure," Freds said. "Why not?" He considered it. "Or if not in this life, then in the next."

Arnold gave him an odd look. "I'm going to ask her along on my next trip, which looks like it'll be China and Tibet. You know how the Chinese have been easing up on the Tibetan religions lately? Well, the clerk at the Guest House gave me a telegram on my way out—my agent tells me that the authorities in Lhasa have decided they're going to rebuild a whole bunch of the Buddhist monasteries that they tore down during the Cultural Revolution, and it looks like I'll be allowed to film some of it. That should make for a real heart-string basher, and I bet Marion would love to see it, don't you?"

Freds and I grinned at each other. "*I'd* love to see it," Freds declared. "Here's to the monasteries, and a free Tibet!"

We toasted the idea, and ordered another bottle.

Arnold waved his cigar. "Meanwhile, this Mallory stuff is dynamite. It's gonna make a hell of a movie."

XXII

Wʜɪᴄʜ ɪꜱ ᴡʜʏ ɪ ᴄᴀɴ tell you about this one—the need for secrecy is going to be blown right out the window as soon as they air Arnold's film, "Nine Against Everest: Seven Men, One Woman, and a Corpse." I hear both PBS and the BBC have gone for it, and it should be on any day now. Check local listings for times in your area.

PART
3

The True Nature
of Shangri-La

THEY SAY IN NEPAL that an early monsoon brings good luck but obviously they are lying through their teeth. The only thing an early monsoon brings if you ask me is more rain than usual in the late spring and early summer. Take for instance 1987, when the monsoon struck in May. Big trouble that year, for a place you probably know as Shangri-La. Now the name Shangri-La is not the valley's real name, that's just what it was called in a movie and they must have heard wrong because the real name is Shambhala. Shambhala is the hidden city of Tibet, the home of the world's most ancient wisdom, the sacred secret stronghold of Tibetan Buddhism. The source of all the world's religions, in fact. I have spent a good bit of time there myself with my teacher Kunga Norbu Rimpoche and so when Kunga came down to Kathmandu to tell me Shambhala was in trouble, I knew it was my duty to help in any way I could.

Apparently word had gotten around that the Nepalis were planning to extend one of their hill roads up to a mountain village that was so close to Shambhala that it represented a serious danger. The road would bring so many people into the area that the secret would eventually get out, and that would be it for the sacred valley.

As soon as Kunga Norbu explained the nature of the problem I knew that my buddy George Fergusson was the answer. George is great at oiling his way through the Nepali bureaucracy to get what he needs for his trekking business, so I figured he had expertise in just the areas we needed.

But when I left Kunga Norbu at the Tibetan camp in Patan and went back to the Hotel Star to approach George about it, he was reluctant. "No way," he said. "Not a chance. You and your guru buddy already nearly killed me."

"Ah come on," says I. "It's just a little road project we need stopped."

"No way, Freds! I have to hassle with the bureaucrats here all the time, why would I deliberately expose myself to more?"

"That's just it, George. We need an expert. And listen, there's more to it than I can tell you. You know, mystical reasons."

George frowned and said "Now don't you go trying to twilight zone me again, Freds," meaning I wasn't to step outside the two-and-a-half-foot radius of his Betty Crocker worldview. But he had already been dragged outside that circle once or twice before and once outside you can never get all the way back in again no matter how hard you try, which was why there was a little crease of worry growing between George's eyes as he wagged his finger at me.

"Come on," says I.

"No fucking way."

It turned out he was in a bad mood because of something he had read in *The International Herald Tribune*. There he was, kicked back in his lawn chair, soaking up the morning rays on the sun deck located on the roof of the Hotel Star lobby, occasionally chatting with two Danish gals in bikinis, stoned and eating Nebico wafers and drinking a Budweiser and reading his week-old copy of the *Tribbie*, and it should have been Kathmandu in Monsoon Heaven but he was sitting there all dejected because of an article he had just read. He tore through the pages to show it to me. "See that? Can you believe it? A group from the University of Washington used a satellite and damned if they didn't find out that K2 is taller than Everest."

"I would have thought that would be hard to judge from a satellite."

"'K2 is now known to be 29,064 feet tall, while Everest's official height is still listed at 29,028 feet.' Can you believe it?" He was really aggrieved. "I mean all those expeditions to Everest, all the heroics and people getting killed, and all for the *second highest mountain*? It's too fucking ironic, man. It's *horrible*."

"Especially since you yourself are now amongst those deluded climbers who risked all for number two," says I.

"Don't say that so loud," he says, glancing around. "But sure I'm disappointed, I mean, aren't you?"

"We had to drag your ass up that mountain, George. You hated it."

"Of course I did, it was a stupid thing the way you guys did it, no support, no *plan*. But, you know—since we did do it, I mean that was the whole *point*. We bagged the biggie."

"We can always take you up K2."

No reply from George.

"In fact," says I, seeing an opening, "Kunga Norbu may just *have* to climb it to fulfill his obligation to Dorjee Lama. And of course his companions would be mystically obliged to accompany him."

"Ha," George said, the crease between his eyes getting deeper.

"And you know one of Kunga's powers is getting people to do what he wants. Like when he convinced you to go for the peak of Chomolungma."

He frowned. "Just don't tell him about this recalculation thing."

"Of course I don't really have time to tell him about that, George. Being as how we've got this other matter we need your help on. Your help here in Kathmandu. Just making a few trips into the government offices, in your spare time. During the monsoon when you got nothing to do and are near dead with boredom anyway."

"All right, all right." He sighed. "So what's this big problem."

"They're building a road to Chhule." I'm going to call the village that even though it is not the village's real name.

"So?"

"George," says I. "They're building a *road* into an unspoiled area of the Himal, where there's never been any road before!"

"Ah," says he. "That is a drag. Chalk off one more good trekking area. But that's not a very popular route anyway, is it?"

That was George all over. Like a lot of Western climbing freaks in Nepal he saw the country as no more than the ultimate mountain playground, with plenty of hash and a lot of exotic quaint cheap local culture on the side. A place where for a couple thou a year you could live like cut-rate royalty providing you didn't mind disease and bad food. So he grooved in the sun and led his treks and climbed the mountains and paid no mind to the rest of it, and like the other longtime regulars he had gotten to a point where he hated the tourists because they were ignorant, and despised the locals because they were ignorant, until in fact there was nobody in Nepal doing it exactly right except him and his buddies, and as the saying goes, even they were suspect.

So he didn't understand at first. But he wasn't as bad as some, or so I believed. "Come on, George, let me take you to Marco Polo's for lunch, I need to tell you more about this in private. There's ramifications, like I told you."

So George put on his T-shirt and his Vuarnets and we went downstairs past the zoned-out clerks in the lobby. It was noonish, hot and muggy, the day's rains about to hit, and everyone in the hotel looked like they were in a trance except for the woman with the kid strapped to her back bent over out front halfway through her daily task of sweeping the courtyard with a hand whisk. Then we were out the hotel gates and past the Tantric Used Book Shop and into Thamel, the hotel quarter of Kathmandu. This area

152

gets pretty dead in the monsoon but that only meant the taxi drivers and carpet shop people and hash dealers and money changers and beggars were all more eager than ever to attract our business. "Hey, Mr. No!" they yelled at George, laughing at him as he hopped down the muddy strip between puddles doing his usual "No, no, no, no," routine to everyone he passed, no matter if they had accosted him or not. He was relaxed and breezy, having a good time, doing his turn and everyone digging it, your typical L.A. thrillseeker, about six two and built like a quarterback, dark-haired and good-looking in a Steve Garvey-gone-to-seed style and so cool you could use him to kill warts, so cool in fact that all the street folk actually enjoyed his No No No routine, and all was well except for the fact that they were as low on rupees after George passed as before. I really should learn to do that myself but I haven't yet and so I usually walk the neighborhood with no rupes at all on me so I can't be giving them all away, but this time I had what it would take to buy George and me lunch, and who did we run into but one of the local beggars we saw all the time, a guy who cruised Thamel homeless with his little daughter in tow, they would stand there holding hands and the man would smile a gap-toothed smile and the little girl about six would do likewise and they would both hold out their free hands toward you and they did tolerably well that way, certainly I could never resist them, and in fact on this day after George noed them I gave them our lunch money, figuring that I would get George to bail me and then it could be said that he had helped out the beggar and his little sidekick, whilst I had bought the lunch as I intended to.

George was unaware of my intentions, but when he looked back and noticed what I was doing he was still disgusted with me. "You only encourage them, Freds."

"Yeah, I know."

George had no sympathy whatsoever for that beggar or

any other, or for any of the rest of the street operators for that matter. Like one time I remember after we had had a particularly bad time getting down the narrow main street he had looked back at the whole crowd of them, all staring at us, and he had flipped out. "They're just like bowling pins in a bowling alley, aren't they Freds? Standing there they look like you could, hey, wait just a sec," and he had rushed into the German Pumpernickel Bakery and come back out with a big dark angelfood cake which did upon reflection indeed resemble a bowling ball in weight and general consistency, and he punched finger and thumb holes in it and took a long run and wind-up, and he bowled that cake right down the middle of them, laughing like a loon.

"You are risking reincarnation as something small and revolting," I told him. But he didn't hear me.

• • •

This time, however, we got to lunch without incident.

"Look, George," I told him as we ate pizza in our little private window nook at Marco Polo's, "you know what happens when they put a road through one of the hill villages."

"People drive there."

"Exactly! People drive there, people drive away from there. The whole village goes to hell. Wiped out forever."

"Don't get too melodramatic, Freds."

"I'm not! You know Jiri?"

"Yeah." He wrinkled his nose.

"That was a beautiful village until the road was built to it."

He didn't believe me. "Freds, they study shit like that before they do it, they make sure it's gonna be okay."

Now this was such a stupid thing to say that I knew he didn't mean it. He was just putting me off. "Cockroach."

"Where?"

"That's what you're gonna come back as."

I stared out the window. Usually the view out the third-story window of the Marco Polo is one I enjoy, the colorful carpets on display at street level, the balconies above covered by tick mattresses faintly steaming in the sun, above that prayer flags and telephone wires tangled in the air, on roofs so old that great lawns of weedy green and yellow grass grow out of them. And then the huge pines of the palace in the background, with maybe a glimpse of the Himal beyond. But on that day the monsoon clouds were lowering the boom, the carpets and mattresses had been hauled in and the buildings looked ramshackle in the dark rainy air. Back in the gloom of the restaurant's main room diners were steadfastly munching away trying to ignore the notion that they had been orwelled off to a world where all food tasted like cardboard, not just pizza dough but also tomato paste and cheese and vegetables, everything in fact except for the big twisty black Chinese mushrooms that writhed on the slices looking just like the bizarre fungoid growths they were and suggesting with every rank rubbery chew that a bad mistake in mycology had been made back at the canning factory.

It was not a cheery sight. And I had a stubborn wily lazy friend to deal with, and it was clear it was going to take a serious breach of security to get him to do what we wanted. "George," I said wearily, "can you keep a secret?"

"Sure."

"This is important, George. This is like Nathan and Buddha, you know?"

"Okay," he said, looking offended. "Did I ever tell anyone about that?"

"I don't know. But you sure as hell can't tell anyone about this. See there's a village just beyond the end of this road they're planning to build, in the next valley over. And this is no ordinary village. It's Kunga Norbu's village."

"I thought he was Tibetan."

"It's a Tibetan village."

"A Tibetan village in Nepal?"

"It's up there on the border, right on the crest where the border gets a little chancy. Up there in ———." Which is one of them semi-independent little old kingdoms that are part of Nepal but stick into the body of Tibet, following curlicues in the crest of the Himalayan range.

George nodded. He knew that a lot of the highland Nepalis were Tibetan in origin, the Sherpas in the east, the Bhotians in the west ("Bhotian" meaning "Tibetan" in Nepalese), so that this situation wasn't that uncommon. "That's near where we let Buddha go," he said.

"That's right. It's a special area." I told him how wonderful it was, like the Khumbu only completely untouched, with Buddha and a lot of other yetis living in the high forest, and all kinds of other special properties, and he chewed and nodded and didn't look at all like he was going to do anything about it.

"So what's the secret?" he said.

He just wanted to know for the sake of knowing a secret, I could tell. But there is a big difference between knowledge that has been pressed on you and knowledge you have asked for, so I leaned over quick and said in a real low voice,

"The village is actually Shangri-La."

"Come on, Freds. That's a made-up name out of a movie. *Lost Horizon*."

"Yeah, that's right. I didn't think you'd know that much about it. The real name is Shambhala. Whatever you call it, it's the same place."

"I thought Shambhala was in northern Tibet, or Mongolia."

"They've spread a lot of disinformation about it. But it's up on the border, and it's in big trouble because of this road they're planning to build."

George stared at me. "You're kidding, right?"

"Was I kidding you about Kunga Norbu being a tulku? Were Nathan and I kidding you about Buddha?"

He chomped away for a while thinking about it. "I don't believe you."

"Why would I lie?"

"You wouldn't lie, Freds, but you could get fooled. I mean, how do you know it's Shambhala?"

"I've been there. I spent about six months there."

He stared at me again. "Freds, just how the hell did *you* come to spend six months in Shambhala?"

●●●

Now you may have wondered about this yourself, and to tell the truth so have I. How did Freds Fredericks, star linebacker for the Razorbacks and all-American vet school dropout, come to be a Tibetan Buddhist monk well acquainted with the sacred hidden valley of Shambhala?

I don't *really* know. Some of us have weird karmas to work through in this life, and that's all you can say about it. But certainly it began for me in a small way when I was in The Graduate in Davis, California. As I tried to explain to George. I was drinking pitchers of beer in there after an intramural football game around 1976, and I overheard a gal at our picnic table explaining how she couldn't eat one of their fine hamburgers because she was a vegetarian because she didn't believe in the killing of animals because she was a Buddhist. And I thought how interesting. And then that night still drunk I was taking a bag of trash from our lab out to the dumpsters behind the building, and when I tossed the bag in I heard a whimper come from inside the dumpster. I checked it out pulling out bags of trash getting spooked by this whimper, and finally I found the source which was a dog that had been used in one of the tutorials. They put them under and then do a variety of surgical work on them to teach how the insides of living animals look, and then they put them down. Happens all the time in vet schools. But this time there had been a fuckup or the dog was especially tough because they hadn't killed it off, and there it was without its hind legs and most of its intestines, whimpering and looking up at me as if I could help it. The best I could do was to try to put it out of its misery and it snapped weakly at me as I tried hands and boots and plastic bags, it fended off every effort until I broke its neck with the dumpster lid and I wandered for a time and found myself on the women's softball field feeling horrible. And then I looked up across the street and the parking lot and I saw the round *The Graduate* sign blinking on and off and something turned in me, what I later understood to be my *bodhi* or awakening to the true nature of reality, and I said to the softball diamond, "God damn it, I am a *Buddhist.*"

I didn't even know what I meant by it. But I quit vet school and as it turned out some of my buddies were going to Nepal at that same time to score some hash, so I went with them. None of us knew the first thing about Nepal except that it was supposed to be big on hash and Buddhism, and we were right about one so we had a fine time in Kathmandu but after a while we got bored so we decided to go trekking as this seemed to be all the rage there. This was around August 1st, right in the middle of a bad monsoon, but we were so ignorant we had no idea there were trekking seasons and nontrekking seasons, and the people in the shops were happy to rent us gear and so we took off on the bus to Lamosangu and started trekking toward Everest. Naturally the clouds were constant and the trails were deluged, and we ate all the wrong food and drank the water from the streams which looked so clear and clean and so we got horribly sick, and we were bit all over by leeches and it seemed to us we were not exactly catching on as to what the appeal of this trekking was. I mean we were so ignorant that we thought when they said "mani walls" they were saying "money walls," we thought that every time we passed a mani wall we were going by the village bank, each stone a thousand-dollar bill or something like that and it seemed to us that they had figured out a very clever way to stop bank robberies, only we were mystified as well, passing wall after wall after wall we said to each other if these folks have got so much cash how come they don't buy no toilets? Which is stupid if you think about it but we didn't we just kept on trekking, sick as dogs but bound and determined to catch sight of Everest or die trying, and it was going to be a close thing.

But one morning I got up early to go out and pee, and I walked out of the teahouse and all the clouds were gone. It was the first time we weren't completely socked in, we'd never seen anything higher than the top of our hats and had hiked through mist and forest like we were in a lumpy Amazon without the slightest idea of what was all around us, so when I walked out the door that morning I was still completely innocent of any real sight of the Himalayas, and I am from Arkansas. I think that everyone gets their sense of how big things should be from their home and their childhood, and where I came from valleys were farm-sized things, rivers were creeks you could ford most anywhere, and mountains were hills a couple hundred feet high at best—the landscape had a certain scale and that to me was the way things were, that was the natural order, that was what I was used to. So when I walked out that teahouse door in the Dudh Kosi and looked around blinking in the dawn light, deep down in this enormous *gap* in the world which apparently was a *valley* which it would take at least a day to cross and a week to walk up—and then, standing behind this mile-deep valley and way, way, *way* above it, these vertical spiky snow-and-rock monster towers that were obviously *unbelievably big mountains*—! Well, if I hadn't clapped my teeth together my heart would have jumped straight out of my mouth. And since that day I have never left the Himalayas.

Anyway, I know this doesn't completely explain how I

became a Tibetan Buddhist monk, but if I told the whole story of how I met Kunga Norbu and became his disciple and went undercover into Tibet it would take me forever, and besides George was going cross-eyed as I told him all this about my past. He was done eating so he waved a hand and cut me off.

"Shambhala, Freds, Shambhala. You were telling me about Shambhala."

"Yes I was."

"You could take me there?"

"Sure. Do you want to go?"

"Do I want to visit Shambhala? Do I want to see Shangri-La? Damn, Freds—why didn't you put it that way in the first place?"

"Because visiting it ain't the point. Saving it is the point, and that's got to happen here. Besides, you wouldn't have believed me if I had just up and asked you out of the blue do you want to visit Shambhala."

"I still don't believe you, Freds. But it's monsoon. There's nothing else to do. And if you're right, well. . . ." He grinned. "You take me there and show me, and then I'll see about helping you out."

• • •

So a couple days later we left the Hotel Star at dawn and woke up one of the taxi drivers whose car was his castle and had him drive us to the Central Bus Stop, and there we located our usual ticket agent who took us through the mud and dead buses to a decrepit old clunker that was packed full. Now in any other season we would have made a beeline for the roof and traveled in style up there, but because it was monsoon we had to jam our way inside. A Rawang man and his wife and daughters were in our seats, so we sat on the floor between the front seats and the partition separating the passengers from the driver's compartment. About an hour later we began the typical Kathmandu departure. Get out of the depot and stop to scrape off the hitchhikers who had jumped on the roof during the run up the mud ramp. Stop for gas. Stop to search through the southern quarter of the city for an engine part. Stop to fix a flat. This time when the spare tire was on they found they couldn't get the flat tire secured under the bus where the spare had come from. They spent an hour trying, and even the driver got down to look at it. He was a big guy with a thick black moustache, looked like an ex-Gurkha and nothing could faze him, he attended to his driving and usually let his flight crew handle all the other problems that every trip presented, so looking at this unattachable tire was a real concession. Finally he shrugged and pointed and the flight crew nodded and came on board and pushed all the aisle passengers back a bit, and maneuvered the flat tire in the door and up the steps and into the aisle, where it stood as tall as some passengers and much muddier.

So we left Kathmandu at noon when we were supposed to be off at seven, which was not bad. Every bus ride in Nepal is an adventure and I enjoy them no end, but George doesn't. On this one he had fallen into a trance to try to escape. Every time he came out of his trance he would look into the driver's area and see the mechanic sticking his head down into the engine compartment with a lit cigarette between his teeth, making adjustments while the engine ran, and George would groan and fall back into his trance again. A wire crate of chickens was set just under the flat tire in the aisle, and every time the chickens looked up they figured they were about to be run over and would squawk madly, then overdose on panic and fall asleep, only to wake up and go through the trauma again. Right beside the chickens sat three Swiss trekkers breathing in the thick fog of cigarette and engine oil smoke like it was ambrosia, they were the kind of Swiss travelers you see in Asia who have been so stressed by the Formula 409 aspects of their culture that their compass has cracked and nothing suits these types better than to be stuck knee-deep in manure and mismanagement in some Asian backwater, whereupon a Ludwig van Ninth look of bliss comes over them as they realize they couldn't get more miserably un-Swiss anywhere. So this bus trip was pleasing them no end.

Meanwhile we were trundling out of the Kathmandu Valley, either east or west I shouldn't tell you which, and it had its usual dreamy look, monsoon clouds filtering the light so that the greens leaped out like Kodak ads, with villages in the distance little clumps of brown, surrounded by trees in pink or lavender bloom. Fields of early rice ran up into the clouds in hundreds of terraces, until it got hard to tell how far away a hillside was because you couldn't believe anyone would terrace a slope so fine. The hilltops were cut off by a cloud ceiling that got lower and darker until finally the pleasures of the view were wiped out by torrents of rain, rain so dense it looked like God had scooped up the Indian Ocean and dumped it on us. Typical monsoon afternoon. I don't think the driver could see past the windshield, but he just hunched forward a touch and carried on as usual.

After that there was nothing to do but meditate or watch the expertise of the driver, who was blindly navigating enormous mudholes and guiding the bus over landslides that had buried the road entirely. These were never cleared off but were driven over so often that a new track was established, weirdly lumpy and canted over. But our driver pushed through at a walking pace, timing every jolt and bounce to get him over bad spots, the engine clunking at about the same rpm as the wheels, and every time we lurched safely back onto the real road and splattered off at our maximum speed of around forty kilometers per hour.

● ● ●

Then just as our bladders were about to blow up and our brains to implode we stopped at a roadside village. The villagers crowded around to greet us and we burst through them like a gang of fullbacks, rushing in both directions down the road to the ends of the village to relieve ourselves. George and I and the Swiss were especially well attended by the village kids, and we peed into the bushes with a considerable audience giggling at us as we tried not to look at or step in the dismal and copious evidence of the intestinal problems of all the travelers who had been there before us. Naturally a road village has shitting grounds vastly larger than your typical hill village, and I knew by the expression on George's face that I didn't have to point this fact out to him.

We returned to the village center and sat at a table under a long tin roof. There wasn't much room between the road and a river, and this open-walled building filled most of it. Buildings across the road and up the hillside had been abandoned and were in the process of being torn down. Silent women served us big steel plates of mushy dhal baat while kids surrounded us to beg for money—one guy who looked about eight but could have been fourteen smoked a handrolled cigarette and kept saying "Candy? Smoke? Dollar? Ballpoint pen?" A gang of younger ones chased a pig from puddle to puddle, yanking on its tail until they were almost run over by a Jeep splashing through. People ran out to greet the Jeep but it didn't stop.

George passed on his dhal baat, and bought a bottle of lemon soda and two packets of Nebico wafers. This was in keeping with his usual culinary strategy while trekking, which he called prophylactic eating. You see he had never really recovered from an early encounter with a plate of dhal baat that had had its rice insufficiently cleaned, so that it tasted "just like taking *raw dirt* and eating it *off the ground*" as he was fond of saying. After that he couldn't even look at the stuff without gagging, so he ended up not only practicing prophylactic antibiotics use, meaning he popped pills daily in hopes of discouraging bacteria from catching hold in him—he also practiced his prophylactic eating, meaning he ate nothing but boiled potatoes that he peeled himself, hardboiled eggs that he peeled himself, Nebico wafers that he unwrapped himself, and water that he both filtered and triple iodinated. It didn't work, but it did make him feel better.

So we sat there and George ate his placebo diet and the clouds pissed on us and the villagers either stood around a little wood stove under the tin roof or rushed out to greet the occasional passing vehicle, and all in all it was like a play put on for George's benefit called "The Degradation of the Nepali Roadside Village" only it was real. Roads were built and people either used them to go and join the unemployed in Kathmandu, or stayed behind and tried to live off the road traffic, which would have worked if only a few of them were trying it, but with all of them trying none could succeed, and all around them the terraces fell to pieces in the rain.

But I never said a word to George about this. I just left him to watch it.

An hour later the bus's flight crew decided it was time to go and we all climbed back aboard and wedged into our places and were off again, at about the hour we had been scheduled to arrive at our final destination. Almost immediately we hung a left onto a road that looked like something out of a civil engineering handbook, a narrow lane of asphalt maybe two buses wide at the widest, black as coal and perfectly smooth, with concrete gutters and abutments and supports and drains, and thick wire mesh covering the hillside above the many switchbacks that the road made. "Hey," George said, cheering up. "The Swiss have been here."

"That's right," I said. "This is the road they're planning to extend to Chhule."

"Is it the Swiss who are going to do it?"

"No, they're done. It's someone else, no one I know is sure who."

The switchbacks marked the slope like sewing machine

stitching, but even so the grade was a bit steep by Nepali standards, and our old clunker only just beat a walking pace up it, slowing down even more in the turns. Each hairpin was a major effort for the driver, because this bus like all Indian buses had a steering wheel that had to be spun three or four times just to dodge a rock in the road much less make a one eighty. Our driver had to twirl his big lasso like Mr. Toad on the wild ride, while one of his assistants hung out the door to tell him how much room there was to spare before we fell off the road and back down the gorge. The assistant's signaling system consisted of shouts of panic of varying intensity so that every time we made a right turn we suspected it was the end and the chickens were positive. This went on all afternoon. We did nothing but vertical distance, so that a full three hours after we had left the roadside village we could still look right down on its roofs, a fact that George couldn't seem to come to terms with. "Look at that," he'd groan at every turn, "it's *still there*." But then we rose into the clouds and couldn't see anything at all.

Hours passed and it got darker. The driver stared through his windshield decals into thick mist, driving by telepathy. I began to feel all warm and cosy, lulled by the bus's motion, as if I was in a teahouse and the engine was a stove. I love trips like this. I mean what is life for, when you get right down to it? Days exactly like this one, if you ask me. We were on our way to Shambhala, after all. No one could expect it to be a simple thing.

Having passed through all transitory emotion himself, George became philosophic. "This had better be the real thing you're taking me to," he said.

"It is," I told him.

He looked doubtful. "I can see how a remote valley could stay hidden up here in the old days, but how do they do it now? I mean, how do they keep satellites from seeing them?"

"They don't. They're in the satellite photos."

"I thought it was a secret city."

"It is, but nowadays it's more of a disguised city. The government in Kathmandu knows it's there, but they just think it's one of their little high valley villages, with a Tibetan population. Someone from the district panchayat drops by from time to time, and everyone is friendly enough, they just don't tell him where he really is. The monastery doesn't look all that important, and most of the lamas stay out of sight when visitors are around. They pay their taxes, and send a representative to the Panchayat and all, and they're left alone like any other remote village."

"So it doesn't look magical?"

"Not to the tax collectors."

"No gold towers and crystal palaces and all?"

"Well, there's some stuff in the monastery. But the truth is hardly anyone from Nepal ever comes by. Kathmandu seems to think of it as a Tibetan village that got caught on the wrong side when they formalized the border with China. Which essentially is true. Besides Kathmandu doesn't pay any attention to villages right next door, much less one as remote as this."

"So it's safe."

"But the thing is, if too many people were to start dropping by, the secret would get out for sure."

"Thus the road paranoia."

"Right."

Much later we began to stop at high villages, lit by kerosene lanterns and the bus's headlights. At each stop a few passengers got off and the rest settled back into a stupor, until finally it was past midnight and we were rolling into a completely dark village that was The End Of The Road. The driver honked his horn and we fell out like cripples, and the teahouse keepers emerged and rounded us up.

After recovering our backpacks from the roof of the bus and finding them soaked, George and I followed a man into a teahouse I had frequented before. As we staggered up to the crowded bedroom on the second floor I looked in the kitchen, and there in the harsh glare of a Coleman lantern was our bus driver, hunched by the stove scooping up huge handfuls of steamed rice and wolfing them down, cleaning off the last of a big steel plate with a stolid expression and a regular movement. Just another day's work as far as he was concerned—seventeen hours of driving a lousy bus over bad roads in horrible weather, surely ten trillion turns of that old steering wheel, and it made me happy to think that such heroes out of Homer still walked the face of this earth. By the time we got up the next morning he and his crew would be long gone, back down to Kathmandu where they would turn around and start the whole epic over again the very next day. Some people really work for a living.

• • •

The village at the end of the road was in the same state as the road village from the day before—focused on the great dirt runway that slashed it in two, new buildings clustered around the road ending, old buildings torn down for construction materials or firewood, and the whole thing surrounded by shitting fields, especially by the river running at the far edge of town. This happens because of the lack of toilet paper but it does no good to their water supply. As we completed our morning business there George said "I don't see why they can't believe in invisible bugs. Air is invisible. Their gods are invisible."

"Germ theory just ain't intuitive, George."

"Neither is religion."

"I'm not so sure of that."

"But why should there be a difference?"

"It may be that the reason for the existence of the universe is a more pressing question for most people than the reason why they get the runs."

"That's crazy."

"Besides," I said, "if you got a good enough answer to the first question then the second one is answered too, right?"

He only squinted at me in a certain suspicious way he has, a look he often gave me.

We returned to our teahouse, and after a breakfast of Nebico wafers and hardboiled eggs we were on our way. Backpacks on, the trail found. Trekking at last.

Now in most seasons this would be the fun part—trekking, one of the finest activities known to humanity. But in the monsoon everything gets very wet. Trails become streams, streams become rivers, rivers become killer torrents. There is a big increase in bugs, mold, rot, damp, and disease.

I like trekking in the monsoon, myself. But I bring along a little umbrella and a pair of wellies with their bottoms carved until they are almost rubber crampons, so I had less trouble with the slick trails than George, who had disdained these accessories and was suffering the consequences. He tended to ski the downhills, and his head was always wet, which I have found is seldom conducive to good humor.

Still, we were trekking. Gone were the long views that in other seasons are such a joy, however. In the monsoon all you see are clouds, mist, rain, and whatever's there in the little bubble of visibility around you, all of it looking green and wet and somehow otherworldly now that your attention is fastened on it rather than the distance. The mossy trees look foreign and fantastical, the trail is a reddish streak of mud leading you through dripping green creepers, and the occasional chorten or mani wall looms out of the mist like something out of the *Bhagavad Gita*, which in a way it is. And every once in a while the mountains appear through gaps in the clouds like live things flying overhead. Oh, it's a spacy thing all right, trekking in the monsoon, and if you've got your brolly and wellies and a stick to knock aside the leeches, it can really be fun.

If you don't have those things, well, you get like George. None of his tour groups ever went out in monsoon and so of course he didn't either, and now he was paying the price because he had forgotten how to do it, if he ever knew. He kept falling on slippery patches and stepping in the streams until he couldn't have been wetter laid out in his bath. Rain got in his eye and he thought there was nothing to see anyway, and since he wasn't looking he kept getting jumped by leeches, which is a painless thing and without negative consequences, but unpleasant if you dislike it. We'd be hiking past bushes or tall grass, and if you watched you would see that some of the little black twigs were wiggling around, trying to feel your heat, and if they did they would leap aboard and weasel through socks or pants or boots and suck your blood. Whenever George looked down at his legs and caught one in the act he howled. "Fuck! Fuck! Fuck! Oh my God, *leeches*!"

"Put mosquito repellent on them, they'll drop right off."

"I *know*." And he'd drop his pack in a puddle and hurry like it was little rattlesnakes latched onto him.

Trying to make him feel better I said, "Hell, first time I came here with my buddies we went trekking and you know back home when you're bit by a mosquito on the forearm some guys will trap them by tensing the forearm muscle, after which they can't get their sticker out of you and not only that they've got no stop valve neither, so they just keep swelling with your blood until they blow up, and where we came from this was considered a big laugh. So one of my buddies gets bit by a leech on the forearm and he says, 'Hail, I'll teach him to bite a Arkansas boy, I'm gonna give him the mosquito treatment' and he tenses his forearm and we start watching, but not only is this a leech it's apparently one of them cow leeches, it's got about ten million times the capacity of a mosquito and so it starts like a tiny little twig but just keeps getting bigger and bigger and bigger till it's like this black watermelon hanging off my

169

buddy's arm. He keeled over in a faint and we squoze the leech to try and get some of his blood transfused back into him before we burned it off, but he was white as a sheet for about a week thereafter. Isn't that funny?"

No reply from George.

We trekked like this for about three days. All the time we were covering the ground that the proposed road would pass through when they built it, something I often pointed out to George, but he appeared unmoved by the prospect. In fact it seemed to me he was getting to think a road there wouldn't be a bad idea.

On the fourth morning he said "Come on, Freds, where is this place?"

"We're almost there. Couple days. But first we have to go cross-country around Chhule."

"What? Why?"

"That's where the Nepali Army outpost is. This is as far north as trekkers are allowed to go, you know, it's that zone they agreed on with the Chinese? The detrekkerized zone, twenty kilometers or some such."

"Ah. They're serious about that, aren't they."

"You bet. They've got a whole battalion based in Chhule, a hundred soldiers or so, all to keep anyone but locals from going any further north."

"But what about this road you're worried about?"

"They plan to build it right to Chhule. That's close enough to Shambhala that it would be fatal to the valley."

"Good."

"What?"

"I mean, good that we're close."

"Yeah, we're almost there."

Which was almost true. The fact was, leaving the trail to bypass Chhule meant going cross-country, and there is nothing harder than hiking cross-country in the forests of the Himal. Wet, vertical, densely covered with leech-infested foliage—it's horrible hard work, in country usually

170

left to the yetis, who make good use of it. But there was a kind of ledge high above the town that could be used as a path if you could find it—people from Shambhala had used it since the time Chhule was founded, but they did their best to leave no trace of their passing, so it was tough locating it in the cloud mist. Late in the afternoon we hacked our way to it, and we even found a nearly horizontal spot for our night's camp.

George, however, could not be convinced either that this was a viable campsite, or that we were on the path to Shambhala.

"What did you think?" says I. "Did you think it was gonna be easy to get to Shambhala? There ain't gonna be no superhighways to it. In fact we've seen the last of the trail. The whole rest of the way is cross-country."

This was true, but once past Chhule we could descend back onto the valley floor. Once there we hiked immediately into the shelter of an enormous rhododendron forest, one that filled a good two miles of the valley. Because the monsoon had hit so early this year the whole forest was still in bloom, every tree an explosion of rich pink or white or lavender flowers, each flower big and bright and water-jeweled. We walked under a roof of millions of these wonders, with mist trailing between the gnarled black branches, and it was so strange and exquisite that even George shut up, and hiked along with his mouth hanging open.

Beyond the rhododendron forest we got into the weird tropical-arctic scrub that covers Himalayan valleys in the zone between about fourteen and seventeen thousand feet. This is God's own country if you ask me, mountain meadows covered with heather, spiky mosses, lichen, little shrubs, and alpine and tundra flowers. The valley here was clearly U-shaped, a glacial thing with steep granite walls, and we crawled up it like ants at the bottom of an empty swimming pool. The valley floor had silvery watertracks snaking all over it, and as we hiked beside these glacial streams we could hear rocks clunking along the bottom, re-routing the streams even as we watched. And towering over the valley to each side were the snowy vertical peaks of the Himal crest, although on that trek we never saw them much because of the clouds.

We were nearing the border between Nepal and Tibet. The general trend of the range is east to west, but there are innumerable spur ranges, all twisted and contorted as you'd only expect when one continent is crashing under an-other at high speed. The political border tries to follow the crest of the range, but in some areas there's a knot of cross-ing ridges and it isn't at all clear what the "crest" is. In those areas the border gets kinky, and it's right in one of those kinks, where twenty-thousand-foot ridges jam into each other and push some peaks to twenty-five, that the high valley of Shambhala is located.

Still some miles to the south of this, George and I came to a Y-split in our valley, offering routes to west and north. The right fork was a long gradual rise to a pass that had served for centuries as a major trading route between Nepal and Tibet. It was this pass, Nangpa La, that explained the Army post in Chhule—their job was to shut it down.

The left fork was blocked by a mean wall, which we climbed, and above that was a long high skinny valley, with a glacier still filling its bottom. We followed the glacier up into a horseshoe ring of spiky peaks. This horseshoe wall was Shambhala's final protection from accidental visitors, and as we hiked to the head of the glacier, looking down at the rubble and melt ponds and blue seracs, and then up at the great curving wall of shattered stone, George said "Hell, Freds, you sure you aren't lost?"

The truth was this was just the spot where I always did get lost. I knew which low spot in the horseshoe ring was our pass, but crossing the glacier and snowfields to get to its bottom was no easy thing, especially when clouds swept in and filled the cirque with cottonball fog. But eventually I got us there, using an occasional line of yeti prints to guide me. These always take the cleanest line across any broken country, but those yetis will leap over crevasses that humans can only stare at shivering, so following their tracks can be unreliable.

At the foot of the wall we had to make camp, in a devil's golf course rock garden. And next morning it was snowing hard, miserable conditions for a nineteen-thousand-foot pass, but there was no advantage to waiting as it might snow for the next two months, so we put on crampons and started up. Soon we were so high there wasn't even any lichen. Every once in a while we saw prints in the snow, of people, and yetis, and snow leopards, and higher yet there were some unobtrusive trail ducks. And midafternoon, to George's surprise, the clouds blew away. You see the Nepal side of the crest catches the monsoon and gets a few hundred inches of rain a year, but just twenty miles north in Tibet they are in total rain shadow desert and get about zero. So on the crest itself there are all kinds of microenvironments where the amount of rain is somewhere between the extremes, and much more livable than either. Shambhala's valley had just about the best climate possible for the area, one reason it was located there in the first place I'm sure.

Anyway we had climbed into the clear, in brilliant cold windy sunshine above a cloud ocean, shadows black as night and each rock sticking out of the wind-slabbed snow just as distinct as if you were holding a microscope to it. We were no more than five hundred feet below our saddle, and now a faint line of footprints was clear, individual prints displaying huge big toes. "Look," I said. "Yeti prints."

"Come on, Freds. I don't believe in that stuff."

"George, you yourself saved a yeti in Kathmandu! You dressed him! You introduced him to Jimmy Carter! You gave him your Dodgers cap!"

"Yeah, yeah." He appeared to disbelieve that particular memory. "But what would a yeti be doing up here?"

"What would a human be doing up here hiking barefoot?"

No reply from George.

We followed the footprints, which disdained switchbacks and headed straight for the pass. The air was thin indeed and it took a while to slog up the last section, but there in the pass was a line of chortens and mani walls and prayer flags strung between poles all ripped to rags by the constant wind, and it was a sight to lift you right up to it, it made the last section like an escalator.

We could only stand to stay in the pass a few minutes, as the wind was brutal. Around us all the ridges banged together, cutting off our view of Tibet to the north, and in fact restricting our views in every direction. High on the wind came a brief squeal, and I pointed out to George what looked like a patch of moving snow. A snow leopard, helping to guard the sacred valley. But George didn't believe his sight any more than his memory.

Then we started our descent into a narrow valley, a fairly high one although since we had an airplane's view it didn't seem high at that moment. On the valley floor was the usual gravel spill of meandering streams, cutting through tiny bits of green and yellow terracing. Above those were abandoned yak herders' huts, some bare brown potato fields, some stone-walled pastures, and a few chortens. Farther downvalley, perched on an ancient butt moraine, was a gathering of stone buildings, all the slate roofs smoking in the midday sun. The buildings were surrounded by nomads' tents. In short, it was a completely ordinary Himalayan mountain village, with nothing to distinguish it except perhaps what looked like the ruins of an old monastery, built into a rocky ridge of the valley's side wall in *dzong* fortress style.

Feeling my heart flapping happily with the prayer flags

174

behind us, I extended a hand. "There it is," says I to George. "There's Shambhala, there's the palace of Kalapa, there's the Lotus Kingdom! Yahoo!"

He gave me a long, long stare.

●●●

Well, I suppose he was expecting the Disneyland castle or a bunch of crystal houses floating ten feet off the ground, but that ain't the way it is. There was nothing to be done but let him get used to it, so I took off down the trail and he followed.

Before long Colonel John jumped us from behind some boulders, screaming "Halt!" at the top of his lungs. George like to died he was so startled.

Standing there before us was a compact wiry Westerner with a wizened lopsided face, wearing camouflage combat fatigues and toting a big old machine gun which he had pointed straight at us.

"It's okay!" I said to both of them. "It's me, Colonel. Me and a good friend."

He stared at us with birdlike intensity. His face was strange, wrinkled like the face of an old monk who had spent too many years at high altitude in the sun—or, given the fatigues, as if he had been fighting a mountain war for twenty or thirty years. A big scarred crease in the left side of his head reinforced the latter notion, as did the 1950s military-style butch haircut. But then the turquoise and coral necklaces and charm boxes hanging over his fatigues brought back the monk image, as did his eyes, which had a little Asian in them. All in all it was as if an old Tibetan monk and a retired Marine drill sergeant had been melted together into a single body. Which was more or less the case.

"George," says I carefully, "this is Colonel John Harris, late of the CIA and the U.S. Marine Corps. He helps valley security these days."

"I *am* valley security," the colonel snapped in a high Midwestern twang.

"Okay, well, this is George Fergusson, Colonel. He's here to help us with the problem of that road extension to Chhule."

"Prove it," the colonel snapped.

"Well," I says, at a loss. Then I switched to Tibetan, speaking it slowly and clearly, as the colonel is one of the few people on earth to speak Tibetan worse than I. I chanted a brief prayer to the Köngchog Sum, the Three Precious Ones. *"Sannggyela kyabsu chio,"* I said, meaning "I seek refuge in the Buddha."

"Ah!" the colonel said, and let his gun hang from its shoulder strap. He put his hands together and gave us a novice monk's bow. "Honored by your presence," he said in Tibetan. *"Gendunla kyabsu chio,"* which means, "I take refuge in the monkhood." Which was very true for John.

"We're off to the valley," I told him, sticking to Tibetan. "Are you coming down tonight?"

"Standing watch," he said. He frowned, said in English, "Down tomorrow at oh eight hundred!"

"See you for breakfast, then," I said, and hustled down the trail with George close on my heels.

"Who the hell is *he*?" George asked me when we were out of earshot.

"Well, Shambhala picks up people from all over the world, you know. If they stumble across the valley and have the right spirit for it, they stay. If they don't have the right spirit they never even recognize it, you'd be surprised how many trekkers come over the pass by accident and just figure they've run across another remote village and leave."

No reply from George.

Finally he says, "So when did this Colonel John arrive?"

"He was in the CIA when they helped the Tibetan resistance fight the Chinese, back in the sixties. You know about that?"

"No."

"They kept it real secret. John spent a few years in Mustang with a guerrilla group. So he must have gotten here sometime in the early seventies. Now he's a monk, and also kind of like Shambhala's defense department."

"Defense department," George said.

We dropped like an avalanche to the valley floor, and got there just after sunset with our knees throbbing. I led George straight to the house of Kunga Norbu's family, and as I walked down the narrow stone streets between the familiar three-story buildings I was breathing in the smells of milktea and smoke and wet yak wool and they went like a knife right to my memory's heart, and I laughed and started yelling hi to the people we passed. A light snow twinkled in the air like mica chips, and I found myself dancing a spinning dance down the street, drunk with homecoming.

Kunga Norbu's oldest sister Lhamo greeted us at their door with a big smile and brought us upstairs to the kitchen and sat us down on a broad bench against one blanketed wall and commenced feeding us. Most of the family crowded in to look at George and talk to me—Kunga Norbu's ancient mother, his younger sisters and their families, some more distant relations they had taken in, and relations of relations until we were jammed in tight. I sat there warming my feet by the fire trying to collect my Tibetan to talk to them. Lhamo fed us a feast, tsampa and butter tea of course but also yak cheese, margam butter, a dried cream called *pumar*, and a kind of cheesecake they call *thud*, maybe for the sound it makes when it bottoms out in your stomach. All the familiar tastes and faces and the smell of the yak dung fire had me purring, and happily I tried to tell them about our trip.

George of course was silent throughout all this, and he avoided his butter tea, and ate as little of his food as he could get away with. Even that amount meant his prophylactic diet was wiped out and it seemed to me he was brooding on this, listening to his digestion and perhaps adding up in his mind the quantity of antibiotics he had brought along. He glanced around the room, at the carpets and sashes and the bowls and pots of bright dented copper and the black iron steamer and the hanging utensils and the brazier and the tall butter churns and the *nyindrog* boxes and the loom in the corner, and he looked tired and low, as if this wasn't at all what he had expected. A crowded smoky little wood and brick room, I reckon he saw, and he was let down by that.

• • •

Well, I suppose Himalayan Buddhist village life isn't the kind to reveal all its beauties right off the bat anyway, especially in the monsoon, although as I said Shambhala's valley is protected from the worst of the weather. Still, it rained or snowed an hour or two almost every day. And ever since the Chinese invaded Tibet Shambhala has suffered from overpopulation, serving as it does as a sort of secret advance refugee camp. That's why the big mountain nomads' yak wool tents surrounded the village, and why all the old stone houses and Kalapa monastery were so full of people. The crowding caused problems, and things were not in great shape to impress George. Lhamo tried, putting us in the best bedroom in the house above the kitchen where it was warmest, but George kept having nightmares that the house was burning down because smoke from the kitchen stove seeped up into our room and made it smell like the house was burning down. So every morning he stumbled out of the house sleepless and exhausted, and there before him was a strangely packed mountain village, as if it was bazaar day except it wasn't, and sick kids were howling with the flu and the monastery head doctor Dr. Choendrak wandered through the rain wringing his hands, because all the great plant and mineral medicines from Mendzekhang, the hospital monastery in Lhasa, were long since used up.

It didn't help George's impression of things when Kunga Norbu came down to say hello and just stared through George in his usual style, and then assigned us to work with a crew rebuilding terrace walls, which is convict-style labor, including breaking up rocks with a sledgehammer like characters in a cartoon. A day or two of that and George was unhappy. "Goddamn, Freds, I coulda been soaking rays in Thamel and here I am *breaking rocks*. This isn't Shambhala and you know it."

I assured him it was.

"Why is it so crowded then? Every house has two or three times as many people as it should, and then there's all these tents. The Sherpas would never live this way."

I told him about the refugee problem. About people crossing uncrossable passes to escape the Chinese, or crawling up the impassable gorge that dropped out of the valley onto the Tibetan plateau, risking death and often finding it in hopes of getting away.

"So it's emergency conditions," George said, surprised.

"If you can call it that after forty years."

That night George looked around him a little more carefully. And for the first time he noticed that there were people sick right there in the house with us. A cousin of Lhamo's named Sindu had a baby boy who was getting weak with the runs. And this cousin Sindu was a young woman, nearly a girl, with a lot of Nepali blood in her so that her face was sharper than the Tibetans', one of those trans-Himal faces that is so beautiful you can't believe it's real. And no husband to be seen. So George sat there watching her as she moved around the kitchen caring for her sick boy, and I could see him adding up his pills in his mind.

Next day Colonel John drafted us to make a firewood run, which meant rounding up a string of yaks and driving them downvalley all morning, to the upper end of the gorge that snaked down into Tibet. Yaks are big hairy delin-

179

quents, sullen and prone to bursts of rebellion and non-cooperation, and the colonel drove them like they were inductees at boot camp, beating them fiercely with his walking stick and getting nothing but looks from their big round bilious eyes.

Midday we left the yaks on the meadow and climbed the steep south slope of the valley wall until we reached a stand of pine. Colonel John took three small axes out of his backpack, Iron Age things with no heft at all, and we set to work cutting down the trees he pointed to. "Man," George said unhappily as he chopped, "this is horrible! This is what they call deforestation, isn't it?"

The colonel and I paused to give him a look.

"No choice," the colonel said. "Yak dung doesn't burn without some wood in the fire."

"But the erosion—"

"I know about erosion!" the colonel shouted, nearly throwing his axe at George. "We leave the stump and roots to hold what they can, and replant with seedlings." He hacked angrily at the tree he was working on. "Three thousand years this valley had a stable population, but with Tibet enslaved what can the Dalai Lama do? This is one of the only escapes."

George asked hesitantly if some of the refugees couldn't be transferred to the Tibetan villages and settlements in India.

"Who would you send?" the colonel demanded. "Send away from the last free and whole place on earth? Send down to some farm in Madras where they die of low altitude sickness? I've seen them down there, take them to a mountain like we did when we brought the resistance to Colorado and they run right out and jump in the snow! We had a yak from a zoo there and they ran up and hugged it!" He brought a tree down with a fierce chop. "I wouldn't want to choose who goes away from here."

"Tell George about your Khampa guerrillas," I suggested.

John sighed. "Got those fellas to Colorado back in the days when you could count on the American government to fight the communists, and I asked a room full of them, How many of you boys would jump out of an airplane to fight the Chinese, and they didn't know a damn thing about parachutes and every one of them raised his hand. And I said these are my kind of boys. This was what the Marine Corps used to be before it went soft! Came over here and wreaked havoc on those killers! Till Birendra betrayed us!"

With that he attacked another tree, chopping as if he were working on the King of Nepal's knees, and muttering in disconnected phrases that I could see meant little to George. "Soup and coffee out of tin cans, running till their hearts popped!" *Chop chop chop.* "Hans on one side and Gurkhas on the other! Scattered to the twelve winds!" *Chop chop chop.* "Dalai Lama said quit but who could surrender to Birendra! Pachen cut his throat instead and I don't blame him! Should have done it myself!" And he brought the tree down, swinging wildly.

Hoping to distract him, I suggested in Tibetan that we had cut as much wood as the yaks could carry.

"We'll carry too," he snarled at me in English, and kept on cutting like a chain saw.

So it was late afternoon before we dragged back upvalley in a cold rain, loaded down with small pines. I let the colonel get ahead of us so I could answer the questions George was eyeballing me. The colonel and some Khampas, I told him, had continued to fight after King Birendra had buckled to Mao and told the Nepali Army to help the Chinese destroy the Tibetan guerrillas based in Mustang. After this disaster the colonel and some Khampas had worked out of the mountains in Tibet until they were ambushed or something—the colonel remembered it poorly because that was when he was wounded in the head, and he wandered out of his mind in the wilds of Tibet for an unknown time until he came as if homing to roost up the gorge to Shambhala. There Dr. Choendrak had cured him and brought back his memory, at least to a certain extent. "He's still a bit mixed up," I said.

"I noticed that."

"Depending on which language you speak to him he acts completely different."

George looked at the little tree-backed figure driving the yaks ahead of us. "I bet he had his language center damaged, and if he learned most of his Tibetan after the injury, it would have to be stored on the other side of his brain. So depending what language you use with him, a different half of his brain is dominant."

"Here they figure it's a matter of incarnations."

"He thinks he's a Tibetan monk whose spirit was most recently in a Marine?"

"Some of the time."

We climbed the ancient terminal moraine and caught sight of the village above us. A shaft of sunlight cut through the clouds and lit the walls of stone and sod, the slate-roofed buildings all smoking, the yaks standing like furry black boulders here and there in the brown potato fields, and it looked like the Middle Ages on some colder planet. We had spent all day gathering wood that would barely keep the village through the night, and every day folks had to go out and do the same, farther and farther away each time. "Man," George said, dropping his trees on the stone-flagged stable yard outside Lhamo's place. He didn't know what else to say.

Lhamo had a big meal ready for us, and we were beat and starving, and helplessly George spooned it in. He didn't have to deal with dhal baat, but the soup was crowded with a vegetable they managed to grow in the lower valley, a vegetable I'd never caught the name of but which on the vine looked like an okra the size of a football, with long flexible tines growing out all over it. Chopped up and floating in the soup it was unappealing to the eye, though the texture was okay and it had little taste. As a side dish they had a curry so hot you could warm your hands by it, and after a couple tries at that George returned sweating to his soup and even tried drinking his butter tea, which is an acquired taste and seemed to give him some trouble. It was the Scylla and Charybdis of foodland for George, but bravely he swam on and finished the meal.

And so of necessity he abandoned his prophylactic eating. At the same time he watched cousin Sindu trying to feed her sick child that night, with little success. And in the morning he dug in his backpack and came up with his anti-biotics, a five-gallon Ziploc bag jam-packed with pills. "Freds, we gotta help these folks," he says. "I don't really have enough here to help everybody, but if we just help a few of them, you know."

"We'll have to tell Dr. Choendrak about it," I told him. So we took the antibiotics to the monastery and George told Dr. Choendrak about them, and he examined the pills and went into a consultation with the Manjushri Rimpoche, the leader of Shambhala, and the Rimpoche decided that every sick child would get an equal share of the pills, which when they figured it out came to about four pills per kid. When George heard that he cried "No! That's too little to do any good, none of them'll be helped by that!"

Dr. Choendrak explained to him that they knew about that aspect of antibiotics, but they figured that in conjunction with the plant medicines they were able to grow it would go better, and it was important to make sure everyone sick got some of the Western medicine.

George was disgusted, but I tried to reassure him. "They're going on the placebo theory, George, and you can't be at all sure they aren't right. Those antibiotics are mostly placebo anyway."

He just gave me that squint.

So all his antibiotics were gone, and he was eating the

183

valley's food, which was clean but certainly had different bugs in it than he was used to. And so he got sick. The usual thing—runs, fever, no appetite, generally feeling shitty. Also bored, fractious, and depressed. Three or four days of that and he was going crazy in the house, so I suggested he go with Lhamo and Sindu to the river to wash clothes.

Now I've been concentrating on the problems Shambhala was having and they were considerable, but still it was Shambhala, mystic capital of the world, and there were some special things about it aside from Kalapa monastery and the lamas and the history of the place. Up in the courtyard of the monastery, for instance, was an eternal holy flame shooting out of the side of the mountain, a strange and impressive sight at dawn or dusk, or in the middle of a ceremony. And down at the bottom of the valley, near the gorge, one whole bank of the river was pure turquoise, sticking out of the mountainside like a hill of solidified sky, littering the river downstream with blue pebbles and boulders.

And most important of all for daily life there, the valley's river began with a hot springs, which like the eternal flame poured out of solid rock mountainside. The hole the water came out of had been carved into a perfect circle, and as it emerged the water steamed and kept the whole area damp, so that brilliant green ferns and mosses grew all over. Chortens and mani stones and prayer flags stood around it, and prayer wheels spun in the stream, wood and tin cylinders painted with bright mandalas, squeaking as they milled out prayers. Moss had covered all the curvy Sanskrit lettering carved into the mani stones and the rockface, so that it always seemed to me like the moss itself was spelling out *Om mani padme hum.* All in all, a spacy place.

They used it for their laundry, by diverting some of the water down a carved runnel which fell into a shallow pool that had a stone-flagged bottom and squared-off sides. Here on sunny mornings people washed clothes, mostly women, though monks and other men often joined them. The women came in their long wraparound black dresses with colorful smock fronts, babies wrapped to their backs or let loose to wander around. The air would be steamy and the sun radiant on your skin, but it was cold in the shadows so the warm water was a blessing. The women wore their black hair pulled back smooth and flat. They mostly had the flat faces of Tibetans, but there were touches of India and elsewhere in women like Sindu, because this was a cross-roads even if it was hidden. Bare brown feet in the water, dresses hitched up around the thighs revealing brown calves harder than baseball bats, smell of milktea and smoke and herb soap rising from the wet clothes as they wrung them out steaming and beat them against the flat smooth black stone flagging to each side of the pool—yes, the laundry pool was a fine place.

And George appeared to like it. At least he came back from mornings there a little less disgruntled. He took to walking there with cousin Sindu and her little boy, and he looked after the kid while she washed, which was easy work as the kid was still sick. And she would talk to the kid in Tibetan and George would nod, saying "Uh huh, yeah, that's exactly what I think," which made her and the other women laugh.

I had asked Lhamo about Sindu, and found out that her husband was alive, off to the west of Nepal on a trading expedition. This kind of thing happens a lot in the trans-Himal villages, and as a result marriages up there tend to have quite a bit of flex in them. So when I saw George fool-ing with the kid, and Sindu laughing at him, I thought, Ho boy. Look at this.

It was odd to watch them together. Sometimes they seemed to understand one another perfectly and to be quite a match—an attractive couple, laughing at something they had seen, and I would think What do you know George has

185

got him a Sherpani girlfriend. His *dakini,* one of the female deities who guide you to wisdom, perhaps. Then just seconds later, for no reason I could pin, there would seem to open a gap between them bigger even than language. Suddenly they would look like creatures from different planets, aliens trying out gestures to see if they would work. But even those moments didn't look awkward—if there was a gap, neither of them seemed especially worried about bridging it. They looked content to stand on opposite banks and wave at each other.

So that was cute to watch, and Lhamo and I and the other gals at the pool got quite a laugh out of it. But meanwhile George was still sick, and so were the kids. He might as well have tossed his pills in the river for all the good they appeared to have done. He himself got thinner and thinner, and I know most nights he had to rush out and stumble around in the dark outhouse, freezing outside and burning inside, crouching over the little hole in the floor. It's amazing what you can get used to, I've gone through times like that myself and know that you can get so used to it that you can do the whole operation almost in your sleep, navigating medieval buildings and doors and locks without ever even waking up—sometimes—while other nights are so uncomfortable and strange that they etch themselves on your mind, and you hang out there in the freezing dark feeling it is some sort of negative *bodhi* and that you are far from home. I'm sure that George suffered more than one night like that.

And the kids bawled, and lay in their beds looking dry-skinned and hot and listless, and shitting watery shit. "Damn it," George said, "diarrhea is serious for little tykes like these, they get so dehydrated they die."

In fact Sindu's boy didn't look good, and a lot of infants in the village were the same. Such a crowded place! Several times folks dropped by to ask George if he had any antibiotics left, and all he could do was throw up his hands. "All gone! All gone! Freds, tell them I'm sorry, all I've got now is Lomotil but that just blocks you up, I shouldn't give them that should I?"

I didn't think he should.

Then he got an inspiration. "Freds, what about that formula you're supposed to give kids with diarrhea, the one the UN wants to spread all over the third world, it's made of simple stuff that everyone has, and it prevents the dehydration. Come on, man, what is it?"

"Never heard of it," I told him.

This drove him crazy. "It's something really obvious." But he couldn't think of it.

Then one morning swirling a glass of milktea he says, "Wasn't it basically salt water? Salt water with maybe a little sugar in it?"

"I thought you weren't supposed to drink salt water?"

"Normally no, but when you've got the runs it helps get the water into your cells."

"I thought that's just what it prevented."

"Normally yes, but in this case no."

"Are you sure enough to try it?"

Long silence. Finally he said "Damn, I wish I had more tetracycline."

But in the days that followed Sindu's son got weaker and weaker, and a lot of the rest of the kids did too. George decided he had the formula right, and he got me to take him to the monastery to see Dr. Choendrak.

In Kalapa's big courtyard George stood staring at the eternal flame, his mouth hanging open. "Just what the hell is that?" he says.

"That is the holy eternal Kalacakra flame," I told him. "Religious shrine since the earliest times here."

"It's gas, Freds. They've got a natural gas supply right here in the valley!"

"So they do."

"Well—" He seized his head in both hands to keep it

from blowing up on him. "Why don't they use it? They've got deforestation, they could pipe this gas down into stoves and solve the problem!"

"I guess since it's a holy shrine and a sign from one of their deities it never occurred to them," I said.

George couldn't believe it. "Here they are cutting down all their trees and watching their soil wash away and this big fucking fire is burning right in their face! What are you all *thinking* here, Freds? What kind of paradise is this anyway?"

"Religious."

"My Lord."

Then Dr. Choendrak joined us, and George got me to act as translator. "There's a lot of flu in the kids here," he told the doctor.

I repeated that to Dr. Choendrak and he nodded. "Their blood has mixed with their bile, and we need to separate it."

"He knows," I said to George.

"Ask him what he's doing about it."

Dr. Choendrak shook his head. They were making medicines as fast as they could, medicines made of plants that I couldn't translate for George.

"Ask him if there are any salts in the medicine."

The doctor said there were.

"How much?" George demanded.

Eventually Dr. Choendrak had to take us to the dispensary and show him. Turned out there was a good heaping tablespoon of pure ground-up Tibetan rock salt in every canister of the water the doctor was feeding the kids.

"Oh," George said, nodding. "Well, tell him he should add a little sugar too."

I translated that for the doctor and he nodded. Turned out they put in about a tablespoon of honey as well.

"Oh!" George said, nonplussed. "Well! Good for him! Tell him the World Health Organization recommends that very same thing!"

Dr. Choendrak nodded, and said that was good.

Suddenly the doctor seemed a really reasonable guy to George. "Maybe their drugs do have some antibacterial action, and the salt and sugar water will give more time for their immune systems to kick in. The little kids need that."

Before we left George made me tell Dr. Choendrak about his plan for the eternal flame—he described ceramic pipes, a big central stove in the village or in the monastery itself, a whole seat-of-the-pants exercise in civil engineering. And in the days after that he started accompanying Dr. Choendrak on his rounds, entertaining the kids while they were checked out, or holding them while the more bitter medicines were administered. And he made all of them drink lots of the water that had generous doses of salt and sugar in it. A sort of language of action grew between him and the doctor, and they got to be buddies even though they didn't understand a word the other said. In fact given the state of their medical theories, that was probably a help.

And in the next couple of weeks the flu epidemic waned, for what reason no one could say—but no one had died of it, and so everyone was happy with Dr. Choendrak and with the appropriate deities, and with George as well. George was real happy too, although his own digestion never did get quite right and he was prone to going cross-eyed and running off in a panic to the outhouse.

• • •

But after that he was friendlier to the monks, which was important, as they were everywhere in the valley. Climb up a slope for firewood and look back down on the browns and grays and the greens of the *chingko* barley terraces, and there would be these maroon dots jumping out all over the landscape. Monks.

They fit into the society in the same sort of way—you saw them everywhere, but couldn't be sure what they were doing. Not exactly authority figures, nor the holier-than-thou types that our preachers tend to be, men who can strike dead any conversation on earth just by walking in on it unexpected—no, here the monks and the smaller group of nuns were woven into things, out in the fields hoeing, stacking yak dung after it had been laid out to dry in the sun, laughing at rude jokes. It was hard for George or any Westerner to understand, coming as we do from a place where religion is mostly ignored or used as a cover for theft. That's why so many were so quick to believe the lies the Chinese spread about Tibet, that stuff about an evil priesthood taxing poor serfs into poverty—that's how it would have been if the system were ours, in fact it is a pretty good description of TV evangelism now I come to think of it. And it was as convenient as hell for the Chinese, who with us looking the other way could not only torture murder enslave rape imprison and starve the Tibetans, but also tell everyone that of course they were only doing it for the Tibetans' own good. Saving them from themselves.

And being more like the Chinese than the Tibetans, we went for it. After all we did the same to the religious elder culture on "our land" not all that long ago, so we want to believe the Chinese, or at least not think about it. George, traipsing all over the south slope of the Himalaya, digging the unbelievable mountains—of course he didn't care to think about the genocide proceeding on the north slope. It would be like tooling around in the Bavarian Alps in the 1940s, and pausing to wonder about those plumes of smoke on the horizon.

So it took him a while to see it, you bet. A while planting potatoes and fixing terrace walls and hunting firewood, with a monk or a nun in the crowd humping a load or cracking jokes. A while of hearing the chants every day at dawn, or seeing a farmer meditating in his field, or women cutting mani stones, or the kids spinning the prayer wheels with loads of firewood tied to their backs. A while of watching the way everyone pitched in on the communal work without tallying who had done what. A while of figuring out relatives, and discovering every family had monks or nuns, that they were not hereditary but came right out of the farmers every generation, the monasteries hoping to get the best and brightest but also taking the feebs and the handicapped, and naturally getting the oddballs too, the religious space cadets. All those dots of maroon in the brown and green, adding the final touch of color to the scene—when George saw that and understood it, he saw everything new.

And so I said to Kunga Norbu, "Can't you show him some little extra, some bit of Shambhala magic to give him that last shove?"

Kunga Norbu said "Freds, you've got it wrong as usual, we don't do tantric exercises to impress people. But he is welcome to visit the Manjushri Rimpoche in his chambers. And next week the Dalai Lama's youngest sister is making a visit here. He will witness that."

"Right on," says I.

• • •

The very next day, first thing in the morning, I took George to his audience with Sucandra, the Manjushri Rimpoche and the King of Shambhala—the equal, in Tibetan Buddhism, of the Dalai and Panchen Lamas.

We were led out of the yellow morning light through a grove of sandalwood trees and into the dark lower chambers of Kalapa monastery, in amongst thick wood beams black with centuries of stove smoke and butter lamps. Every beam on these floors was covered with festival masks, each a brilliantly colored pop-eyed toothy demon face, heavy on green and red and yellow, with splashes of blue and white and gold. Bönpa nightmares they were, the scariest faces you would ever want to run into. Seeing them it was no mystery to me why the Buddha had been so welcomed in Tibet.

Then it was up stairs for flight after flight, because Kalapa was a *dzong*, a fortress monastery built back in the days when they had to worry about invasion by Genghis Khan or Alexander the Great. So it was plugged into a steep rocky ridge of the valley wall, looking like a squared-off outcropping of the ridge itself. Each level was set back from the one below it, and as we climbed higher on steep well-worn stairs we passed through larger and larger rooms, each with more light pouring into it than the one below. We passed through the library, where thousands of volumes of the *Kalacakra* and the *Tengyur* were set against the wall—short wide thick loose-leaved black-bound volumes, and scrolls in boxes like player piano rolls. Then through a music room, where drums and cymbals and long horns were kept. Then up into the sunniest room yet, where the walls were painted white, and the smooth wood floor had a sand painting mandala at its center. "What's this?" George asked, looking in as we passed by.

"That was Essa's room," I told him.

"Essa?"

"Jesus, you know."

No reply from George.

Finally we were led into what appeared to be the highest room in Kalapa. Its walls were hung with carpets that showed the history of Tibetan Buddhism in bright mandala patterns. Other than that the room was empty. The south wall was made of big sliding panel shutters, and the monk who had led us up the stairs slid these back to let in cool crisp morning air, and the sound of chanting from some floor below.

The monk left, and after a bit another one entered. Then I saw the new monk's face, and realized it was Sucandra, the Manjushri Rimpoche.

I had never seen him before, but I knew. I wish I could explain how. He was a reincarnate, a tulku like Kunga Norbu, only infinitely more powerful—he was the reincarnation of Padma Sambhava, the Indian yogi who brought

Buddhism to Tibet in the eighth century, and he was also the Manjushri Bodhisattva, the bodhisattva of wisdom, meaning he had worked right to the edge of nirvana but had then chosen to return to subsequent incarnations in human form, just to help other people along the way.

This time around he looked much like any other monk. Old, head shaved, face wrinkled into that map of wrinkles that old Himalayan faces take on. But the look in his eye—that calm and friendly smile! Out of his presence it's hard to put my finger on what it was, but with him in the room there was no doubt of it—a feeling flowed out of him into us, both sharp and soothing. Invigorating—as if the chill sunny morning air had been suddenly turned into a state of being.

He asked us to sit, in English that had a strong Brit accent. He sounded like our buddy Trevor's grandpa. We sat and he brought over a tea tray, and poured us some hot tea, no yak butter in it.

We drank the tea and talked. He asked us about our lives in Nepal, and back in the States, and had us tell him the story of our climb with Kunga Norbu up Chomolungma, which gave him a lot of laughs. "The Diamond Path is hard," he said. "Climbing the Mother Goddess! Still, it's better than getting beat in the head with a shoe." He laughed. "I would like to make that climb myself."

I could see George was trying to decide whether to tell the Rimpoche that the Mother Goddess had actually been K2 all along—there was something in the Rimpoche's face that made you immediately want to spill the beans, about anything at all. So I quick changed the subject. "George here is going to help us try to stop the construction of the road to Chhule," I said.

The Rimpoche looked closely at George. The attention he brought to bear on you was intense, but so suffused with friendliness that you couldn't help but be warmed by it. And his voice was so relaxed. "That would help us," he said. "For a long time we lived at the end of the earth, but the world has grown until the danger of being discovered and overrun is very real."

"In a way it's already happened, hasn't it?" George said. He gestured out the window, down at the village and its skirt of refugee tents.

The Rimpoche nodded. "In a way. But we couldn't hide from our people when they were in need, in danger of their lives. And when the time comes they or their children or their children's children will return to their real homes. But to be discovered by the world at large—to be connected by road to Kathmandu, and its airport. . . ." He cocked his head and looked at George. "Do you want to help us?"

"I'm not sure I can do anything."

"This is not what I asked."

"Well. . . ." George struggled, looked away. Finally he met the Rimpoche's patient gaze. "Yes. I do."

"Gotcha!" I exclaimed, and they both laughed at me.

After that they talked of other things. I went through the open wall onto a narrow balcony to look down at the village, smoking away in the morning sun. Inside George and the Rimpoche laughed at something George had said. "The Chinese are a test," the Rimpoche exclaimed in response. "We have to love them too."

"Freds says they're going to be reincarnated as leeches," George said.

And they laughed and talked some more. I went back inside and joined them. At one point the Rimpoche leaned over to refill our teacups, moving like a dancer miming the filling of teacups. They had been talking about the road again, and he murmured as if to himself. "The pure is powerless in the face of the impure. Only the sacred vanquishes it."

Quiet minutes, sipping tea in the sunlight—that's how you spend time with a bodhisattva, and while you're doing it, you understand why.

Afterwards, on our way back down, George was silent. Once outside the monastery he said, "You know, I asked him how old he was."

"You did?"

"Yeah, weren't you curious? He's a hundred and twenty, Freds. A hundred and twenty years old."

"That's pretty old."

"He says he's gonna die in three years. He says that if he's reincarnated in Tibet as they usually are, the next incarnation is sure to be a strange one."

"He should aim himself somewhere else."

"I suggested the same thing myself, but he told me it's not easy to do. The Bardo is a dark and dangerous place. He told me that once back in the forties, a lama tried to reincarnate himself as the King of England—"

"Prince Charles? So that's the explanation."

"No, no. He missed. Got lost. The Rimpoche thinks he may have been reborn as Colonel John. That's why the colonel came to Tibet, and got so wrapped up in the resistance, and why he's so confused now about his past."

"That would explain it."

"True. Although I still think it's a case of learning a new language after damage to the speech center of the brain."

"Did you tell the Rimpoche that?"

"No. But I wish I had."

• • •

And then the next afternoon Colonel John appeared leading a string of ponies over the pass, the second pony carrying the youngest sister of the Dalai Lama. Suddenly everyone in the village was rushing out of homes and off the slopes, from upstream and down, all converging on the procession until there was a crush around the ponies and they couldn't move, and everyone crying, the Dalai Lama's sister and all her party crying, Colonel John crying, everyone there calling out her name and the tears running down

195

their faces like monsoon flooding. George and I stood back from the crowd, feeling like we had accidentally stepped in on an intense family scene, a reunion that no one had ever really expected, but never stopped hoping for.

Later we were brought to meet the Dalai Lama's sister, Pema Gyalpo. She spoke excellent English, and looked supremely happy to be there in the valley. She laughed and gave each of us the traditional white scarf of welcome, and a little picture of the Dalai Lama, and we had a big meal and all the locals dressed in their Sunday best and all their jewelry, spreading it out among refugee relatives so everyone had some, and we drank chang and sat around the stoves singing until late in the night. George and I didn't know the songs so we drank chang and provided a bass *auoum* to every tune, singing until we were practically unconscious with it. George kept his portrait of the Dalai Lama in hand, and every once in a while he would look at it and say, "Now I see why the Chinese don't allow tourists to wear Phil Silvers T-shirts in Tibet. Look at that!"

And the next morning we were sitting on the rocks that made a lookout point over the hot spring. Water clattered down the stone chute into the empty laundry pool, and steam rose from it and drifted onto all the ferns and mosses, giving them a coat of fine dew. Downvalley the village was just waking up, gray-brown smoke rising from the roofs out of the shadow of the mountain into the sun where it turned bright gold, and George turned to me and said, "Okay, okay, okay. Let's go see what we can do about that road."

● ● ●

So we returned to Kathmandu, hiking hard for days and then driven by Colonel John, who had a Land Rover stashed with a family in the village at the End of the Road. We dug it out from a tower of yak dung, and he drove us down the Swiss road faster than I would have liked, putting the Land Rover in four-wheel drifts at every hairpin and looking like he would have preferred to ignore the switchbacks entirely and take off straight down the mountainside, using the road as an occasional take-off or landing ramp. He had us down to the old dirt road inside an hour, and then he ignored ponds and mudslides and the sad roadside villages and drove like a suicide until we reached Kathmandu's Ring Road, covering the distance that had taken our bus eighteen hours in just over four, but leaving us just as exhausted if not more.

After the weeks in Shambhala Kathmandu looked like Manhattan, only noisier and more crowded. The taxi horns and bike bells and the heat and rain and mud and all the cars and shops and faces drove us immediately to the Hotel Star, where we collapsed in our rooms, overwhelmed. Colonel John declared he was driving back to The End of the Road that very night and we couldn't dissuade him. "I'll be back soon," he said as he disappeared down the stairs. "You'd better have results by then."

So we were on our own, and after George sat under his dwarf shower and ran through two tanks of hot water and burned a couple bowls of hash he felt better about everything. "Let's go to the Old Vienna and eat like pigs," he suggested. "I'm so sick I don't care anymore, water buff, milk, I'm having it all." So we went to the Old Vienna Inn and had Hungarian goulash and wiener schnitzel and beer and apple strudel and it was so good we almost died, literally for George unfortunately as he spent most of that night on the toilet moaning.

So he started his dive into the public administration of Nepal feeling a little peaked, which couldn't have helped. First day he spent talking to contacts, visiting the Oriental Carpet Shop, where the owner Yongten had gotten word through the Tibetan exile grapevine that we were to be given all aid. Then he found an American friend of ours named Steve, who worked for the Peace Corps. And finally he visited some buddies of his in Central Immigration, who had prospered heavily in the past from baksheesh provided by George's employer. All of them told him about the same thing, which was "good luck." Yongten suggested he start by going to the Department of Public Works and Transport in the public administration building over on Ram Shah Path. "Don't be in hurry," Yongten told him.

George said he wouldn't be, that he had had a lot of experience in Central Immigration getting trek permits and the like.

"Immigration very quick," Yongten told him. "Very efficient."

This paled George a bit, but he was determined, and the next morning he hopped on his Hero Jet and took off into traffic ringing his bell enthusiastically.

He came back that night just before sunset, completely beat. "Starved," he said. "Food."

So we went to K.C.'s and I asked him how it had gone.

He shook his head. "I found the right department, I think. There's a Department of Old Roads and a Department of New Roads, if you can believe that. They're both in Singha Durbar, which is a big place."

I nodded, having seen it before—it was a pile set back from Ram Shah Path by a park and a ceremonial circular driveway, and looked like the Lincoln Memorial with a Hindu temple roof.

"The whole civil administration is there. It took me a while to find the Department of New Roads. It was empty."

"You're kidding."

"No. And then somebody walked by and when I told him what I wanted to find out, he told me that since this road was an extension of an old road it would be the Old Hill Roads office I wanted. 'For new hill roads that are extensions of old hill roads you need Old Hill Roads department and not New Hill Roads department.' So he sent me in that direction. Didn't know where it was exactly. After a while I found it, but it was three by then and they had closed for the day. So I came home."

"Hey," says I, "good progress."

No reply from George.

Next morning he was off first thing, and he got back even later. I asked him how it had gone, trailing him to Valentino's for Chinese food.

He shook his head as he scarfed eggroll. "Old Hill Roads told me that since it's a new road I obviously had to go to New Hill Roads. They acted like I was stupid. They said they only do maintenance and they don't know a thing about extensions."

"You're kidding."

"No. So I went back to New Roads and asked someone else, this time with baksheesh. He told me they don't know anything about this road, that it is a very special road."

"Say it again?"

"You heard me. 'Oh, sir! We are knowing nothing about this road you speak of! It is a very special road!' They recommended I go talk to the Department of Information in the Ministry of Communication."

"Ah ha. Progress."

That night he was in considerable distress again—all the exotic Kathmandu food was disagreeing with him. And the next day he found the inhabitants of the Department of Information knew nothing about our road, not even when primed with baksheesh. They recommended the Department of Roads. Or possibly the office of the National Planning Commission.

Next day the people in the planning commission sent him to the Ministry of the Panchayat, which had a Local Development Department. There he was directed to the Department of Roads.

"We're making progress," I told him. "Now we know where not to go."

He snarled.

The next week he started in again. But he was still sick, and appeared to be getting sicker, so it got harder and harder to put in a full day.

One day someone in the Department of Information told him the road was being paid for by the Chinese, but the King didn't want the Indians to know about it. That got us excited, and only a day or two after that, someone in the Local Development Department told him that one of the ministers in the cabinet had gotten the construction contracts for his family, and so he didn't want anyone to know about it.

A couple of days later a third official in the Department of Old Terai Roads informed him that the road was a secret because it was being paid for by the Indians and the King didn't want the Chinese to know about it.

A few days after that, an informant in the Panchayat took a packet of baksheesh and told him that the Ministry of Finance had gotten both the Chinese and the Indians to pay for it, so they didn't want anyone to know anything at all about the matter so that neither side would find out what he had done.

"That's so likely it's probably not true," our friend Steve told us.

But there was no way to tell for sure. And all the while George was wasting away in those Singha Durbar offices, waiting to be received by one official or another, until one day he came home and I asked him where he had been that day and he said "Don't know."

"What do you mean, don't know? Where did you go?"

"Don't know."

I waved my hand in front of his face. "What's your name, George?"

"Don't know."

I suspected he was starting to burn out, and took him to dinner. Afterwards when he had roused a bit I said "Hey, man, I should go along with you. That way you'll have someone to talk to while you're waiting."

"Freds, you just don't look like an official person."

"Well no more do you! You look like a trekker who died of altitude sickness."

"Hmm," he said, studying a window's reflection of him. "Maybe so."

So we went to Yongten to get more baksheesh, and some haircuts. "Make us look just like we got off the plane," George told him.

"Sure."

"Aid agency types," I said, "with lots of money."

"That will take longer," he said. But he worked away on us with a little set of carpet scissors until he had us looking almost like Young Americans for Freedom.

So I began to accompany George, and we went back to another branch of the Department of Roads, both of us spiffed as aid agency types, and in fact that's what we said we were. The office looked like Central Immigration only bigger, the walls covered by bookcases filled with giant black ledgers which were also stacked on the floor and on the desks in the room, the ledgers collecting dust while the desks were manned by Hindu bureaucrats in bucket caps and worn baggy soft beige suits, doing nothing as far as I could tell but chatting among themselves and glancing at us. Finally one of them gave us an audience, but he denied that the Department of Roads had anything to do with this road we mentioned, new or old, hill or Terai.

That night over dinner I said, "Let's ask the Swiss what they know. Since they built that last extension, they should know who's gonna do the new one."

"Good idea," George said.

The fact that I was the one coming up with ideas struck me as a bad sign. George was looking discouraged, and his intestinal troubles continued to disrupt his nights. And Colonel John had returned to town, and every night when we came home he grilled us about how the day had gone and gave us a tongue-lashing about what miserable progress we were making. George would snap back at him and he would bawl us out, and I would start chanting in Tibetan trying to calm John down, and sometimes he got mellow and joined me and other nights he just got mad and yelled louder at us in English, and occasionally he got confused trying to do both and went into a sort of catatonic fit. Our neighbors in the hotel were displeased with us, and George was getting exhausted.

But we kept at it. Next day we biked south across the Bagmati River into Patan, the old holy city. There the Swiss Volunteers for Development and the Swiss Associations for Technical Assistance had their offices.

After Singha Durbar the Swiss were so efficient we couldn't believe it. It was like talking to aliens. Two of them brought us immediately into a bright shiny white room with prints on the walls and sat us down at a couch before a coffee table and gave us espresso, and they stayed and asked what they could do for us. It was so amazing that George at first forgot what we were there for, but he collected himself and asked about the road extension.

Unfortunately they couldn't tell us much. They had heard of a proposal to extend the road to Chhule, but they didn't consider the area in question to be suitable geologically. They suspected the project might have been taken on by the Chinese. They suggested we try the Ministry of Administration, but they warned us that each government that gave aid to Nepal was a semi-independent power in the country, so the regular Nepali government might not know much. They really weren't sure—in the usual Swiss style they were as unconnected to any other government as they could be, making most of their aid arrangements directly with local businesses.

So they were no great help. And the next day we found no one in the Administration offices wanted to talk to us, no matter the baksheesh.

George threw up his hands and went back to our friend Steve. "Give me a contact," he asked him. "I don't care who it is."

Steve gave him the name of a guy who wrote for the *Nepal Gazette*, the paper that publishes notices of all the official actions of the government. Apparently this guy had been a supporter of B. P. Koirala, the Prime Minister jailed by King Birendra's father back in the sixties. This was a good sign, and indeed when we went into this guy's office in Singha Durbar and George plopped five hundred rupees on his desk and said, "Please let us take you to lunch and ask you some questions, nothing secret, only some information help," the man actually seemed interested, he looked at his watch and said "Well, sir, I am just going to lunch now. If you came along I could try my best to answer your questions, if I am knowing the answer."

So we took him to lunch and he sat there looking at us with some amusement. Little Hindu bureaucrat with a red dot on his forehead and all the rest. His name was Bahadim Shrestha, and he had been born down in the Terai. He had been to Tribhuvan University in Kathmandu, and had chosen to go into public administration. All this was good, because most of the administrators in Singha Durbar were Brahmin or Chetri, born in Kathmandu, and fallen into their jobs through family connections as an easy way to make money without working. Bahadim was outside this crowd, and naturally he disliked it. "Poverty and bad administration are Nepal's two big problems," he told us, "and we will never solve the first until we are solving the second. Every year or two we have foreign administration expert come design for us a new system—organization, promotion, all very much detailed and with points and an absolute end to corruption, and these systems the Palace Secretariat orders us to use and then they are forgotten before anyone understands them." He shook his head gloomily. "It is a veritable museum of systems."

"No lie," George said fervently. "So, if I want to find out who in Singha Durbar is responsible for building a certain road?"

"Oh, sir, it will not be anyone in Singha Durbar at all!"

Bahadim looked shocked at the thought. "That is the government house."

George and I looked at each other.

"You must understand," Bahadim said, rubbing his hands with somewhat ghoulish pleasure. "There are three centers of power in Nepal. Singha Durbar and the Panchayat are one center, foreign aid community is another center, and Palace Secretariat working directly for King Birendra is the third center. It is not determined officially who is responsible for what, but in practice, nothing can be done without the King and his advisors."

"But what about the *government*?" George said, grimacing at the thought of the work we had put in.

Bahadim spread his hands. "The Panchayat government is not important for your interests. As the King says often, in Panchayat system is no danger of one being lost in a labyrinth of democracy. It is the real administration you must be dealing with."

"But that's what we've been trying to do!"

"Yes. Well. You must go to Palace Secretariat, then." He saw the expression on George's face and shrugged. "It is confusing."

"You aren't kidding!" Pretty soon George was going to grab his head to keep it from exploding. "But why, Bahadim? Why is it so confused?"

"Well." Bahadim made diagrams with a finger. "In administration there are eleven ministries and twelve departments, headed by ministers or directors. All have assistant directors, deputy secretaries, assistant secretaries, and gazetted officers. But there is no chain of command. Each person is reporting to any superior he likes. The superiors then give orders to subordinates at any level, without the knowledge of immediate supervisors. This creates problems, and to deal with them many new positions at every level have been created and filled, without the knowledge of the Finance Ministry in most cases. The civil service therefore grew so much that the Finance Ministry refused to disburse funds to the agencies, agreeing however to do so to individual officials. To deal with this a Civil Service Screening Committee was formed, but it became defunct after a time without tangible result. Similarly the importation of Indian experts." Bahadim shrugged. "Responsibility for decisions is therefore difficult to determine."

George put his elbows on the table and held his head. "My Lord. How did it ever get so messed up?"

Bahadim smiled at George's innocence. "It is a long story," he said.

And with that same mordant pleasure he began to explain. He took George all the way back to the Ranas, the family that had run the country for over a hundred years. They held the prime ministership and all the important posts, while keeping the royal family on a leash and siphoning the country's wealth to private accounts in India. Being Hindu they had over time set up a caste system within their own family, so that you could be Rana A, B, or C, depending on whether you married in the family or out, etc. Finally enough Rana Cs got disgusted by the As that they were willing to help kick them out of power, and in 1951 there was a successful revolution that booted the whole family. The King at that time, Tribhuvan, naturally loved this revolution with all his heart as it unleashed him and his family, and he helped to write a new constitution that set up a democratic government based on the Indian Congress Party model.

But then Tribhuvan died and his son Mahendra became King, and Mahendra wanted to run everything himself. He kept trying to take over, and the Congress Party kept resisting him, until in 1960 he got the Army to help him stage a coup and he arrested and jailed Prime Minister B. P. Koirala, and disbanded the Parliament. To make that look less like what it was he started up the no-party Panchayat Raj, a classic rubberstamp government. He also began to use the Ranas as his ministers, the better to keep an eye on them, and so they weaseled back into things, except under the King rather than on top of him. They took up their old ways as quick as they got in, and under them the Palace Secretariat became the real source of power.

Then when Mahendra died in 1972, his son Birendra took over. Now Birendra had been educated at Harvard and had learned a number of modern vices there, and people assumed that he wouldn't be as interested in absolute monarchy as his father, which was true but didn't matter as anything that Birendra wasn't interested in his Rana secretaries grabbed. So it was back to the Ranas, under a King who was nearly useless. "And I am very sorry to say that the disease of corruption is worse than ever," Bahadim said grimly.

George was looking a little desperate. "So what the hell do we *do*?" he asked.

Bahadim shrugged. "Whatever you do must be done in the palace. All the ministers there of any importance hold a durbar every morning."

"What's that?"

Bahadim explained that people who wanted to get the ministers to do anything had to show up at little receptions in the mornings and lay on the baksheesh and flattery as thick as they could. Then something might happen.

George considered. "Well listen, could you try to find out for us which agency is doing this road? They must have published the information in the *Gazette*, didn't they?"

"No, they did not," Bahadim said. But he agreed to look into it for us.

• • •

The very next day he confirmed one of the stories George had been given during his time in Singha Durbar. The Indians were building the road. Definite fact. No doubt about it. And it was being kept strangely hush hush.

So I says, "What's your plan, George? I mean when you get hold of the right person, do you have a plan?"

No reply from George.

But he did take me down to the Human Fit Tailor Shop on New Road, so we could upgrade into two perfectly fitted young-executive-off-the-plane Western suits, which were nearly convincing. And we went to the Palace Secretariat to find out what we could.

The Secretariat was a big new squat white concrete building on the edge of the palace grounds, which was the best thing about it—it was just outside of Thamel, so every day we could walk down the street in our Wall Street pseudosuits with our forged paperwork dodging the cows, and in ten minutes we were there and could dive right in.

But once inside it was much like being in Singha Durbar, except everything was upscale—new offices, new furniture and typewriters, snappy dressers in fresh white jackets. We shuffled from office to office and waited till we had counted every crack in the poorly set concrete walls, only to find out that the functionary we were waiting for was happy to talk about or take our money, but knew nothing and didn't know who did.

And every night Colonel John gave us hell. And George continued to suffer from the runs. It all was beginning to get to him—one day we staggered out into the rain and George looked up into the tall pines in the palace grounds, and he saw the flock of enormous bats hanging head down from the branches and said, "That's them! That's where they go when they get out of the office! Hey!" He yelled at them. "Where the fuck is the office responsible for the road, you vampires!"

People stared at us. The bats didn't stir.

"George," I said, "you got to remember that these people are under pressure to be corrupt. They aren't paid much, and this city is expensive. And they get into an office, and everyone there is on the take and they're given some of the group take, and what can they do? There's hardly any way to avoid it."

"Don't give me that Buddhist mellow trip," George snarled. "They're crooks, and Colonel John is right, there are times when you've just got to kick some ass! If they're not vampire bats, they're vultures. I just wish one would land on me so I could wring his fucking neck for everything he knows."

The next day he got his wish, almost. A secretary in the National Development Council, Foreign Aid Office, India Branch, took one look at George and his eyes lit up. George smiled and explained that we were from the William T. Sloane Foundation for International Development of Houston, Texas, and laid some baksheesh on the table and asked after the road project. Oh of course, the secretary said, nodding. Naturally we would want to speak directly to the deputy minister, Mr. A.S.J.B. Rana, who spoke with visitors and interested parties every morning in the south patio of the Palace Secretariat.

"Rana," says I to George as we left. "That's *the* Ranas, you know. All the real Ranas have the same last four names, that S.J.B.R. stuff."

"I didn't know. But that's good, very good. Getting into the power structure at last."

So we dropped by A.S.J.B. Rana's durbar next morning. Again we were the subject of great interest, and George went at it in his usual style, explaining who we were and looking like money was weighing him down like millstones he wanted to get rid of. A. Rana, a slick character in the usual white jacket, allowed he was interested, and would let us have an audience later in the day.

So we met with him, presented him with a token of the Foundation's appreciation, and George laid his rap on him. Foundation grant, road construction in Nepal, feasibility study of current projects. Questions we wanted to ask about the extension to Chhule. A. Rana was accommodating, and told us he would look into it and we should come back later, putting his eye on the Foundation gift as he said this.

So we came back later.

I didn't always accompany George, but he started going every day. And A.S.J.B.R. seemed more interested every time, asking all sorts of questions about the Foundation and asking outright for money help for his department, and from time to time dropping a tidbit of information, confirming that the Indians were building the road, or giving us figures about the cost, or sending us to one of his colleagues, who also asked for money.

But as he saw he could string George along he got a bit suspicious, and then high-handed. One time we attended a durbar where the group spoke in Nepalese the whole time, and A. Rana laughed and glanced at us or away from us, until it became obvious we were the object of his jokes. And he wanted us to understand that. That made me think that he knew we were bogus, and was just milking us for cash and entertainment value. But George thought we should continue to try.

Then another time George was there alone and another minister came in shouting angrily at A. Rana, and Rana pointed at George and said loudly It's this American's fault, he insists on pestering me! Oh, the other minister said. So this is the one. And they stared at George, giving him the strong feeling that he was well known in the Secretariat. "You know I think we're being set up as scapegoat for something A. Rana is doing on the side," George growled when he told me about it.

But that was nothing compared to the following day. Apparently A. Rana had passed by George on his way out and they had bumped legs, and before he could stop himself Rana had snapped "Don't touch me!" looking disgusted. George didn't get it. I explained to him that as foreigners we were technically untouchable. Our touch was unclean.

"Ah come on," George said, face darkening.

"That's what some Hindus think."

George scowled. And the next time I went with him, I noticed that after checking to see if A.S.J.B.R. were watching from his inner office, he was slipping a hand into the outer office's desk and snatching stationery and the like. One time when A. Rana left us alone he even typed on some of it. "We'll see who sets up who," he muttered as he slipped the typed pages into his briefcase.

But meanwhile A. Rana was soaking us for baksheesh, demanding payment for his time and then putting us off again. George had to keep visiting Yongten to get more cash, and Yongten started shaking his head. "Not working," he said.

Colonel John was furious. "The bulldozers are there and they'll be starting construction as soon as the monsoon ends! We've got to get something *done*!"

Really, it was worse than Singha Durbar. A. Rana and his buddies in the Secretariat were entertaining themselves by playing volleyball with George's brains, bump, set, spike, hilarious! and meanwhile he was still suffering from the runs, losing a lot of weight. He was just about to break.

And so one day A. Rana plopped us in his outer office and got busy ostentatiously ignoring us, talking to somebody on the phone in Nepalese and laughing a lot, and then he put down the phone and emerged from his inner sanctum, yawning. He dismissed us with a wave. "I must leave now. Come back later."

I could hear the cables snapping inside George. All of a sudden he was standing in front of A. Rana, blocking him and saying in a real intense voice, "Listen you little tin god, you either give me the records for that road extension or I'll break your fucking neck."

Which of course is exactly what you must never do with a Kathmandu bureaucrat, as George himself well knew—usually he was Mr. Valium with these guys. But as I say, he had snapped.

And A. Rana immediately huffed up like a cobra in a corner, crying out "Do not think you can threaten me sir! Leave this office at once!" and George took a step toward him, threatening to touch him with his forefinger and growling "Who's gonna make me? Gimme those records right now!"

A. Rana picked up his phone and cried "Be gone or I will call the police to eject you!"

"What makes you think they'll come!" George shouted, furious at the idea. "You'd have to bribe them to get them to come! And then they'd have to bribe the people at the door to get in, and where are you all gonna get the money for *that*? Gonna skim another foreign aid project? Gonna rip off another development agency to pay for throwing me out of your office? It'll take you *ten years* to throw me out of this office!" and then I had him by the shoulders, and I kind of lifted him out of there, holding A. Rana away with my foot while they screamed at each other and everyone else came out into the hallways to watch.

Scratch that opening.

• • •

That night George was inconsolable. "I blew it, Freds, I blew it."

"Yes you did."

We smoked several bowls of hash and went to K.C.'s to get over it. Once there George started to down enormous quantities of beer.

Pretty soon he was shitfaced. "I just don't know what to do, Freds. I just don't know what to do."

I nodded. Truth was, my bud was overmatched. I mean what could he do? The people he had taken on were eating up the foreign aid agencies of the entire world, the World Bank, the IMF, all the giant cash cows.

And then Steve came in and joined us and we sat there drinking and Steve told us some of his Peace Corps horror stories, how once the palace had run short on cash when they needed to buy the panchayat elections for their candidates, and so they had gone down to the Terai and cut down a huge swath of hardwood forest and sold the lumber to India to raise the bucks, and then gone to the World Bank and said Oh, sir! Deforestation, what a horrible problem for us, come look! and took them to the piece of the Terai they had just finished wiping out and sure enough the soil was already in Bangladesh and so the World Bank gave them money, and they quick reforested about thirty acres and put an airstrip in the middle of it and pocketed the rest, and after that they took people down to see the great reforestation project every chance they got, and soaked every visitor for money to help finish the task, which money went immediately to tux uniforms for the Army and other less crucial things.

And this was the crowd George was going up against. With limited funds, and no Nepalese. What was he going to do against guys like these?

He was going to get drunk and smash beer cans against his forehead. At least on that night. No mean feat given that the beer cans were from India and still made of tin. "Thass all right, I'm used to it," George said. "Beat my head against a brick wall for a month now, gotta big callus up there." He demonstrated. *Crunch*. I took him home.

We stumbled through Thamel's narrow streets and George stepped in all the puddles as he looked around. "Look, Freds. Look at these poor fuckers, I mean look at them."

Someone said "Hey, Mr. No!"

George shook his head and almost fell over. "I'm Mr. Yes! Mr. Yes! Yes yes yes!"

I waved the curious kids away and helped George walk. He staggered along unsteadily. "Wouldn't it be great if Tibet and Nepal just changed places, Freds? If they had just started on opposite sides of the Himmies? See what I mean?"

"China would have conquered Nepal."

"Thass right! Then they'd be the ones diving into this bu-reaucracy! They could use it for population control! Send people into it and watch them disappear! Pretty soon China'd have only a few people left, and the Ranas could take over Beijing. Have 'em begging for mercy."

"Good idea."

"And meanwhile the Tibetans and the Dalai Lama woulda been on the south side and they could've kept on doing their brother from another planet trip in peace and quiet, and wouldn't it be wonderful, Freds? Wouldn't it?"

"Yes it would, George. You're drunk. You're crying in your beer. Let's get you home and smoke a few bowls and sober you up."

"Good idea."

But Colonel John was back at the Star waiting for us, and he was not amused. He did not approve of our obvious dereliction. That didn't stop us, but whilst we were getting high he paced back and forth in front of us like a mummy drill sergeant, spinning a hand prayer wheel and snapping "What'll we do now? You've spent two thousand rupees and we don't have a thing to show for it! All we got is the most suspicious gang of bureaucrats on earth! What'll we do now?"

George took a huge hit and held it till he turned blue. "Gahhhhhh. Dunno. Dunno! Dunno. I mean what can we do? We got an Indian road, that's all we know. Swiss don't want. Why not? Dunno. Indians building it. Chinese can't be too thrilled, I mean the Indians weren't happy when the Chinese built that Lhasa-to-Kathmandu road. Right? All these roads are nothing but attack corridors far as New Delhi and Beijing are concerned, they're both paranoid about it. I suppose we could try to scare them out of doing it, I dunno. Fake a raid, or something like that—"

The colonel grabbed him by the neck and lifted him bodily. "YES!" he shrieked, and let George fall back to the bed. "YES!" Quivering like he had stuck his toe in an electrical socket.

"Yes what?" George said, massaging his neck.

Colonel John bayonetted him with a finger. "Raid! Raid! Raid!"

"Doesn't work. The little bastards crawl back under the door."

The colonel ignored him. "We dress up some of the Khampas as Chinese, and make a night raid on the Army barracks in Chhule."

"How'll you get Chinese uniforms?" I asked.

"We've got a lot of those," he said darkly. "Just have to sew up the holes." He thought more about it. "We go down into Tibet that same night, and attack the nearest Chinese Army post. Cross over Nangpa La, so it looks to both sides like the attacks came from the other side. Keep Shambhala out of it. Border incident, Chinese complain, Birendra chickens out like in '72, and the road project is stopped for good. YES!" He leaned over to yell in George's face. *"Great plan, soldier!"*

But George had passed out on the bed.

• • •

Next morning he couldn't even remember what the plan was, and when we told it to him he wouldn't believe that it was his idea. "Oh no you don't, Freds. You're doing it to me again, and I don't want any part of it!"

Colonel John was already packing.

"Think about Singha Durbar," I said to George. "Think about Birendra and the Ranas. Think about A. Shumsher Jung Bahadur Rana."

That got to him. He would have growled, but he was too hung over. He crawled to his window and looked out at the rooftops of Thamel.

"All right," he said after a while. "I'll do it. It's a stupid plan, but it's better than *this*—" waving out at all of Kathmandu.

So we got ready to leave again, which for Colonel John meant jumping in the Land Rover and for me meant packing my backpack, but George had a list of Things To Do. First he bought a couple big canisters of kerosene. Then he bought near all the antibiotics in Kathmandu, a search that took him not only into the little drug stores around Thamel but also to the many dealers on the sidewalks, who sat there on cloth spreads next to folks selling candied fruits or incense and yet stocked state-of-the-art drugs because they were supplied by returning climbing expeditions. Among the finds was a load of Tinnidazole, which is a treatment for giardia not approved in the States—you take four giant horse pills of the stuff all at once, and next day all the giardia in you is dead, along with much of the rest of your insides no doubt. George bolted down a dose of this poison himself on the off chance it was giardia he was suffering from, and staggered on through his tasks.

One of these was to drop by our friend Bahadim and confer with him, giving him a notice he had written for the *Nepal Gazette*, along with some letters that looked to me like A.S.J.B. Rana's stationery.

Then after quick visits to drop off more paperwork at the Swiss office and the Palace Secretariat, he was ready. Colonel John drove us up to the farm near the End of the Road, and we hid his Land Rover and took off practically running for three days straight, then around Chhule, through the rhododendron forest with all its flowers now fallen and matted on the ground, and up the high valley, now roaring with monsoon runoff. Then over the glacier and up the ridge into the snows, over the pass and down into Shambhala.

Once down in the sacred valley the colonel told everyone about George's plan. All the Khampas went wild for it, but the Manjushri Rimpoche was not so enthusiastic. "By no means can you harm anyone doing this. That would be an injustice so serious that it would overwhelm any good that could come out of it."

Colonel John was not pleased to hear this, but he agreed to it, sounding just like Eddie Haskell—"Of *course* not, holy Rimpoche, no killing whatsoever. We'll direct our fire against property only."

"We just want to scare them," I explained.

"Yes!" Colonel John said, seizing on the concept. "We only want to *scare them*," and he went away fizzing over with plans to terrify the border posts on both sides so thoroughly that some of them might die of fright, which would be too bad but not our fault, not directly. Not as directly as bullets, anyway.

So with the organizing of the raid he fell back completely into his Marine Corps mode, setting up the two forces and drilling them and making up maps and charts and battle plans. His idea was that the two forces would time their attacks on the border posts in Nepal and Tibet so that they could retreat up into Nangpa La from each direction, meet, and then slip away, leaving any pursuing Chinese and Nepalis to face each other. He thought this was great. Every day he came up with a new twist to add to it. "Okay," he'd say after one of these brainstorms, "we'll come down on Chhule dressed in Chinese Army uniforms, but every fifth man will be wearing one of the monastery's festival demon masks, which'll give the Nepalis a subliminal shock. Consciously they'll think it's the Chinese, but corner-of-the-eye-wise they'll think it's all the demons of Yamantaka coming at them."

George would frown heavily at these ideas. "Don't you think that's overdoing it a bit?" he would suggest. "I mean, it's really important that the Chhule soldiers think that it's the Chinese attacking them. I'm not sure festival demon masks will help support that."

"Of course it will," Colonel John would say, dismissing the objection. "It's their subconscious minds we'll be tampering with. Psychological warfare. I didn't spend ten years in the CIA for nothing, you know. You just leave that part of things to me."

"If there's any Gurkhas stationed there they aren't gonna care what we look like," George warned. "They're gonna come out firing."

"There's no Gurkhas up here!" Colonel John snapped. "They're Nepali Army police, the worst troops on earth." And he stopped telling George his plans.

Eventually all was ready. Two raiding groups were to go out on the same night, one led by Colonel John into Nepal, the other by Kunga Norbu into Tibet. The Manjushri Rimpoche had given us permission to use some of the tunnels in Shambhala's ancient secret tunnel system, so that we could emerge well away from the valley—just up the ridge, in fact, from the saddle of Nangpa La itself.

Now Nangpa La, as I said, was the old salt and wool traders' pass between Tibet and Nepal, exactly the pass that would be used by the Chinese or the Nepalis if an attack were to be made on each other—not that the Nepalis would ever be so stupid as to attack China, but the Chinese were convinced the Indians would use the route, ignoring the existence of Nepal. So it was perfect for our purposes—it fit with our cover story, and there would be nothing to lead any pursuit into the area of Shambhala itself. So we could make our attacks and be back to Nangpa La by dawn, and when we had disappeared, any pursuers could sort it out in mutual extreme paranoia.

"I don't know," George kept saying. "Maybe we should just try the Nepal side. I mean what are they gonna think when they *both* get attacked?"

"They'll both think the other side is lying," the colonel said, "and they'll both have years of good reasons for thinking it."

The only question in the colonel's mind was whether he was leading the right group. His deepest hatred was directed against the Chinese, and it was likely that their Army post would be the more dangerous when attacked. But these were in fact good reasons for staying on the Nepali side, because if he and the Khampas were to get in a firefight with a Chinese platoon, they were liable to go crazy and kill them all. Even the colonel recognized this. The chance to scare the daylights out of the craven Nepalis, on the other hand, sounded both satisfying and safe—as good a revenge as the Manjushri Rimpoche would allow for Birendra's betrayal of the Tibetan resistance back in '72.

So three days after our return, we assembled in the monastery courtyard at noon. Demon masks were distributed, along with a collection of rifles and mortars that looked like they had come out of a museum of the Kashmiri Wars. I was loaded up with a mortar, and George was given a backpack filled with its ammunition, rocks by the feel of it. The colonel told us how to use the thing. Turned out the mortars were in fact antiques, and the Khampas had long ago run out of ammunition for them, so they made their own explosive charges by gutting bullets stolen from the Chinese. Once these charges were in the mortars you then stuffed in yak wool wadding, followed by cannonballs or birdshot or rocks, whatever was at hand and fit the barrels.

The Manjushri Rimpoche came out and gave us his blessing, and Colonel John gave a pep talk. Then the Kalapa *kuden* joined us, looking stunned and about to die as usual, all dressed in his gold ceremonial robes, and suddenly he fell in a seizure and swole up, and they struggled to tie on his helmet which weighed around a hundred pounds and looked like it would keep him floored, and they tightened the strap under his chin till he should have been strangled and then the spirit of Dorje Drakden entered him fully and suddenly he was strutting around the courtyard with his eyes bugged out, hissing in strangled Tibetan that I couldn't understand, swinging a giant wooden sword and taking short rushes hither and yon that forced us to clear the way for him. It was as clear as the nose on your face that Dorje Drakden had possessed him and was snarling at us—a fierce deity, rushing among us under the dark sky and the strange light of the eternal flame, and damned if some of that spirit didn't arc across into every one of us, so that when Dorje pointed his giant sword at the lower entrance to Kalapa we all tore into it.

Down and in we ran, until the walls of Kalapa had run out and the room we were in was made entirely of stone, and we continued down a tunnel that was lit by butter lamps until we clattered down a set of dark stairs into a huge underground cave, walled with gold. This apparently was the Grand Central Station of Shambhala's vast tunnel system. "Whoah," George says. "You didn't tell me about this."

"I didn't know about this," says I. The few points of light coming from butter lamps didn't show us much, but it seemed to me that around twenty tunnel entrances opened out of this golden cave. "Hope we don't have to make our way back alone."

"Don't say that."

We took off along one of the tunnels, following Kunga Norbu and a few Khampas with torches who ran ahead in the dark filling and lighting the butter lamps. The lamps were in niches which held statues of Bönpa demons or Bodhisattvas, so that we were either shrieked at or cheered on as we passed. There were occasional splits in the tunnel, and usually we turned right, but not always. We moved along at a jog, uphill most of the time, even stairs in some places, so it got to be hard work. Except for puddles and little drip waterfalls and the lamp niches the tunnels were nearly featureless, so that it was impossible to tell how far we were going. But it must have been several miles over and about four thousand feet up, because that's how far away Nangpa La was.

Then we stopped all bunched up together while the leaders opened a door made of stone, and we stepped out under billowing monsoon night clouds, on a steep ridge some three hundred yards above Nangpa La. Down in the pass was a line of decrepit chortens, and tall skinny poles that had once held prayer flags. Watching them I caught sight of movement, and a faint high whistle wafted past us, making the hair on my forearms stand out from the skin. "Whoah," says I, and George hissed "Ambush!" But the colonel only shook his head.

"Yetis," he said. "The Manjushri Rimpoche has enlisted their aid."

"Shit," George said. But there was nothing he could do about it at this point. Down in the pass shapes shifted and disappeared and that was all we saw of them anyway, and quickly we were down in the pass, stepping on exposed rocks so there would be no footprints to indicate where we had come from.

Among the chortens we split into two groups, and took off down both sides of the pass. After that it was a matter of keeping up with the colonel, who was pretending he was in his Land Rover, running everywhere he could, shouting at us and hauling ass over talus slopes and through cold clunking glacial streams, following the ancient traders' trail.

A few hours later we reached the rhododendron forest above Chhule. Rain had knocked down all the flowers and they lay matted on the forest floor like busted birthday balloons, thousands of them so that the ground was pink and the sky was a billowing cloudy white, strongly backlit by a full moon. Between the pink ground and the white sky hundreds of black gnarly rhododendron branches twisted up into a light wet snow that began to fall. It was a weird place, and when the moon shone through the wrack like a streetlight it only looked weirder—pink ground, twisty black shapes, falling snow, clouds racing across the moon, and every once in a while, shapes moving in the corner of the eye.

At the low edge of the forest we were on the outskirts of Chhule, and the barracks that housed the Nepali Army were on our side of the village, just on the other side of a narrow clearing—three long two-story stone buildings with sheet-metal roofs and wood-frame windows, all peacefully asleep in the depths of an ordinary village night. Somewhere in the village a mastiff was barking, but that happened every night in every village in Nepal, so there was nothing to worry about from him.

Silently we began to spread out along the forest's edge, following the colonel's instructions. He set the mortar teams in a semicircle facing in on the barracks, putting me and George at one end of the semicircle, behind a short fat old rhododendron. He chuckled grimly at the sight of the barracks roofs. "Gonna sound like we're bashing them in the head with trashcan lids. Here, take masks—you'll be off in their peripheral vision."

He gave us demon masks and flashlights and we put on the masks, and luckily our demons had pop eyes so enormous that the cut holes of the pupils were big enough to see through. George was transformed into a green red blue and gold horror, grinning with three or four times as many teeth as he should have had. And I suppose I looked much the same. Once the fracas began we were supposed to shoot two mortar rounds off, and then slink around amongst the trees, flashing the flashlights up at our faces for some subliminal negative advertising and then dropping behind trees to dodge any fire that we might draw.

Great plan. Although George didn't think much of it. And when he took the cannonball rocks out of his backpack to load our mortar, he was even less impressed. "Freds, what is this? Can you see this? These rocks, they're blue! Aren't they blue?" He shined his flashlight on them for a second. "Freds, these are turquoise!"

He ran through the trees and caught up with the colonel and dragged him back. "Colonel, what the hell are we doing bombing these guys with *turquoise*?"

The colonel already had on a particularly grotesque demon mask, but somehow it was obvious that the wild grin on its face was perfectly matched underneath. "Beautiful, isn't it?" the colonel said. "They'll come running out of those barracks and see this stuff scattered everywhere, and *they'll think the sky is falling.* They'll go stark raving mad with fear."

No reply from George.

Finally he shook his head violently, skewing his mask, and in a muffled voice he said, "Colonel, doesn't it seem to you that, you know, perhaps bombing these guys with turquoise is going to make it *hard* for them, tomorrow morning, to *understand* the night as a *raid by the Chinese Army*—"

But before he had managed to finish the question and get his mask readjusted the colonel was off, and had given the whistle that was the signal to start the attack, and one of the Khampas wearing a mask that had been beat particularly hard with the ugly stick had snuck up to one of the windows and put his face up against it and flashed his flashlight into the room and then at his face and shrieked, and that was the signal for all of us to fire our mortars, in a ragged volley that lasted about half a minute. The Khampa at the window hauled ass back into the trees and the riflemen opened fire and shot out all the barracks windows, and then a dozen mortar loads of turquoise came whistling down out of the sky and a few of them at least landed on those metal roofs and they began to boom horrendously under the impact. All the while we demons were dancing between the trees flashing lights on our faces, and from inside the barracks there came cries of mindless panic to warm the colonel's heart for several incarnations to come.

So everything was going great for a couple of minutes at least, but unfortunately one of the demons got carried away and ran up to the nearest barracks to stare in a broken window, feeling a demonic invulnerability that was sadly misplaced because someone inside shot him. He fell back and being nearest to him George and I ran out into the clearing and grabbed him up. His right arm was bloody and it seemed to me he was in very serious pain until I recalled his mask. Black clouds had rolled overhead and it was as dark as it got that night, snowing hard and crazy with the sound of gunfire, and our demon comrade was just indicating he could walk on his own when *whump*, there was rock falling all over us. Hit by friendly fire, we were. I got whanged hard in the shoulder and back and the Khampa jerked sideways, but George took the brunt of it. Luckily the colonel's turquoise cannonballs tended to shatter into fragments on being fired, so that they came down like birdshot rather than bowling balls. Still, enough landed on George that he crashed to the ground, felled by what looked to be the raw material for several dozen turquoise earrings.

He was cut up around the back of the head and the shoulders, and was lucky to have been wearing his mask, because it was all bashed up. Knocked out cold, too. Now our wounded Khampa buddy had to help us, and he used his good arm and I got on the other side of George, and we dragged him back into the rhododendron forest right quick.

After that things got confused. Loud ceremonial fireworks were going off over the Nepali barracks, and their roofs still banged horribly, but I could only begin to conclude that there were in fact some Gurkhas stationed in Chhule, because a group came charging out of one of their barracks unimpressed by our firepower and unaware that the sky was falling, and they started shooting at us with very loud *brrrp brrrps* that seemed to indicate very big guns indeed, and rhododendron branches began to rain down left and right.

Now since the Manjushri Rimpoche had ordered us to avoid killing any of these Nepali soldiers there was nothing to be done at this point but to beat a very hasty retreat, while shooting back all the while in demon Chinese Army style. Our comrades did this, but the wounded demon and I were having a tough time of it with George, who had come to but was clumsy and confused, staggering along be-

223

tween us mumbling incoherently as if his drubbing had put him on the very short path to enlightenment, but I doubted it. He was simply stunned, and we were losing ground on the colonel and the Khampas.

I crashed into an abandoned mortar, still steaming in the snow. *Brrrp brrrps* spiked into us like nails of fear, and branches snapped overhead to emphasize that this reaction was not inappropriate. I decided we had to fire another mortar round at the Nepalis, although now I am not sure why, and I had the explosives charge and wadding jammed down into the barrel before I discovered there were no chunks of turquoise or rock of any kind left in the area.

So we were crouched behind a tree trunk letting George catch his breath and thinking it was all over when without a sound we were suddenly joined by short dark figures, with long arms and funny heads. I had almost melted from under my mask with fright, when I saw that one of them was wearing an L.A. Dodgers baseball cap.

"Buddha!" I said.

"Na-mas-tayyy," he said in his squeaky little voice.

I took off my demon mask and grabbed up his skinny hand, too overwhelmed to be surprised.

"What?" said George. "What?"

"We've got some help," I told him, and in a considerable hurry I indicated to Buddha that the mortar should be loaded with rocks, using a wadded handful of fallen rhododendron blossoms as an example. He misunderstood me and he and three or four of his bros quickly stuffed the barrel entirely full with matted blooms. "What the hell" said I and fired them off, and then the yetis had us picked up and we were hauling ass uphill through the forest, leaving the Gurkhas behind to figure out why it was snowing rhododendron mush.

Halfway up the glacial valley we caught up with the colonel and the Khampas and our yeti companions dropped us, suddenly skittish at the proximity to so many strangers with guns, Shambhala allies or no. "Thanks, Buddha!" I called after their disappearing forms, and then the wounded Khampa and I hustled George upvalley after the rest of our band. The Khampa called to them in Tibetan and they waited for us, and then the Gurkhas were within firing distance again and we were off to the races, headed for Nangpa La as fast as we could.

It began to snow and rain both, and an hour later we found that one stream we had forded on the way down was now unfordably high. We struck out upstream and found a stand of trees near a narrow spot in the flow, so the Khampas cut down two trees and dropped them across the water onto a prominent boulder on the other side. The colonel crawled over first and secured the tips of the trees the best he could. Then we sent George across this impromptu bridge, but in doing so he shoved the trees apart and was about to slip between them into the stream, wrecking the bridge in the process. He caught an arm and a leg over each tree, and was stuck. "Hold on!" the colonel shouted at him furiously. "Don't move! Don't let go!" And in Tibetan he ordered the rest of the Khampas to come on across. Most did it without stepping on George but by no means all. When we were all over the colonel and I crawled back out and dragged George over the two trees to safety.

The experience seemed to have roused George from his stupor—he had shifted from muttering "What, what, what" to saying very distinctly, "Fuck. Fuck. Fuck."

"Well," I said, trying to cheer him up, "at least we weren't wearing crampons."

No reply from George.

Now we were over the largest of the streams, and could beat a retreat up to Nangpa La without too much trouble. In fact, we got into the pass with everything timed so nicely that you would have thought it had all been going according to plan, and who knows maybe the colonel thought that it had, because we arrived in the pass with the Gurkhas hot on our tail, and Kunga Norbu's party came hauling up out of Tibet with the Chinese Army hot on their tail, and we slipped up the ridge and ducked into our tunnel and slammed shut the door, leaving the Gurkhas and Chinese to sort things out if they could. "They'll end up killing each other," I said to the colonel.

"Good," he snarled.

So then it was back through the tunnels, dragging every step of the way. It was lucky for George that it was a downhill run, because when we got to Grand Central Station and then the basement of the monastery, we walked out into clear morning light, which meant we had run all night long. This was standard Khampa guerrilla raid style—I suppose we had done about fifty miles in the previous eighteen hours, and been shot at for fifteen of them. I was beat, and George was devastated. He looked like he still had his demon mask on, and one of the gorier ones at that, face all puffy and bruised and bloody, mouth clenched in a scowl and eyes popped out with disbelief that he had taken part in any such expedition as ours had been.

But we were back.

• • •

Lhamo and the rest of the villagers took good care of George. For several days he crashed at Lhamo's house in a fever, moaning and groaning, and Sindu and her kid hung around helping Lhamo feed him and wipe his face, being careful to avoid the cuts and bruises which Dr. Choendrak was tending in standard doctor style, stitches and everything.

Dr. Choendrak also decided to take on George's dysentery once and for all, and he dosed him with the *rinchen ribus*, the Precious Pills. These pills are composed of a hundred and sixty-five ingredients, including precious metals ground to powder as well as a great number of medicinal plants, and they come wrapped in colored cotton tied with rainbow-colored thread sealed with wax. It takes twenty druggists up to three months to concoct them, and they are so strong that generally they wipe the patient out for a day while they rearrange the balance of his interior. George was wiped out completely for five days, and for a while Dr. Choendrak was really worried about him. But eventually he got up and around, a mere shadow of his former self, stick-limbed and with a scraggly bearded face that looked like midget axe murderers with tiny axes had been after him.

• • •

We got a break in the monsoon, several sunny days in a row, and George spent the time on the lookout rock above the laundry pool, watching the locals live their lives. He was still kind of sick, and he didn't have much energy, but up there he didn't need it. New arrivals at the pool would greet him in Tibetan and he would reply in English, and everyone was happy with this arrangement. A lot of the time he slept on his rock like a cat.

In the meanwhile Colonel John went down to Kathmandu, and when he came back, I went up to George all excited. "Hey," says I, "do you want to hear what we did?"

"I know what we did," he says darkly.

"But do you want to read about it in *The International Herald Tribune*?"

"What?"

I held out the battered issues of the paper that the colonel had brought back with him. "Looks like there was a fair bit of fallout," I said as George hustled down off his rock and snatched them up.

The first one was from July 29th, three days after our raids. Back on one of the inner pages was a little article titled "Nepal Protests Alleged Border Incursion by Chinese," and the headline basically told the story.

The very next day it had moved onto the front page—"Beijing Accuses India of Attack on Tibet," on top of a pretty sizable article, describing the charges and counter-charges of the two countries. Apparently the Chinese felt that the attack on their border post had been made by the Indians' Special Frontier Force, going through Nepal so as to make it look like it wasn't them. And the Indians felt that this whole charge was a lie to cover a Chinese attack on Nepal, which being on their side of the Himalaya they considered to be an attack on their own security.

So far so good. But the *Tribbie* for August 2nd had a big top-of-the-front-page headline which read "TROOPS MASS ON CHINA-INDIA BORDER."

"Oh my God," George said as he ripped through the article, and as he read it he kept on saying that, in higher and higher keys.

A good portion of the front page was devoted to that article and related side articles, describing the disappearance of the DMZ on the India-China border in Kashmir, the unprecedented deployment of Indian troops in Sikkim, and also how the Pakistanis had warned the Indians not to mess with their buddies the Chinese, while the Soviets had warned the Chinese not to fuck with their buddies the Indians. "Oh my *God*," George kept saying.

And then the next day's paper was practically nothing *but* the border crisis, all in big type, and even allowing for the fact that this was the Hong Kong edition of the *Trib*, with a resulting emphasis on Asian affairs, it still had to be admitted that this was a major league crisis. Clashes between Indian and Chinese and Indian and Pakistani forces had been reported, some of them really serious. And American satellite photos showed massive troop build-ups on the Soviet-Chinese border.

"Oh my GOD," George said. "Where's the next day? Where's the next day?"

"That's all the colonel brought back."

"*What*? He left in the middle of all this? Without telling anyone that we started it? It's been, what?" He checked the date. "Five days! Oh my God."

He ran back down to the village and called Colonel John an idiot. "Damn it, we could have just started World War Three!" he shouted at him.

It turned out the colonel didn't much care. He figured that World War Three was one of the few ways Tibet could get out from under the boot of the Chinese, and if that's what it took, it was okay by John.

George ripped him for this. "What would the Manjushri Rimpoche say if you told him that! He'd throw you right out of this valley!"

Which was probably true. But the colonel just stuck out his lower lip stubbornly. He knew the Rimpoche would kick his ass for such a selfish sentiment, but he wasn't going to lie—that's how he felt about it. If the world wouldn't stop a case of genocide when it was staring them in the face, then fuck 'em. Let them eat nukes.

George was so furious he couldn't talk. He went over and kicked one of the stone and sod walls lining the village street so hard that several stones in the top row fell off. Then he threatened to go tell the Rimpoche of John's murderous hopes, if the colonel didn't drive us back down to Kathmandu *immediately*.

John was agreeable, and so that night we were over the pass and down to the Land Rover, hustling all the way until I feared George would drop, and the next afternoon we were back in Thamel, where life seemed to be going on just as if we were nowhere near the brink of World War Three, although in Kathmandu that meant nothing. Armageddon could have happened the week before and Kathmandu would probably not yet be aware of it. It would be the last place to know.

So George rushed around the used bookstores trying to find the latest *Tribbies* and failing, which made him paranoid. "Maybe that'd be the first sign," he kept saying. "Maybe that means the end has already come."

Finally he found one, as usual dated four days before— August 5th, and the front page was still full of the crisis.

The main article described an emergency meeting of the UN Security Council, very acrimonious from the sound of it. A side article reported as to how our President had been over-heard saying that if the Russkies and the Chinese really had a disagreement well then maybe they ought to duke it out man to man. He could think of worse things happening. This view had apparently displeased the Russkies who immediately declared that they considered the USA to be allies of China, and party to any aggression by same.

And so things stood. Not for anything could George find any later *Tribbies* in Kathmandu, and besides, the situation was clear. The world was on the brink.

The only question was, what were we going to do about it.

"We've got to hit it from every angle possible," George said. "I've got some groundwork laid already, thank God."

It seemed to him that the letters he had typed on A.S.J.B. Rana's typewriter and passed around could be adapted to the present emergency. "I figured Rana was trying to use us as a cover for something he was doing in the Secretariat," he said as he sketched out flowcharts on the floor. "Remember how someone once told us they thought the road to Chhule had been contracted to the family of a minister? I decided it might be useful to make it look like Rana was that minister. He's probably the one who approved that road, after all, and he was keeping us coming back as if he needed to keep an eye on us to prevent us from finding anything out. So I wrote up a bunch of memos implicating him, and spread them around before we left. Now if we can connect that stuff to the right people. . . ."

So the next day he dressed up in his foundation suit and charged into Singha Durbar, and with his face chopped up like it was he looked so bizarre that no one dared stop him. He went to the offices of the *Nepal Gazette* and found Bahadim, and told him to slip the word to the relevant ministers that the attack on Chhule had not been made by the

Chinese Army, but was in fact the work of a faction in the Palace Secretariat, which was feuding with another faction in the Secretariat that had stolen all the contracts for the Chhule road.

That same afternoon he went to the Swiss agency. The letters George had left there implicated A.S.J.B. Rana in a plot to sabotage the Chhule road, as part of one of the Rana family's endless tussles among themselves for higher ground at the palace. George told the Swiss that the border incursions had in fact been faked as part of this Rana family struggle, and he said that the Swiss should use that information to try to cool things down in Geneva and on the international scene generally. The Swiss told him they were already working on it.

Last thing that afternoon he cracked the Palace Secretariat and found the Ministry for Development, Chinese Friendship Agency office. This, as Bahadim had told him, was run by a Rana who personally and departmentally was a rival of our A. Rana, and George had primed him before our trip with the information that A. Rana was accusing him of trying to sabotage the Chhule road. Naturally this had gotten the other Rana paranoid, and when George returned to tell him that A. Rana had gotten people to fake the border incursion, and was now telling foreign aid agencies that the raid had been organized by this guy in the Chinese Friendship Agency, the Rana there sat down abruptly before his telephone and got to work.

That evening George was utterly beat, but he lay there on his bed figuring out the ramifications of the day's work—who was likely to tell what to whom, and what it would mean. And the next morning he dropped by the Chinese embassy with another letter written on A. Rana's stationery. This one asserted that the incursion into Tibet had been made by Tibetans desperate to escape a mopping-up operation run in secret by the Nepali Army, which had hoped to make the Chhule road completely safe for use by the Special Frontier Force of the Indian Army, by forcing all Tibetan guerrillas over into their home country.

Lastly he biked over to the American embassy, and told them he was a friend and representative of one faction of the outlawed Nepali Congress Party, the party that had formed the legal government until the royal coup of 1960. They wanted the Americans to know that both border attacks had been part of the internecine warfare in the corrupt Palace Secretariat, that one group in the palace wanted to stop the Chhule road by creating friction between China and Nepal. Now that the hoax had gotten way out of hand the perpetrators were too frightened to confess. George told the Americans that the Congress Party had spies in the palace who had found all this out, and they wanted everyone in the world to know so that tensions would be eased.

Then when the embassy official George had been talking to went to get the ambassador, or some higher-up like that, George quick got up and asked a secretary for the bathroom, and then slipped out the front and biked away, joining me at the corner and then leading the way at high speed. When he told me what he had told the embassy I said "Hey, that's almost the truth."

"Best kind of lie," he panted.

On the way back to Thamel we biked down Naxal road, past the palace itself. We stopped to let some cows cross, and George craned his head back to look up at the bats hanging from the pine trees on the palace grounds. "They're in conference," he said, laughing weakly. He was pale and his face sweaty. "Trying to work it out. I just gave them some of their own medicine. Exactly Birendra's technique. Put enough contradictory information out there, it's interference. Like wave tanks in physics class. So much cross-chop . . . all goes to. . . ." He stopped, and I thought he was considering his next words. But then he keeled over, bang up against a cow and then down into the street. Fainted dead away.

I flagged a cab and stuffed him in it, and took him to the Canadian health clinic, back up near the American embassy. This was a Western-style clinic that looked like it had been lifted out of Glendale, and when you were sick the sight of its white walls and pastel prints and old magazines and the smell of disinfectant was enough to make you weep.

They took George in and gave him some intravenous stuff—he hadn't eaten that day, and was still suffering from dysentery despite the Precious Pills. So he was dehydrated, and some of his cuts were infected—obviously his immune system had been shredded by years of antibiotic abuse. In short, he was completely fucked up.

They made him stay in their little two-bed hospital to pull back together. It took a while, and I brought him *Tribbies* every day.

And slowly, with our four-day delay on real time, we watched the crisis simmer down and go away. Everyone decided it had been a false alarm. Rumors of secret American and Swiss diplomacy were rife, especially in George's room in the clinic. Critical intervention, no doubt. And so George would finish the day's read, and give a little shudder, and then fall asleep again.

One day I slogged through a downpour to K.C.'s with the Swiss guys, and over some beers they told me that the Chhule road was deader than Mussolini. The Indians wouldn't build it for anything, and Birendra and his gang wouldn't build it for twice anything. Too dangerous.

So the next afternoon I went to collect George, as the Canadians were releasing him. "You did it, George. They'll never build that road now. Aren't you happy you decided to help us out?"

No reply from George.

We cabbed down to Thamel and walked the main street toward the Star. George was such a ghost of his former self that the street merchants didn't even recognize him, and they laid their rap on as if he were a stranger rather than their beloved Mr. No. "Change money? Hash? Carpet? Pipe? Change money?" and he would stare at them as if he were considering their offer, or trying to understand it. I've often tried to understand that money-changing bit myself, I mean the street folk pay you more than the official exchange rate for traveler's checks. They then sell the traveler's checks for more than they bought them. Whoever they sell them to must also sell them for more than they bought them, I assume, and so on up the line, and what I wonder is, how does it end? Doesn't someone at the end finally get stuck selling them for the official exchange rate, and losing lots of money?

Anyway, George stood in the street just staring at people as if he were having trouble focusing, until they gave up and moved on.

"Look," he kept saying. "Look, Freds. Look. That's a pile of garbage. Right there in the street."

"That's right, George. We dodge that pile every day."

"Cows eating it. Rats. Dogs. Kids."

"That's right."

We walked on.

"Let's go to the Old Vienna," he said suddenly.

"Are you sure your system can take it?" I asked.

"I don't care."

But in fact he did care. He had suffered so much that when the food hit the table he got cautious and decided that actually he shouldn't really eat the meat, because we had never been able to decide for sure where Eva got it. He spooned a little of the goulash broth up and left the chunks of water buff for me, and sat there trying to sniff the meal down, looking mournful as I had my schnitzel Parisienne and apple strudel buried in whipped cream.

So when we rolled out of there George was feeling a little low, even though the latest *Tribbie* we found in a used bookstore seemed to consider the border crisis pretty much over. But as I was folding the paper up I saw a little filler article on the back pages, headlined "Everest Is Still the Highest." "Hey dig this," I said to George, and read— "'Early this year University of Washington scientists stunned the mountaineering world, recalculating K2 to be 29,064 feet. Now an Italian team has used satellite measurements to put Everest back where it should be, in first place at the new height of 29,108. The team rechecked K2 and found it to be 28,268 feet above sea level. U.S. mountaineers are willing to accept the Italian measurements,' you ain't kidding! Great news, eh? Now you won't have to climb K2 with Kunga Norbu and me."

"Good," George said.

"And you saved Shambhala," I told him. "You saved the holiest most important hidden valley on the whole earth."

"Good," he said. "But we still need to get some kerosene stoves up there."

"Not necessary. Didn't you hear? The Rimpoche is going to try that idea of yours—they're making ceramic pipe to put the eternal flame down into a communal kitchen, maybe even several of them. Dr. Choendrak and some of the other monks are really getting into the design and all."

"Good."

But he was still low, and still looking around as we made our way through Thamel toward the Hotel Star. "Freds, that's *grass* growing on the *roof*."

"I like grass on the roof."

"Freds, this is one of the biggest streets in this nation's capital, and it's *mud*."

"That's right."

"And this is the nation's *capital*."

"That's right. Kinda like parts of Washington, D.C., as I recall."

He sighed. "Yeah, but still . . ."

Then we ran into the beggar and his daughter. They stood there hand in hand, both with free hands extended toward us, looking just the same as always except wetter because of the monsoon, the beggar with his gap-toothed smile and the little girl in her shift looking like a UNICEF poster and not all that different from Sindu's little boy up in the valley, and George said, "Oh, man," and ransacked his wallet to pull out a fistful of rupees and give them to the beggar. The beggar took them and stepped back, looking shocked.

George pursued him, looking back at me. "Freds, we gotta do something, don't we?"

"You just did, George."

"Yeah, but something more! I mean, couldn't we hire them to clean our rooms, or sweep the halls out front, so they had a job?"

"The clerks hire that gal with the baby on her back to sweep, I think it's the same kind of thing." And actually the beggar had a good thing going, his little girl was worth lots of rupees to him in this neighborhood. There were other beggars hurting bad compared to him. But I didn't say that.

"But couldn't we . . . couldn't we tell them to do just our rooms?"

"They wouldn't understand you."

The beggar and his little girl retreated cautiously from us, and then wandered off. George's shoulders fell.

"There's nothing we can do, is there?"

"No. Just what you did, George."

We reached the Star and went up to our rooms, and read the rest of the *Trib*, and smoked a nightcap, and laughed over the great adventure of saving Shambhala, not to mention world peace. And we recalled our climb of Everest and the time we unkidnapped Buddha and set him free, and I told George for the first time about how Buddha and some of his bros had showed up during the battle of Chhule to help us out. "No," he said. "You're kidding." And he wouldn't believe me. "YOU'RE KIDDING!"

It made me giggle. "Ain't that my line?"

And he laughed, and we talked some more, about Nathan and Sarah, and Jimmy and Rosalynn, and all the rest, and it was fun.

But George wasn't easy about things, not really. He was restless. When I was about to crash he decided to take a walk down to K.C.'s and have a beer. I told him not to overindulge so soon after his recovery because he still looked like death, fresh scars and black rings under his eyes, the envy of every anorexic in the world, but he assured me he was fine and took off.

A couple of hours later fleas in my mattress woke me, however, and I checked in George's room and found he hadn't returned. It was late for K.C.'s. Worried that he might have gotten shitfaced and passed out, I went down to the streets to have a look for him.

Thamel was dark, it was late and the narrow streets were near empty. No noise but the dogs barking some neighborhoods away. K.C.'s was closed, that whole area really pitch-black.

And so I almost stumbled across him. He had found the beggar and his daughter, who slept against the wall of the German Pumpernickel Bakery under a wide eave where they were sheltered from rain and caught some warmth from the ovens on the other side of the wall. George and the beggar were sitting back against that wall on each side of the little girl, who lay stretched out between them. All three fast asleep. George's head was canted back against the brick and he was snoring like a crosscut saw, his face all dessicated like he'd been dead in a desert for forty years. Lightly I kicked the bottom of his boot and he jerked a little, cracked his lids, stared up eyes glazed, not seeing a thing. "Wake up, bro," I said quietly. "Come on home."

No reply from George.

PART
4

The Kingdom
Underground

I

IT IS REMARKABLE HOW short a time the innocence of youth lasts.

Actually it lasted nearly forty years in my case, but I never noticed it until it was gone, and so of course it didn't feel like I had had it long. A couple seconds at the most. And after that I was experienced. I knew. I walked the crowded streets of Kathmandu, which used to give me such joy—perverse joy, but joy nevertheless—and now all I saw was squalor and poverty and lame civic planning.

And you know whose fault it was.

So one night I was in my room at the Hotel Star kicked back on my bed with the *Tribbie*, wondering if it could really be telling the truth about the world; and knowing, now, that it probably was. And someone knocked at my door. I opened it and there stood Freds Fredericks, looking like he had just gotten out of the Himal.

Quickly I slammed the door and locked it. "Get out of here, Freds!" I said loudly. "I never want to see your face again!"

Muffled protests from outside. I ignored them and returned to the bed, picked up the paper and stuck my nose in it. "Go away!" I shouted at the door. *Bang bang bang.* "Get the fuck out of here!"

My door shares the front wall of the room with a window, and the window has three panes—one big one flanked by two narrow ones, which are mounted on swivel posts. These can be turned like little revolving doors if you want to open them, to encourage a breeze or let out smoke. Now as I tried to read I saw Freds's hand rotate the narrow pane nearest the door, then reach in and find the doorknob. With a twist he had the door unlocked and opened.

Thus security at the Hotel Star.

It was hopeless anyway; no doubt Freds had already checked in, probably to the room next door, which was his regular. I wouldn't be able to avoid him. "What do you want," I said, throwing the paper down.

"Nothing, George. I just got back from the sacred valley, you know, and thought I'd check in and see how you're doing."

"I'm doing fine," I said. "I'm almost back to my eighth grade weight."

"That's good, George, real good. You look good, too. Can't hardly see those scars even."

"Wonderful."

Freds sat on the room's only chair. "Listen, George, I got a little favor to ask—whoah—hey!—no!—*hey!* Real little, George! *Real* little!"

By this time we were out in the hallway, and I had him by the throat. I couldn't remember exactly how we had got there. This was a tendency I had developed recently that gave me concern. Blank-outs. Periods of amnesia, or undue emotion. Insanity—yes, that's what we're talking about here.

I eased my grip on his throat and said carefully, "Do I have to do anything?"

"No! Nothing at all!"

"Good." I trailed back into my room and sat heavily on my bed. Ever since my last encounter with Freds I found I tired easily.

The truth was, I was sick of Freds Fredericks. He was the snake in my Garden; he had taken the rotten apple of knowledge and slam-dunked it down my throat, and I had choked on it. And now nothing in Nepal was fun anymore.

"What is it, then," I said, feeling like I was waiting to hear a judge sentence me.

"Notning, George, really. Nothing. Relax. It's just that my friends Gaubahal and Daubahal have just opened a new jungle camp down in Chitwan, and they need customers to get it going. You know, a place like Tiger View, only cheaper. They'll give us eighty percent off if we go down there for a week."

"No," I said. "I hate the jungle."

"Me too," Freds said, "but Gaub and Daub have got a really cute place right on the border of Chitwan National Park, a bunch of new bungalows and viewing towers and all that. All we gotta do is eat and drink and lounge around watching birds and animals and all."

Dread began to fill me. "No way." Of course I knew he was leaving something out. I wasn't sure what, or why, but I knew it. The last time Freds had asked me for a favor, things had worked out such that I could still fit my whole body through one of the sleeves of my shirt. I knew I wasn't ready for whatever he had in mind this time.

"Come on, George. You look like you could use the R and R. I'm gonna do it, and it'd be a blast to have you along. They'll take us on elephant rides and everything."

"No way. Not a chance."

II

So I WENT VACATIONING in Chitwan. We were picked up bright and early by a Land Rover already stuffed with West Germans who insisted they were not Germans but *Bavarians*, and the driving team took us west and south down onto the Terai, the lowlands of southern Nepal that are part of the Ganges plain. I used to enjoy drives in this direction, toward Pokhara and the wild west of Nepal; but now all I saw were roadside villages in ruins, with hungry faces staring in our windows.

We arrived at the end of the road, deep in the boonies,

and were met by our camp administrator Daubahal, who was looking worried. Apparently the camp's Jeep was out of commission. The camp was on the other side of a shallow but wide river, and without the Jeep we were cut off from it, and without a place to spend the night. Crossing the river in the Land Rover was out of the question; it would have drowned. Daubahal, a small intent Hindu, conducted an anxious conversation over a walkie-talkie, and after an hour or so a line of elephants appeared on the other shore, drivers seated behind their heads. They forded the river slowly, at one point going shoulder deep. "How great," Freds said. "We're gonna cross on elephants."

So we were. The elephants were made to kneel, and we climbed up the rubbery skin of their bent legs onto enormous wooden saddles strapped to their backs. These saddles were actually square platforms, with wooden railings held up by wooden posts at the four corners. We sat with our legs wrapped around the posts, arms hanging over the railings, four to an elephant—not counting the drivers, who whacked the elephants when we were aboard to get them to rise, then climbed up their trunks and swung into position behind their heads. And we galumped into the river.

It was the first time I had ever been on elephant back, and I was impressed by how high we were—say twelve or fifteen feet—and by how irregular our motion was. The platform had no flex, and our elephant's gait tossed it around unpredictably. I learned that as elephants walk they put a leg forward, and hold it as stiff as a post as they move over it; then when the leg is somewhere past the vertical they let go and the leg gives abruptly at the knee. The platform's corners, sitting on the creature's four shoulders, rise slowly and then drop with the breaking knees, in a rhythm that I couldn't discern. It was random motion, as if we were on a little raft and waves were rolling under us from every direction. If you were prone to seasickness it would have given you trouble, and an hour of it was likely to give anybody back pain for the rest of the day.

So we made our way into the Chitwan jungle, moving under tall trees that Daubahal told us were saal trees. These were about forty or fifty feet tall, and spaced fairly far apart. Below them the groundcover was relatively sparse. It wasn't like the jungle I had imagined, Amazon or Congo-type thick lush greenery; but it was pretty thick, and fairly green, and enough for me.

We hove into camp around sundown and found it a pleasant circle of new wooden bungalows, with gravel pathways and flowering bushes and an elephant mounting platform and a mess hall with a big bar, which everyone descended on happily. It was the first time I'd ever seen a bar decorated in African Queen style where it didn't look completely bogus, and we sucked down mai tais and fruit punch kamikazees until it seemed like a real good idea to have come down here, and went to bed by lantern light. Freds and I shared a bungalow.

And for a while things seemed what they claimed to be. We vacationed in the jungle. As a fellow professional in the Nepali tourist industry I felt a little sorry for Daubahal, who functioned as our social director. Up in the Himal there is a lot to do just getting from place to place; here, we were here, and there was nowhere else to go. You couldn't wander off by yourself, because it would be easy to get lost in the jungle, and something out there might trample or eat you. The Jeep was out of commission, so we couldn't drive around on the little dirt tracks that someone had cut into the bush at one time or another. And the camp's viewing tower had for some reason been built a good distance away from the circle of bungalows, so that getting to it at night would be a risky business, and they had no lighting system anyway, so you wouldn't have been able to see any nocturnal activity even if you had ventured across to it. Since there was nothing to see from it by day, it stood there unused.

That left elephant rides. Every morning we were awakened at dawn, and given a pre-breakfast elephant ride around the jungle. It was like spending hours on a somewhat dysfunctional painted metal horse in front of a K-Mart, one that bucked hard and irregularly. No one over the age of five likes to ride those things even when they're working right, and often even little kids begin to wonder mid-ride if it is a really fun activity or not. An hour of it would tell them.

Supposedly we were doing this to look for animals, but the truth is that most wild animals are shy creatures, and will run away if they hear you coming. So riding an elephant is not the best way to sneak up on them. And in fact we never saw a living thing. Except, that is, for an occasional rhino. Apparently their hearing and eyesight are poor, and judging by their expression, their IQ is no great shakes either; one look at a rhinoceros and you know immediately why the dinosaurs are extinct. It didn't take a comet to kill those guys off.

The rhinos we came across didn't like our elephants, and the elephants didn't like the rhinos. Whenever we sighted one the elephants would stop, and the rhinos would lumber out of their mudhole baths, then stand and squint at us. We would all go really silent, and the drivers would gently urge their beasts in the direction of the rhino, and there we would be, within twenty or thirty yards of a truly bizarre rubberoid creature, something like a cross between a tank and Mr. Magoo, with a dinosaur's face and a deeply suspicious expression, looking just as out of place as if he'd been dragged up from the bottom of the sea and dropped there in the grass. No sound but the clicking of camera shutters. It was almost worth the elephant rides to see something as strange as that.

Then the rhino would lumber off, and we would continue jouncing across seas of grass, back to the camp for a welcome breakfast and a return to bed. After a big lunch we would sit around, watching Daubahal squirm, and he would hunch his shoulders, and consult his clipboard, and finally raise his ballpoint as if he had just had an idea, and say brightly "Okay! For afternoon—elephant ride!" And everyone would groan loudly and complain about kidney injury or the lack of chiropractic coverage in their insurance, and most would refuse to do it, spending the afternoon in the bar drinking like sensible folk.

But Freds of course loved the elephant rides. And he often talked me into coming along. It wasn't all that hard, actually, because as a fellow tourist handler really I felt sorry for Daubahal. You tend to take it personally when clients groan and scoff and retch at your planned activities. So we would climb the stairs of the mounting platform and step on board, and ride an elephant around the jungle all afternoon—aimless, uncomfortable, bored.

But I have to admit there were moments. We learned that the Chitwan jungle had distinct zones; a lot of it was saal forest, but then there were denser knots of smaller brush and trees; bamboo thickets; open stretches of elephant grass, which was aptly named, as it looked like ordinary grass, but fifteen feet tall (Freds said, "When I buy a house in suburbia I'm gonna plant this stuff, can you imagine?"); and a number of open gravel zones, seamed by shallow rivers. Occasionally we'd come across a rhino, or see a spotted deer running away. Once we caught a glimpse of a jackal. Colorful birds flashed by, including one blue and bronze thing that looked like it was made of jewels. And down by one of the streams, imprinted deep in the sand, were the perfect tracks of a tiger. A cat-print as big around as my outstretched hand. "Holy moly," Freds said, leaning over till he was almost falling off. "That's one big tabby, eh?" The Bavarians took photos of the prints; that was as close as we were going to come to a tiger at our camp, and looking down at the prints, I wasn't sorry.

And then one afternoon, galumping home at sundown, we came to a clearing by one of the streams and could see a range of hills to the north, one of the first thrusts of the

Himalayas, mere green hills but probably ten thousand feet tall for all that, and as I jolted along it occurred to me that I was on the Indian tectonic plate while that range was on the Asian plate, and I could sort of see it, sort of feel the collision (an up-and-down bump and grind), and the last rays of the sun turned the air a dark smoky red, and bronzed the elephant grass, and Freds looked at me with his crazed grin, and a bone-jarred little glow filled me. I could have been stuck in traffic on an L.A. freeway at that very moment, and instead I was in the middle of Asia, on elephant back in the jungle. I couldn't help grinning back at Freds.

So, aside from the damage accruing from twelve hours on elephant back in only three days, there really was nothing wrong with our vacation in the Royal Chitwan Jungle Camp. Compared to what Freds had put me through the last couple of times we had traveled together, it was light-weight indeed. Naturally this made me extremely uneasy. Suspicion and unfocused dread grew in me nightly as nothing in particular happened. The tiniest incidents fueled my alarm—Freds disappearing for an afternoon, for instance. Or the sight of him talking to one of the elephant handlers. "Freds, I thought you said you don't speak Nepalese."

"I don't, George, I speak Tibetan."

"And that elephant handler is Tibetan, I suppose."

"Right."

A Tibetan elephant handler. Think about it.

I did, one night in the bar, and it made me nervous. To stave off nameless dread I drank kamikazees, and soon I felt better. Then it seemed I felt a little too good, and I staggered to our bungalow and crashed.

I don't know how much later it was that Freds roused me, by rolling me out of my bed onto the floor. Sometime in the middle of the night; I was still drunk, so much so that I couldn't remember where I was. But when Freds said "Come on, George, I need your help," I had enough of my wits about me to cry "No!" and try to crawl under the bed.

But Freds dragged me out. Unfortunately I had retired with my clothes still on, and he jammed my feet into my boots. "Come on," he said in an excited whisper. "We just need you to look after Sunyash for an hour or so whilst Dawa and I check out this cave we've found."

"Sunyash?"

"You know, the biggest elephant."

III

I DID NOT KNOW the biggest elephant. But when Freds dragged me out to the mounting stand I recognized her, having spent several hours on her back getting well acquainted with her—with the loose wrinkled gray skin that slid back and forth over her massive shoulders as she lumbered along, and the pink splotches on the back of her neck, and the dozen strands of hair on her head, each as thick as a pencil lead. An impressive beast, and very well handled by her driver Dawa, who was already in position, seated on her neck with his bare feet hooked behind the tops of her ears. Elephant drivers control their charges with an iron rod that looks a lot like a fireplace poker, except it is sharper at the business end. Many of the drivers at the camp used their rods ruthlessly, whacking the elephants on the left or right side of the head to get them to change direction, and poking them with the sharp end to make them go forward when they were reluctant; some drivers drew blood on every trip. There were a couple that were gentler, however, and Dawa was one of those; he drove Sunyash by talking to her, or at the most kicking her lightly with his heels. I had never seen him use his rod.

Now he and Freds conversed in Tibetan, and suddenly I could see even in the dark that he looked Tibetan; he looked like the Khampas of Shambhala. Suddenly it finally penetrated that Freds had said something about investigating a cave.

"Freds," I said as we lumbered off. Though I was sobering fast I had to hang on tight to the platform railing, my saddle-sore legs wrapped around a corner post. "What are you doing to me this time."

"Nothing, George. Just a ride. Besides, when have I ever done anything to you?"

I wanted to hit him, but couldn't spare a hand. "You stuck me in a snow cave for a night on the south summit of Everest," I said angrily. "You made me crawl in the Kathmandu bureaucracy for a month! You used me for a *bridge*."

"Not on purpose. Besides tonight ain't gonna be like that."

"Tell me what's happening or I'll jump overboard right now."

"Now don't be hasty, I was just about to tell you, as soon as we got good and away from camp."

"So spill. What's this about a cave."

"Well, you know the tunnel system that we used when we made our attack on Chhule? That is one big tunnel system, bigger than you might expect, and there's a whole lot of it under Kathmandu itself, but with all the recent construction there most of the entrances have been built over or blocked up. That's making trouble for the folks in Shambhala, because they've been using the tunnels to transport things and get down to Kathmandu unseen—"

"Wait a second," I said, feeling kamikazees slosh around inside me in a sickening way. "You're telling me that there are tunnels from Shambhala all the way to Kathmandu?"

"Oh yeah! Yeah! There's tunnels everywhere under the Himal. And a big network under Kathmandu."

I tried to comprehend this.

"But now they've got a problem with the Kathmandu exits all getting blocked up," Freds said, "and they want to relocate an old opening down here in the Terai. This one was pretty much forgotten in the last few centuries, and Dawa and I have been cruising around a little trying to find it, and we think we have, but damned if it isn't right next to Tiger View."

"Right next to Tiger View."

"Yeah that's one of the big expensive camps over in the park, like Tiger Tops. There's a little rock outcropping just to the south of this Tiger View camp, and there's a cave there that Dawa is pretty sure is one of the entrances to the tunnel system. So we need to check it out at night."

"Aren't there a lot of tigers around Tiger View at night?"

"Yeah, but Sunyash will keep them away."

I sighed. "Freds, why am I here?"

"To do good on this earth, George. That's why we're all here."

"I mean why am I here with you tonight? Why did you bring me along?"

"Dawa and I are gonna check out this cave and make sure it's the tunnel entrance, and while we're doing that we need someone to stay with Sunyash so she doesn't wander off. It'll be simple."

I was feeling too queasy to answer for a while. Finally I said, "You lied to me. You said this was just a vacation."

"Well, I thought I'd better leave this part out so you wouldn't worry. Think of it as a treasure hunt."

"A treasure hunt at night, in a jungle with tigers. On the back of a stolen elephant."

"She ain't stolen, we're only borrowing her."

I gave up.

Sunyash continued to crash through the forest, under the canopy of saal trees. There was a half moon up, so there was a bit of light—shapes black on black, and the occasional moonbeam defining eerie trees and drooping vines. Sunyash made too much noise for us to be able to hear anything else, but when Dawa stopped her to have a look around, the sound of the night jungle wrapped around us like a good soundtrack: creaks, rustles, insect chirps, the distant cry of a bird, the low cough of an animal. It was much junglier than in the light of day, and the knowledge that tigers were making their nocturnal rounds added an edge that wasn't there when the sun was out. Freds was probably right in saying that no tiger was going to stick around while an elephant walked by, but still, it made me nervous.

On we rocked for a long time, so long that I almost fell asleep. Then Freds nudged me and I saw a glow off to our right; "Tiger View," he said. "Those are the lights they put on so they can see tigers."

"Ah."

"We're getting close. It's somewhere up here."

"Fine."

Through the dark we moved. I settled in over my post and railing.

Eventually Dawa brought Sunyash to a halt. At first it looked the same as anywhere else to me, and then I noticed that there in the moonlight was a small dark hill—a stony knoll covered by shrub, with several small saal trees growing out of its top. The spotlights from Tiger View were still nearby, but now behind us—between us and our camp, I judged.

Freds and Dawa slid off Sunyash. "Hey!" I said.

"We're tying her to this tree," Freds said up to me. "Keep your feet on her back so she knows you're there. We'll be back as soon as we can, probably won't take more'n an hour."

"Hey!" I protested. But they were gone. I was left alone on the back of an elephant, in the middle of the jungle at night. Classic Freds operation, here. Still, as nervous as I was, it struck me as minor compared to the situations he had thrust me into before. I settled down with my boots placed firmly on Sunyash's broad back, and she settled down before a clump of bamboo to indulge in a midnight snack, and drunkenly it seemed to me that I was getting out of this one pretty cheaply. It wasn't even that cold. I was used to going outside at night in Nepal and immediately freezing, but down here in the Terai it was only a bit cool and clammy, and I was sitting right on top of a pretty effective heater at that. So I put my chin on the rail and tried to ignore the night jungle noises, and catch some z's.

I was just about to succeed at that when I noticed that in fact there were no night jungle noises. This seemed odd. And Sunyash had raised her big head before me, and she had her trunk extended, it seemed, and was snuffling the air in big wheezes.

And all of a sudden she raised back her head till we almost bumped foreheads, and let out a blast like forty French horn players punched in the stomach, and then she was off. Never even noticed whatever Freds and Dawa had used to tie her up with, and for all I knew we were dragging a saal tree in our wake, but in any case we were thundering along through the jungle. I had to hang onto the front railing of the platform for dear life, and nothing I shouted at Sunyash had any effect on her rampage. She wanted out of the area, and I thought I could guess why. Tiger! Would it chase us, leap aboard and eat me? Branches slashed my body as Sunyash brushed through trees, going faster than I would have thought possible. An elephant can run hard, and when they get up to speed it is like being on a train, a train that has skipped the tracks and is jouncing badly across uneven ground. A branch caught me in the forehead and after that things were blurry. It seemed my survival depended on slowing her down, and I saw no alternative but to slip under the front railing and slide down onto the driver's seat, straddling her neck with a boot under each ear. I managed this and found it was not a very secure seat; there was nothing to hang on to. I leaned forward and grabbed hold of her ears as they flopped up and down, and yanked back on them as hard as I could. Sunyash tossed her head and almost got rid of me, but my back crunched into the platform railing and all that was lost was my breath.

And then she slowed to a fast walk. "Good Sunyash," I called down to her, wishing I knew more Nepali elephant driver talk. "Sunyash," I said, in as calming a voice as I could muster. She would recognize that. I repeated it like a mantra. She slowed her pace a little, but did nothing else. I didn't know if she knew where she was or not. Perhaps she was headed back to the camp stables; on the other hand she could have been lost. Over my left shoulder I thought I could still see a distant glimmer of the Tiger View spotlights.

I felt no compunction about leaving Freds and Dawa there on their hilltop, at least until daylight. But if Sunyash were just wandering, then I'd be as lost at dawn as I was now. So tentatively I tried directing her. Kind of like learning to drive a car while it was rolling out of control down a hill, but there was no immediate danger except for the occasional low-flying branch. A kick under the left ear got her to veer a bit to the right, I thought. More kicks under each ear confirmed that she would swerve a few degrees if you kicked her hard enough to convince her you meant it. So I kept belting her under the flap of her left ear until we were headed back the way we had come, at which point she slowed down, and even stopped. "Come on, Sunyash." Not a budge. "Go!"

She didn't want to understand. No movement. This was where the harsher drivers would raise up their rods and literally stab their beasts in the top of the head, alternating that with broad whacks right behind the ears, on both sides. I'd seen an elephant that refused to cross a small bridge coerced by these methods into stepping straight down into the gully that the bridge crossed and running up the other side, both moves awkward in the extreme. And other drivers had used these methods on flats to get the elephants to do their version of a gallop, so the tourists could feel how fast an elephant could run.

I suppose I would have used one of those things on Sunyash at that moment, but I didn't have one. She was impervious to my fists and boots, and tweaking the delicate flaps at the back of her ears only made her toss her head irritably.

Finally I leaned forward and whispered into those monster ears. "Bistarre," I said, which means "slowly." This is a word most trekkers learn on their first day in Nepal from their porters. "Bistarre, Sunyash, bistarre." Meanwhile whopping my boots together on the sides of her head, like a rodeo cowboy trying to get extra points out of an unenthusiastic horse.

She began to move forward.

After that it was just a matter of slow navigation, using the spotlights at Tiger View as a reference point. When I got to where I thought the hillock should be, there was nothing. I just kept wandering in circles until I ran into it. The Tiger View spots even gave me an idea of which side of the outcropping we had been on when Sunyash decided to depart the area.

We were just settling down when suddenly Sunyash jerked and I cried "No!" thinking we were off to the races again; but it was just Dawa, climbing up her trunk. Freds hauled himself up the platform straps on her big round sides.

"Hey bro," Freds said. "Sorry we took so long, but we did find what we were looking for. Hope you weren't bored."

"No," I said.

IV

THEN ON THE WAY back Freds decided he wanted to take a look at the Tiger View operation. "Hey we're right next to it and aren't you curious? I mean we might get to see one of the tigers they get visiting."

"Sunyash doesn't like tigers near her."

"We'll keep our distance. Here, right over here." He spoke briefly to Dawa, and slowly Sunyash moved through the night toward the gleam of the spotlight. We stopped when a gap between saal trees gave us a view of the lit clearing, spread below the vague shapes of the big camp's viewing towers.

In the clearing was a young sheep, a lamb really, tied to a stake in the middle of a swath of trampled and bloody grass. The dismembered and half-eaten body of another lamb lay at the edge of the circle of illumination. The lamb still alive huddled in on itself miserably, reaching down with its head from time to time to nibble at the broken grass. The rope tying it to the stake was taut; it had pulled away as far as it could.

"My God," I said, repelled. "Bait?"

"Guess so," Freds said. "I've heard that's how they guarantee you'll see tigers if you stay at Tiger View. They do it almost every night, and the tigers know it and come by for a snack. Pretty sick, eh?" In the dim light Freds's grin was fierce. "I remember one of the guys in my frat house kept a gar in a big fishtank, and he fed it little minnows or goldfish or whatnot, and that gar would be laying at the bottom of the tank and then suddenly there'd be a swirl and one of the goldfish would be missing, you know, and we'd get high and sit around watching it and feel like Nazis. But this!"

"People are in those towers watching?"

"Sure! That's the whole point! And tigers are messy killers, too, they're liable to commence eating before the little thing is completely dead and all."

"Yuck. Let's get out of here before we see it."

"Yeah okay. Although it just occurred to me that we oughta . . . you know what we oughta do is we oughta . . ."

"We oughta what, Freds?"

But he was already involved in a conversation with Dawa, at the same time leaning far over the side of the platform. "Freds!" I whispered sharply, pulling him back up by his belt. "What the hell are you doing?"

"Looking for a rock or something." Dawa interrupted him with a quick stream of Tibetan, pointing all the while at the spotlight.

"Freds," I said warningly, "I don't care what you have in mind, I don't like it." But Freds was listening to Dawa, and nodding, and muttering "Great, great, good idea, I shoulda thought of that myself," and I don't think he even heard me.

When Dawa started Sunyash off in the direction of the big camp, I seized Freds in both hands and shook him. "Freds, *what are you doing*?"

"We're just gonna give these sickos a little scare, George, it won't take but a minute. I was gonna throw rocks at the lights, but Dawa suggested going for the generator which is a much better idea. Come on, jump down here with me, use the straps to let yourself down partways."

"No, Freds!" But he was hauling me over the side behind him, and there was no alternative but to grab onto the platform straps and let myself down as gently as I could. When I hit the earth Freds was already reaching up to get something from Dawa. A dagger the size of a machete. Maybe it was a machete. "Oh my God," I said.

"Shh!" Freds said. "Follow me."

Dawa and Sunyash were lumbering away, and I had no choice. "Freds you tell me what you're doing or I'll tackle you and hold you down till you do."

"Shh, George, we gotta be quiet now." He was really whispering. "Dawa's gonna circle around and cut off their generator, and when the lights go out we're gonna rescue that little lamb and give them rich folks something to think about."

"Shit."

"Shh."

"You've been spending too much time around Colonel John, you know that Freds?"

"*Sshhh!*"

We stopped in the darkness just outside the illuminated area. Once again I noticed that there were no animal or bird noises in the surrounding jungle, and I punched Freds in the arm and whispered into his ear, "Freds, listen! There's no sound! There's probably a tiger around here somewhere!"

"Better hurry," he muttered.

We crouched there for what seemed to me several years. The sheep out in the clearing stared around wide-eyed, occasionally letting out a bleat. I sympathized with it completely.

Then all of a sudden the big spotlights went out. Voices from the viewing tower exclaimed unhappily. Freds ran out into the clearing and I followed him. The sheep was bleating with fear. Freds cut the rope, then tackled the sheep before it could move. "Here, George," he said in a quick whisper. "Hold onto it for a second, I'm gonna just sling some of the dead one up onto the tower steps so they can get a real close-up on any tiger that comes by later." He giggled like Colonel John and slammed a live lamb into my chest. I held onto it and heard more than saw Freds picking up some pieces of the slaughtered sheep. It occurred to me that the sheep and I made a very nice two-for-one package deal for any tiger who happened to wander by and wanted to take advantage of the dark, and so I hurried after Freds just to keep near his dagger, or at least make sure that he too got eaten if it turned out that way; but the sheep had other ideas. It struggled furiously to escape, and just as I reached Freds it pushed away from me with all four legs and we pitched forward into Freds and all three of us went down in a heap. I landed on a squishy spot that appeared to be the entrails of the sheep Freds was carrying to the tower, then was yanked out of it by the live sheep, whose rope had gotten wrapped around my middle and my right arm. "Just about ready here," Freds was whispering under his breath, "no need to be so impatient," and I would've screamed but I couldn't be sure it wouldn't increase our risk. So I hauled the lamb back to my side and avoided its fierce kick; in fact I kicked it back, right behind the head, and picked the poor bleating thing up and tried to squeeze all the air out of it as I stumbled after Freds toward the viewing tower.

Up above us there were still a number of voices: high voices complaining, low voices reassuring. Freds tossed whatever he had recovered right up onto the steps, and they landed *thump thump*, completely killing all noise from above. In the dead silence we could hear distant jungle noises, and a rustle that I fervently hoped was Sunyash; and above us in the viewing tower, furious whispering, and a couple of clicks and thunks that sounded to me suspiciously like shotguns or rifles being deployed over the railings above. No doubt if we tried for sanctuary in the tower they might shoot us. If we didn't and tried to run they might shoot us too, and if not we were wandering around on foot at night in a jungle containing tigers, covered with sheep blood and carrying a live lamb in our arms.

It was not a good situation and I was ready to try calling up to the people in the tower and asking for sanctuary, but Freds was already off, and so with a moan I punched the lamb behind the head again to subdue it and took off following him. Try as I might I still felt like I was making noise like a car crash, and Freds was no quieter, and my shoulder blades were rigid with the expectation that bullet or claw was about to smack between them. Then there was a noise in the bush to the right and I opened my mouth to scream my last scream and swung the sheep back to throw it forward in sacrificial offering, when the big black bulk of the approaching thing revealed it to be Sunyash, lumbering right at us. Dawa didn't even have to stop her; Freds leaped up onto the platform with what looked like a single bound, and then I threw the lamb up to him and leaped aboard myself, hauling up the platform straps and vaulting over the rail. I landed on the sheep so hard I was sure I had killed it, but it bleated and kicked me to show it was all right.

And we were off full tilt through the jungle.

V

"HA!" FREDS SAID WHEN he had caught his breath. "Wasn't that great?"

I couldn't think of anything to say to him.

He started giggling. "Any tigers go by Tiger View later tonight, hopefully they'll climb right up the steps and scratch on that tower door. Give those sickos inside a close-up. Maybe one'll even try to rip down the door, give them some cardiac arrests in there."

"You've been hanging around Colonel John too long."

"Maybe so."

Then Dawa reached back with a hand and gestured for silence, at the same time that he got Sunyash to come to a halt. We sat there silently. We were out from under the saal canopy, in elephant grass and on the edge of a meadow. "What now," I breathed, but Dawa waved at me again, vehemently.

Freds put his mouth to my ear. "Jeep there, see it?"

He pointed, and I recognized the squarish mass to one side of the meadow. I nodded.

"Poachers," Freds whispered. "Be real quiet—this could be dangerous."

This could be dangerous? I mouthed.

Freds was over the side before I could stop him. I moved to his side of the platform, but Dawa put a hand on my arm and shook his head. We sat there for three or four minutes in silence. Then Freds was back. He held up a large conical object; I took it from him, finding it heavy and with a weird texture, and lifted it onto the platform next to the stunned sheep. "What the hell is this?" I whispered as Freds climbed up to me.

"Rhino horn," he said under his breath. "They chopped it off, see?" He had a quick conversation with Dawa and we took off again, retreating as slowly and as quietly as Sunyash could, then circling around the poacher's meadow.

"Bastards," Freds said. "It was an Army Jeep, too. Nepali Army."

"What did you do?" I asked.

"I slashed all their tires and the ignition wiring, and snatched this horn out of the back. And took down their license plate number."

"They kill the rhinos just for the horns?"

"Yep. It's the damn Chinese again—they think ground rhino horn is an aphrodisiac."

"An aphrodisiac?"

"Yeah. I guess the Chinese don't think they reproduce well enough."

"And it was a Nepali Army Jeep?"

"Yeah, but that could mean anything. Coulda stole it, borrowed it—could be Army folks out on the sly."

Suddenly there was a shout in the trees to our right, and a *bang! bang! bang!* We were being shot at. One bullet zipped overhead like a fast horsefly, and then Sunyash was off again, running full tilt. Even when she ran from the tiger she hadn't gone as fast as this; Dawa was leaning over shouting into her ears and she really pounded along, faster than anything but a rhino could have been in terrain like that. I could still hear shots behind us, but we seemed to be leaving them behind.

Then I noticed that our platform was listing to the left, sliding farther down Sunyash's broad flank with every surging step. "Straps loose," Freds exclaimed, hanging onto the downside rail. "George, grab the rope next to the strap and hold on!"

So I leaned out under the platform rail and reached down, and located a rope that apparently circled Sunyash front to back. With a hand clenched around the rope and a knee hooked over a corner post, I was able to keep the platform from listing any farther down her side. Once in position, however, I had no choice but to stay there. And Dawa, worried about the poachers, ran Sunyash all the way back to our camp, with me hanging head down, draped across the elephant's right side, scraped hard by every passing branch. Above me the sheep bleated, and Freds called out "That's it, George—hang in there—almost home."

Eventually we reached our camp, and slowed to a silent walk. At the mounting tower they disentangled me from the platform and the straps, and slid me down and caught me. Dawa took care of Sunyash and the sheep, while Freds got me to our cabin. I fell onto my bed, and soon descended into the deep sleep of denial.

An hour later the camp attendants came around banging on all the doors to wake us up. Daubahal stuck his head in our room; the rising sun ringed his smiling face.

"Elephant ride!" he announced.

That night we had mutton for dinner.

VI

THE FOLLOWING DAY WE turned the rhino horn in to Nepali policemen that Daubahal had called in, and gave them the license plate number Freds had memorized: 346. I couldn't help but wonder if the rhino horn wasn't going to end up in China anyway, but by a different route.

I peered in the busted mirror in our shower, and saw that I looked like the martyr who had tried to convert the Malays and had been flayed alive with whips of bamboo; and felt worse. But we returned to the Land Rover on the other side of the jungle river, in one last painful elephant ride, and drove away. And that evening we were back at the Hotel Star in Kathmandu, and so far as I was concerned, our jungle adventure was over. Finished. No more. All things considered, it hadn't been too bad. Compared to the previous outings with Freds, where I had been ground up like a human sausage, it was nothing. A night out. Big deal. End of story. Great. Happy me. Sorry this one was a little bit short.

But they weren't done with me yet.

Because the day after we got back, there was a knock at my door.

People rarely visit me in my room. So I picked up my Bluet stove, planning on heaving it at Freds's face if it was him and then making a run for it, and I yanked the door open shouting "What do you want!" and it was Freds and I let fly with the stove and he ducked and it went sailing down into the courtyard of the Star, clanging across the cobblestones.

But there was a couple there standing beside Freds, and who was it but Nathan Howe and Sarah Hornsby. "Nathan!" I said. "Sarah!"

"George!" they said, taken aback by my welcome.

Other than that, they looked the same as the last time I had seen them, two years before. Nathan still had his perfect seal-fur beard, and now he wore the jacket with leather patches on the elbows that the beard demanded, so that I assumed he had gotten tenure or would get tenure as soon as an academic committee spotted him; as upright, clean-cut, straightforward and true blue as they come, our

Nathan. And Sarah still looked like the sexiest librarian on earth, which as those of you who frequent libraries know means very sexy indeed, but with that added owlish touch that drives you wild. I am not into New Age greetings myself, but I decided to change my ways in order to give Sarah a big hug, and it was inspiring. Shaking Nathan's hand I caught sight of rings on their fingers and said, "What's this? Married?"

They nodded. Big smile from Nathan, the lucky devil.

"Fantastic!" I said. I recollected myself and waved them into the room. "Come on in!"

"What happened to you, George?" Sarah asked as they entered. "You look like you were in an accident."

"I was," I said. "I agreed to do Freds a favor."

"We had a blast," Freds said, sitting in his usual spot on the floor.

"That's funny," Nathan said as he and Sarah and I sat on bed and chair. "We wanted to ask you to do us a favor too, and we found out last week from Freds that you were still living here at the Star—but we haven't been able to find you at home."

"Well, that's because Freds and I . . ."

I noticed the blush flaring on Freds's cheeks. I stared at him, and he hung his head and tried to sink down into the floor. "It's because Freds needed my help keeping some friends' jungle camp in business. Didn't you, Freds?"

Freds nodded, head still bowed onto his chest. "Uh huh, that's right," he muttered.

Now Freds is a bad liar. That is not to say that he isn't great at evading the truth, or omitting it, or twisting it to serve his purposes; as someone who has been manipulated more than once by him into maniac deeds, I have a healthy respect for his cunning and unreliability. But at the actual act of bald-faced lying, he is inept. He blushes, his face contorts, he squints at you like Popeye to see if you are watching him, he stammers. He tells howlers so stupid a five-year-old would doubt them.

So I stared hard at him. "If Nathan and Sarah asked you where I was, they probably mentioned to you that they were going to ask me to do them a favor, right?"

"I don't recall," Freds muttered.

"But Nathan probably does," I said, shifting on the bed so that I was hanging over Freds a little better. "Don't you, Nathan? Didn't you tell Freds what you wanted with me?"

"Why yes," Nathan said, tilting his head curiously. "I think I did."

"And as soon as you did, Freds here ran and got me and dragged me off to the jungle. It's enough to make you suspect that he doesn't want me to help you"—and I leaned over and shouted into Freds's ear—"*isn't it?*"

"I forgot," Freds said. He raised his head to look at us, and it was like there was a big lie detector right behind him with a whole bank of red lights strobing and a siren going off. His eyes looked like they were about to spin in their sockets. "I just plain forgot, that's all, and when my buds down at Chitwan Camp asked me to bring some friends down I naturally thought of George here." Reddened southern country face, long blond hippie hair tied back in a pony tail: there couldn't have been a worse liar in the world. He was blinking a hundred times a minute, he looked desperately from one face to the next trying to find some iota of belief in us; his mouth hung open. "Besides," he cried to me, "you just hear what they want from you and you'll see I wouldn't of needed to take you away anyway!"

"Nathan," I said levelly, "what is it that you want me to do?"

"Well," Nathan said, looking with concerned alarm at our mendacious friend, "I'm working now for the South Asian Development Agency, trying to help improve conditions for the people here."

I nodded. It sounded like Nathan, and in fact I approved completely. "Good for you," I said. "And you?" I asked Sarah.

"I've got some more animal studies I'm doing," she said. "It's worked out well, so that we can both be here."

"It's great," Nathan said. "Currently I'm working on an aid project to put a sewer system into the northwest quarter of Kathmandu. They don't have sewers and it's something they really need—you know how the garbage gets piled up in the streets and all."

"I know," I said. "It's a good idea."

"Thanks. Anyway the plans are set, and everything was going fine until the proposal got to the Palace Secretariat. It's been stopped there, and we don't really know why. And I remembered how well you handled Royal Nepal Airline, and how much experience you had with the Kathmandu bureaucracy, and I was hoping we could hire you as a consultant to help us get this proposal approved and into action."

I kept a straight face and said, "I'd love to help you, Nathan."

"*What?*" Freds cried, leaping to his feet. "What do you mean 'I'd love to help you'? I come and ask you to help me with the Kathmandu bureaucracy and you tell me I can go to hell and then Nathan asks you to help *him* with the Kathmandu bureaucracy and you say 'I'd love to help you'?"

"That's right."

"It ain't fair!"

"I don't care. I want to help do something for this city, and putting in sewers is just about the first thing you'd want. It doesn't change the character of the town any, except in a way that would help keep the kids healthy. Like my beggar buddy and his little girl. Why would you want to stop such a thing, Freds?"

Freds stared back and forth at us wildly. "George won't be any help to you anyways," he said to Nathan. "He's horrible with the bureaucracy, he spent a month trying to help us and all he did was spend two thousand rupees and get a lot of people mad at him. He's useless."

"You ask A.S.J.B. Rana if I'm useless," I said sharply. "I nailed that guy! Besides, if you don't think I'd help them, why'd you slip me off into the jungle where they couldn't find me?"

"I didn't."

"You did."

Sarah stood and went to Freds, put her hand to his arm. "Freds," she said, "we're your friends. You don't have to worry so much. You can tell us what's bothering you."

She squeezed his arm. He took a deep breath. "Well," he said, wiping his face with his hands. "I reckon I'm gonna have to. I've told George about it already—"

"You have?"

"Yeah. The tunnel system, remember?" He turned to Nathan. "Nathan, you're my oldest friend, so I'm gonna trust you with this, but it's gonna put you in a hard spot, because I've got to swear you to secrecy, and that may be a problem for this project you're working on."

Nathan frowned.

Freds took in another huge breath, blew it out. "Hell, I'd better show you. You ain't gonna believe me unless you see it anyway."

VII

FREDS LED US DOWN into the section of the city between Thamel and Durbar Square, a fairly prosperous commercial district composed of narrow streets lined by two- and three-story buildings, made of brick and wood in a style that is slightly ramshackle and somehow nineteenth-centuryish, but quite solid. The thoroughfare has no official name and is called Freak Street by the Westerners, because of all the bustle and color and hash dealers. It is lined by a great number of open shopfronts, busily hawking food and books and carpets and mountain gear.

Freds turned off Freak Street into a narrow alleyway that led to our friend Yongten's carpet shop. Yongten did a lot of money-changing from his shop, and between the customers getting confused over which carpet to buy and the ones lined up to change traveler's checks into rupees, we had to wait awhile. But finally Yongten nodded at us and exchanged a word with Freds, and led us into his back room, then through a door that was a piece of the room's back wall, cut open and stuck on hinges.

We found ourselves in a narrow room that looked like an air space between buildings, except it was roofed. It was perhaps used for storage, as dark old boxes were stacked against one wall. Yongten lit a Coleman lantern and handed it to Freds, and then closed the door to the shop. By the light of the lantern he and Freds moved one stack of boxes to the side, revealing another rough wood wall, with a door cut into it that was no more than waist high. Huge black iron hinges and a matching clasp and lock kept this door secure, and Yongten took a key the size of my hand out of his jacket and unlocked the lock. He and Freds pulled back on the door together to open it.

Cool dank air gusted out at us, from a dark square hole. "Follow me close," Freds said, and crouched to enter the hole. The three of us followed, and Yongten shut us in.

"Watch out, the ceiling stays low for a stretch."

We ducked along behind Freds, hands out to protect us from any low points in the wooden ceiling above us. The walls hemming us in were brick, the floor packed earth. Then we stepped onto flagstones and down steps, until we could stand upright.

The lantern revealed what seemed to be a low, roundish gallery; in many places the light showed nothing at all, so it was hard to tell the shape of the cavern we were in. "This is the old tunnel system," Freds said in a low voice as we huddled around his light. "What we came down was just cut recently, because the only entrance left in Kathmandu that hadn't been covered up long ago was on the palace grounds, and it got covered by the foundation of a new building a couple years back. That's why the Manjushri Rimpoche wanted Dawa and me to relocate the jungle entrance. No one's too happy about this one here being in Yongten's store. He just rents that space, you know, and anything could happen."

"Who's the Manjushri Rimpoche?" Nathan wanted to know. "And what does all this have to do with our sewer project?"

"It's a long story," Freds said. "George, do you want to tell them?"

"Hell no."

So Freds led us farther into the tunnel system, and as he did he told Sarah and Nathan all about our recent adventures in Shambhala. Nathan and Sarah listened speechlessly; I couldn't see enough of their expressions to figure out what they thought of the tale, but I thought I caught heavy vibes of amazement and disbelief, confirmed by the occasional wide-eyed glance they shared.

We continued to descend, into a large squared-off tunnel, worked stone on all sides of us. Then things opened out again; we couldn't see a wall in any direction. Freds led us to a staircase that descended in a long curve down the side of what must have been an immense boring. It was impossible to believe that human labor had built it. Perhaps a natural cave had been worked smooth.

The stairs had a thick wooden bannister on the open side, for which I was grateful. The wood of the bannister was slick with hand oils. The bannister posts were carved and painted. The wall of the cavern was pocked with niches containing statues of Buddha, or Bönpa demons; it reminded me of the tunnel up in the mountains, extending from Shambhala to Nangpa La. Part of the same system, if Freds were to be believed.

We must have gone down several hundred steps when we came to the bottom of the cavern. Here the light of the Coleman lantern caught gleams from a long gallery; we followed this passageway, and found little chambers cut into the rock, some walled with highly worked bronze, others with silver, one with what appeared to be pure gold.

Freds led us into this last one. The walls, floor and ceiling were curved, so that it was like being inside a giant egg. The lantern light glowed in the soft yellow metal surrounding us. It had been worked with the Tibetan letters spelling *Om Mani Padme Hum,* repeated over and over so the inner surface of the chamber was covered with them, the tiny hammer marks black or bronze or a darker yellow or even white, depending on how the light struck them. *Om Mani Padme Hum*—the jewel in the heart of the lotus—it seemed that we were actually there, inside the jewel itself.

"Hermitage," Freds said matter-of-factly. "Padma Sambhava, the guru who brought Buddhism to Tibet, came down here once. They say the walls turned to gold when he left, with the writing already on them."

Nathan and Sarah were staring around, mouths open like fish in air. No doubt I looked much the same.

The tunnel system, Freds went on, had its center in Shambhala, and from there it radiated out in every direction. "It's not just under the Himalayas," he said, "and it doesn't just come here to Kathmandu. It's thousands of years old, and it's been very important to Shambhala—you know, in influencing the course of things, trying to keep the world from self-destructing."

I could see Nathan and Sarah trying to digest this news, and only partially succeeding. Even with the advantage of having visited Shambhala, and run for miles through its tunnel system, I had a hard time comprehending it; for them it was harder. I approached one wall and ran my fingertips over the letters. The metal was cold, the curved letters in bas-relief, with tiny chiseling marks etched at the border of the letters. Touching the wall, it seemed to me I could feel a faint vibration. The flame in the lantern flickered, the walls very slightly trembled, there was just the faintest ambient hum in the air; you could just barely sense the crowded city of Kathmandu, pounding with life over our heads.

VIII

"LISTEN, FREDS," NATHAN SAID, when we were safely back in my room at the Star—when he had had a chance to recover from the experience a bit. "Those tunnels are very interesting, and I'm sure the archeological community would be fascinated by them. But you can't allow something like that to get in the way of improving the health conditions for the people living here today! You've got to keep your priorities straight. I mean that gold-lined cave is impressive, sure, but it doesn't really matter where Padma what's-his-name hid thousands of years ago. What's important is that the people in the city now have a better chance to live healthy lives! A decent sewer system is like a minimal step in that direction, I mean without it they're living in their own garbage, and it's impossible to avoid disease in those conditions. The sewers have got to be built!" He turned to me. "George, you've got to help us get that approval over the final hurdle in the Secretariat."

"Hey no!" Freds said, reaching across the bed and shaking me by the arm. "You've gotta help stop it for good! The tunnels ain't just ancient history," he insisted. "They're still being used and they lead straight to Shambhala, and if they start digging and run across them they'll strip them and they'll follow them up to Shambhala and strip it too, and everything we did this summer to save the valley will go to waste! Nathan just don't understand what that *means*."

"I do understand," Nathan said. "But it's a question of helping the people in the city. You know what it looks like without any sewers under the streets—the streets themselves are the sewers."

"That's true," I said.

And Nathan nodded, and Freds shook his head and said "Come on, George, remember the valley," and Sarah looked at me, her eyes big behind her glasses. Freds and Nathan argued with each other, until they got pretty heated about it. Sarah tried to calm them down; they were glaring at each other, and raising their voices.

She got them to stop and then they both stared at me, hard, as if I'd better take their side. As if, in fact, it were all my fault in the first place.

"Hey," I said, hands up. "Don't look at me."

"You gave a lot to the valley," Freds said to me hotly.

"That's true."

"You know perfectly well they need sewers here or they'll be sick forever," Nathan told me with a solemn glare.

"That's true too."

And I kept agreeing with everything they said until they were both furious at me. They couldn't stand my wishy-washiness. But I wouldn't budge. Or I couldn't. They were both my friends, and they both had a point. I didn't have a clue what I was going to do. Except put them off while I tried to figure something out. So I did that, and they got extremely disgusted with me.

IX

FINALLY THEY LEFT AND I went to bed, and was sixty fathoms under when Freds rolled me into the wall and sat on the bed beside me. He stuck a lit hash pipe in my mouth, exhaled noisily. "Get prepped bro we got to take another journey to the center of the earth here."

"Wha?" I pushed him away and lit chunks of hash bounced out of his pipe and spilled all over me and the bed, glowing like tiny charcoal briquets and smoking fiercely. By the time we had leaped up and slapped them all out my one sheet was ruined, but I was wide awake, and considerably stoned, so I suppose Freds was happy.

"Freds, God damn you! What time is it?"

"Time to go, bro. I got to show you some parts of the sacred tunnels that Nathan and Sarah weren't supposed to see."

"Now?"

"Yeah, come on. It'll be a real adventure, you'll love it."

"I hate your adventures, Freds."

"Not this one. Come on, you'll see."

So I pulled on shirt and pants and blearily tied my bootlaces, and we were off, into the dark empty streets of Thamel and down to the alley and Yongten's shop. It was closed and boarded up, but when Freds knocked on the door Yongten opened up for us; like a lot of residents of Kathmandu, he slept in his place of business, on a hard cot set right next to rolls of thick carpet. He appeared unsurprised to see us, and told Freds quite a lot in Tibetan before waving us through to the back room. There we took two flashlights instead of a Coleman lantern, and followed the narrow way to the low door, and the tunnels below.

It was weird down there by flashlight. Whenever we took them off the rough stone under our feet, the beams lanced hither and yon in the blackness and caught things I hadn't seen in the localized glow of the Coleman lantern: a massive wooden lintel over one intersection, carved and painted in an intricate red green and yellow pattern; a snarling blue pop-eyed demon face, down one dead-end; a thick post of spiraling silver; and everywhere, unexpected depths where the flashlight beam never touched a thing before dissipating in the blackness. Big caverns, endless tunnels—I stayed right on Freds's heels and hoped that my flashlight would exceed the usual half-hour lifetime that these Indian models had, because if by any chance I got separated from him, I would never find my way out.

Freds stopped as we descended the cavern staircase. "George, you're kicking me in the calves."

"Oh. Sorry."

"Here. We head north up this one."

We hiked for what seemed an hour, though it could have been as little as twenty minutes. We passed rooms and niches on each side, and if I flashed them with my light they burst with the crude colors of mandalas, or the gleam of burnished metal. Our footsteps and breathing were the only sounds we heard; but at one point we stopped, and from far ahead of us wafted a faint clank, then a scrap of whispery voices.

"Hey," Freds said. "You're gonna break my arm you grab it that hard."

"Listen!" I hissed.

"I hear. That's who we've come to see, I reckon." He whistled like Star Trek, then pointed his flashlight down the tunnel and turned it off and on three times, leaving it off. "Point your flashlight at the ground," he told me.

Steps approached. We could hear them a long way off, and it took them forever to reach us, growing louder and bigger as they did. It was all I could do to keep from turning my flashlight up and blinding whoever was approaching, but Freds held me still until the steps were just down the tunnel from us, and we could make out a dim figure, just beyond the glow of my wavering light, holding a lowered flashlight of its own.

Freds switched his light on and aimed it at the wall. By the reflected light the figure could see us, and we could see him, suddenly smaller—

It was Bahadim Shrestha, our friend from the *Nepal Gazette*. "Mr. Freds," he said. "Mr. George! So good to see you again."

"Bahadim!" I said, amazed. "What the hell!"

"Indeed," he said with a small smile.

Freds quickly explained why we were here, and Bahadim frowned when he heard of the proposed sewer system. "That would be most inconvenient, yes indeed."

"Here, show George what you got going, will you? I want him to see it himself."

Bahadim looked at me closely, considering it. Then he nodded. "You must promise not to tell anyone about this. And from this point we must be very, very quiet. We have just made a noise accidentally, and it would not do to be making another so soon after it. Those above might hear us."

So we tiptoed after Bahadim down the tunnel, and came upon a group of men working by the light of a single candle. We extinguished our flashlights, and after a while I was surprised to see that the single flame actually illuminated a great deal. We were in a broad, circular room, with a low earthen roof held up by a number of wooden crossing beams. Piles of raw dirt pyramided under some new holes in the ceiling, and spindly ladders stuck up into these dark holes. Bahadim led me to one of the ladders, which appeared to have been made on the spot, the rungs lashed onto two long poles with rope. He tugged on a piece of string hanging down between the rungs, and shortly thereafter another small Hindu man came down the ladder, moving slowly and silently. Bahadim pointed up the ladder, then whispered in my ear, "Go to the top and look in the mirror tube."

So I tested the bottom rung and found it would hold me, and skinnied up the hole into the dark until my head bumped dirt. The top of the tunnel was illuminated by what I thought at first was a little penlight, but which actually turned out to be the mirror tube Bahadim had mentioned. I put my eye to the end of this thing, and saw in a tiny chip of mirror a small part of a well-lit room: a desk, apparently, with an empty chair behind it, and a wall. A blurry tan shape moved before me and then it was the same scene again. After a while I figured that was it, and descended the ladder.

"You saw?" Bahadim whispered in my ear.

I nodded. "What was it?" I whispered in his ear.

"That was the working office of the King."

I whipped my head back and stared at him.

He nodded. "Truly," he whispered.

I waved my hand around at the other holes in the ceiling, each with its ladder.

He nodded again, and the red dot on his forehead gleamed. "Offices of the Palace Secretariat," he whispered. "Ministers' council room. King's private quarters. We have been finding all the important places in the palace."

I looked around again and saw that a group of men seated in a circle on the floor were busy constructing another mini-periscope, made of taped-together cardboard tubes and the tiny circular mirrors that are sewn into local dresses. Other cardboard tubes, cut and shaped like antique hearing trumpets, served them as microphones.

Bahadim saw that I was miming questions at him, and led me back down the tunnel the way we had come, then off into a side tunnel and into a little chamber. There on the floor were a candle lantern and a tiny primus stove, teacups and a teapot. He sat cross-legged before the stove and began to brew us a pot, just as if we were in his office at the *Gazette*.

"Yes," he said when he had poured us steaming cups of tea, "we are under the palace grounds. The tunnels themselves have always been here, but lately we have been sending up the observation posts, to be seeing better what goes on in the Secretariat."

"You're spying on them?"

"Yes. You see, as I told you when we met before, it is impossible to tell from the outside how decisions are made in the palace. But without that knowledge we cannot oppose these decisions successfully."

"So who are you?" I said.

"We are a wing of the Nepali Congress Party, the largest opposition party. Nepal is officially a no-party system, you see. The Panchayat Raj. But there are opposition parties despite that, and the biggest is our Congress Party. We would like to see Nepal changed into a parliamentary democracy, with a real government—something besides the people over us." He jerked a thumb at the ceiling. "Unfortunately, the Congress Party itself is highly factionalized. There is a wing led by G. P. Koirala, another by Ganesh Man Singh, a third by K. P. Bhattarai. All somewhat at odds with each other, and that combined with the fact that we are officially illegal means we do not do very well in the elections. So—" He whispered a sigh. "We lose the elections to the Panchayat Party. And the palace Ranas rule, and nothing is ever changing in Nepal."

I nodded. I had seen that up close and personal, in my miserable and completely futile attempt to kill the road to Chhule by diplomatic means.

Bahadim's face brightened. "But now we have hope! When one of us discovered the tunnels here, our wing of the party decided to take direct action, pending the day when we are having more of a voice in the legal government. We have constructed this system for observing the palace Ranas at work, and when we discover their plans, we do what we can to aid or obstruct them, depending what they are."

"It's a great idea," I said.

Bahadim nodded. "We have also constructed a kind of underground government, you might call it." He fingered diagrams on the colored cloth spread under us. "Most of the foreign aid in Nepal comes from big international agencies or other countries, and most of it goes where the Ranas direct it. Often to businesses they themselves own. Big money, big projects, big delays—little results. This is always the story in Nepal. The people never see any of it. So we have begun aid projects ourselves, funded by a few

277

prosperous Nepalis who support us. The amounts are small, and they are given to the smallest kinds of projects— the irrigation of a single field, the beginning of a basket shop or a carpet loom or the like. Our headquarters are kept down here in the tunnels for secrecy's sake. And in time we hope to become the real government of Nepal—because we are the ones actually helping the people of our country, do you understand?"

"You bet!" I said.

Grinning, Freds put a finger to his lips. "Don't talk too loud, guys, you'll give it all away."

Bahadim smiled. "Sorry—it gets me excited. You understand?"

I nodded. "Listen," I whispered, "there's a beggar in Thamel, a beggar with a little girl, and they don't have anywhere to stay, or any work. Could you help them?"

"We can try," Bahadim whispered back. "Give me their name— Ah. You don't know it. Well—I will visit you, and you can perhaps take me to them." I nodded. "We will see what can be done."

Impressed, I looked at Freds. He grinned and said, "See what I mean?"

X

I SAW WHAT HE meant. And as we made our way through the dark, back to the entrance behind Yongten's shop, the huge system of tunnels took on a different appearance for me. It was still the lost ruins of an ancient and long-forgotten kingdom, sure; but it was also, it seemed, the vestigial network of a new government of Nepal—an underground government, created to work against the corrupt rule of King Birendra and the Ranas in the palace. It pleased me no end to learn that such a thing existed.

So when Nathan woke me with a knock at my door early the next afternoon, I felt awkward with him, and tried my best to put him off. But Nathan is not the kind of guy you can put off easily, and he wanted to show me what his sewer project was hoping to do.

So we walked around the northwest quarter of Kathmandu, not only in Thamel, but also in the less-visited areas outside it, on the banks of the Vishnumati River. Here there were hardly any foreigners; it was home for the locals. Many of these people worked in the tourist trade in Thamel, but it was clear they didn't make much from it; the neighborhoods were packed, the buildings old and small, their bricks handmade and irregular so that the buildings tilted crazily. The streets between them were mud runnels, and all in all it looked like I imagine Elizabethan London must have looked, except for the sacred cows and the little Toyotas zooming by honking their horns. This was the home of Kathmandu's poor, a dirty, cramped, squalid zone, utterly unlike the funky and picturesque downtown. In this district any Westerner was as rich as a king. It was a sensation I had enjoyed, once upon a time.

Here and there in corners or wide spots in the street piles of refuse had accumulated for years, worked down by the rain and by foraging cows, goats, dogs, rats, children, and beggars. As we watched the crowds swirl around these dumps, Nathan told me more about the project. Apparently the South Asian Development Agency, the sponsor of the project, had been one of the worst-run aid agencies working in Nepal. Lax accounting practices had made it one of those money funnels that rumor speaks of, wherein money intended to help the people of the country actually ends up lining the pockets of bureaucrats along the way.

Nathan had taken the job offered by the agency determined to end this kind of thing, and the first step had been to establish a full-time Kathmandu office, which he manned himself. Before that the agency's business had been done on short visits from the main office in Manila, which of course meant that no one really knew what was going on in Nepal. This had resulted in some horribly inappropriate aid programs, some of which had even been vetoed by the agency's donors, which was a rare event. "But everyone's been enthusiastic about this sewer project," Nathan said, "and you can see why."

"Yeah."

We had reached the banks of the Vishnumati River, and there under the bright sun and the scattered cottonball clouds we could see the whole story: women washing clothes in the shallows; trash being dumped from a cart onto a big pile on the bank, which was undercut by the stream; makeshift huts set right on the water's edge; spindly kids scavenging empty lots or the gravelly floodlands; and there around us, the spoor of old shitting grounds. And this river merged downstream with the Bagmati, which ran by the university and a couple of the city's hospitals. Polluted as it was, it was inconceivable that the city's population could ever become healthy.

Then on the way back we navigated the crowded muddy lanes into the hive of Thamel, and all around us it was clear that the locals were doing their best to make a living from the inexhaustible fortune that the Western visitors represented, and some were succeeding and others were marginal and others still were for whatever reason flat-out failing, living in the streets and begging to avoid starvation. I had been doing what I could to help two of these people, a man and his little girl, until Freds had wagged his finger at me one night when he was stoned and told me that those two were relatively prosperous because of people like me fixing on the cute and pathetic little girl; that there were old men, old women, alone and ignored and several steps down the ladder even from the man and his girl; and after that I had, in effect, given up. I didn't know what to do, I didn't know how to help. Kathmandu wasn't the same place it had been: And now Nathan waved a hand at the garbage pile just up the lane from the Hotel Star and the Kathmandu Guest House, and said "See what I mean?"

And all I could say was, "Yeah, yeah. I see what you mean."

XI

So THERE MATTERS STOOD when Nathan and Sarah dropped by my room to see if I had made up my mind, and Freds and I were sitting in there working on a bowl of hash and Nathan naturally assumed that we were conspiring together and his upper lip lifted with hearty disgust for me. "I don't know why I thought you would want to help the poor of Nepal anyway," he said bitterly. "Just another trek guide, exploiting the country for all it's worth. I wish I'd never even met you!"

"Well hey," I said, aggrieved. "I wish I'd never met you neither! In fact I wish I hadn't stolen your letter to Freds and read it because then I'd never have gotten involved with you guys, and I'd still be having fun over here, and my face would still be in one piece, and I'd weigh more than a hundred and thirty pounds!" It was hard not to shout at him. "But you!" I shouted. "*You* wouldn't ever have found Freds, or saved your brain-damaged yeti, or gotten it together with Sarah here!"

"You stole that letter?" Nathan said, ignoring everything else I'd said. .

"Well, yes. I did: It looked interesting."

He threw up his hands. "No wonder you won't help us! I mean, what kind of principles—I mean, who would steal a *letter*?"

"I would."

Freds exhaled noisily. "He's worthless with the bureaucracy here anyway. You're better off without him. We tried to get him to help us and they only use his brains for a volleyball. Can't you see that by the look on his face? Worthless. Watch. *Singha Durbar!*" he snapped at me. "See that? He flinches if you even say the name."

"Ungrateful bastard," I said to him. "You just ask your Manjushri Rimpoche if I was worthless. You ask Colonel John if I was worthless."

"If we'd be better off without him," Sarah pointed out to Freds, "then you wouldn't be trying to convince us not to get his help."

"That's right," I said. Sarah seemed to be the only one to have paid attention to what I had said about helping to get her and Nathan together, and she watched me through the argument with a little smile, which made me feel rambunctious. "You'd better show more appreciation," I growled at Nathan, "or I might actually help Freds, and then you'd really be in trouble. Here, sit down and smoke the pipe of peace with us."

"No way," he said, folding his arms. "I'm trying to have a serious conversation."

"Spoilsport."

"Degenerate."

"Bridge smasher. Liar. Home breaker. Pet thief."

The skin of Nathan's cheeks was turning a bright red, except for a narrow line at the top of his beard. I found this phenomenon interesting, and was trying to think of more names to call him when Sarah stepped in, and ordered us to stop being silly. "We're just wasting time here, and there isn't that much time to waste."

"That's right," Nathan said, anxiety and indignation battling in him. "That Rana is about to turn us down—"

"Rana?" I said. "Which Rana?"

"You don't care about him," Freds began, but I waved him off.

"Not A.S.J.B. Rana, by chance?"

"Why yes, I think so. Do you know him?"

"I thought I had ended his career."

"Why no—he was just recently made head of the foreign aid office in the palace."

"Promoted! It can't be the same one."

"You don't care about him," Freds told me.

"The hell I don't!" I yelled loudly.

"Quiet!" Sarah said loudly. "Stop this bickering!"

We all looked at her.

"It isn't necessary," she said, laughing at us. "I can see by the look on George's face that he's got a plan." She sat down next to me on the bed and put her arm around my shoulders. She gave me a hug. "I can just tell. You've got a plan, right George?"

The funny thing was, a plan was kind of coming to me. It was like inspiration. "That's right," I said, feeling warm. "I've got a plan."

Nathan and Freds stared dubiously at me.

"The first part of the plan," I said, thinking about it, "is that you both get me maps—Nathan of the proposed sewer sytem, and Freds of the old tunnels. Can you do that for me?" They nodded. "Good. The second part of the plan is that we go have dinner at the Old Vienna, and look them over."

"That's no plan," Nathan complained.

"Yes it is. I do have a plan." And really, it was coming to me even as I spoke. I put my arm around Sarah and gave her a hug back, and it all fell into place like a long string of dominos. "I just don't know if it will work or not."

XII

AND SO THAT EVENING, after one of Eva's sumptuous Austro-Hungarian feasts, we found ourselves seated in one of the big booths at the back of the Old Vienna Inn, warm in the steamy sauerkraut-and-Strauss air, nibbling at the last of the apple strudel and sipping schnapps and/or cappuccino. I got out one of my yellow Lufthansa maps of Kathmandu, and a pencil, and carefully transferred the information from Nathan and Freds's maps onto it. "See, look," I said. "They only intersect in three places, and none of those places are really major parts of the tunnel system."

"Yeah, but they connect the big rooms together," Freds said. "Besides it's all one—if you run into them, you discover the whole system."

"I know that, I know that. But say you filled in your tunnels, in just those places." I illustrated by erasing those sections of Freds's system. "Then if they built the sewers, they'd find some strangely loose dirt, but that's no big deal, the underside of a city is bound to be weird. So they lay the sewers and they never notice a thing."

"But the different parts of the tunnel system would be cut off from each other!" Freds objected.

"Sure, sure, but you can always go deeper, see—after they're done you can dig under the sewers, put in another nifty staircase system, and when it's all over the sewers are laid, and your tunnel system is back in action, and no one's the wiser!"

"That's a lot of labor," Sarah noted. "Where is Freds going to get the manpower for something like that?"

"Freds has got friends up north," I said. "The very people who use this tunnel system, in fact. If they went to work on it, it could be a matter of days. Put Colonel John on it and it could be a matter of hours."

Freds was nodding. Nathan was nodding. Sarah leaned over to give me a kiss on the cheek. We toasted the plan, and I agreed to go in and see exactly how old A. Shumsher Jung Bahadur Rana was using this sewer project to further himself.

XIII

Mʏ ᴘʀᴇᴠɪᴏᴜs ᴇɴᴄᴏᴜɴᴛᴇʀ ᴡɪᴛʜ A.S.J.B.R. had ended on a bad note, and so when I entered his durbar one morning soon after our dinner I had a whole pile of baksheesh from the South Asian Development Agency ready to hand over to him, along with an elaborate apology for the little incident that had ended our last meeting; I planned to explain to him that I had been stressed out as a result of serious illness and a case of insanity in my immediate circle, figuring it is always best to use the truth when you can.

But when I approached A. Rana he turned in my direction, nodded shortly, and then waited to find out who I was, and what I wanted. *He didn't recognize me.*

I had spent five billion hours in his office; and the last time we had seen each other we'd ended up screaming in each other's faces; but he didn't remember me. I stood that far outside his system.

This was such a shock that it took me a while to collect myself. Given the nature of our last meeting, it was of course a good thing he didn't recognize me; but I couldn't help feeling pissed off. That he would *forget* me, after all that *pain* . . . I choked off my irritation and went with it. I declared myself a representative of the South Asian Development Agency, which caught his interest immediately, no doubt because of the agency's reputation for shoddy accounting practices. I told him about the sewer project, and he nodded and told me to come by his office during the afternoon.

I had seen this movie before. I did not care to see it again.

Nevertheless I gave it a try, and started the familiar round of visits and payments. Nothing came of it, although

I was able to confirm some things about his new position in the Secretariat. It was true; somehow he had weaseled out of the whammy I had laid on him with the Great Border Incident, and more than that—he had gotten a promotion out of it. I couldn't imagine how. "Oh, sir! It seems I am being responsible for a crisis that has nearly brought the Indians and Chinese down on our heads! Perhaps even begun World War Three!" "Good. You are promoted to head of the department controlling all foreign aid help." Okay. Another Great Mystery of Nepal.

It increased my already healthy respect for A.S.J.B.R.'s Machiavellian ability to fall upward, and I dealt with him as cautiously as I could. But after only a week of the hold-and-extract routine I found that my patience for sitting around in his office had *completely* disappeared. I couldn't stand it. I still harbored a lot of ill will—hatred, in fact—for him from the last time, and even though it was useful that he didn't remember who I was, that still rankled bad. I just couldn't stand waiting around for him.

So I arranged a meeting with Bahadim, and asked him whether his spy system included observation of A. Rana's offices.

Bahadim nodded. "You know how it is in Nepal—the foreign aid community is one of the biggest centers of power we have. A. Rana is not the most important person in this area, but it appears that he is rising fast, and we had a tunnel built under his office. Would you like to join us in watching him?"

"Oh, man—" I put a hand over my heart. "I can't *tell* you how good that sounds. It's the best news I've heard in *years!*"

Bahadim regarded me oddly, and I refrained from kissing him. But I was awfully pleased by this news, and couldn't have been happier the following day, when Bahadim and one of his cohorts took me through Yongten's shop and down into the tunnels again. I followed them to their under-palace complex, and skinnied up one of the ladders with Bahadim ahead of me. There was scarcely room at the top of the ladder for both of us; it was a small low earthen cave, with a section of the roof that was higher than the rest, and made of wood. This was the corner of the floor of A. Rana's office. A little mirror periscope and earhorn were inserted into cracks where the floor met the wall. I looked in the periscope, and after a while perceived a corner of a desk and a wall. No people on view. But when Bahadim took the plug out of the earhorn we could both hear voices above us, conversing in rapid, loud Nepalese.

I had arranged for Nathan to visit A. Rana's offices, in the hope of stimulating some inner sanctum conversation on our case. After Bahadim and I had been settled in place for some time, I heard his name spoken in the midst of a burst of Nepalese: "Mr. Nathan Howe." All the voices receded into the outer office, where I could just hear the sound of Nathan's voice, in conversation with A. Rana—I couldn't make out what they were saying.

Finally A. Rana returned to his office and got on the phone. Bahadim shifted around so he could put his mouth to my ear, to whisper a partial translation. "He is speaking to a friend in the Department of Public Works . . . about the sewers, yes. He is planning to give the contract for this work to the friend." Suddenly Bahadim stopped whispering and listened hard for a long time. I stared at his face in the gloom. A. Rana hung up the phone, and Bahadim whispered in my ear, "Actually the contract is already awarded, and the work will soon begin. They only delay telling Mr. Howe to obtain more money from the agency."

"Did he say when they're going to start?"

"No."

I scurried down the ladder to the cavern, and we retreated to Bahadim's little underground office chamber. While he cooked up a pot of tea I pounded fist into palm nervously. "What does it mean, what does it mean?"

"It means only that the project has been approved, and yet A. Rana has delayed informing the agency about this. It is a fairly common tactic with agencies like that one, to generate more baksheesh. The South Asian Development Agency is known to harbor loose accountants."

"Damn," I said. "That A. Rana is such a *crook*."

"It is not likely it is just him doing it."

"Who, then? Who makes the decisions up there?"

Bahadim poured our tea, shrugged. "No one can be sure. Anyone who tells you that he knows how the Palace Secretariat makes its decisions is a liar. The palace is like what you call a black box. People go in—information, money, requests go in—decisions come out. What happens inside is secret. They do not want you to know, you see. No one from the outside. It is a habit we have in Nepal, a desire to be holding some secrets to ourselves. It is a big world, and we are small, and so we feel the need to have something of our own. Some secrets, if nothing else."

"But the corruption it allows!"

"I know."

"You need laws, Bahadim. You need some kind of legal system. A constitutional monarchy or whatever."

Bahadim was sipping at his tea, but he waved a finger at me vigorously. "Oh my! Those are very bad words in the palace, you must believe me. Constitutional monarchy, oh! It has caused great trouble when other governments innocently use this phrase, because it is a code for us, you see. To the royal family it is a fright because it reminds them of the days when they were controlled by the Ranas, and could do nothing. And to the Ranas it is a fright because it suggests an open system, and an end to their power."

"But I thought the Ranas were overthrown in the fifties! Isn't that what you told me?"

He wiggled a hand ambiguously. "It was almost true. But in the years since they have slipped back into power. Because the Shahs are always marrying Ranas. The Queen is a

Rana, you see. And the King's two younger brothers, they married the Queen's two younger sisters. And the heads of the Army are Ranas. And all over—" He waved his hand to indicate the palace above us. "Ranas. That family runs this country. We need desperately the constitutional monarchy you speak of, but the Ranas will stop it if they can."

I shook my head. "It can't be good for the country."

"No, of course it is not good!" Bahadim's mouth tightened. "In 1951 at the time of our revolution Nepal was the same size, economically speaking, as South Korea. And South Korea suffered their war, and yet only thirty-seven years later, South Korea is what it is—while here we are, still among the poorest nations on the earth. Now you can say Korea has a seacoast and we do not, but still, it is more than that. We simply cannot advance economically until we advance politically! A constitutional democracy, yes. It is what we work for down here!"

His eyes gleamed in the lantern light, and when he put down his teacup, his hand formed a fist. I could see he was dead serious, and I knew I had found the team I wanted to play on. "Can you keep a watch on A. Rana's office for me?" I asked.

"Oh, yes. We will be keeping someone under it whenever it is occupied. We would like to know what is going on with this sewer project. It seems it is just as always; the contract is being given to a friend of the Ranas. It was probably not the lowest bid, if bids were entertained at all, and now it has not been announced yet, so that maximum amounts of baksheesh can be taken from the source of funds. Much of the money will no doubt be ending up in India, in Rana accounts and with subcontractors. And there is no telling what kind of horrible sewers we might get for this."

I nodded. "We'll need to know when they're planning to begin."

"I will let you know what we learn."

When I got home to the Star, Nathan was already there. "My gosh, George, you must really be some operator. I talked to the foreign aid officer you made the appointment with, and damned if he didn't tell me the project was approved!"

"I had nothing to do with it," I said. "Did he say when they're going to start?"

"Why, no. There's a lot to be done, a bidding process and all—"

"They've already done that," I told him sourly, and gave him a truncated version of the news. He was shocked.

A couple of days later Bahadim called me on the phone. His listeners had found out that the digging for the sewer was supposed to begin soon. The contractor had hired a Swiss technician to help, meaning everything would happen three times faster than it would have otherwise.

So it was time to go into overdrive. Freds took off for Shambhala, to recruit Colonel John and the Khampas for help in rearranging their tunnel system under the city. It would take them a while to get down to Kathmandu and get started; meanwhile there was little for me to do. I surveyed the tunnel system, and determined exactly where the sewers' trenches would cut through it, and marked up the tunnel system to show where it should be filled; I spent hours lying under A. Rana's floor, listening to him lying up above me, getting angrier and angrier at him; I even cleaned my room, something I hadn't done in months.

While I was doing the cleaning I came across a little bag of junk from my first trek in Nepal. I had been hired to assist with that trekking group, even though I hadn't known a thing about it; our Sherpa sirdar had taught me everything. Among the mementoes in the bag was a folded piece of paper, worn at the creases. Curiously, not recalling what it was, I unfolded it.

It was a letter, in a strange spiky handwriting that I found hard to read.

Date. 27/9/1981

Respected Sir,
        Namaste.
    Today I am writing a letter for you and I hope and saw you are living at school play ground so that I am very happyness to you and your guides. I want to tell you about this primary school poor condition excuse me sir here are not responsive person and rich man so that they can't give a lot of money for school. In my school here aren't enough furniture to sit student and I hope you help for this primary school by money. If you have money but I am very sad to writting this letter for you. Sir I have to much problem in school. What can I do? because I am also a poor teacher in this social. Now I stop my pen.

                                your credible teacher
                                Ramdas Shrestha
                                headmaster

I sat on my bed with the note on my knee, remembering. We had come in late one night to a teahouse and a school, straddling a steep ridge next to the trail. Sangbadanda, that was it. It had rained hard that night, and our group was exhausted, half of them sick already, and so we had spent the next day drying out and recovering. Sitting there in the morning sun I had been approached by a young guy from the school, who had handed me the note with a smile. After reading it I'd given the young man some rupees, and they had invited me into the school to talk to the head-master and all the teachers. The headmaster was an old re-tired Gurkha, who ran the school on his pension. As we had noticed that morning, he drilled the kids like they were in boot camp. His teachers were young guys who all had a little English, and they were happy to talk to me about America and American schools, and about their own school. They had no books; they taught on blackboards. Coming out of the meeting with them I had yelled at one of

291

my clients for peeing against the back wall of the school-house. But there's shit all over the place, he had protested.

I folded the note slowly, and put it back in the bag. And I made my way through the streets and down to Bahadim's underground headquarters still thinking about that headmaster and his school.

Bahadim joined me in the listening post under A. Rana's office, and we lay there in the dark while A.S.J.B.R. operated just inches above our heads. During one of his interminable phone conversations Bahadim grabbed my hand and squeezed. "He is dealing with an Army friend," Bahadim whispered in my ear. "They are selling rhinoceros horns to members of a Chinese trade group. It is poaching in Chitwan, for sure."

I lay there and physically held myself back from punching A. Rana's floor. Sleazy slimy son of a bitch, pocketing bribes in a country without school books, poaching in a country with hardly any rhinos left—failing to recognize me!—I wanted to scream, I wanted to kill him; he'd remember me then, just punch his floor so hard that the shock scared him to death! I could barely stop myself from doing it. It was the first obvious sign that I was losing my grip.

XIV

AFTER THAT SIGNS OF this problem came more frequently. In fact much of the following week is blurry in my memory. I ran around in the streets of the city and the tunnels below it, doing a very primitive and often clandestine surveying job to mark the spots in the tunnels that needed to be filled; and while doing that I fizzed over with plans, scenarios that I worked out in tremendous detail (except for certain critical moments). I brooded deeply over these plans, and jumped nervously whenever anyone asked me what I was so deep in thought about. "Nothing! Nothing! Get back to work!" I would yelp, and we'd be back to it. The Khampas arrived with Colonel John in the lead, shouting loud enough to be heard on the streets above, if life up there didn't run at a constant hundred decibels. They brought with them a whole system of little mine carts like something the seven dwarfs would use, which apparently were standard equipment in the long-range tunnels they had traveled in to get down to us. These carts ran on permanent iron tracks in the long-range tunnels, Freds told me, and they could lay temporary tracks under the city as needed.

So we all started running back and forth in the tunnels, digging with picks, shoveling dirt onto carts, and staggering around in the dark as we pushed them back and forth along the new tracks. The digging for the sewer had already begun above, and they were going to break into the first of the ancient tunnels in a matter of days. They were closing off back streets and digging them up with Indian machinery, and with the Swiss engineer on the scene every day diving into the holes and running the backhoes and exhorting the workers in bad Nepalese, they were making remarkably good progress. Down below we had more to do and less to do it with, although every day additional Khampas arrived out of the dark tunnels to the west. And Colonel John was more than a match for the Swiss guy above us; he reverted to full dress Marine Corps mode, and screamed at us all so loudly that I was sure they'd hear us on the streets. If it weren't for the fact that the extremely noisy festival of Dasain had begun, I'm sure they would have. But they didn't and we pounded away, driven slavelike by the lash of the colonel's tongue. "John Wayne meets Ben-Hur," Freds muttered one time after the colonel had blown through. "Don't take it personal, George, he doesn't really mean it's all your fault."

"Then why did he say 'This is all your fault'?" I muttered. It wasn't fair. I shook my head hard but couldn't seem to clear it. I'd been underground for most of several days, and every time I emerged from Yongten's shop it turned out to be nighttime, and the Dasain celebrations were in full swing, with fireworks going off overhead and underfoot, and masked nightmare figures crashing blindly through the streets, drinking and yelling in the intermittent light. Dodging them and the fireworks I came to feel that it was more normal underground than on the surface, and I decided to just stay below for the duration. Sarah and Nathan brought down meals, and we ate in the gold-lined chamber, which was only a short distance from one of our filling operations. A single candle could light that chamber like a naked 150-watt bulb. We slept in one of the bronze chambers nearby, catching only a few hours at a time.

The fill was coming along, although it proved difficult to ram dirt right up to the ceiling. Colonel John solved that by erecting a wall at one end and then shoving dirt up to it. He went all out, re-creating what he thought the earth under an old city like Kathmandu should look like—shards of old pottery, rotted beams, a lost silver spoon—a whole archeological fantasia of false strata and old finds, until it got so bad we had to drag him out of there and let the Khampas and Bahadim's Congress Party rebels fill the space up to the ceiling, and then wall off the other side.

Just after they'd finished the first of those, we heard a low rumble, and the tunnels quivered around us, and we got our first test; they had reached our new fill, and were digging through it. Nathan kept running up to street level to see that they were keeping on track, but I was confident they would; they'd have to burrow under buildings to leave it. The only question was, had I surveyed the tunnel correctly, so that we had filled the area underneath the street? I was worried that they might excavate right into one of the new retaining walls, and burst right through the whole plan. What Colonel John would say to me then! But they didn't, at least not at that first intersection.

The next one was only a couple of blocks away, and so we had no rest. And this was more than a tunnel; it was one of the big circular chambers, and to be safe we were going to have to fill it entirely, and at the same time build a new passageway deep beneath it, because otherwise we would be blocked off from one whole section. So we ran down narrow tunnels extending to the west, toward Shambhala, and hacked madly at the walls while making sure we didn't bring the roof down on us; then carted the dirt back into this chamber, which seemed like a bottomless pit. Bahadim's crew did this while simultaneously celebrating Dasain, so that they were draped in streamers and confetti and their foreheads and the parts of their hair were dotted and streaked with red dye and colored grains of rice, and they were drunk most of the time. Freds considered this a good plan and joined them in it. Meanwhile the sewer builders were churning on above us with unusual efficiency, dropping lengths of concrete pipe like they were in a race. They were about to reach the chamber, and so we went into overdrive, everyone working round the clock to get it filled. Colonel John was furious. Freds was ecstatic. "Isn't this a blast?" he kept saying during our breaks. I gobbled down the sandwiches Sarah and Nathan had brought down and declined to respond. The truth was I was feeling weird; I hadn't yet recovered from my weight loss of the summer, and besides my Shambhalan dysentery was coming back a bit, leaving me light-headed and sometimes a touch delirious.

When we were done with one meal Freds popped a bottle of chang and lit up his pipe. "Here," he choked, puffing away, "have a hit of this, digging's a lot more fun with a little buzz on." Unfortunately I took him up on the offer and sucked down a lungful when he added, "I just scored this from a guy on Freak Street, supposed to be cut with opium," at which point I coughed till I almost broke ribs. Then immediately on leaving the chamber I ran into one of the low beams in the tunnel, smacking my forehead, and between that and Freds's opiated hash I found myself deep in the dreamtime. Like, were the miners hauling those overfull carts of dirt rather short, and hairy, with long arms, and peculiar heads? Did I see one of them wearing a Dodgers cap? Were there in fact a whole *lot* of them zooming around in the dark like gnomes, and saving the day as far as filling the big chamber goes? I can't really tell you for sure. I only know that I felt extremely strange, and that we were working like fiends, with the rumble of bulldozers overhead, and even if we did get the chamber filled in time we still had another tunnel to fill farther to the west, and I was staggering around doing all this when Bahadim passed me and said "We have just overheard your friend Mister A. Rana telling the South Asian Development Agency that the sewer project is running behind schedule, and asking them for another million dollars to help with that. And then he telephoned those Chinese traders to make arrangements to supply them with what he called a permanent source in Chitwan, so that they can run their factory reliably. A Chinese aphrodisiac factory no doubt! Isn't that funny!"

And I flew into a rage and dropped the pick from my blistered palms and took off running through the tunnels, north to the palace. I had lost my mind.

XV

This was the plan: I would skinny up the ladder into the little space they had cut behind the King's quarters, and break open the narrow crack in his closet's back wall that we had been listening through, and crawl through into the closet and from there into the King's private chambers. Threatening the King with something (I hadn't quite worked out what), I would force him down into the tunnels below and turn him over to Bahadim and the other members of the Congress Party splinter down there with him. With the King in hand they would be able to take over in a quick bloodless coup, the same kind of coup King Mahendra had laid on the country back in 1960. The Congress Party would take over and the Ranas would be kicked out on their asses, and everything would be better.

It worked like a charm. A crowbar snatched from one of the work sites sufficed to break open the crack in the King's closet. Below me some of Bahadim's crew of observers were whispering up at me fiercely, "What are you doing!" and the like, but I ignored them and wedged my way through the crack and into a black closet, which was lined on both sides by impressive royal or military jackets. It was not an Imelda Marcos–type closet, you understand, but big enough to walk in, which I did, to a door that I opened just a little.

And there he was, standing with his back to me. I threw open the door and grabbed him around the neck and held the crowbar out before him so he could see what he would get hit with if he struggled. He didn't resist, and I hauled him back into the closet and spun him around, growling "Don't make a sound!" in a low murderous voice. "Here—through this hole—go!" And I shoved him ahead of me through the break I had made in the wall. "Down a ladder!" I added quickly, but apparently not quickly enough, as there was a *thump thump thump* sound descending our little manhole.

I hurried through and dropped down the ladder and found the King just getting to his feet. He was straightening his jacket and looking around at the circle of Bahadim's associates, who now ringed us. I caught sight of his face for the first time and for a second I reeled, thinking How in the hell did they get Jerry Lewis into the palace? But no—he only looked like Jerry Lewis, or at least as much like Jerry Lewis as the Dalai Lama looked like Phil Silvers; in other words not much, but enough to give you a start if you ran into him at the bottom of a poorly lit cavern.

So there we were; we had him: His Majesty King Birendra Bir Bikram Shah Dev, standing right there, blinking at us. The Congress Party guys, most of whom had been working themselves ragged to plug the tunnels, stood there speechless. The King was speechless. I was speechless.

Bahadim broke through the circle. "What is this, what is going on oh *my*!" He had caught sight of the King and stopped, frozen like Lot's wife. His mouth was a perfect O.

Then he broke the tableau and rushed to my side. "What are you doing?" he gabbled. "What is this?"

"This is the King," I said, gesturing with my crowbar.

"Yes I know this but what is he *doing* down here, what have you *done*?"

"Coup," I said. "This is a coup. We're taking over."

"*Aggh!*" he said loudly. He grimaced. He hopped up and down in place, he slapped me wildly back and forth on my upper arm, he wrung his hands till I thought his fingers would break off. He sucked in a breath, and then shuffled over to face the King, who had watched the whole performance with a dazed expression. His tinted glasses couldn't have helped him any down there in that gloom.

"Your Majesty," Bahadim said, "we are most sorry, this man here has made a most horrible error in trying to help us, you must forgive him, he is an American."

"Ah," the King said.

"Please," Bahadim said. He reached a hand toward the King, withdrew it, then reached out again and took the King gently by the forearm. He shifted into Nepalese and they had a quick conversation as he led the King back to the bottom of the ladder and started him up it.

Noises from up the shaft. Shouts. Bahadim sucked in air

again and explained something to the King in the most rapid Nepalese I had ever heard. The King nodded at him and continued climbing.

Then the shouts began to descend the ladder, and Bahadim turned and said something fierce to his cohorts, who immediately disappeared in the blackness, and then he ran at me and gave me a tremendous whack on the arm. "Fool! Fool! Aggh! Fly, come follow—we must fly—"

And suddenly there were big black boots hanging down out of the hole, scrabbling for the ladder rungs and kicking the King in the head, and Bahadim yanked me by the arm and we were off into the dark.

XVI

WHEN WE LOCATED THE rest of our companions, still working like dervishes in a mad dance, Bahadim shouted for their attention and told them quickly what had happened, in English and Nepalese. Everyone stopped and stared at me in disbelief. Then Freds and Colonel John stepped forward, and after a quick conference everyone was running around, some apparently to try to block off tunnels in hopes of concealing the extent of the system from the King's soldiers; others, including the platoon of yetis, simply to get out of the way. Freds led us to an obscure side tunnel entrance, one I had never been down. "Stay here," he told me and Bahadim, and then he and the colonel were off.

We stood in the dark listening. There was an eerie silence in the tunnels, punctuated by shouts from the direction of the palace—the King's security people, no doubt. Every once in a while Bahadim punched me in the arm, muttering under his breath. Then Freds rejoined us, breathing hard.

He cupped his hands and yelled back the way he had come. "Oh! No! Here they are coming! Run!" We heard shouts and took off running down the narrow side tunnel.

"What are we doing?" I asked Freds as we jogged along.

"We're the decoy," he said. "This is the tunnel that goes down to Chitwan, you know, the one we found. The colonel's gotten the bodyguards who came down from the King's palace to follow us, and he figures he can block off a lot of the system while they're doing that, hide some of what's down here." We came to a fork and Freds led us left. A few minutes down this hole and he yelled back the way we had come: "Oh! No! Here they are coming!"

"This will not be necessary once I get a chance to speak with these people," Bahadim said. "It will only take a conversation."

"That may be so," Freds said, "but meanwhile they appear to have their guns out, and I don't think you want to try talking to them just yet."

"No," Bahadim agreed, and whacked me on the arm again.

"Freds," I said. "Isn't it like a hundred miles to Chitwan?"

"I think so."

"Are we going to run all the way there?"

"No, there's more of them little rail carts up here. Ah! Here they are."

By the light of our flashlight beams we saw them; we were in a circular widening in the tunnel, and against one wall was a line of the small wooden carts, their iron wheels gleaming. Freds ran to the one at the far end and pushed it; it squealed over the tracks set in the floor of the tunnel. "Come on climb on hurry," he said, and so we jumped on and were off into the dark. Freds pumped up and down on something like an old railroad handcar pump, and we rolled faster and faster. "Pull up on that lever there when we turn," he instructed me. "That's the brake."

I pointed my flashlight forward into the rushing dark, but it made a poor headlight. "How will I know when we're turning?"

"You'll feel it."

"Are you going to pump us all the way to Chitwan?"

"This is the downhill trip. We drop about three thousand feet, so it's more a matter of braking than pumping. Coming back up must be hard work. Here, don't brake as much as that, we're on rails and those soldiers'll be coming after us."

"You think so?"

"Look."

Behind us, a brief gleam of light. Our car's wheels were too loud to let us hear anything but ourselves, and then only if we shouted in each other's faces; but obviously there was another car following us. Freds moved me aside and took over the brake.

"Let's see how fast we can get this old bucket rolling."

Judging by the squeaking of the wheels and the air rushing over us, and the sight of the walls flying by in the cone of flashlight illumination, we could go pretty fast. Really fast. Occasionally we passed statues of the Buddha, or long murals of Bönpa demons, looking like vivid nightmares as we zoomed by them. In places the tunnel dropped more steeply, and we must have got up to about eighty or ninety miles an hour. Freds became used to this speed, and when the tunnel's pitch laid back a little he would pump away to try to get us back to it. He put Bahadim on the brake because he didn't like the way I overused it.

I don't know how long we fired down the tunnel like that; sometimes it felt like we had been doing it for days, other times it seemed only minutes had passed since the King and I had stood surrounded by Bahadim's gang. One problem I never would have anticipated was the cold. The air down there was probably forty or fifty degrees—not too bad—but at the rate we were moving there was the equivalent of a sixty- to eighty-mile-an-hour wind rushing over us, and I believe you are supposed to subtract one degree for every mile per hour to get a windchill factor, meaning that for us it was about twenty below zero. And it felt every bit of that. Even Freds declared it was a bit uncomfortable, and I caught him trying to warm a hand by holding it over the side just above one of the brake pads. "It doesn't really work all that good," he admitted, teeth clattering. Eventually we all ended up on the floor of the cart hiding behind the front wall, traveling blind and literally freezing to death.

Finally Freds pushed up to look forward into the dark, then leaped to the brake and hauled up on it, causing a deafening screech. When we came to a halt and shined the flashlights around, we found ourselves in another circular chamber filled with cars. We hopped out as stiff as frozen pork chops, and followed Freds down a tunnel on the other side. "I cannot feel my hands," Bahadim said. I couldn't feel my hands or my feet.

"It's only a couple hundred yards," Freds said, teeth hammering together in great shivers. "God, wasn't that *great*? Like a monster roller coaster—I wanna do it *again*."

Far up the tunnel we heard the faint low roar of iron wheels on iron rails. "Hey, those guys went for it pretty hard. Come on, let's hurry."

We staggered along, slapping our arms at our sides to warm up. Bahadim warmed up by slapping me. Soon we came to a long rough set of stone steps; we had to swing up them like Frankenstein, as our knees hadn't quite thawed. But the air was getting warmer, and then we were colliding together as Freds had stopped and extinguished his flashlight.

"Okay," he said. "This is the entry."

"Where?"

"Right here."

"Where?"

"It's still night, George." He flicked his flashlight on and off, and I caught a brief glimpse of saal trees.

"Oh, no," I said. I didn't want to go into the jungle at night, on foot; I absolutely refused. But behind us, down the tunnel, there came a distant *screech,* and some faint screams, and then a short sequence of crashes. The King's bodyguards had arrived.

"Come on," Freds said, and took off.

XVII

BAD AS IT IS to be on the back of a rogue elephant in the jungle at night, it is infinitely worse to be there on foot. We snuck between trees and through bushes and tried to be as quiet as we could, and the quieter we were the more we could hear: creaks, rustles, quick scurrying sounds; the occasional bird cry, brief and to the point. And then there would be the sound of a branch snapping, and every other sound out there in the blackness would go away, leaving a heavy vegetable silence in which you could tell any number of living things were hunkered down waiting for something big to go away, sniffing the air and listening with noses and ears much sharper than ours. It would have made better sense to go crashing along singing at the top of our lungs or making martial arts sound effects, but with the King's soldiers out of the tunnel and moving around in a group, flashlights lancing through the trees and sometimes illuminating spots very close to us, we couldn't do that. Like all the rest of the hunted, we had to keep low and scurry along as quietly as we could.

Luckily it is impossible for humans to trail anyone or anything in the jungle at night, and the bodyguards seemed to be decoyed by the lights of Tiger View. They were moving in that direction when Freds stomped a bush several times and yelled out "Ah!"

Their flashlights turned in our direction and we took off running, Freds making as much noise as he could.

"Damn, Freds," I panted as we followed him. "Why did you *do* that?"

"Just follow me," he called back at us. "I got a plan."

We led the soldiers through the saal forest for about half an hour. Then all of a sudden Freds stopped and crouched down. "Okay," he whispered. "Be quiet. We're there."

"Where?"

"This is the poacher's meadow. See? The Jeep's back. Now if we can just sic them soldiers on the poachers, wouldn't that be great. Here, find something to throw. Here, here's some rocks. Start throwing them at the Jeep."

He started firing away like Sandy Koufax, and after a while there was a *whang!* and then another. Voices came from behind us, then from off to one side. The soldiers were crashing through the jungle rapidly now, and a flashlight beam caught the Jeep and held on it. More voices, off in the jungle beyond us.

"Let's get out of here," Freds whispered, and dropped to his hands and knees. Bahadim and I crawled through muck and shrubbery, following him. Behind us there were indefinable crashing noises, then gunshots. Then volleys of gunfire. We crawled faster.

Eventually Freds stood up.

"I think we're in the clear, boys!" he declared.

"It does not seem so very clear to me," Bahadim opined. "It is jungle."

"That it is. But no one's chasing us." And he took off at a jaunty walking pace.

Once again we followed him. But after a while I said, unhappily, "You mean no humans are chasing us."

"Well—yeah. Why, do you think . . . ?" He stopped to listen.

"It's awfully quiet," I pointed out.

We started off again, as silently as we could.

"*Awfully* quiet." I was whispering now.

And before us, off beyond some trees, a branch clicked. It seemed there was a sound, like breathing: a low, quiet, rasping kind of breath. The kind of rasping breath that could have growled, or roared, or purred.

"Maybe we oughta take refuge," Freds whispered, his voice sounding worried.

"Any suggestions?"

"How about up a tree?"

"I think tigers can climb trees," I said.

"Nah."

"Cats can climb trees," I said. "Why not tigers? They've got the claws, and the power. Leopards climb trees for sure."

"I still think we're better off up a tree than down here."

And in fact while we were having this conversation we were circling a big double-trunked saal tree, trying to find a way up it, so apparently it was a moot point. Bahadim offered the opinion that some tigers could climb while others couldn't. Freds complained that saal trees were not good climbing trees, which they weren't; the trunks tended to rise for thirty feet or more before extending their branches. The double-trunker we were circling looked our best bet, but I still wasn't sure we weren't heading up a dead end, so to speak. So there we stood for a few minutes, arguing bitterly in sharp undertones about the climbing ability of tigers.

Finally Freds broke the deadlock by saying, "Hey, whatever, I'm going for it. Better to make the damn tiger work for us, even if it can climb."

"How do you plan to get up this thing?" I asked him.

"Kind of like bouldering," he muttered. "Can't be worse than five eight or nine." And he gave it a try.

It took a lot of attempts, and he kept sliding back down. "Okay, okay. Five eleven, five twelve. Maybe a six." Finally he got past the crux and hauled himself up into the cleft between trunks. I boosted Bahadim up on my back, then climbed up after them. Freds led the way, up the more mutant-looking of the two trunks, over broken bark and what felt like big crawling ants.

Once we had skinnied up to where the branches began there were a lot of them, and we could spread out a little as we climbed higher. This took us a long time, however, and all the while Freds and I were bitching at each other about tigers and their climbing potential. The jungle was still dead quiet, except for the horrendously loud noises that we seemed to make from time to time; so it was a serious issue for us. "Shit, you don't know a thing about it!" Freds said. "Didn't you ever watch *Wild Kingdom*?"

"Of course!" I replied. "And I'm sure I remember tigers up in trees, with whole deer dragged up there after them. They sleep up there!"

"Those were leopards, George. The spotted ones are leopards, the striped ones are tigers. And tigers only use trees for scratching posts. They're too big to climb them, they break the branches I guess, or it's like the thing of why can't there ever be giant nuclear ants, you know, double the size and quadruple the weight or whatever."

I didn't see how that applied. "They've got the strength and they've got the claws."

"Claws ain't no help when you've got to go down the damn tree! That's why cats are always getting rescued out of trees by firemen! There ain't no firemen out here to get these tigers down, and they know it. They're not as stupid as cats. Their brains must be ten times bigger."

"Brain size doesn't have anything to do with intelligence."

"You tell that to a worm."

We climbed some more. Bahadim mentioned that he thought Chitwan jungle contained leopards as well as tigers.

"Well shit!" Freds said. "You got any better suggestion than this?"

"No, no," Bahadim said. Besides, he admitted, climbing trees was the recommended refuge from tigers. If nothing else you would be safe from rhinos. And it was said that if you climbed high enough you would get up into branches too slender to hold either leopards or climbing tigers, if they did indeed exist.

So we climbed as high as we could.

Eventually I found myself wedged in a narrow crook, hanging on to small branches on both sides, swaying very noticeably. No view whatsoever of the ground. Above me through leaves I glimpsed the stars. Freds and Bahadim were clattering around to either side of me, partly visible through intervening branches. "This is as high as I can go," I said, and tried to get more comfortable. The swaying was really very noticeable. "Jesus, Freds," I said. "The things you get me into."

"It is not Freds who has gotten us into this horrible position!" Bahadim burst out. "It is you, George Fergusson, who has done this to us! You have assaulted His Majesty King Birendra!"

Apparently in our hurry to escape Bahadim had not gotten the chance to fully express his displeasure with me about this. It had been too loud to talk during the cart run, and at all other times we had been too busy. Now we were at leisure, so to speak, and he really laid into me. He called me every kind of fool he could think of. A lot of times he had to lapse into Nepalese to get just the right phrase.

"Interfering in the affairs of Nepal! Messing about where you don't know what is going on! Stupid! Fool! Idiot! You are just another arrogant stupid American, putting in your hand where you are not wanted, with terroristic actions no better than a bomb thrower like Ram Raja Prasad Singh, *aggh*! And what is the justification for this stupidity! Are things so perfect in your country that you must come to ours to solve our problems? No! No! No! You are going all over the world pretending to solve everyone's problems and meanwhile you are making half these problems yourselves, sending out soldiers and practicing usury and exploding your chemical factories on us! And back in your country, are there not poor people to help? Are there not political problems? Do you not have any corruption there in your own military? Yes you most certainly do! Why don't you mess with your own country's affairs and leave the poor rest of the world alone! I invite you to kidnap your own king if you are feeling a need for such a thing! Kidnapping the King of Nepal! Stupid! Stupid! STUPID!" And then a long string of Nepalese.

"Hey," Freds said. "Give him a break, why don't you. It was just an idea."

"Just an idea! Just an idea, to kidnap the King and overthrow the government!"

"Well sure," Freds said. "Why not?"

Bahadim couldn't believe this.

"No, really," Freds said. "That's basically what you're doing, right? You're running an alternative government there under the city, right? So why shouldn't you take over? The King's father did the same thing. If you guys had been ready for it, you might have been pretty damn happy to see George hand the King over to you as easy as that. You might have liked it."

"No!" Bahadim said. "Never! You do not understand."

"I guess I don't," Freds said.

Bahadim took a deep breath. His set of branches was shaking, he was so upset.

He pulled himself together, calmed down. After a while he tried to explain. "We in Nepal, we are loyal to the King. We love our King. He is our King, the King of an independent Nepal, which has never been ruled by any other country."

"Yeah, but he's a crook."

"*No!* This is not true. King Birendra is not a crook. People say this because he is King, perhaps, or because his youngest brother is a wastrel. And the Ranas, they surround

308

him—the Queen, the Army, his advisors—they are everywhere around him, and they make it impossible for him to act as fully as he might like to act. He is not a forceful King like his father was, I admit that. But he is a thoughtful man, and he knows where the problems in Nepal are coming from. He *wants* things to change."

"He does?" Freds and I said together.

"Yes, yes. King Birendra would like political reforms, to be aiding the economic reforms. He is only frustrated by all these aid programs, by the bureaucracy and the corruption and the Ranas. He wants a constitutional country, you see. But it is not in his power to accomplish this. Many many people like to have the palace in charge. The King is captive of the caste system, of the power of the Ranas. They are richer than him, and they control the Army, you see. So he must work with us."

"With you!" I cried.

"Yes. You remember, I told you that we are working under the city to help the people, with funds provided by rich Nepalis who are sympathetic to our cause?"

"Birendra?" I was amazed.

"Yes," Bahadim said. "We have contacted him, and he knows what we are doing. He helps us. It is one way that he can be starting to change things, without the Ranas knowing about it. He is our patron. We communicate with him through that crack in his closet. He is our King, we love him. He has his flaws, but he is trying, and what is wrong with Nepal is not his fault, or not entirely. He does what he can, now, and so do we."

"Why didn't you tell me?" I said, shocked.

"It was not your business! I told you, in Nepal we keep some things secret, some things that belong to Nepal alone. Naturally it cannot spread about that the King works through an underground government! If that were to happen the Ranas would stop it. So I kept it a secret from you."

"So then it's all your fault, ain't it," Freds pointed out. "If you had just told George, he would never have tried to help you out in that particular way."

Bahadim's only response to this was in pungent-sounding Nepalese.

I sat there swaying, thinking about it. "So if the King knows about you," I said to Bahadim, "then you should be able to patch things up about the tunnels and all."

"Yes," he said shortly. "Some of his bodyguards are in his confidence, and know about us. They probably were assuming that we had been overwhelmed by Ram Raja Prasad Singh, or some other terroristic group. When they are less nervous and we have time to explain, we can clear things up, and hopefully the tunnel system will not be exposed."

"Good," I said. I sighed. "I'm sorry, Bahadim. I just lost it there for a while, I guess. That God-damned A. Rana drove me insane. And when you told me the latest, about that poaching business—"

"You need not worry about that," Bahadim said shortly. "We have traced the Jeep Freds reported to a motor pool in Chitwan, one used by A. Rana's nephews. Now that Freds had led the King's bodyguards into a fight with these poachers, the King will take a very close interest. We will stop A. Rana, and probably get him into very big trouble indeed. Although it may take some time, because of confusion caused by your kidnapping."

"I'm sorry," I said. "I blew it."

He sighed. "It is all right," he said reluctantly. "You were only trying to help." A pause. "Although I must tell you that we do not want your help in this matter, thank you. And it seems to me that there are as yet many things still to be helped in your own country."

Another hesitation; then he said, "You know, ours is not the only underground government in this world. We have contacts, some by actual tunnel, some only by information, and they extend to many many countries. Including your own. Under the cities of Washington, D.C., London, Moscow—"

"Tunnel systems?" I said.

Freds called out, "Subways, remember George?"

"No no no," Bahadim said. "They are under the subways and the like."

"It's like what I told you, George," Freds said. "Shambhala's tunnel system is older and bigger than you could ever imagine. It was a really great civilization. Thousands of years, thousands of miles."

"Very extensive indeed," Bahadim said. "And now being used again to bypass the Ranas, you see. Or whatever equivalent exists."

"Well," I said. "I'll have to look them up. If I ever go back."

"I recommend it," Bahadim said, and I couldn't tell if he meant looking them up, or going back.

I let it pass, feeling a bit overwhelmed. Also my butt had gone to sleep. I had to change position. During our crawl through the jungle we had warmed up and more from our hypothermic run down the tunnels, but now the sweat was cooling us down too far, and I was growing cold again.

The horizon that must have been the eastern one was going a little gray, but there was a long way to go to daylight, and there was nothing to do but sit up there, swaying in a slight breeze and shivering. From his perch Freds kept up the never-ending narration of his life, his voice a familiar staccato pattern that faded in and out of my consciousness. "Shit, it is freezing *ass* up here. Could you believe how cold that roller coaster ride was? My eyeballs were freezing open! Reminded me of the time I was doing my novice training under Kunga Norbu at the secret Rongbuk, and we got to the test they have of your tumo powers where they take you up at night to one of those glacial creeks at about fifteen thousand feet and strip you naked and pour a few buckets of creek water over you and soak about twenty white sheets and leave you there, and see you're not only supposed to keep warm but you're supposed to keep *so* warm that you dry out the wet sheets, as many of them as you can and the more you do over the course of the night the better you do on the test, it's a numerical thing kinda like your SAT scores and very accurate in finding out who's gonna be the best lama. Well, I mean to tell you when they dumped that ice water over me I had every bit of my tumo training shocked right out of me, I mean I just plain *forgot* it and there I was buck naked and sopping wet at fifteen thousand feet in November at eight P.M. and nowhere to go, I didn't know *what* to do. . . ."

On and on he rattled. I think I fell asleep a little, although every shift in my perch brought me bolt upright as I recalled where I was.

The sky got lighter and lighter. My hands got horribly sore, and I realized I had been clenching the branches the whole time I had been up there.

". . . so when they showed up I had the sheets all folded and looking ironed practically and dryer than toast, but Kunga Norbu was suspicious and when he found the ashes he beat the shit out of me with a stick—"

"Freds?"

"What? Hey, George! Good morning! Sun should be up any minute, hey? What a day! Boy, it's gonna be great to get out of this tree, isn't it? Gonna be great to get down and over to Daubahal's camp and then back to Kathmandu, man, we can go to the Old Vienna I'm starved aren't you? I'm gonna have wiener schnitzel and goulash and apple strudel, maybe two apple strudels, sure, and Dasain should still be going and Kathmandu is such a blast during Dasain, we can get out in the street and just party our brains out to celebrate."

"What exactly is it we will celebrate?" Bahadim croaked wearily.

"Why—well—well, getting out of this tree for one. I don't know about you, but my legs are falling off. I think I got frostbit on our ride. Kind of reminds me of the time we decided to bicycle to Makalu—"

312

"Freds!" I said.

"What!"

"Shut up."

"Oh, hey, sure bro. Never let it be said that I bothered anyone, not that you'd want to go to sleep up here or anything, I probably *should* bother you. . . ."

I let his voice drift into the background of jungle dawn sounds. I was tired—very, very, very tired.

But something in the way Freds had talked about Kathmandu had brought the image of the city strongly to my mind, crawling all over the insides of my eyeballs. And as the red sun cracked the horizon and the thick humid air filled with light, and we started trying to descend the tree ("Where's them firemen? Maybe cats ain't so stupid after all!"), I kept thinking helplessly of the city, of the crowded streets and the open-front shops and the corner temples and the street operators, and I knew that it would never change—that when we got back the cows would be in the streets blocking the crazed traffic, and the giant bats would be hanging upside down in the pine trees on the palace grounds, and the lines of people would be stretching hundreds of yards out of the post office and Central Telegraph, and the peddlers would be sitting on the sidewalks selling candies and incense and antibiotics and unidentifiable fruit and bolts of brilliant cloth, and crows and clouds and rainbows would be flying overhead with the Himal to the north and bike bells ringing and everything aswirl in the ramshackle old streets of the town, and I found I couldn't wait to get home to it again.

XIX

OH, ONE LAST THING; about those underground governments: keep your eye peeled. And tell everyone you trust about them, okay?

ACKNOWLEDGMENTS

A trek to Everest is a pilgrimage of sorts, and I'd like to thank some of our fellow pilgrims, who contributed so much to the spirit of this book: Lahure Tenzing and Bahadim Bahadur and Dol Bahadur, Tenzing Sherpa and Pemba Sherpa, Larry and Chet and Kathy and Roger, Bob and Karla, Tron and Thor-Erik, Kim and Lisa, Ernest and Christiane, Mishka and Melka, Barb and Sarah, Trevor and Tom and Tom and John, Ivan, Thomas, Kitty and Joe, Ray and Anna and Kya, Len, Gilbert and the French crew, Pasang Kami, Bob and Lorraine, Brent and Sue, and all the guys at the Hotel Star.

While I was writing the book I was helped by my friends Patrick Delahunt, Gardner Dozois, Pat Murphy, Beth Meacham, Lisa Nowell, Paul Park, and Ian Watson. My thanks.

A special thank you to the man who helped in 524 ways; and to Kabir Saxena, who, one night at the Blue Moon Lodge in Junbesi, told us of Shambhala.

This book is for all of you.